THE REWIND FILES

By Claire Willett

AXIŌMATIC
PUBLISHING

ISBN: 978-0-9861157-4-5

Published by Axiomatic Publishing
A Retrofit Films Company
5455 Wilshire Blvd #1406
Los Angeles, CA 90036
www.axiomaticpublishing.com

WE WANT TO HEAR FROM YOU!

Please let us know what you think!

Leave reviews for First Fleet on Amazon.
Your feedback helps us make better books.

Email us typos or other notes to:
editor@axiomaticpublishing.com

Thank you!

AXIÖMATIC
PUBLISHING

*To Christopher, who believed in this book
before it was a book.*

*To my grandmother Lydia, our family's
original Watergate junkie.*

To Dad, for everything.

\

"*There is nothing more deceptive than an obvious fact.*"

— *ARTHUR CONAN DOYLE,*
The Boscombe Valley Mystery

TABLE OF CONTENTS

PART I
MANUAL OVERRIDE RECOMMENDED

PART II
PAST IMPERFECT

PART I

MANUAL OVERRIDE
RECOMMENDED

PROLOGUE

THE REPAIRMEN

Washington, DC. August 2112

Time travel sounds much more glamorous than it really is. On paper, I'm Regina Bellows, a member of the elite, highly-trained team of history and technology specialists known formally as Government-Authorized Time-Slip Field Agents (Historical Realignment Division).

We call ourselves the Repairmen. (I just go by Reggie.)

So here's what happened. About 80 years ago, there was an event we call the Great Rift – that's when Li Chidong and Martina Garcia Lopez finally solved the time travel equation for transit of solid bodies and Lopez performed the first successful Chrono-Splicing to send herself back to 1995. Chrono-Splicing means you create a tiny rip in one small section of the General Timeline and insert yourself into it, temporarily merging it with your own permanent timeline.

Eventually it would allow us to create maps with agents' GC (Garcia-Chidong) Map Coordinates.

I don't want to bore you with all the math, but basically it meant that with the right equipment, anyone could send anyone anywhere.

The result? A giant goddamn mess.

And so began a massive global free-for-all as every government on earth dived headfirst into an epic international shoving match with one goal: To be first in line to send some bow-tied college professor back to whatever point in their own national history they felt like rewriting.

The Germans, being particularly motivated (and who can blame them), bribed their way to the front of the line and sent their first field agent back to 1907 to arrange for a fully-funded scholarship to the Vienna School of Fine Arts for a modestly-talented eighteen-year-old painter named Adolf Hitler.

It worked – Hitler's totalitarian career was over before it even started, though at the cost of some truly ghastly paintings – but it knocked over the first domino. The entire 20th century began to unravel.

See, the U.N., NATO, all the great global policing agencies were founded during and after the Second World War. No war, no United Nations. No United Nations, no peace agreement in any country the U.N. ever brokered.

So Germany redeemed its reputation at the expense of genocide in Bosnia. Meanwhile, the American government took a clumsy swing at erasing slavery and ended up almost singlehandedly destroying the economy of the Western hemisphere for three hundred years.

Enter government regulation. The U.N. sent representatives from every delegate country to form a committee on global policing of time travel. An uneasy truce was declared.

No one nation was permitted sole provenance over its own country's history, and they all agreed to leave the General

Timeline alone. After that, for the most part the governments left time travel to the experts – meaning, us.

That's where the Repairmen come in. We're the ones sent in to clean up the mess and restore the General Timeline. After the practices and restrictions of time travel were codified, every member nation set up an official government-supervised bureau with registered agents trained both in system science and history.

Over the years we learned, through trial and error (sometimes fatal), how best to gently nudge history back on track when it slides off the rails, with minimal interference. You learn the rules on Day One at the Academy, so we've all had this drilled into our heads for years.

But it's not necessarily common knowledge for civilians, so let me just very quickly run you through the basics.

1. The General Timeline (that means the real course of history the way it's supposed to play out) does its best to self-correct when things go wrong. But it's a big, slow, lumbering animal, and its attempts at repair can be cumbersome and sometimes insanely overcomplicated. Letting it correct itself is like performing a heart transplant with industrial logging equipment. Using an agent allows you to be accurate and surgically precise. Quick and clean. Get in, make the fix, get out.

2. Have you ever wondered what it would be like to go forward in time and see what your world will be like in fifty years, or go backwards to talk your past self out of marrying that loser? Well, too bad. You can't.

   One of the first things you learn in agent training is that your own permanent timeline (meaning your natural birth to natural death) is off-limits. That timeline is locked until you die. You can go back and tackle Lee Harvey Oswald on the floor of the Texas Schoolbook Depository to keep him from shooting John F. Kennedy, but you cannot stop yourself from attempting ballet in the seventh grade all-school talent show.

Being in two places at once creates what's called a Double Incongruity, and it can be deadly. A Chronomaly (that's basically any incident that occurs which is not part of the General Timeline) can be very minor, or it can be significant enough that we send an agent in to repair it.

But an Incongruity is full of peril. It's a Chronomaly on a scale so massive that it doesn't just affect the way history plays out.

It risks affecting time itself.

It makes the Slipstream around you terribly unstable. Agents have died trying to transport out of an Incongruity. So whatever narcissistic fantasies you might have had about hopping around to watch the Greatest Hits of your own life play out in real time, just ask yourself if reliving that three-pointer from half-court in the junior varsity basketball playoffs is worth total organ failure.

3. Death is death. Even time travelers can't circumvent it. Your *real* death, I mean. You can't prevent it and you can't undo it. Sure, if you're trampled by an elephant while trying to patch the General Timeline around Alexander the Great, the tech monitoring your vitals will spot it, sound the alarm, and

send somebody back to your initial transport site to pull you out before the elephant gets too close.

That's because that rampaging elephant wasn't really how you were supposed to die. In its own way, it's a Chronomaly. Which means it can be repaired. But if you die in your own timeline, that's it. You're gone.

~

We learned all of this through trial and error, of course. Everybody wanted to believe that the possibility of time travel was somehow a magical ticket to immortality.

But the thing people don't really understand about time is how fragile it is. We still have continuous aftershocks from that first era of disastrous intervention; you'll think you plugged a hole but bits and pieces of chaos slide through.

So we do a lot of tedious, low-level patching. Napoleon leaves for battle and forgets his sword at home, so you have to sneak one into his scabbard before he realizes it. Abraham Lincoln cancels his theater tickets at the last minute because Mary Todd has a headache. Things like that.

Little dumb human things, all the tiny, meaningless moments that make up a life, only they aren't meaningless because these people have no idea how important they will turn out to be.

And of course, you can't tell them. "Abe, you have to go see the play tonight so you can get shot by an out-of-work actor." That's not how it works.

"The first rule of patching," a professor said to one of my first-year classes, "is this: 'For God's sake, *don't make it worse.*'" To that end, every field agent is equipped with a monitor for their Holistic Interference Output (HIO) Levels; that's the tool we use to measure how much our presence and actions are impacting the General Timeline.

You have to keep it as low as possible. Dress in flawlessly period-appropriate clothing and walk through a busy, crowded public place like a town square or subway station? Good job, your HIO meter is ticking peacefully at a 1 or a 2. Your mission is a success and your patch will probably stick.

Land a plane in the middle of a Wild West shootout? That thing is blinking red and shrieking twelve different alarms in your ear, and your ass is getting *so* fired the second you step off that transport platform.

Anyway, I know this is all a little inside-baseball and the general public doesn't really know or care that much about all of this. In fact, a lot of new Academy recruits don't know or care that much about it either.

They come waltzing in with stars in their eyes, dreaming naïve little dreams about getting to hang out with Dorothy Parker and Oscar Wilde, and then they're cruelly disappointed to learn that their glamorous fantasy career is like, 90% paperwork. That's why only about ten percent of the new recruits actually stick around to get hired.

Me, I'm different. In the world of the U.S. Time Travel Bureau, my parents are like, mega-famous, so I grew up with this stuff. I could read an HIO meter by the age of five. There was no way the daughter of the legendary Carstairs and Bellows was not going to be among that ten percent of her class.

I didn't exactly have a better plan — nor, to be quite frank — *any* plan for my life after graduation. So I figured I'd let my mom pull her strings to land me a boring desk job where I could sit in front of a computer screen all day until I figured out what I actually wanted to do.

Sounds okay, right?

Not so much, if you've heard of Watergate. Have you heard of Watergate? Of course you have.

That's because I screwed up.

CHAPTER ONE

LOOK PAST THE EGGS

It was 2:30 a.m. Four hours and sixteen minutes since my last break. Yawning, I stretched and tried to work out the kinks in my back from sitting hunched over the screen all day.

My eyes started to blur, and my whole body was experiencing that feeling you get from intense and prolonged lack of sleep, where you're sort of hungry and sort of cold and sort of nauseous and every muscle in your body feels either too tense or too relaxed.

But it would be over tomorrow. Director Gray was coming for the report at noon. Once it was submitted, we could all go home, with an extra half day to our weekend. I just had to survive nine and a half more hours without screwing up.

There were twelve of us who had studied Mid-20th and been assigned to this floor. They discovered early on that the best way to keep track of agents in the field was to have a permanent data technician assigned to each one, continually monitoring any unusual activity in the General Timeline around the agent's location.

I worked for an agent named Harold Grove, the senior agent on our floor whose field covered most of the latter half of the 20th century, alongside a tech named Calliope, an impossibly-gorgeous young woman with springy golden curls who looked like she didn't have two brain cells to rub together, but was actually one of the smartest people I knew.

At the moment, Grove was in the field on a fairly routine mission to mend a troublesome patch on the 1968 Presidential election. According to the General Timeline — that is, the way unaltered history is supposed to play out — President Johnson announces that he won't run for reelection, leading to a melee of Democratic candidates splitting the votes eight ways to Sunday and giving Republican Richard Nixon a clear run at the field.

Johnson's health is failing and he'll die just a few days after Nixon's first term ends. Half a century ago, after the Great Rift, a group of well-meaning but clueless historians convinced themselves that a second Johnson term would have put an end to the Vietnam War, so they went back posing as campaign consultants and pushed him to run for re-election.

Well, no matter how many attempts they made, the system self-corrected; he was beaten in the primary, or he died of a heart attack on the campaign trail, or his wife threatened to leave him if he didn't quit.

Once, he was hit and killed by his own campaign bus crossing the street. Something would always intercede to keep him from getting anywhere close to reelected.

Finally, growing desperate, the historians had Johnson's Vice President, Hubert Humphrey (who was supposed to end up winning the nomination) assassinated and spread rumors that the Republican Party was to blame.

It worked. Johnson was reelected in a landslide of sympathy votes, and the entire system began to collapse in on itself in a staggering net of self-corrections that didn't stop until another agent went back in time and shot our own guys before they shot Humphrey.

Don't worry, the agents didn't mind. There's a certain cachet among some of them about Rewinds — otherwise known as Emergency Manual Re-Edits. That's when you're killed in a flexible timeline you're visiting and another agent gets sent back to retrieve you before your mission starts. It creates a lot of residual interference, though there's no long-term impact on the agent.

Also, some of the more chest-thumping guys at the Bureau like to brag about it as a measure of how many risky missions they've taken. Myself, I prefer to take it as a measure of stupidity, and how many times a colleague had to put their own work on hold to go back and pull your ass out of the fire. It's this attitude that made me very unpopular at school.

Three weeks ago, Grove spotted a news headline in the archives saying "JOHNSON ANNOUNCES RE-ELECTION BID" and immediately packed his bags to go fix the decaying patch.

While Grove was in the field monitoring President Johnson, Calliope and I were monitoring Grove. Or, she was anyway. I was trying my damndest to finish Grove's field report in time to present it to the Director. And I was stumped.

Like I said, I'm the math girl on my floor. Grove usually hates his apprentices, and he *really* didn't want to be the agent who got stuck with Katie Bellows' daughter ("The last time you stuck me with a nepotism case I had to go back *twice* to Rewind that scrawny Ambassador's kid out of the same air raid," I overheard him snapping at the Director on my first day).

But even he's not as fast on the computer as I am.

Without a degree in 22nd-century Chrono-Engineering, it will probably be hard for you to understand what I do, but essentially it boils down to this: the Garcia-Chidong Map marks the exact location in time and space where any given event takes place, and continually updates those coordinates against the General Timeline.

Tiny aberrations in the system occur on a near-constant basis, 99% of which are non-significant. It's terrifying the first time you see it — graphs constantly shifting in the blink of an eye.

But you learn to filter out the stuff that doesn't matter, the way astrophysicists learn not to think too hard about all the space debris hurtling towards Earth because the odds of any of it actually crashing and killing you are very slim.

But until you get used to it, it feels like you're hovering on the brink of disaster nearly all the time.

The trick, my mother always said, was to look not at the moments but at the patterns, to take in the big and the small at the same time.

Let's say that a thirty-two-year-old accountant in Queens in 1986 has eggs for breakfast three days in a row and then on the fourth she changes her mind and decides she wants oatmeal.

Does it matter? Maybe it doesn't. Maybe she's just tired of eggs. Maybe she's craving something sweet that morning. Maybe she wanted something easier to eat on the train. How hard do you think the thirty-two-year-old accountant is really thinking about it? Not that hard. It's April. It's tax season. Breakfast is the last thing on her mind.

She would be astonished if she knew that a century in the future, we were watching her open the cupboard and take down the oats while lights flashed, alarms blared, panicked data techs sprinted from their desks with tablets in hand, and an emergency beacon commenced its frenzied blinking over the desk of the Director.

That's because what the accountant didn't know was that she was supposed to have eggs this morning. That way, tomorrow morning she would wake up and realize she was out of eggs, run to the store before work, meet a twenty-eight-year-old veterinarian who was also buying eggs that morning, marry him three years later and give birth to a child who would grow up to discover the cure for Lou Gehrig's Disease.

Fortunately, the General Timeline carries within it a complex set of self-corrections. Maybe the accountant would miss the veterinarian at the grocery store but catch him two days later at the dry cleaners instead. Maybe she would come home from work that night and spill a whole quart of milk, sending her to the right aisle in the right grocery store at the right time tomorrow morning anyway to make sure she had milk for her coffee.

That's how you can tell the good agents from the great ones. The best agents — the ones like Grove, like my mother — can look at that picture and see past the details to find the pattern, to understand that it's not about the eggs. It never is.

So there I sat in my cubicle outside Grove's office, staring at a dizzying array of coordinates, trying to look past the eggs.

"How's it coming?" I dimly heard Calliope ask from what felt like forty thousand miles away. I gave her sort of a mumbly grunt in response, my brain too busy to shape sounds into actual words.

A few minutes later, I felt her shimmer into my peripherals as her white coat and golden hair emerged beside me from behind. She placed a giant mug of hot black coffee, God bless her, on the desk, wrapped my hand around it, and perched on the desk next to the screen.

"Stop for five minutes," she said firmly. "I can see your eyes glazing over."

"I'm fine," I muttered without looking up.

"Look away from the screen and up at me, and then drink your coffee. Five minutes. And let me call down to the kitchens and get you something to eat. You haven't had any food since you had dinner. It's after two now."

"I'll be fine." Pause. More seemed expected. "Thanks."

"Regina Bellows, un-fry your brain or you're going to fall asleep in this chair. Or worse."

"What's worse?"

"You could make a mistake. In front of your mother."

That did it. I sighed, paused the screen, and turned to her. She had the giddy look of pleasure she always wore when she had some particularly juicy gossip for me.

"All right, who did what?"

"*Well*," she began confidentially in her this-is-totally-a-secret-so-keep-it-better-than-I'm-about-to voice, "I just ran into Yasmina,"(she was my mother's tech)"and she told me that Naomi on Six told her that there are ten apprentices getting fired tomorrow."

"Holy shit! *Ten*? What happened?" Apprentices got fired all the time; the whole point of the job, after all, was a brutal two-year elimination process to see who really had what it took to be an agent. We usually lost one or two a week out of the several hundred in the building. But ten at once was a big deal.

"Naomi says that they were sending themselves back to two weeks ago to give themselves more time to finish their reports for the Director."

This was a major infringement. Besides the ban on unsupervised transport use, and the obvious fact that this was *cheating* and an apprentice who couldn't finish their work on time didn't deserve a chance to qualify as a field agent, there were few things more dangerous to the General Timeline — or to an agent — than a Double Incongruity.

I said as much to Calliope, and she nodded.

"They ran diagnostics and it doesn't appear to have caused any lasting damage," she said. "But they got busted on the return transport. A tech spotted interference in the Slipstream and told his supervisor. By the time they arrived back in the lab all their agents were waiting for them. And the department heads. And the Director."

I shuddered a little, temporarily feeling a twinge of compassion for my dishonest colleagues at the thought of how terrified they must have been to step out of the Slipstream and find themselves staring at those stony faces. They must have been so sure that they would get away with it, and now their careers were over before they even started. Poor cocky idiots.

"Any of ours?" I asked.

"Only one from this floor. Harriet Chao."

"*Harriet?*" I was astonished. "No way did Harriet need an extra two weeks for her report; she turns everything in three days early."

"It wasn't her idea. The ringleaders were the Weston brothers, on Six. She was the only girl. The other nine were the Westons and their rich, white, asshole friends. That's how Naomi found out, she's their tech. They both got placed in Late Medieval and they've been struggling to keep up, so they got desperate to buy themselves some extra time."

She continued, "And then Chris Weston told a couple other people, and Jess Weston roped in his roommate, who is dating

Harriet, so she went along with it. A bonehead move. But in her defense, I think she decided if she couldn't stop them, she might as well make sure there was one person along for the ride with a brain to make sure they didn't all totally kill themselves. I feel bad for her."

So did I. "She was never going to pass the practical exam, though," I pointed out. "She declared for Mid-20th with an emphasis in World War II, but that era is a level 8 for Asians at *best*. Japanese-Americans were being rounded up and sent to internment camps. It's way too dangerous. They were never going to put her in the field."

Calliope sighed. "Don't you do anything stupid," she said pointedly.

"Like screw with the Timeline to cheat on a test? Not likely."

"Or give yourself a nervous breakdown. Or work thirty-six straight hours with no sleep and then get run over on your way to work because you were too tired to see where you were going. Or die of malnutrition. Or —"

"I get it, Calliope."

"Did you know that after the first twenty-four hours without sleep, the human body —"

"Yes, thank you, Calliope."

"I'm just saying," she tossed over her shoulder as she bounced away. "You should take better care of yourself. This floor can't afford to lose anymore apprentices."

She was right. Harriet Chao was a big loss in an already-depleted department. Mid-20th had been my mother's specialty. Back when she was a field agent, apprentices used to line up around the block to train with her.

But five years ago, she had been promoted to Deputy Director, and once she was no longer an active agent, those showbiz-hungry newbies — the ones who wanted the glamour-by-association of the most high-profile Repairmen on their resume — found other mentors, just as flashy.

Slowly Mid-20th began to revert to its pre-Katie Bellows state: a permanently exhausted and criminally understaffed department of overworked scholars who worked round-the-clock to patch one of the most chaotic 30-year periods in American History. There were at present only seven actives in our department, and only five of them had apprentices. After today, four.

I understood why Mid-20th was unpopular. You didn't get to fight with swords or ride horses or wear spectacular clothes. You didn't get to hobnob with historical legends like in Renaissance or Colonial. Those are the gigs most apprentices wanted.

Not me. This was my first and only choice. It wasn't flashy, but its complexity fascinated me.

∼

We took a class trip once to visit the 20th-Century History Museum at the Smithsonian. I think I was nine or ten but I remember it like it was yesterday.

I spent the entire afternoon in the Early Computer Technology wing, running reverent fingertips over acrylic models of a 1977 Commodore PET, an 8-bit Apple II prototype, an original Jacquard loom, a Turing machine, and a whole evolutionary timeline of IBM processors before stopping short at the vast glass case enclosing the holy of holies.

It was the centerpiece of the entire exhibit, the entire reason I had awoken cheerfully and uncomplainingly at 5 am to eat breakfast in the dark with my mother in order to beat the morning train rush and meet the rest of the class outside the museum before it opened at 7.

The Colossus.

Oh, how I revered the Colossus Mark II. The granddaddy of decryption, the original code breaker, the unappreciated genius whose brilliance went unnoticed in its time due to pesky UK national security concerns.

The computer that ended World War II.

It was a thing of beauty, the size of a small room, all metal pins and vacuum tubes and paper tape that seemed both ageless and ancient at the same time.

Built in 1944 to decode German telegraphs sent by the Lorenz SZ 40/42 machine, the Colossus was kept under the highest security until the 1970s. Hardly anyone had even known that it existed.

My mother, who had walked up the block from her office to meet us at the museum for lunch, (much to the starry-eyed delight of the café staff, my teacher, my classmates and random passersby who kept stopping her for autographs), peppered me with questions about the things I had seen and learned that morning.

As I swooned to her, my mouth full of sandwich, about how the Colossus was the first machine to use vacuum tubes to perform Boolean operations, I could see the familiar weary puzzlement in her eyes, a sort of "Joke's over, I'd like my real daughter back please" expression I had seen thousands upon thousands of times.

It was the look I got when she came home from work to find Leo and his friends playing gladiators, Viking warriors or pirates in the living room while I sat primly on the couch with a math textbook.

Leo Jr. and Regina Bellows, the only children of the late great Leo Carstairs and the famous Katie Bellows, two of the greatest legends in the past, present or future of time travel.

Adventure should be in our blood. We were supposed to be made for bold, heroic things.

Well, I can't speak for Leo, but I certainly wasn't.

~

A pencil hit me in the back of my head, startling me out of my fuzzy-brained reminiscences. "You're staring into space," Calliope shouted from across the office. *"Go home."*

I sighed. "Can we compromise?" I asked. "If I go downstairs and eat some post-dinner, will you let me come back and work?"

She gave me a suspicious look, but finally nodded in agreement. One of the things I like about Calliope, and why I count my lucky stars every day that I landed in her department, is that she never complains about the hours or the workload.

Apprentices aren't supposed to be logged into the system without a tech present, which means she's supposed to be here whenever I'm here. So the fact that I've been at the office for almost a full day and a half without a break means she has been too. And yet, she never complains.

Though, just to play devil's advocate for a minute, she did just throw a pencil at my head. So there's that.

CHAPTER TWO

JUST A GLITCH

I had used the word "post-dinner" to Calliope, but it would technically have fallen more accurately somewhere in the dead zone between "midnight snack" and "early breakfast."

It was three in the morning, and the commissary was empty. Behind the metal counters I could see into the huge, gleaming kitchens. There were only a few staff members at this time of night.

Kenny, the night manager, was washing out a big pile of baking pans in the industrial sink. As I walked up to the counter, I could hear him singing quietly to himself as he blasted the angry, steaming nozzle at chunks of crusted cheese from whatever the pans had originally held.

Lindsay, his assistant, spotted me from her chair in the corner and set down her book. (It will tell you all you need to know about my work habits that I'm on a first-name basis with the night staff in the kitchens.)

"How's the report?" asked Lindsay. Kenny turned at the sound of her voice and shut off the faucets.

"Hey Reg," he greeted me.

"Hey Kenny. It's going okay," I said, turning back to Lindsay. "I think I'm going to finish in time to maybe get a nap and a shower before I have to actually go hand it in."

"That oughta make Calliope happy," said Kenny.

"That's the idea," I said. "You know how she gets."

"Well, what can we fix for you? If you're going to power through until morning, let's get some protein in your system. We've got some lamb stew left from dinner that I can heat up for you if that sounds all right."

"It sounds great."

"She has low standards," Lindsay pointed out, going to the cold storage case and pulling out the pan of stew. "She only eats when Calliope makes her and she couldn't care less how it tastes."

"Gets it from her mama," Kenny laughed, turning back to his scrubbing. "Carstairs was the food snob of the family. Isn't your brother a cook somewhere?"

"Dubrovnik," I said. "He has a little seafood place on the water."

"I've been there," said Lindsay. "My mom and I went on Opening Day when they launched the high-speed to Croatia and your brother's restaurant was on the tour. There were lines around the block."

"What did you eat?" I asked.

"Crostini with scallops, this totally to-die-for lemon shrimp stew —

"I've had that stew. Amazing."

"It was perfection. And then a grilled sole in herbed butter. And lots of wine."

"You chose wisely," I told her.

～

Mom and I were regulars at Leo's. Though fairly catch-as-catch-can cooks on our own time — I frequently subsisted on government-issue nutritional supplements or took my meals standing in front of the refrigerator, and I know my mother did the same thing at her own house — we do appreciate good food when it's put in front of us, contrary to Kenny and Lindsay's teasing.

Mom's rule is that she won't eat anywhere that it would take more time to travel to than to eat a good dinner at. The High-Speed Transatlantic Underground put Leo's Croatian bistro just slightly outside that margin (with a transfer at Lisbon it was just over two and a half hours), but Leo was so busy that if we didn't make reservations at least once a month, we would never get a chance to see him.

Leo was something of a puzzlement to my mother, I knew. He had never expressed the slightest shred of interest in joining the family business. He listened politely and with occasional interest to our stories about Repairman work, but it was an alien world to him.

In some ways, my brother was a creature of another time.

He had fallen hard for Croatia, one of the few developed Western nations that had never lost its Old World charm. You could take the Underground into Dubrovnik, but there was only one stop. You had to walk or ride bikes inside the city walls. They still built houses out of stone and mortar, so new houses matched the thousand-year-old castles and cottages lining the white sand beaches.

In the military bases and expat outposts, they lived like we did, with food supplements and hydration tablets, but outside those walls the city still felt untouched.

Time Travel was fortunate to be the only government bureau with a full-service cafeteria serving fresh food, but our agents wouldn't have allowed it any other way. Try getting an agent who's been posted in 18th-century Provence on a three-year assignment to come back to 22nd-century Washington D.C. to work behind a desk.

No, our food service department had gleaming flatware made from real silver, a diverse international menu featuring our field agents' favorite recipe discoveries — the lamb stew Lindsay placed in front of me, in a steaming copper bowl, was clearly North African in origin, exuding a dense steam of warm, heady spices — and even a sommelier in the executive dining hall on the top floor.

Fresh produce wouldn't transport through the Slipstream, but nonperishable items traveled just fine.

About thirty years ago, an agent discovered the curious fact that spirits brought back through the stream would age correctly in transit — meaning, an agent who brought a bottle of newly-bottled whiskey back from two hundred years ago would arrive with a bottle of two-hundred-year-old whiskey.

There was an entire department on the third floor dedicated to regulating and policing the antique liquor trade; you had to maintain proper permits and licensing and the bureau would tell you how many bottles per year you were allowed to bring through. It was rife with corruption, of course, with agents permitting scandalous license violations in exchange for cuts of the profits; the black market for Chrono-Imported spirits was epic, and one bottle could fetch millions of dollars.

Leo had given me some once, a glass of ninety-two-year-old Irish whiskey a customer had (legally — Leo was still his mother's son) brought him as a gift. We had it for Christmas.

Leo opened the bottle and poured the amber liquid into three heavy crystal tumblers, each with one perfect square cube of flawless ice sitting in the middle like a sculpture. The whiskey shimmered down the sides of the ice and settled in the bottom like ripples of golden silk.

He handed a glass to Mom, and then to me, with the reverent air of an acolyte performing a religious ceremony. He drank, eyes closed in orgiastic bliss. Mom drank, and I could see her hold the liquid in her mouth, savoring it before she swallowed.

I drank.

"This shit tastes like charcoal."

Mom gave the tight, pointed sigh she saved for my most violently inappropriate social *faux pas*. Leo looked hurt, like a sad puppy I had just kicked in the face.

"It does!" I said defensively. "It tastes like peat moss smells when it's burning."

"That is the idea," said Leo tightly.

"It's nasty."

"I'll drink hers," Mom volunteered, and I willingly passed it over.

"This is the last time I waste Chrono-Imported liquor on you, heathen," said Leo. "This bottle would cost six thousand dollars in the open market."

"Just give me a beer or something."

"You eat like a raccoon," he sighed, pointing me towards the kitchen. And true to his word, that was the last time he had wasted any of "the good stuff" on me.

～

I scraped the last of the stew out of the bowl and sighed contentedly as the hot spiced broth slid down my throat. I felt like a functional, living human being again.

Unfortunately, I still had twelve pages of data to process

before Director Gray came by at noon to collect all the apprentice reports, so this good feeling wasn't destined to last.

When I got back to my desk, Calliope was standing there, her face worried.

"What is it now?"

"He hasn't called in," she said, brow furrowed.

"What do you mean?"

"I mean he hasn't called in. He was supposed to buzz me at 6 pm local. That was half an hour ago. I tried his Comm and couldn't reach him." I could see panic beginning to dawn in her eyes, and I patted her hand reassuringly.

"I'll check it out," I said. "I'm sure it's just a glitch. Give me a second to log in and we'll get this all sorted out."

I was trying to sound confident, but it actually was really disconcerting to have Grove — nitpicky to a fault, neurotically obsessed with punctuality — miss a scheduled check-in. Especially knowing his perpetually-worried tech's personality as he did.

Grove and Calliope had been working together for ten years; she had been placed with him as an apprentice and never left. She was his right hand. If he had said he'd call her, he'd call her.

It's nothing, I told myself firmly, sitting down to the computer. *This is Grove we're talking about. He's done this a thousand times. He's patched this exact date at least twice a year since he started. He has it together. It's just a glitch, Reggie. Just a glitch. You can fix it.*

Calliope went to grab us both more coffee. I entered my security code and endured the annoying retinal scan.

This thing was installed on all of our computers last year, thanks to a boondoggle government contract with United Enterprises, who received a giant government handout to provide us a ton of security systems we didn't need.

Then, I logged into what we affectionately refer to as the Hive — a massive, ever-fluctuating data-tracking system which logs every agent currently in the field based on their GC coordinates against the General Timeline.

The readout defaults to the current year, so I had to scroll back to 1968 to find Grove. As I scrolled, I watched the familiar undulating peaks and valleys of the moving graphs — a brief pop in France in 2145, another in New Mexico in 2014, a third in Dubai in 2009, indicating agents from around the world transporting in. All steady. Nothing to see here, folks.

That was until I hit the screen for 1960-1970 and saw what Calliope was talking about. The readouts were going crazy, with the GC coordinates for Grove's location spiking off the charts.

What was happening? What had he done? Had he been spotted transporting in? Was he injured? Was the patch decaying? What was causing this level of instability? I had never seen anything like it.

Not really expecting a response, I paged his Comm — mostly just so I could tell Calliope I had — and was surprised to see his face pop up on the screen, though the image kept freezing up and blacking out.

"Grove! What the hell is going on?" I snapped, sharp-tongued and insubordinate out of sheer relief. Logically, I knew that if something really terrible had happened, we would have been paged for a Rewind, but I still hadn't admitted to myself until I saw him alive how afraid I was.

"Bellows, thank God. I've been trying to reach Calliope —"

"She said she tried you after you missed the check-in and she couldn't get through."

"The interference is playing hell with my Comm connection," he said. "I saw her incoming message but I couldn't connect. And when I tried to get her back, it almost died altogether."

"What's going on?"

"The patch isn't working, Bellows," he said grimly. "We've tried everything in the playbook and Johnson's still alive and well and running for President."

"Oh my God, Grove, when are you? Is it —"

"Yes," he said. "It's Election Day." A klaxon shriek from my computer diverted my attention away from the Comm. The General Timeline was a mess.

"Grove, you have to get out of there," I said. "I'm getting some seriously demented readings. There are reverberations from your GC location filtering up as far forward as mid-21st."

"Something could still happen," he said stubbornly. "Johnson could lose. We can't manipulate millions of voters. We have no way of knowing what the results will be —"

"IMPENDING TRANSPORT SHUTDOWN," said the angry red letters flashing on my computer screen. "MANUAL OVERRIDE RECOMMENDED."

"Sir, get out now or you'll be trapped there!"

"That's not your call, Bellows," he snapped back as the computer continued to go crazy.

"But sir, you have no idea what's causing the Incongruity. If you don't get out now, you could get stuck mid-transport —"

"I know what I'm doing, Bellows. I need to stay until they call the election. If Johnson wins I'm going to have to —"

"If Johnson wins the whole General Timeline will be in shambles," I told him. "This has never happened before. Just get back to the lab and we can deal with it from here."

"IMPENDING TRANSPORT SHUTDOWN. MANUAL OVERRIDE RECOMMENDED."

"Bellows, my portable transport is malfunctioning. I need you to short-hop me back to last week. I need to talk to the President."

"Sir, I can't do that. Any further transports inside this timeline will just make the Incongruity worse."

"Stop giving me excuses, Bellows, and do it."

I hung up on him. I had never done that before, and however much it startled him on his end, it couldn't be half as much as I startled myself.

But I knew there was only one thing to do. There would be time later to address the consequences, but right now my boss was trapped in an Incongruity with a patch that was breaking down, and he was refusing to leave.

"IMPENDING TRANSPORT SHUTDOWN. MANUAL OVERRIDE RECOMMENDED."

"I'm on it," I muttered grimly to the computer as I shoved back my chair and bolted from the desk, nearly knocking Calliope over.

"Where the hell are you going?"

"Transport lab! Now!" She turned on a dime and sprinted down the long hall after me.

The lab was on the same floor as the 20th Century department, down a long, long hallway full of offices and conference rooms, all spookily empty at this time of night. We sailed past them, running like our lives depended on it.

Once standing behind the console, I felt a little calmer. Resigned. I would probably get fired for this — unauthorized transport was a big no-no and I hadn't filled out any of the paperwork required for a jump this big. Without Grove present I'd need a ranking officer or department director to sign off on it.

Not to mention the fact that Grove's concerns were not invalid — if he left before his mission was completed, it could wreck the General Timeline. If Johnson was re-elected, the entire second half of the century would be reshaped, and the bureaucratic nightmare of cleaning it all back up again would cost the Bureau millions of dollars.

But if I didn't bring Grove back, he could die.

Transport of solid bodies is nowhere near as risky now as it was in the early days, but the first Garcia-Chidong reports warned of terrifying dangers. A traveler caught inside an Incongruity could be killed — essentially, two versions of yourself meet in the Slipstream coming and going, forcing both your bodies to begin deteriorating.

Grove was running a terrible risk. Without knowing what had caused that major spike — what unplanned event was taking place within the range of his GC coordinates and throwing the system into shambles — he was in increasing danger of getting stuck with every passing minute he stayed there.

"Run a trace on all agents currently in the field within a hundred-year radius," I told Calliope as she took her station. "See if there are any other aberrations."

My fingers flew over the keyboards, trying to get a lock on Grove's maddeningly elusive signal. Vital signs were still stable, that was good news. He was still whole and healthy, just stubborn as hell.

"Twenty-six agents within those coordinates," she said after a few moments. "No Chronomalies. Whatever it is, it's only affecting Grove."

"Or it's only affecting 1968," I pointed out. "It could be local interference. Check the registry. Any other agents in a concurrent timeline?" She clicked a few times.

"Closest is '66, Argentina. Too far to have any impact."

"I can't get a lock on him," I complained. "It's like his signal is ping-ponging back and forth because of the interference. Whatever's happening where he is, the instability is growing."

Out of the corner of my eye I could see my Comm buzzing on the counter. Grove was ringing in, no doubt to yell at me. Calliope moved towards it but I shook my head. "He's gonna be pissed," I told her, "but we have to do this. Are you with me?"

"Can you get him out?"

"I think so."

"Then I'm with you," she said. "Just tell me what to do."

"Can you get a lock on any of the other agents in the field?"

"All of them. Everyone else's signals are clear. It's just on his end."

"Then this might work," I said, pulling off my ratty sweater and stripping down to the plain white undershirt beneath as Calliope looked on in puzzlement. "If you can lock on to them, hopefully you can lock onto me. Give me your coat."

"What?"

"Your coat, your white coat. Give it to me."

"What are you doing?"

"Trying to shave a few points off my HIO reading. Take the controls," I said, pulling my messy hair back into a hasty knot, grabbing one of the micro-cams from the bin and clipping it in over my temple. "I've set a lock on Grove's exact location, just before the interference started."

"Wait, what? Reggie, no. You're not going in after him."

"Of course I am. What did you think I was doing?"

"I don't know, I thought you were going to work some computer genius magic or something."

"Unfortunately not."

"You have no experience! You're not cleared for field work outside the classroom! And that's two unauthorized transports without proper documentation —"

"This is literally the only idea I have left, Calliope," I said.

"It's 3 am. There are no agents from our floor in the building. Either waking one up to drag them down here, or pulling somebody from another era and mission-briefing them, would take time we don't have. We're just going to have to do this ourselves. Keep a lock on me, and as soon as I make contact, bring us both back. I want to see if I can figure out what's causing the Chronomaly, but if I can't, at least I'm going to get my boss out of there before he gets stuck."

I knew she wasn't happy. But I also knew she would do it. Hopefully in my now-nondescript outfit with a generic white lab coat over it and my hair pulled back, I could reduce my HIO level enough to get in and out with as little mess as possible.

I stepped onto the transport platform and felt the familiar buzzing vibrations as the Hive locked onto my signal.

"We who are about to die salute you," I said dryly.

"Not funny," she snapped, punching in the coordinates. "Get back here as soon as you can. Both of you."

And with that I was gone.

CHAPTER THREE

ELECTION DAY

I felt solid ground beneath my feet and opened my eyes, to find myself in a toilet stall. "Very funny," I hissed. I pushed open the door to the toilet stall, heart pounding. My Comm showed no human activity nearby, but I didn't want to take any chances. All clear.

"You try coming up with a low HIO transport site with fifteen seconds' notice, smartass," she snapped back. "It was the only empty room in the building. And no one will look funny at someone walking out of a bathroom."

"Well, they might," I said, turning my head so my micro-cam could give her a full view of the row of urinals behind me, "since, you know, *this is the men's room.*"

"Oh."

"How far am I from Grove?"

"He's right across the street," she said. "Go out the bathroom door, turn left and then left again, and you'll be on the front steps."

"Can I do it without being noticed?"

"God, I hope so."

"Calliope!"

"It's a public building. People go in and out constantly. Just merge with the crowd."

I caught a glimpse of myself in the mirror — nondescript gray pants, dingy white shirt looking almost yellow in contrast with Calliope's spotless white lab coat, messy knot of curls in the back of my head. *Please don't force me to go inside the White House dressed like this,* I prayed.

Grove's vitals showed that he was outside, which was safer. On streets, people keep moving. They don't look around as much. Indoors, people move less, and more slowly. It's harder to go unnoticed.

"Time check?"

"You're twenty-two minutes ahead of the Chronomaly. Plenty of time."

"Okay. Here goes." I took a deep breath, opened the door, and stepped out into the tiled hallway of a big stone building, mercifully unnoticed.

By the light coming in from the big arched windows, it was about midday. A steady stream of men in suits, and a handful of women, ebbed and flowed from the offices around me.

I was struck immediately, as I always had been doing field study for my classes at the Academy, by how different the people smelled.

We talk all the time about evolutions in ideology, fashion, hairstyles, architecture, slang terms and colloquialisms, cuisine, and all the other features that determine the personality of a society, but the one thing school can't prepare you for is the tactile. How things smell and taste.

Inside this building, 1968 smelled like old brick dust and coffee and strongly-spiced perfumes, with a fresh airy breeze the closer I got to the front door. But the heavy D.C. car exhaust stench I was expecting was curiously absent.

I merged with a small cluster of gray suits and followed them out the door, like a salmon swimming upstream. As we stepped out into the chilly sunlight, I stopped short at the top of a flight of big stone steps and looked around.

I had expected to land somewhere within walking distance of the White House. Instead, I was staring at the bustling Main Street of a bucolic Midwestern town, all brick storefronts and cheery red street clocks and open blue skies.

"Calliope, where the hell am I?"

"What do you mean, where are you?"

"This isn't Washington, D.C."

"Your dazzling powers of observation are —"

"*Calliope.*"

"This is Ohio," she said. "You didn't check the coordinates before you jumped?"

"What the hell am I doing in Ohio?" I snapped.

"I ask myself that question every day," sighed a bored-looking woman as she passed me going down the steps, and I winced a little. Apparently I was not exactly as stealthy as I thought.

"For God's sake, Reggie, walk around the block or something. You can't just stand there staring into space and talking to yourself."

I sighed. I hated it when she was right. I walked down the grand stone steps and turned around to look behind me.

"It's the Belmont County Courthouse," said Calliope's voice in my earpiece. "You're in St. Clairsville, Ohio. Election Day, 1968. Turn left and keep walking."

St. Clairsville, Ohio. What was he doing here? More to the point, why was there a Chronomaly here? What was so important about this sleepy little town? The outside world faded away, my feet moving mechanically beneath me of their own volition, as I opened the mental compartment entitled "1968 Election" and rifled through it.

And then it came to me.

"This was one of the turning-point states," I said to Calliope. "The '68 election came down to California, Illinois and Ohio. Nixon only won Ohio by about 2% of the vote and that's what put him over the Electoral College majority he needed to win. Pull county-by-county polling data for me."

"I'm looking at it now. Belmont County went like 2-to-1 for Nixon."

"He's checking to see if the votes have changed," I realized suddenly. "He's using St. Clairsville as a bellwether, trying to test the waters. If Belmont County is sliding left, it might be a sign that the rest of the country is too."

I had circled the block by this time and returned to the front steps of the courthouse. Across the street, outside a brick building labeled "ST. CLAIRSVILLE PUBLIC LIBRARY," festooned with red, white and blue bunting, a long line of people snaked down the block and around the corner.

The library must be the town's polling place, I realized. The line filed into the building through the left of two double glass doors, and out on the right.

That's when I spotted Grove.

"I've got him on visual," I whispered. "I'm looking at him right now."

"Where is he? Oh! I see him! Over by the door to that building. He looks okay, don't you think he looks okay?"

"He looks fine, quit worrying. Time check?"

"Eleven minutes. What's he doing? Why is he talking to those people?"

"God, he's good," I murmured approvingly. "He's posing as a reporter doing an exit poll. He's asking everyone coming out of the booths how they voted."

"Is that legal?"

"Oh, yeah. Happens all the time."

"How reliable is it?"

"Hard to say," I said. "But he doesn't look happy."

"No, he doesn't."

Grove had positioned himself just outside the right-hand exit door so everyone leaving the building had to walk right past him. I saw him asking questions and making notes as they passed.

As I crossed the street, my heart sank. A stream of voters exited the building, and one of them held the right-hand exit door open, beckoning Grove in. No doubt on account of the chill in the air, Grove smiled and obliged. Now he was inside, which meant I somehow had to get inside to get to him.

"Well, that's inconvenient," said Calliope, annoyed.

"I'll say. Can you do a building scan? Give me some options."

Technically all I had to do was grab him and then jump out; my Comm would latch onto him the moment I made physical contact.

But there was no way to vanish into thin air, in such a crowded place, without screamingly high HIO levels, and anything above a twenty would send a red alert to the absolute last person I wanted notified of my screw-ups. She would find out eventually, but you can't blame me for wanting to stall the inevitable shitshow as long as possible.

"Pickin's are slim," said the voice in my ear. "The library used to be a bank, so it's not exactly an embarrassment of riches in terms of unsecured entrances. You're going to have to go in the front door. That's the downside. But the interior is pretty crowded, and the shelves are high. If you can get him away from the polling booths and into the stacks, you should be able to get a little cover."

"Thanks, Calliope."

"Nine minutes, by the way."

With only one entrance to the building, and with the queue passing through it nearly two blocks long, I decided my only option here was to play to my strengths — namely, being a gigantic pain in the ass.

So I cut to the front of the line.

"Excuse me, ma'am," said the gray-haired man about five spots from the entrance who I had just stepped in front of. "I was next."

"I'm not really in line," I said. "You're fine."

"The line ends over there," said the woman next to him, pointing back to the corner of the block.

"I'm not really in line," I said. "I'm not here to vote."

"The library is closed. You can't go in unless you're voting."

"I'm not going in, I just need to talk to that guy over there," I said, pointing to Grove, who was now about twenty feet away with his back to me.

"We've all been waiting patiently," said the gray-haired man. "You can't just cut in front. That's rude."

"Yes. I'm a very rude person. It's terrible. But look, seriously, I just need to go talk to that guy. I'm not going to slow down your voting."

"You need to get out of this line," said a woman behind me. "This isn't fair to everyone else who's been waiting."

"Holy shit, can you calm down!?" I snapped. "I'll be out of your hair in like two minutes."

I don't know whether it was the soft tick of the HIO meter on my Comm, notching up a dangerous few levels, the exasperated sigh from Calliope, or the horrorstruck faces of the people standing next to me that penetrated first, but I knew I'd gone too far.

"Oh," I said. "Sorry. Do women not say 'shit' here?"

"*Ladies* don't," said the woman behind me frostily.

"Well, sorry," I said. "I'm new."

"To *civilization*?"

"Listen, lady —"

"Oh my God Reggie — stop talking — stop talking — *stop talking*!" Calliope screeched in my ear, so loudly that I winced. Hard. Like in a full-body flail kind of way. The HIO meter ticked up again as everyone stared at me.

"This is going well."

"Shut up, Calliope."

"Who is Calliope?" asked the woman. *Tick.* "Who are you talking to? Why are you dressed like that?" *Tick, tick.*

"Oh, look, the line's moving!" I exclaimed, faint with relief, and shoved the people in front of me through the doorway.

"Four minutes," said Calliope. "By the way, if I get fired I'm taking you down with me."

"Oh, I think I'll be able to get myself fired with no help from you," I murmured, shoving into the front door behind the annoying Ohioans.

"See the tall shelves to your right? About five feet behind Grove? Don't say anything, just nod if you see them."

I nodded.

She continued, "No human activity, blocked sightlines to the rest of the room. If you can get him behind the stacks, you're clear to transport. Just stay out of the line to the actual polling booths, they're asking everyone to show their voter registration and they'll throw you out the door if you don't have it."

I nodded again, and as the line of voters inside the library moved closer to the check-in table I spotted a woman wearing a badge that said VOLUNTEER.

"Excuse me, where's the ladies' room?" I said politely, and thanked God for my first stroke of good luck all day when she pointed in the direction that Calliope had indicated to me.

"You'll lose your place in line," she cautioned.

"It's okay, I didn't feel like voting anyway," I said. "One old white guy or another old white guy, what's the difference really?"

And I stepped out of the line to make a break for Grove, leaving her shocked face behind me.

Once in the stacks, hidden from view, I relaxed a little bit. All I had to do now was creep up behind Grove, pull him behind the shelves and jump.

I checked my Comm. Three minutes. I was so close.

That was when it suddenly occurred to me what I had missed. Somewhere, in this quaint small-town library full of ordinary men and women, something was *not right*. I was three minutes from the crisis point, which meant that whoever or whatever was about to cause the Chronomaly was right here. Something in this room was causing interference so intense that Grove couldn't transport. But I had no idea what it was.

I hung back slightly, out of Grove's line of vision. There was a break coming up in the line of exiting voters; there was a woman talking to him now, but nobody in line after her had emerged from the voting booths yet.

"Two minutes."

"I'm going in as soon as that woman leaves," I murmured, heart beginning to accelerate. We were so close. Whatever was going to happen was about to happen.

Grove, deep in conversation with the woman wrote

something on his notepad and nodded as she moved away. Still, no one coming out of the booths. Nobody on Grove's side of the door. It was now or never.

I pounced.

Grove was a big guy, and in a fight he would have overpowered me in a heartbeat. Very few people, however, are at their best when taken by surprise, so when I stepped up behind him, grabbed his arm and yanked him back into the stacks — rather neatly, I thought, and almost entirely unnoticed — he was too startled to resist.

"Incoming," said Calliope. "Turn left and then right and you're clear." I followed her instructions, dragging Grove with me.

"Bellows, what the hell are you doing here?"

"Saving your ass, sir," I said. "We're one minute out from a massive Incongruity. We have to jump before it hits."

"Let go of me right this minute, Bellows, you are jeopardizing the completion of this mission."

"Due respect, sir, right now Calliope is staring at a giant TRANSPORT SHUTDOWN error message flashing on her screen. You could have been stuck here permanently, or ripped in half if you tried to jump back with busted equipment. Calliope?"

"Clear."

"Signal locked," I said to her, grabbing tightly to Grove's hand. He was furious.

"Goddammit, Bellows, you have no idea what you've done!"

"Yell at me later," I said. "Let's go." And the library shimmered into nothingness and was gone.

We hit the Slipstream, and I felt the familiar tingling sensation. I counted to five and waited to land. Suddenly I felt a jolt to the stomach and a drop in pressure. This was taking too long. We should have landed by now. Something was wrong.

I opened my eyes but saw only darkness. We were falling. I clutched tight to Grove. He was heavier, dragging me down, but I held on. I felt the air around me expand, become dense and heavy, as though it were pressing on me with a physical weight, and I realized we were trapped inside the Incongruity. If Calliope didn't have a lock on our signals, we were dead.

Grove's eyes were wide with panic and I opened my mouth to yell at him to hold on, but nothing came out. Cold fear shivered down the back of my neck. *Breathe, Reggie, breathe,* I told myself sternly. *Come on, Calliope!*

I began to feel shaky all over. Lack of oxygen was a common side effect of getting trapped inside a Slipstream for too long, much like when divers who spend too much time in the deeps of the ocean get "the bends." It could be lethal, and Grove's system was already weakened by coming out of a mission with so many interior drops. If we didn't get out soon, it could cause us both permanent brain damage.

The blackness softened slightly around the edges and a small, telescoping point of light slowly opened up in the center of my vision. My eyes were fuzzy and my brain was beginning to swim. It was either the lab, or I was about to die. At that point I felt so faint that I didn't really care.

"Oh, thank God!" Calliope's shrill voice pierced through the fog in my brain as I felt the comfortingly solid floor beneath my feet. My legs buckled beneath me and I began to sway, pulled down to the ground by some unseen force.

Dimly, I could see three green-uniformed medics standing at the ready (Calliope, ever prepared). One of them caught me as I started to collapse. That was when I noticed the thing that had been pulling me downward.

I had not let go of Grove's hand.

Grove was not moving.

"I've got you, ma'am," said the medic comfortingly as he scooped me up in his arms. "You're gonna be fine."

"He isn't moving," I said haltingly, remembering as I spoke them how words were formed in my mouth. My entire face felt like it had been shoved full of cotton balls and sand.

"His vitals are stable, he's just unconscious. He's gonna be fine too. We need to get you up to Medical. I need you to let go of his hand."

"But he'll fall," I said sleepily, my head lolling back into the medic's arms. "I came back to save him. I can't let go of his hand."

"You saved him," said Calliope's voice, from inside Calliope's now upside-down head. "You did it, Reggie. Everything's going to be okay."

I let go of his hand.

CHAPTER FOUR

CALLED TO THE PRINCIPAL'S OFFICE

I came to in one of the hospital beds in the thirty-sixth-floor Medical bay, feeling like I had been run over by a marauding Viking horde. Everything hurt.

A blazing golden shadow shimmered into view, which turned out to be Calliope's blonde hair caught in the bright sickbay lights.

"How do you feel?" she asked. "Are you all right?"

"Fine, I think," I said, sitting up and stretching myself. "How long was I out? What day is it?"

She gave me a curious look. "What?" I asked, beginning to panic.

"I didn't want to have to be the one to tell you," she began. My heart turned over in my chest at the sad, serious look in her eyes.

"Tell me what? Tell me what?"

"Reggie. You've been unconscious for ten years," she said quietly.

"*What?*"

"Ha! I'm totally kidding. It's been like an hour."

"I hate you so much right now."

She laughed, sitting down on the bed next to me and handing me a glass of water.

"Drink this. Thanks to you, Grove made it," she said, answering before I could ask. "He's in a coma. But he's alive. The doctors said to congratulate you on your quick thinking. I don't know what kind of malfunction kept him from being able to spot that Chronomaly, but every short-hop he took just made the Incongruity worse. If he'd tried to jump out using his own equipment, he'd have ended up with massive organ failure the second he entered the Slipstream."

"What about the election?"

"Johnson lost the Electoral College. Landslide. Wasn't even close. The Chronomaly repaired itself and 1968 is back to normal. We still don't know why it took so long, but the patch eventually worked."

"Thank God," I sighed, lying back against the hospital pillow before sitting bolt upright again. Calliope laughed, seeing it on my face before I even asked.

"Your report has been waived," she said. "The data's not relevant anyway, since the mission was terminated and Grove is back. And he can give a full report when he's awake again. Right now you need rest. You just combined thirty-three hours of no sleep and very little food with a massive Slipstream malfunction."

"Calliope Burns, that is the greatest of all your great ideas," I said agreeably, and allowed her to settle me back into bed.

"Sleep until I come get you," she said. "Do not, under any circumstances, get out of this bed until I or a medical professional say you can. Deal?"

I was already asleep.

~

It felt like only half a second later when I felt someone gently shaking me awake, but in actuality it had been almost nine hours. The longest I'd slept in a month, at least. I still felt groggy and bleary-eyed, but much more sane.

"Agent Bellows?" said a warm male voice. I opened my eyes and saw the medic from the transport bay.

"Mmmmmmmghhhhhhh," I replied.

"And good morning to you," he grinned. "You're cleared to go, and you're needed back on your floor in an hour. Wardrobe cleaned your clothes, and there's a shower just down the hall."

The shower was a brilliant idea, and I told him so — profusely — on my return. I stayed there for ages, hot water pounding my knotted shoulders and neck into submission. I stood in there until my skin was flushed and pink, then dried my hair and got dressed, thinking idly that it felt like another lifetime ago when I took off that sweater and traded it for Calliope's lab coat. The medic smiled when he saw me.

"You look much more human," he said.

"I feel more human."

"Good luck down there," he said as I headed for the elevator.

"Thanks," I tossed over my shoulder, then stopped and turned back around. "Wait. Good luck with what? What did you mean?"

He looked uncomfortable. "Sorry, I didn't — I know she's — I just meant, I would be intimidated if it was me. That's all."

"Intimidated by what?"

"I thought Calliope told you."

"Told me *what*?"

"They just rang me before I woke you up," he said, an

apology in his tone. "You've been called in to meet with the Deputy Director."

"The Deputy Director," I repeated.

"Yes."

"Tall, brown hair, ice-cold eyes of judgment? Passed on only the shittiest half of her genetic material to the daughter she's probably about to fire? *That* Deputy Director?"

"Good luck," he said again, more weakly this time. I sighed.

Well, it's not like I didn't anticipate this, I thought to myself as the elevator plunged downward. I knew it was unauthorized. I knew I could get in trouble.

I had known that before I brought Grove back. I had been willing to take my lumps with him, but somehow it hadn't occurred to me to remember that this was Katie Bellows' turf, and shame-inducing lectures on breaches of government ethics were her favorite way to unwind at the end of a long day.

~

I don't know whether or not you've been raised by a celebrity parent. If you have, I'm so sorry. Come to D.C. and I'll buy you a drink. If you haven't, you should know that it's the kind of thing that sounds like a whole lot more fun than it is.

For one thing, most of my professors at the Academy were colleagues of my mother's, greatly reducing my opportunities for slacking off, tardiness, or fun. Everywhere you go, people are watching you, eager to report back and score some points with the boss. To her credit, she was a perfectly reasonable amount of strict — a little firmer with Leo, the renegade, and a little looser with me, the placid bookworm — but reasonable either way.

At sixteen, however, I did not have quite this pragmatic

attitude. Getting caught misbehaving and being forced to sit for an hour in some unforgiving metal chair in some drab office while waiting for my impatient mother to stride in, tall and majestic, impervious to the giddy swoons of the receptionist, shoot a look full of daggers in my direction and say, very quietly, "I was called out of a meeting with the Director for this, Regina Theresa, *what did you do*?" was a mistake I made exactly one time and never again.

Looking back, I can see that it could have been worse. I'm sure she knew early on that I had decent enough judgment to avoid any really stupid situations — I never went home with the bad boys, I never tried mystery drugs at a party, I never got less than a B on an exam — but it still drove me crazy.

This is the most important thing you should know about my mother. She may be a feminist hero and the most iconic legend in Bureau history, she may be able to Chrono-Jump six hundred years round-trip without mussing her hair, and she may be the rumored top pick to replace the Director when he retires this year, which would make her the first woman Director ever. (Oh, you thought because this is the 22nd century, the patriarchy has been dismantled? That's adorable.)

But she has one huge, all-encompassing trait that to me, her daughter, outweighs everything else, which is that *she is my mother* and every time some junior apprentice gushes to me about what it must have been like to grow up "in the shadow of a legend," I flash back to that metal chair in the school office and I want to tell them, "You have absolutely no idea."

Katharine Silverton Bellows, six-times decorated for injuries suffered in the line of duty, youngest field agent in Repairman history and current Deputy Director of the United States Time Travel Bureau, is one of those rare living legends who actually lives up to the hype.

My mother is very tall and very pretty. I got her huge green eyes, my one point of vanity — the Silverton women all have them — and Leo got the impossibly shiny, dark-chocolate hair she inherited from her Iranian grandmother. Mom's has a little bit of gray at the temples – not nearly as much as there ought to be given that she's well on the other side of fifty, but just a perfect, aristocratic sweep of silver at the brow and temples.

I did not get Mom's hair. I would also have been fine with Dad's — thick and cornsilk-blond — but I wasn't even that lucky. I don't know which blight on the Silverton-Bellows-Carstairs family tree bestowed their coiffure on me, but it is a goddamn nightmare, coarse and curly and a dull mousy brown, impossible to do anything with except tie it back in a knot and forget about it.

So to all my various mother complexes, please add to the list the fact that she is prettier than me by such a dramatic margin that people meeting us side-by-side for the first time are palpably startled.

I've lost count over the years of every government official who looked me over and then instantly dismissed me as a frumpy low-level aide until my mother introduced me, at which point they would look from me to her and from her to me and from me to her, and then cough awkwardly and extend a too-hearty handshake to cover their discomfort.

Other mothers, I learned from books, said comforting things to their plain daughters like "You'll grow into your looks" or "Boys love curly hair" or "Don't worry, it's just an awkward phase."

Katie Bellows stood for none of that nonsense. When her teenage daughter cried in the mirror and lamented that she would never be as pretty as that blonde volleyball player who sat behind her in Advanced Algebra, Katie Bellows would fire back the same crisp retort, "So what if she's prettier? You're better at math."

"That doesn't matter!" I wailed.

"It ought to, in math class."

"Mom, you know what I mean!"

"You're being ridiculous."

"You've always been pretty, you don't know what it's like," I grumped. My mother laughed at this, actually laughed out loud. Nothing could have stung more.

"Listen to me, Regina. I'm going to tell you a secret. I'm not pretty at all."

"Yes, you are, dummy."

"No, not the way you mean. When you say 'pretty' what you're thinking of is a very narrow definition of how a woman is meant to look which is basically defined by whatever traits fifteen-to-thirty-five-year-old men currently happen to be attracted to." (I hated when she talked like this.) "Look at me. Really look." I did, reluctant to humor her but curious to where this was going.

"My eyes are proportionately too big for my face," she said. "I have a very long nose. I have a sharp jaw. I'm taller than most men. I have the body of a woman who has birthed two children, which means my ass has a mind of its own sometimes. But none of that actually *means* anything. First of all, what people are attracted to varies dramatically, and my very long nose and your father's terrible mustache did not stop us from falling in love. Second, if you have a good haircut and good shoes, you're clean and neat, 90% of the entire human race will find you perfectly presentable and you can accomplish anything you want to."

I thought "perfectly presentable" sounded not that much of an improvement on "hideous," and I said so. She sighed the particular and specific sigh of the feminist mother.

"You will be astonished, Regina, at how little any of this matters in the real world. You're kind and competent and unbelievably smart. You work hard. You're trustworthy. Those are the things that count."

"Not to boys," I pouted.

"They're idiots at this age," she said calmly. "The right things will matter to the right boy. In the meantime, math is more important than boys."

"But I want Jamal to like me!"

"Well, maybe he will and maybe he won't," she said, her voice annoyingly reasonable. "But there's nothing you can do to control that, so you might as well spare yourself the headache." And with that, impervious to my I-hate-you glare, she sailed out of the room.

∼

The elevator door slid open and I saw Calliope waiting for me, tapping her foot anxiously. She knew as well as I did that in my entire career, my mother had never once called me into her office.

"Are we getting fired?" she mouthed. I shook my head.

"She's my *mother*, she's not going to fire me," I said, hoping to God that it was actually true.

"Is she going to fire *me*?"

"You didn't do anything wrong. You just did what I told you to do."

"But she's never —"

"I know."

"And you had to —"

"I *know*."

We looked at each other for a long moment. Finally she

sighed, straightened my jacket, made a valiant attempt to tidy my un-tidy-able hair, and shoved me down the hall like a military general sending troops to certain doom.

The clomp of my shoes down the white tiled floor felt unbearably loud, like the whole department had fallen silent to watch my walk of shame to the solid wooden door with its elegant brass nameplate at the end of the hallway.

Clomp. Clomp. Clomp. Clomp.

It was the longest hallway in the world. It went on for eons. Whole civilizations were born and died in the time it took me to round the corner away from the hot uncomfortable stares of my coworkers. I knocked on the door to the Executive Wing.

Yasmina, my mother's tech of the past seventeen years, opened the door and let me in. I could tell from the stoic set of her jaw and the way her dark eyes avoided contact with mine that she was thinking what Calliope was thinking.

"It's gonna be fine," I whispered, and Yasmina's face relaxed ever so slightly.

"Heads up. They're in the Council Chambers," she said under her breath.

"What do you mean, 'they?'" I asked, heart sinking.

"It's not just her. The committee is in there too."

"The *Congressional Time Travel Committee* is here?" My voice came out high-pitched and squeaky, and Yasmina hushed me with a sharp gesture. "What is *happening*? Is this about Grove?"

"Nobody knows," she whispered back. "Promise you'll tell me. If you can."

"Promise."

She patted me on the back with the same pitying expression I had gotten from Calliope. Nothing instills confidence like well-meaning people looking at you like you're about to die.

I sighed and followed her through the anteroom, down the short hall where my mother's office adjoined the Director's, until we stopped in front of the door that led to the Council Chambers. She knocked three times, waited a moment until an unfamiliar man's voice uttered a brisk "Come in!" then opened the door.

~

The last time I had been in this room, I was six. My friend Ruth, whose dads both worked in Wardrobe, had come upstairs to play with me and Leo while they finished outfitting six agents for a patch on F. Scott Fitzgerald.

It was late in the evening and we mostly had the run of the place while our parents worked. Someone from the cleaning staff had left the Council Chamber's back door unlocked; on a dare, Ruth opened it and we all stared in.

We were strictly forbidden to go inside, but were unable to resist temptation when it was dangled right in front of our faces. Ruth, infinitely braver, tiptoed in, and after a few breathless moments of silence, heart pounding, I crept in after her, Leo close behind.

The chairs seemed like empty thrones to us, waiting in hushed anticipation for the return of the kings and queens and heads of state who belonged there.

We crawled under the table, hid behind flags, chased each other in and out of the maze of chairs, and generally scampered around like puppies who have been trapped in a small room too long, until suddenly Ruth knocked something off the table — a pen or something — and the crashing sound it made on the hard wooden floor made us freeze with terror as all the awe and panic of that daunting room fell down around us at once.

~

It was the same now.

The first thing I registered about the room was how full it seemed. My first impression was of an absolute sea of faces staring at me in stern disapproval.

I took a small step forward, tripped over the doorframe, and stumbled into the Council Chambers with a drunken lurch, flailing around for the doorknob to steady myself. Once the world slid back into focus and the hot waves of mortification subsided, I noticed that what had looked like a mob of angry faces was in fact only fifteen, sitting around the large central table.

But they were all staring at me. Except my mother, who was studiously examining her notes. I sent her a little psychic I-hate-you wave, gathered up what little dignity I had left, and took the empty seat at the end of the table which was clearly reserved for me.

"Thank you for joining us, Agent Bellows," said a familiar voice, and I looked up to see Director Gray at the head of the table directly opposite me.

I opened my mouth to respond, closed it again quickly after nothing came out but a nervous squeak, coughed in an attempt to cover it, caught the tail end of a repressive glare from my mother, glared back, coughed again, just to be on the safe side, and then carefully responded, "Thank you, sir."

Though why I was thanking him if he was about to send me packing, I wasn't sure.

"Medical informs us that Grove is unconscious but stable, and that you are fully recovered. Are you well?"

"Fine, thank you."

"Do you know why you're here?"

"I'm being fired for bringing Grove back without proper authorization," I said promptly, and was completely befuddled as the room burst into laughter.

"You're not in trouble, Agent Bellows," the Director said kindly. "Just the opposite, in fact. The Council has called you here because we need your help."

"I'm not getting fired?"

"No, Agent Bellows, you are not getting fired."

Well, this was an unexpected development.

"Even though I violated like" — I tried to count in my head — "*every* rule about transport usage?"

"Would you like a reprimand? All right. It's been noted on your record," he said, smiling. "Try not to let it happen again."

Confused, but at least slightly less petrified now, I took the glass of water he offered me and took several long, slow sips to buy myself a few seconds of time to catch up. I looked around the room.

Director Gray was across from me, then the Speaker of the House, the House Majority Leader, and eleven members of the U.S. House of Representatives.

One of them, I noticed with mixed emotions, was a man named Benjamin Arthur Holmes. He had served in Congress for nearly forty years representing the good people of Boston. Twenty-five years ago, as a member of the Government Oversight Committee, he had chaired the investigative hearings on the Sharpeville Massacre.

Our eyes met for an uncomfortable moment, as he saw that I knew who he was. And what he had done, or failed to do. Nobody was ever held responsible for the death of Leo Carstairs, and my mother had never stopped blaming Congressman Holmes for that.

~

I have no actual memories of my parents together. When I was younger, my mother talked about my father so much that I began to feel like I had really known him, and sometimes, in my childlike confusion, would tell a story about his life as though I had actually been there. Leo never did this, only me.

He had died on assignment while Mom was pregnant, only a few years into their fairy tale office romance. He had been a green recruit, pulled from Late- to Mid-20th to help with a particularly troublesome patch, and ended up making such a good impression that the Director assigned him as the new partner to my mother, then 26 and the department's rising star.

Despite her clinical assessment of her ass and nose, it was clear from every photograph that young Katie Bellows was as beautiful as she was brilliant, and as brilliant as she was completely unbearable. Nobody wanted to work with her.

Director Graham had burned through half a dozen promising candidates before plucky Leo Carstairs drew the short straw and became in rapid succession Katie Bellows' right hand, best friend, lover and husband. He was the last partner she ever had. After he died, she worked alone.

Obviously I remember none of this since my brother and I were fetuses at the time, but it's been documented so often and so thoroughly that I can tell you about the Sharpeville Massacre like I was there.

I've read the Congressional hearing transcripts so many times I had them practically memorized before I was fourteen. Leo thought it was morbid, but I needed to know.

See, the Director at the time (a desk jockey known familiarly and without affection as "Lazy Daisey") had never seen field training beyond his required stint at the Academy.

He was also completely ignorant of mid-20th-century politics, his father having essentially bought the position for him with a massive campaign donation.

So he was out of his depth from day one.

There was a massive anti-apartheid protest in the township of Sharpeville, South Africa, which according to the General Timeline and all contemporary documentation was supposed to be peaceful — a few thousand black citizens voluntarily turning over their government IDs to the police (thereby preventing them from passing through white South Africa to get to work), which would cripple local businesses.

Just a long line of people handing over pieces of paper, that's all that was supposed to happen.

But something went wrong — nobody ever found out what — and the protest turned into a bloodbath with white police officers indiscriminately firing at black citizens. Daisey had to send an agent back to stop it, and he sent my dad. My blonde, blue-eyed dad.

Alone.

What he should have done, I heard my mother say thousands of times over the ensuing years, was send a second agent. Send a white agent to blend in with the cops, to keep them cool and keep their guns in their holsters, and send a black agent who could move freely through the crowd and absorb whispers and information without arousing suspicion or fear.

That's what she would have done.

But every black agent on our floor was already in that same timeline a few years away, part of a massive task force to patch the arrest of Nelson Mandela, and nobody could be spared to come back.

Plus Daisey had pulled a total dick move on Mom the week before and she found herself benched because of one tiny blip on a routine physical, where pregnancy hormones (AKA Leo and me) had thrown off one section of her stress test. So she wasn't there for Dad's mission brief and she didn't know anything was wrong until Dad missed his scheduled call-in.

So she broke protocol to come into the office and check on him, which is how she spotted the *insane* HIO readings at his location and realized that all hell was about to break loose. Which it did.

The five thousand peaceful protesters Dad was briefed to expect had swelled to twenty thousand, and the dozen small-town cops had suddenly and inexplicably received backup from a heavily armed unit of nearly a hundred police officers with armored cars.

None of which was supposed to happen, and none of which Dad could stop by himself.

By the time the livid pregnant woman screaming in Daisey's office had convinced him to pull an agent off Mandela right this second and send him back for her husband, it was too late to stop it.

Poor Agent Jenkins arrived and found a bloodbath. He put the pieces together later for the official report, fat lot of good it was by then.

The policemen were young and skittish. They had heard tales of officers murdered by rampaging natives. Fear and distrust towards a crowd of black faces was hard-wired into them. They had been there for nearly 24 hours straight and were hungry and tired and at their wits' end. The tension was rising on both sides, so thick and hot it pressed down on them like a blanket. Suddenly, from somewhere in the crowd, a rock sailed through the sky and cracked neatly into the police station's metal roof, startling everyone.

One idiot cop thought the crowd had started shooting, and fired back. His bullet hit a young black man in the shoulder, and then the world went crazy.

The crowd began to panic and flee. The cops began firing left and right. Bullets were flying everywhere. One of them hit Carstairs just before he and Jenkins opened the Slipstream. Less than a minute later, nearly 200 people (including dozens of children) were injured and 70 were dead.

If my father had died in Sharpeville, Jenkins could have simply made a Rewind, popping back to Carstairs' transport coordinates from the day before, and pulling him back to the lab to reset long before a single bullet was fired.

But Jenkins didn't know my dad was dying when he yanked him back through time to bleed to death on the lab floor at the feet of his eight-months-pregnant wife. Jenkins charged headfirst through a fleeing mob and a hail of bullets to bring Agent Carstairs home, and that's exactly what he did. None of us ever blamed him. He did everything right.

But that didn't make it better. The damage had been done. Not only did my father die, but so did all of those other people. The bullet that killed Agent Carstairs tied a knot between his own permanent timeline and the permanent timelines of all those innocent people in South Africa. The Sharpeville Massacre was real. Jenkins couldn't save them.

During the epic Congressional hearing into Dad's death, Mom wanted Daisey hung out to dry for criminal incompetence. But of course his rich dad paid off all the right people, so the evidence was deemed "inconclusive" and Daisey was quietly let go with a giant severance package and half a dozen offers for jobs in the corporate sector. Mom and the rest of the devastated agents were left to pick up the pieces.

Leo and I were born just six weeks later and she refused to take any of her maternity leave beyond what was medically required. She brought us to the office with her. The new Director tried, with increasing urgency, to send her home to either mourn or raise two newborns in peace and quiet, but she would have none of it. "I am mourning," she told him once. "This is how I do that. I am honoring the work my husband died for. I am not sitting on my sofa staring at family photos and crying into my brandy."

No one ever mentioned it again.

~

"Agent Bellows, Director Gray has shared your most recent field report with the committee, and we'd like to ask you some questions," said Holmes, snapping me back to the present. He paused, politely, as though waiting for me to assent to further questioning — like I had any choice — so I nodded for him to go on.

"Agent Grove, as you know, is still in unconscious and under medical care, so no field report has been filed on the 1968 Chronomaly," said the Director. "The committee would like to hear, in your own words, what happened and what you saw."

"I didn't see anything," I said. "Or, if I did, I don't know what it was."

"You were right on top of it," said one of the congressmen — Fletcher, Democrat, Oregon 1st, said the catalog of useless data in my head.

"I know."

"And nothing looked out of place?"

"Look," I said a little defensively, "I'm an apprentice. I'm in training as a desk agent. Do you want to talk about math? I can talk to you about the math. But the people stuff, that's not what I do."

"The HIO readings were astronomical," said the Director. "If a Chronomaly is so massive that it causes a Slipstream Incongruity, there must have been some sign of it. We've been over the footage from your micro-cam several times and have been completely unable to detect what the event might have been. Anything you can tell us — anything unusual that you might have spotted — would help tremendously. We know the spike was within about thirty seconds of the moment you transported out with Grove, and definitely inside that building, but that's as narrow as we can close in."

"Believe me," I said, "if I had seen anything I'd tell you. I wanted to find it too. I don't like math problems I can't solve." This amused him, and he smiled at me as he refilled my now-empty water glass.

"Agent Bellows," said another congresswoman I didn't recognize, "what would you say if I asked you to tell us in one sentence what caused the Third World War?"

I was startled at the change of subject, and thought for a moment. It was a tricky question, and my brain began doing the thing it does when I have to sift through my mental library of historical data to put facts in order.

"Well," I began cautiously, "The simplest one-sentence version would be to say that it officially began with the Chinese bombing raid on Washington D.C. in 1982."

"But the truth is more complicated than that?"

"Almost always."

"So what would you say if we asked you your real opinion?"

"In more than one sentence?"

"In as many sentences as you need."

"We'd be here for hours," I explained. "It wasn't a

straightforward action/reaction. It was a big messy tangled knot. The U.S. economy, the '68 Republican Convention, Communism, Ronald Reagan —"

"And Nixon?" said the man at my elbow, and I turned to him in surprise. He smiled at my expression.

"You weren't expecting that," he said. I smiled back.

"I wasn't, to be honest," I admitted. "President Nixon is mostly only of interest to historians these days. He's a footnote, mostly of significance because Reagan was his Vice President before being elected in 1976. Ask any high school student about him and that's the only thing any of them will know."

"You're a Nixon specialist, I'm told. You studied him in-depth at the Academy."

"That's correct."

"What kind of politician was he?"

"Stubborn," I said. "Taciturn, a little grumpy, but solid. Stable. No nasty baggage, you know? No secret mistress, no drugs, no gay rumors, no mob ties. He was Quaker. He didn't drink that much. He didn't swear. He didn't sleep in the same room as his wife. Just very self-contained. Thoroughly unexciting from most people's point of view."

I went on, "But I've always found him fascinating. It's always seemed to me — and this is my personal opinion, by the way, not my professional one, so feel free to ignore it — that something about his personality seemed...I don't know. Too crafted. Like someone trying to keep their true self very contained. But of course there's no evidence that he had any more of a secret dark side than the average politician."

Another voice spoke up from the far end of the table.

"Agent Bellows, do you know who I am?"

"Yes, ma'am, I do," I said, her serious voice causing me to tense up for no clear reason I could think of. "Adeline

Ondwudiwe. Speaker of the U.S. House of Representatives. It's an honor to meet you."

"Thank you, Agent Bellows. Now, I need to ask you a tremendously important question, so please think carefully about your answer. Is it your considered opinion, as an expert scholar of mid-20th century history — which I understand, from your record, that despite your young age you certainly are — that the course of history would have been changed significantly had Richard Nixon not served out a second term?"

"You're asking about the war, aren't you?" I felt suddenly cold. She nodded.

For some reason my eyes drifted back to Director Gray, and he nodded too. This wasn't theoretical. Something was happening. The strange tense energy in the room suddenly coalesced around this one single question and I realized what they were asking.

The penny dropped.

"You're not on the Time Travel Committee," I said, turning to Congressman Holmes as the truth dawned on me. "You never have been."

He nodded. "That's right."

"What you are, I believe, is the chair of the House Intelligence Committee."

"Right again."

"So you're not here so much as a congressional specialist on time travel as you are the guy responsible for oversight of Homeland Security and the CIA." He didn't say anything, just nodded again, confirming my worst fears. I looked from him to the Director to Speaker Onduwidwe and back. All three of their faces had the same expression.

"You can't possibly be thinking what you're thinking,"

I said, perhaps more accusingly than I meant. "You can't possibly. It's insane. No one has tried this in sixty years. The last time somebody tried to redirect a historical event of this magnitude, it messed up the timeline for generations. The whole reason our jobs *exist* is to repair errors caused by First-Gen agents with this exact crackpot idea."

"Crackpot or not," said my mother, who I had literally forgotten was there, in a repressive tone that made me slink a little lower in my seat, "it's actually a bit more complicated than that." She slid a handheld screen across the table to me. "Take a look."

I picked it up and looked at the screen and said the first thing that popped into my head.

"Holy. Shit."

They all looked awkwardly at each other, startled and a little flustered at my poor manners. All except my mother, who nodded serenely like I had given the correct answer to a question she already knew. She hit a button below the table and the chart I was seeing on the handheld appeared on the screen behind us.

"Tell them what they're looking at, Regina," she said, and I stood and walked over to the screen to show them.

"Okay. Look at this," I said, pointing. "This horizontal axis here, this represents the course of history as past events unfold. This vertical axis represents the significance of those events, as measured by how many people they impact. So in places where some major historical event occurs, you'll see a spike. Everybody with me?"

They nodded.

"Okay, so let me scroll back and show you the Revolutionary War for comparison," I said, sliding my finger over the screen of the handheld to roll back a couple of centuries. "Here. You can see a very, very slow buildup over decades before, then an abrupt acceleration."

I pointed to the first big peak. "This is 1765, right here," I said. "The Stamp Act. Americans begin to rebel against the Crown in earnest. It keeps ramping up, and you can note here that the rate of acceleration increases every year. That's fairly standard. The colonists are angry. They're frustrated. Something that might slide by their notice twenty years ago sets off a boiling point now. Emotions are running high. The gap between incidents narrows. This is how wars traditionally start."

"And this big peak here?" asked one of the congressmen, pointing to the beginning of the steep plateau.

"1775."

"Lexington and Concord," said one of the others.

"That's right," I said. "The official beginning of the war. So you can see that it spikes here pretty dramatically — 'shot heard around the world' and all that — and then stays at a high peak until here. 1783-ish. Treaty of Paris is signed, British troops empty out of the U.S., life goes back to normal."

I continued, "Now, amidst the overall trajectory you can see a healthy amount of random scatter — data points all over the map, high and low, throughout the entire war. That's normal. Even during wartime, the war isn't the only thing going on in everyone's lives. Other events are taking place all over the country, some with major significance and some perfectly ordinary."

I took a breath. "So you have a trendline here but it's still knee-deep in ordinary data. That's what a regular war looks like."

I scrolled forward to the Third World War. "Now look at this again," I said, pointing so they could see. "Do you see it now?"

"It's not the same kind of pattern at all," said the congresswoman sitting next to my mother, who nodded. They all leaned in closer to see.

"Look," I pointed. "The irregularity comes out of nowhere. There's no buildup. It's just a massive spike."

"Higher than any of the other spikes you showed us," said Holmes.

"Exactly. This isn't what a natural crisis point looks like. Actions don't take place in a vacuum. Nobody just bombs a country for no reason."

"So what is that big spike?" asked one of them. I looked at the date and frowned.

"That's strange."

"What?"

"It's not the bombing raid."

"It's not?"

"It's ten years before the bombing raid. It's June 1972."

"What happened in June, 1972?"

"Nothing," I said. "Or, nothing connected to this, anyway. But this spike isn't the important part. What's important are these smaller ones."

"Why?" said the Speaker. They were all curious now.

"When you throw a rock in a pond," I explained, "you get a ripple effect of concentric circles that start strong in the center and then fade out the further they are from where the rock hit. Yes?" They nodded. "That's what this means. But that's not what Lexington and Concord look like. Lexington and Concord were simmering for a long time at a higher and higher temperature until finally the tension boiled over. World War II is the same way. Long slow build after World War I, big spike after Hitler starts invading, another big spike after Hiroshima and Nagasaki. Action stays elevated for a long time."

I paused to make sure they were all with me, then went

on. "But what we're looking at here is one massive, off-the-charts irregularity with decreasing symmetrical irregularities on either side of it. Look, the pattern is pristine. Each subsequent spike decreases on the x-axis by the same ratio. It's too clean to be natural. Real life doesn't look like that. And look, the random scatter we saw during the Revolutionary War? Nonexistent here. This pattern can only mean one thing: the timeline is self-correcting. This is the fallout of a massive Chronomaly. Bigger than any I've ever seen."

"You're sure?"

"I'm sure. A historical event that's synced properly has a wildly irregular pattern of up-and-down spikes. There's a random scatter to the coordinates that shows you it was a real-time event. Once the chronology has been altered, though, you see patterns begin to emerge that show the system correcting itself. So what you're seeing here is the pattern that you would expect to see after a direct intervention. There's a huge jump, here. That's the rock that gets dropped into the pond. The ripples spread out from there, forward and back. The levels stay high right around the event and taper off gradually before and after as the system repairs itself."

I pointed to the screen. "Look, here. This spike in 1968? That's Grove and me. Whatever went wrong with the Johnson election, whatever almost trapped us in the Slipstream, it was only an aftershock from a much, much bigger original event."

"So what does it mean?"

"Well, if I'm reading this graph right — and I'm definitely reading it right — this means…" I froze as the true significance of what I was looking at crashed down on me all at once.

I looked at the Director. He nodded at me soberly.

"How did we not know?" I said softly to him. "How could we possibly not know?"

"You did know," he said. "You just didn't know you knew. We pulled all these numbers from your field report for Grove. The reason you kept beating your head against the wall to make the pattern fit was because the pattern didn't fit. It never did. Everyone else chalked it up to crisis point interference. Wars are always messy. You're the first agent to see what all the rest of us should have seen decades ago."

"Oh my God," I said. "*The war itself* is the Chronomaly."

"Yes."

"It was never supposed to happen. And look — once you know it's there, once you know what you're looking for, you can trace the ripples forwards and backwards, all the way up to — " I scrolled forward and leaned in to read: "December 2113."

I stopped suddenly. "That's *next year.*"

"Yes."

"We're still inside the chronomaly fallout, even now."

"We believe so, yes."

"That's why you're all here," I said, looking at my mother. "You want to send an agent back to the crisis point to stop a war."

"Not just somebody," she said calmly, and I felt a slow cold terror spread over my body as she and the Director looked at each other.

No, don't say it, don't say it, don't say it …

"You," she said.

The last thing I remember was the annoyed look on her face as I slumped to the floor.

CHAPTER FOUR

HOW TO STOP
A WAR THAT ALREADY
HAPPENED

"Miss me?" said an amused male voice, and I opened my eyes to find myself back in the medical bay, in the exact same room I had just left. The medic grinned at me.

Calliope and my mother were sitting in the visitor chairs, deep in conversation. Calliope spotted me first.

"Oh good, you're awake," she said, relieved. More audacious than I had ever seen her in my life, she boldly turned to my mother and said, "You took a big chance elevating her stress level so soon after she almost got trapped in the Slipstream."

"She's fine," said my mother. "Aren't you, Regina?"

"Your concern is touching," I snapped. Or tried to, but it came out "Mmmmmglllfllphhhhh." My head was fuzzy again.

"She needs sleep," said Calliope.

"I agree," said the medic. I thanked him silently. "At least four days' bed rest. No work and no transports."

"We don't have four days," said my mother. "We're sending her back out in the field."

"Really?" he said. "You want to take that chance? You want to send her into the office of some historical dignitary and have her faint all over the floor?"

My mother was silent. "I'm not making a suggestion," he said firmly. "I'm giving an order. On every other floor of this building your word is law, but up here on Thirty-Six the only thing that matters is the patient's health. Your field mission will have to wait four days."

My mother gave him a long stern look before nodding in agreement, a small hidden smile on her face. She enjoyed having this effect; she got a kick out of prodding dissent out of the handful of people still left in this building (or, you know, the *world*) who dared to publicly disagree with her. I could see this young medic rising in her estimation as he stood there and pointedly held his ground.

"Four days then," she said. "No more." Her tone would have frozen lava, but as she left she was smiling.

~

The visits started immediately. Apparently my mother did not believe that work was work if I was doing it in my pajamas, so she sent an endless parade of staff members over to my apartment with files to review. I did not feel this qualified as "bed rest," but I knew better than to bring it up.

The Director was first. In his defense, he had clearly been bludgeoned into it by my mother.

"I told her to give you a break," he said. "But since that

obviously wasn't going to happen I thought I should be first in line to give you your mission briefing before the conquering hordes descend."

"I'm really fine," I protested, slightly half-heartedly. He smiled.

"You're like both of them, you know," he said. "You're a pragmatist like your mother but you're also fearless like your father."

"Fearless? Hardly."

"Really? How did you feel when you were standing on that transport platform, breaking all the rules in the book to go in and rescue Grove?"

"I didn't really feel anything by that point," I admitted. "There just wasn't another way. I figured I'd deal with the consequences later."

"You were certain you were going to get fired," he said. "But you went anyway. You don't think that's bravery?"

"Anyone could have done it," I protested. "The problem was only Grove's signal. Anyone could have jumped him out, it's just that it was 3 am and nobody else was there."

"Trading clothes with Calliope was quick thinking," he said. "The white lab coat. That was a very Agent Carstairs move." I looked away to hide a smile, irrationally pleased by this.

"And you conducted yourself impressively in the committee meeting — intermittent obscenities aside," he added dryly, and I winced. "It was a pleasure to watch your mind at work. You stand in front of a dilemma and you watch and wait and you flip through a mental file of possible solutions until the right one pops up. Isn't that right?"

I stared at him. "How did you know?"

"That's how Katie always explained it to me. You have her brain. She never has to force it, your mother. She just closes her eyes, and takes a deep breath, and waits. She always told me it was like turning the pages of a book. And sooner or later it would flip to the right page and she'd have an answer. Your father was less patient," he laughed. "He'd want to jump in right away."

"They were good together," I said, though it was more a question than a statement, and he smiled.

"They were," he agreed. "We don't come across a pair like that every day. Your mother is the most brilliant person I've ever met — one of the great minds of our time — but she had to learn from your father to be able to trust her instincts. She lived in her head."

"When we first paired her with Carstairs, oh, she was livid. She stormed into the Director's office and screamed that she refused to work with such a brash, reckless puppy dog who would get them both killed some day. But I think secretly she was a little pleased to have finally met someone who would stand up to her. We'd had the devil of a time finding anyone who would set foot in her office twice. But she loved Carstairs because he wasn't afraid."

"That's what he gave you," he said, smiling kindly. "You think you want to be a desk agent for the rest of your life, but you don't. You only tell yourself that because it seems like the easy path. But you showed yourself who you really are on that transport platform — in that Ohio town — pulling Grove through the Slipstream just in time. We would have lost one of our top agents if it weren't for your quick thinking, and whatever you tell yourself now, it took great courage to do all those things. You thought you would lose your job and you did it anyway."

"What's intriguing about you," he said thoughtfully, "is that you have the best of both of them in one person. Your parents needed each other to be the complete package. You have it all in yourself."

He smiled, patted my hand affectionately, and pulled a handheld out of his bag to set on the couch.

"Give yourself a day before you dive in," he warned. "Don't read this until tomorrow or it will make your head hurt again. We'll see you on Friday for your staff briefing."

"I don't suppose there's any way I can get out of this," I said, half-pleading, and he stopped at the door and turned back.

"I know this isn't what you wanted," he said. "This isn't what you came here to do. There are plenty of other agents who love field work, who love the human element, who love the unpredictability and adventure. You don't. You love the math. That means you're the one we need. We need someone in the field who can spot a Chronomaly the second it happens. Or, ideally, before," he added dryly. "You're an apprentice and you have a more intuitive grasp of GC coordinates than ranking officers twice your age."

"This is partly a test, isn't it?" I said. "You want to know if I can do this before you promote me."

"I know you can do this, Agent Bellows," he said. "The only person who doesn't think you can stop a war before it starts is you."

True to his words, nobody else came to bother me that day. I spent a blissful afternoon in total silence, slumped on the couch watching old movies and drinking beer with no pants on.

Mark from Wardrobe came the next morning, along with Mrs. Graham from Etiquette & Customs. They were both 20th-century specialists who I vaguely remembered from my final exams. Mark was tall, handsome, and gay, with a shaved head and an incredibly elaborate glossy black handlebar moustache which together made him look like a 19th-century carnival barker.

Mrs. Graham ("I don't think anyone actually knows her first name," my mother had told me once, "even the Director calls her Mrs. Graham") was slight and bird-like, with impeccable white hair and the pep of a woman seventy years her junior.

I was a little embarrassed to let them into my messy bachelor apartment, but they were completely oblivious; Mark bustled around with fabric swatches and outfits on metal hangers, creating a mini boudoir in my dining room while Mrs. Graham briefed me on social customs.

"You're going to Washington D.C. in 1972," she said. "Have you been over your file thoroughly?"

"I have."

"Tell me what you know about your identity."

"She's a junior-grade secretary —"

"Wrong."

"What?"

"Not 'she.' You."

"Fine. *I'm* a junior-grade secretary at the White House who just moved to the city from Kansas City, Missouri. I have wealthy Republican parents, a degree in American History and a typing certification, and I came to the city to get a job with the Nixon administration."

"You came to the city to meet eligible men," she said. I rolled my eyes.

"I refuse to use that as my cover."

"It's much more plausible."

"Not for me."

"You're not being you, Agent Bellows," said Mark, holding up three identical-looking fabric swatches to test them against my hair. "The first secret to successful field work is to inhabit the character. Regina Bellows the 22nd-century time travel agent and Regina Bellows the 1970's secretary are two completely different people."

"With the same brain," I pointed out. "And the same body. And the same voice. And —"

"Yes, yes," said Mrs. Graham impatiently, "but we're getting off-track. Your job, Agent Bellows, is not to saunter into the past and condemn it as primitive. Your job is to *get information.* And if people are suspicious of you — if they find your manners alien, your attitude off-putting, your motives suspect — you will get nothing and you will be of no use to us. We all saw the micro-cam footage of your little adventure in Ohio. On a long-term mission, such shenanigans are unacceptable."

I shut my mouth, chastened slightly. She was right, of course. I was there to do a job. *A giant, terrifying, history-changing job with incalculably massive geopolitical ramifications,* the traitor voice in the back of my head whispered evilly. But this was the part that had always challenged me with field work — I wasn't a particularly good actor, and I didn't really like people that much.

My father had been charismatic, engaging, and wildly improvisational. There was no tight corner he couldn't talk his way out of. If he had lived, I thought suddenly, it would probably have been him right now being fussed over by Mark and Mrs. Graham. This was right in his wheelhouse.

My mother was chillier and less charming, true, but she was also so prudent and unflappable that she was impossible to trap in a tight corner to begin with. Some people are good at getting out of traps. Some people are good at not falling into them. Together they had been indestructible. And here I was, sharing their DNA in equal parts, but completely at a loss in this situation.

"The hair works as it is, I think," said Mark contemplatively, interrupting my thoughts.

"I believe it does, yes," agreed Mrs. Graham. "A chignon for evening, my dear."

"I have no idea what that is." They ignored me and went on talking to each other.

"You're a Republican government employee," said Mark. "So this is not going to be the beads-and-bell-bottoms look here."

"Nixon distrusted anyone who looked too countercultural," said Mrs. Graham. "She's going to need to look polished and conservative and just ever-so-slightly behind the trend. Not dowdy, but not flashy either."

"You need to blend in," she said to me. "A White House secretary wouldn't wear anything too attention-getting."

"No trousers," said Mark thoughtfully.

"In 1972, in the workplace? Most definitely not. Skirts only, hems at the knee with stockings. Let's give her a dark skirt suit —"

"Chocolate brown, I think. She can wear blouses or turtlenecks with it."

"What about a wrap dress?" she asked.

Mark shook his head. "Diane von Furstenburg is just now showing them on the runway. A secretary wouldn't be able to buy a knockoff version yet. Too fashion-forward. I think a sheath dress with a matching coat for evening," he said thoughtfully, "something that looks like a pricey investment piece she saved up for and bought five years ago and keeps in pristine condition."

"Perfect. Just the thing."

"Has anyone talked to you about underwear?"

This was getting ridiculous. "My mother told me I should

always leave the house in a clean pair in case I got in an accident and had to go to the hospital." Neither of them was amused.

"The lines created by period undergarments are very important," said Mark seriously. "A 1940's bra and a 1970's bra look very different."

"Well, yes, to a period fashion expert they probably do," I said, "but what are the odds anyone I meet is going to see my bra? I'm not Mata Hari here, I'm not seducing men for information."

"The wrong bra will affect how all of your blouses fit," said Mrs. Graham sternly. "Pay attention."

This went on for hours. I'll spare you an account of Mark's self-guided tour through my underpants drawer and my ensuing mortification, but I did eventually end up with both a complete wardrobe and the conviction that I was apparently failing at being a woman on literally every level. By the end of the day I had four suitcases packed with the following:

- One chocolate-brown wool skirt suit, with a knee-length skirt;

- A green-and-yellow checked day dress with a green jacket lined in the same fabric;

- A pair of crisp khaki slacks and a pink cotton button-down shirt ("Only for the weekend," Mark had warned me in foreboding tones. "You *cannot* wear these within five hundred feet of the White House." "Why, will they detonate?" I asked, suddenly interested, only to receive another death glare from Mrs. Graham);

- A powder-blue silk blouse with short sleeves;

- A long-sleeved red silk blouse that tied at the neck;

- Three turtlenecks in burgundy, white and teal;

- Two knee-length pencil skirts, one in gray and one in black;

- A black sheath dress for evening with a cream wool coat lined in a sharp emerald green;

- A pair of comfortable cotton pajamas for regular wear (it seemed like the wrong moment to tell Mrs. Graham I slept naked) and a flimsy black lace thing you could literally see right through, which I caught Mark sneaking into one of the suitcases with a wink while Mrs. Graham wasn't looking ("The best agents are prepared for any situation," he said primly when I thrust it in his face after she left);

- Two bras, four pairs of underwear, a black slip, a white slip, a nude half-slip and two pairs of hose (black and tan);

- Brown heels and black heels for day, fancier black shoes for evening, and a pair of flat penny loafers for my weekend khakis.

Their early enthusiasm for my curly hair faded a little as Mark valiantly attempted to actually style it. "What do you use on this?" he said in horror as his comb snagged for the fifty-fourth time, causing a yowl of pain.

"I usually just shower at the gym before work," I said. "I use that pink stuff in the stalls."

"You put that in your *hair*?"

"It says 'For Hair, Face and Body' right on the dispenser!" I said defensively. He gave a truly award-winning exasperated sigh and looked at me with pitying eyes.

"Nobody *actually uses that on their hair*," he said witheringly. "You have curls, you need something that weighs down the hair follicles to prevent frizz. How has no one taught you this?"

This got an *enormous* laugh from Mrs. Graham. "Come now, Mark, cut the girl some slack," she said. "You've met her mother." They both found this utterly hilarious, but I was not amused.

"I'll leave you some products for your hair and face," he said. "There's a diagram in the suitcase to help you do the makeup. It has brands and colors you'll be able to find in any period department store."

"Um, I think I can handle putting on my own makeup without a diagram," I said a little too sharply. "I do have an advanced degree in 20th Century culture, you know."

"All right, smart girl," he said dryly. "Then tell me what you do with this."

He pulled a bizarre implement made of twisted wire out of his bag and handed it to me. I looked at it. Then I turned it upside down and looked at it again. It had a handle a little like a pair of scissors, but it ended in a strange curved clamp instead of blades.

"What would you use that for?" Mrs. Graham asked. I considered it carefully.

"Well, it depends if this padding on the ends here is flame-retardant," I said. "If it is, I would assume this is some kind of archaic tool for a very delicate welding operation. Look, you would grasp the handles here and the clasp would lock onto the metal — maybe needles or wire or something very fine — so you could pull it out of the forge and —"

"It's an eyelash curler," Mark said coldly. I was silent. "The diagram is in the smallest suitcase," he said after a long, uncomfortable pause.

I thanked him meekly and shut up for the rest of the day.

In between patronizing visits from various colleagues who all began by apologizing for intruding on my bed rest but immediately proceeded to stuff my brain full of more information than it could currently hold, I read the file the Director had left me over and over and over again.

To reassure myself, I pored over the chart readouts until I had them memorized. "This is just a math problem," I said to myself every time I felt my heart start to clench in panic. "All of this is just window dressing around a math problem." But deep down, I wasn't sure I believed that.

I don't want to get too deep into theology here, but one of the things time agents tend to wrestle with quite a bit is the notion of human agency. Free will.

If I can look at a chart two hundred years in the future and see what you're about to do, does that mean it was predetermined? That it wasn't your choice to do it? That you have no free will?

What if I go back in time and alter the course of your life to ensure a specific action, like I was doing now? Was I interfering with the God-given free will of real living and breathing people by helping Congress make a permanent structural reconfiguration of the Timeline, even if it would prevent a war that took millions of lives?

Not if the war was the Chronomaly all along, I told myself. *If the war was never supposed to happen, then we've all been living in the fallout of someone else's interference and all I'm doing is resetting the clock. That's all. I'm taking us back to where we were supposed to be.*

For it had become clear to me, as I ate, slept and breathed those pages of GC coordinate charts, that our first instincts had been right. There was absolutely no way the Third World

War was a naturally-occurring event. Once I knew what I was seeing, it was all so clear. And as soon as I sat down at my desk on Friday morning to pull up the field site coordinates, I realized why nobody had spotted it until now.

"Are you absolutely, positively, 100% sure?" said the Director, frowning. We were on a park bench about ten blocks from the office. I had asked to meet with them both outside, paranoia perhaps beginning to get the best of me.

"If she says she's sure, she's sure," said my mother crisply. "Regina knows this data like the back of her hand."

"We've sent in agents to patch during World War III before," I explained. "Just small stuff. If the system had read it as a massive Chronomaly, the transport wouldn't have opened automatically. You have to do a manual override to send an agent into a hot spot like that, and we have no reports of manual overrides in that era. Not ever. World War III is actually pretty quiet. Which, knowing what we now know, is suspicious in and of itself. There are only two explanations. One is that for some reason, nobody in the early days ever really messed with it. Which, given the levels of interference in the first two world wars, is unlikely."

"And the other is —"

"Manual data reconfiguration, sir."

"You mean someone has been adjusting the readings on a daily basis to obscure the patterns so we'd never detect the spike."

"Yes."

"That's impossible, Agent Bellows. That would have to be done internally, from the central GC control room or from a handheld that's directly linked to it."

"Yes, sir. By someone with a deep well of technical knowledge and high security clearance."

"Not a prankster, you're saying," he said. "We weren't hacked."

"No, sir."

"It was one of us. We're talking about treason."

"Yes, sir. It was one of us. Nobody else would know how."

He leaned back against the back of the park bench and rubbed his temples wearily. A couple of kids were splashing around in a fountain on the other side of the park. We watched them in silence for a few moments, nobody wanting to speak first. Finally the Director broke the silence. "Who?" was all he said.

"Any agent in the field has the technical capability," said my mother. "Their handhelds sync to the central database automatically every seven minutes. Provided someone had the technical knowledge, it could be done from anywhere."

"Without being spotted by a tech?"

"If the tech was right there as it happened, they'd spot it," I said. "But field agents always know when their techs are scheduled for breaks."

"Still, one of them might have noticed something," said my mother. "If I tried to log in from the field and manually rewrite a signal while Yasmina was monitoring me, she'd definitely register a few minutes of skewed readings before the patch took. She might not know what it was, but she'd have flagged it."

"I suggest you begin quietly meeting with each tech and asking some discreet questions," Director Gray said to her, and she nodded. "It's most likely someone from Early, Mid- or Late 20th Century, so start with those departments. Bring them in all at once, quickly and quietly, before word has a chance to spread. Don't mention sabotage. Tell them you're investigating a server malfunction. If any of them have seen something, they might not know what they know. Go canny, Katherine, and use a light touch."

"It shouldn't be you," I said suddenly. "If it's you, they'll know something's up. It should be someone with a much lower rank. I'd send a tech, actually. Yasmina or Calliope. Play it off like it's a purely administrative meeting. Give them an agenda with five topics on it and make this one the fourth. Sneak it in. Blah blah sick days, blah blah the thing that happened with the Weston kids, blah blah Grove is fine, blah blah server malfunction, blah blah other made-up thing."

"I agree," said my mother. "We don't want to spook anyone. They're a loyal bunch. Any of them would clam right up if they thought their boss was in trouble."

"It is worth mentioning," I pointed out, "that it could be a tech who did it."

"Do you think that's likely?" asked the Director. I thought for a second.

"I wouldn't think so, no," I conceded. "They're all too disciplined."

My mother nodded. "I think Regina is right," she said. "Yasmina *could* do it — she would certainly know how — but she wouldn't unless I ordered her to."

"But if you had," said the Director, "she'd do it and she wouldn't ask any questions."

"Yes," she said. "That's why it's imperative that we handle this right. If a tech knows something, and hasn't come to us yet, either they think it's nothing —"

"Or they were told not to tell. Which means we need to walk softly."

"I don't want to be the one to say this," I said, "but somebody has to. What if —"

"What if it's one of the three of us?" said the Director, his voice sober. We all looked at each other.

"I'm sorry," I said helplessly.

"Don't be," said my mother. "Obviously it has to be considered. You're being thorough."

"Look," said the Director, "as far as I'm concerned, the facts we have so far clear only two people. Bellows and Grove. You landed right smack in the center of one of the aftershocks from the Chronomaly and barely came out alive. If either of you were the culprit you'd have known it was there and bypassed it."

He paused, then went on. "I'm also inclined to clear your mother straightaway, since she never would have risked calling you out of sickbay to come meet with the committee if she didn't want you to spot the Chronomaly and tell them about it. Clearly I'm confident in both of you, but I fully recognize you have no such reassurance that it wasn't me. So for fairness, I think we should submit all our techs and all their records for review. Katherine, I'm assigning this to you while Agent Bellows is in the field."

He turned to me. "Agent Bellows, you will report back only to your mother and to me. We will never contact you with anyone else in the room and we ask you not to speak to any other staff about your findings until this has been resolved. The only staff member aware of your true mission is Calliope, who has arranged to discreetly spread it around that you were called to your mother's office to meet with the committee for a disciplinary hearing in which I threatened to fire you but only relented because the department can't spare any more apprentices after losing Agent Chao."

He smiled slightly. "So instead, as punishment you have been assigned a lengthy and tedious mission to the Nixon White House to gather information on the evolving roles of women in public service. If anyone asks, the words 'If you're so enthusiastic about field work, I'm sure something can be arranged' were uttered, and you and your mother are not currently speaking. Clear?"

"Perfectly, sir."

"That's all for now," he said, nodding meaningfully at my mother. They exchanged a look I couldn't read, but she promptly stood and walked away, through the park and back towards the office. Once we were alone, he looked at me for a long, appraising moment.

"I meant what I said," he told me. "I'm confident the mole isn't you."

"Wait. You think it's *her*?" I said, aghast. "You wanted to get me alone to tell me you think my mom is a traitor?" He shook his head hastily.

"No, no, that's not what I meant at all," he said. "I have the utmost faith in both of you. I am confident in your loyalty to the country, to the Bureau and to me. There is, however, another possibility you may not have considered. I wanted to prevent your mother from dwelling on it unless it becomes necessary, but it's something for which you ought to be prepared."

I felt a chill at the soberness of his tone and waited expectantly while he took a deep breath and gathered himself to go on.

"When you were going through your mission file, how many other agents did you spot in the field in your timeline?"

"Just one," I said, "but only a Ghost."

The official term was "Nonsignificant Human Variable (Deceased)," meaning an agent who had been dead in our timeline for over ten years. They popped up from time to time in our readings, a slightly spooky reminder that in our line of work the past and the present were always connected.

"What year?"

"I don't remember. '59? '60? I'm sorry, I didn't pay a lot of attention. It wasn't anywhere near my GC coordinates so I didn't think it mattered. It was only a Ghost." I looked at him. "Was I wrong? Is it important?"

"You could potentially make the jump from there to the crisis point with Short-Hops," he said, "and it would be difficult, but not impossible, to hack an outdated Comm device and log into the Hive undetected."

"You think a dead former agent created an Incongruity to trap Grove in 1968?"

"It's a possibility we need to consider," he said. "You're going to need to keep your eyes open. It may be that the person we're looking for isn't one of us. It may be someone we don't know yet. It may be someone we knew once and have long forgotten. It may be someone we can't trace using data and technology and math. You're going to need to use your gut, Regina."

The penny dropped. I looked at him, my heart in my throat. "Why did you send her away?"

"The chances are very faint, but I do think we need to keep our eyes open to all the —"

"Why did you send her away?"

There was an uncomfortable silence. Finally he sighed and his eyes met mine, sadly.

"Because that agent in 1960 is your father."

~

It was an uncomfortable dinner, to say the least.

Leo's place was closed on Mondays, so he was hosting us in his apartment, an airy white stone loft on the third floor above the restaurant, a few blocks from Dubrovnik's Old Harbour. He had outdone himself, serving a five-course feast with oceans of wine and a singularly impressive cheese course, but none of us had much appetite.

We were all behaving like this was a celebratory family dinner, but nobody was fooling anybody. My brother knew as well as anyone else did how little interest I had in field work. Having grown up with me, he also knew firsthand what an absolutely terrible liar I was.

Though the briefing details were classified, he knew I was hunting for an enemy agent of some kind, and the notion of his sister even remotely engaged in espionage probably didn't give him a great deal of reassurance in the future of humanity. It was hard for me not to agree with him.

Mom was the least mopey of the three of us, and to her credit I do genuinely believe she had a higher estimation of my powers than I did. But she had spent thirty-five years at the Bureau and she knew about ten thousand times more than me about what I was getting into.

Not counting the Ohio catastrophe with Grove, I had done this exactly three times before, all under the supervision of senior agents in non-crisis timelines as part of my final exams at the Academy. It's true that the Nixon White House was my specialty, but my knowledge was completely theoretical.

How she could sit there so calmly, sawing the head off her grilled fish, knowing that her daughter was about to go off on a secret mission with massive geopolitical stakes, was beyond me.

"Regina, are you listening?"

I wasn't, as she obviously knew. She sighed and started again.

"I was saying," she continued, "that we have a permanent research Embed in '72 that you should make contact with as soon as you get there. He's been briefed on your mission parameters and will have a great deal of helpful information for you."

"How do you know he's not the mole?" asked Leo over his shoulder from the kitchen, pulling a second loaf of bread out of the oven. "If he's in the same time period."

"We thought of that," said my mother. "We ran an aggressive trace on all his Comm activity and we gave his tech a thorough going-over. No suspicious activity. The Director feels confident that he's safe. He's an asset we've worked with a number of times in the past and he'll be a good resource for you."

"What's his name?"

"I can't tell you that."

"Where does he work?"

"I can't tell you that."

"Oh, for Christ's sake."

"It's for your own good, Regina," she said. "His position is fairly sensitive, and the whole thing would go up in smoke if you blew his cover. Don't worry. He'll find you."

I nodded. There was a long silence.

"It wasn't your father," she said finally, startling Leo and making him spill the water pitcher in his hand. "I know what the Director thinks, and it's a perfectly reasonable theory, but it wasn't your father."

"What the hell are you talking about, Mom?" said Leo, his voice shaky.

"She's going back into the same timeline where we lost your father. Carstairs is —" She took a sip of her wine, seemingly impervious, but I saw a flicker of emotion in her eyes which she quickly hid.

"Carstairs is the only agent in the field in that timeline who's close enough to have short-hopped up and back to Grove. And Regina is only going in a few years later. The Director thinks the mole could have been a past agent — and actually, it certainly could be — but it wasn't Carstairs. Not in a thousand years, not ever."

"Then Reggie will just have to find out who really did it and prove the Director wrong," said Leo, but I could tell his heart wasn't really in it. Thanks, family.

Mom was silent for the whole two-and-a-half-hour Underground ride back from Croatia. She tapped irritably at her handheld from time to time, but I could see her mind wasn't really on her work.

I wanted to ask her how she knew, how she was so sure. I wanted to ask her what would happen if she was wrong. I wanted to ask her to tell me again the story of that last day in South Africa. I wanted to ask her if she thought he would believe me if I did meet him and I told him I was his daughter. I wondered if that kind of thing had ever happened before.

I wanted to ask her why, if she was so confident Carstairs wasn't the traitor, there was such a tight, cold expression on her face when it had come up at dinner.

But I didn't.

Instead I sat in silence with her, all the way home.

CHAPTER FIVE

LIE AS LITTLE AS POSSIBLE

I hadn't been able to fall asleep, no matter how hard I tried, so around 4 a.m. I gave up and got out of bed. I paced in my underwear for a bit, made some coffee, puttered around, made a half-assed attempt at cleaning my kitchen (since who knew when I'd be back) and read through my mission briefing again.

Forty-five minutes later, I threw the handheld down onto my suitcases in frustration. I had four and a half hours left to kill before go time and if I didn't find something to distract my brain, I would go crazy. I grabbed some clothes from the top of the dirty laundry pile and decided I had to get out of the house.

My apartment was in a big steel-and-glass monstrosity on 7th and H Street, in what used to be Chinatown — before the bombing raids in the early 1980's that leveled D.C. to the ground.

It used to be lively and colorful, packed with fish markets

and hole-in-the-wall dim sum shops and brightly-painted storefronts. Now it was just rows upon rows of utilitarian concrete block housing, with the occasional apartment tower thrown in as a feeble attempt to give the city some kind of a skyline again.

I was on the seventeenth floor — I'd always liked heights — but D.C. from above wasn't much to look at. Still, it was my home, and a small strange part of me found myself wanting to say some kind of goodbye to it — to *my* D.C. — before I stepped back in time 140 years to Richard Nixon's.

It was still dark out as I closed the lobby door behind me and turned left down 7th. The streets were largely deserted — a few exceptionally motivated runners, a few delivery trucks, one or two stray cats, and me.

Mom still lived in Old Georgetown, in the condo where Leo and I had grown up, so this was the first place I'd lived on my own and I knew it like the back of my hand. I loved this sea of concrete in the weird, desperate way you love ugly, broken things simply because they're yours.

I walked down 7th, then absently turned right on Constitution and kept walking. I don't think I consciously realized where my feet were taking me until we arrived there.

Once upon a time, a century and a half ago, a vast green parkway sprawled through this part of the city, stretching along Constitution Avenue from 1st, where the Capitol Building used to be, all the way down to 23rd, by the Lincoln Memorial.

It was called the National Mall. Monuments to the presidents and wars that shaped America were housed here. In the springtime, the streets were dazzlingly pink with flowering cherry trees. In the summer, the National Gallery and the Natural History Museum were packed with crowds of school children. It was a beautiful place.

I stared out over the vast expanse of dead earth and dark craters that now stood in its place, ringed with tall iron security fencing and bronze plaques.

The World War III Memorial.

~

The first bomb in the 1982 air raid had struck, with near-surgical precision, on the site of the vast white obelisk that had once been the Washington Monument, right at the heart of the National Mall and just blocks from the White House.

The second, just six minutes later, flattened the U.S. Capitol into dust, killing everyone inside. President Reagan and his senior staff made it into the security bunker safely before the third bomb blew a hole the size of a brontosaurus in the side of the White House. That was how the war began.

Those first three strikes were the big ones, though smaller bombing raids went on for five more days throughout the city. Communications went down so fast and so thoroughly — phone lines out, news stations destroyed, and remember, this was decades pre-internet — that it was days before the handful of surviving government officials in Washington realized the extent of the damage to the rest of the country.

C.I.A. headquarters in Langley, Virginia, was gone. So was about half of Manhattan, the U.S. Air Force Academy in Colorado, and the U.S. Military Academy in West Point, not to mention sizable chunks of at least a dozen other cities.

There were just under 232 million people in the U.S. then, and nearly ten percent of them died. In a red haze of fury, heartbreak and vengeance, the United States — under the leadership of President Reagan, then in the middle of his second term, who suspended the 22nd Amendment and served another eight years unopposed as the nation rebuilt itself — swiftly took the upper hand and flattened China's three biggest cities.

First Chongquing, and its fourteen million citizens. Gone in a flash.

Reagan sent a message to the Chinese government telling them to surrender. They ignored him.

Shanghai went next – population, eleven million. All dead.

Reagan was sure that would be the end of it. Instead, another handful of Chinese bombs peppered the Midwest crop centers, setting fire to thousands of acres of industrial wheat fields and decimating the country's food supply.

Next stop, then, Beijing. 9 million citizens and the seat of government for the People's Republic of China.

Once this city, too, had been turned to nothing but smoke and dust and piles of bones, it seemed both sides had had enough. Russia had begun the war as a stalwart ally of China, but had promptly switched sides after the destruction of Beijing, as had the rest of the Chinese allies.

With no friends left, no government, and 34 million citizens dead, China agreed to a cease-fire and was annexed by the United States. Many people more idealistic than me credited President Reagan's sixteen years in office — his firm hand in military dealings, his forceful leadership as Commander-in-Chief — with the revitalization of the American economy in the 1990's and the resurgence of the U.S. as the world's dominant superpower.

～

That might be true. But all I could think, as I stared out at that massive, shadowy crater where the Washington

Monument used to be, was about those 22 million Americans and 34 million Chinese.

All dead. And for what?

I walked around the circumference of the crater until I reached the front, where a twenty-foot-long bronze relief embedded in the cement below my feet showed a map of the old National Mall. I sat down on the ground next to it and watched the sun come up over the water, idly tracing the outline of the Old Smithsonian with my fingertip and thinking.

If the war was really a Chronomaly — if it really was never supposed to happen — then that meant 56 million innocent people were counting on me to find out what had gone wrong and stop it. 56 million people, killed in their offices and schools and homes and streets. Two nations' histories turned into piles of rubble, from the Library of Congress to Beijing's Forbidden City.

And me, a twenty-five-year-old computer tech who hates people, expected to fix it.

You know, no pressure or anything.

I sat there staring into the yawning dark chasm as the misty early morning light hardened into bright sharp sun, crisp and clear, with a snap in the air and a blue expanse of cloudless sky. The kind of day meant for a long country drive, or baking an apple pie.

Obviously it's not like I'd be doing either of those things if I was staying — I would be sitting at a desk staring at a screen all day and then coming home to sprawl on the couch with a beer and no pants — but something about knowing that I was being forcibly ejected from my real life gave a little glow of nostalgia to everything I saw.

Finally I stood, dusted off my pants, and slowly made my

way back home. *Just window dressing around a math problem,* I whispered to myself as I walked. *You can do this.*

I only had time to brush my teeth, pee, and run a decidedly half-assed comb through my hair before the knock came. I opened the door and was unpleasantly surprised to find — instead of Calliope with an enormous vat of coffee to tide me over on the drive — my mother instead.

Or, more accurately, my mother's uniformed chauffeur Moulson, who shot me an apologetic glance as he stepped inside, wordlessly picked up my suitcases, and motioned me towards the elevator.

"I thought I might escape this hellish morning without a parental lecture," I muttered as he pushed the button marked "LOBBY" and we descended. He chuckled.

"Well, that was pretty optimistic of you."

"Shut up."

"You Bellows women, you're all a real treat in the mornings."

He stashed my suitcases in the capacious trunk of the big, sleek black car parked outside my building and opened the door for me to slide into the roomy backseat next to my mother.

"I wanted a word with you in private before we left," she said. "To the office, Moulson, please."

"And a good morning to you too," I said. She ignored me and went on as if I hadn't spoken.

"Field work requires a specialized set of skills that take years and years to develop," she said. "You lack many of those skills. You've always hated field work and you only have the barest minimum of experience needed to competently perform as a tech."

"Your support means the world to me, Mom. I sincerely hope you know that."

"But what you do have," she went on, sailing blithely right past me again, "is instinct. I could send another agent on twenty drops in the same timeline with reams of research data memorized and she'd still miss something you wouldn't. Your problem is that you don't trust your instincts because you'd rather have the data. And in this situation, that could be fatal."

"This is just the *worst* pep talk."

"You've been prepped on all the facts and figures, so I won't bother drilling you on any of that. I'm fully confident in your grasp of all the relevant material. But I have one piece of advice for you that you won't have found in your files or heard in your mission briefing. This is the most important thing I can possibly teach you."

This got my attention, and I briefly paused making exasperated faces at her and turned to listen. Once she saw that she had me, she nodded and pressed on.

"Field work forces you to make decisions quickly," she said, "and then stand by and watch the consequences of those decisions play out in real time. It is not theoretical. You do not have the luxury of crafting a perfect solution to each problem. Situations will be thrown at you and you will be forced to adjust as they come. And the most crucial thing for you to remember, the thing that is most likely to get you through it unscathed, is this: *lie as little as possible.*"

"That's good advice, I think Moses said that."

"This is not a joke, Regina," she said, and there was a steely urgency in her voice that shut me up. "I don't think you have any idea what you're up against here. Do you know what field work is? *Talking to people.* All day. Every day. Interacting with them. Trying to get information from them without ever looking like you're trying to get information. You don't get a file. You make your own data, and *then* you analyze it."

"You will be asked questions you can't answer. You'll be in situations you haven't prepped for. You'll have to improvise. You will panic. And your brain will say, 'Quick, make something up.' But this isn't a three-hour, teacher-supervised field drop for your Academy exams. You're embedded. You *live* with these people." She paused and looked at me seriously, to make sure I was listening.

"That means if someone asks a question, you don't just have to give a plausible answer; you have to give a plausible answer *and remember it every time*. Say you make a contact who might have helpful information. Say you meet him in a bar, and he offers to buy you a drink. He asks what you'd like, and your logic brain clicks into gear and begins sifting through the lengthy list of period-appropriate cocktails you memorized, and you decide that a Republican junior secretary in 1972 would drink a martini, so that's what you order. So all the while, as he's getting to know you, he's building 'martini drinker' into his mental picture of you along with everything else you say. Where you're from. What you like to read. What church you went to on Christmas as a child. And the next time you see him, he'll order you a martini."

She continued. "And if you run into him at a cocktail party at someone's house and the hostess is pouring he'll tell her, 'Regina would like a martini.' Now it's built into his sense of your identity. Except for one thing — you hate vermouth. But now it's out there, you've said you like martinis, so every time he puts one in front of you you'll have to pretend you like it."

Her eyes were more steely than usual. Her voice matched. "And not just barely manage to choke it down without grimacing, but enjoy it like a real martini drinker, enjoy it with flair in the way that someone who really loves gin martinis would do. It has to look real at every moment. And if *even one time* you slip up, it's over, because then that becomes embedded into his mental picture of you — that you lied about a stupid small thing, that you kept on lying and lying about it — and then he'll wonder what else you might have lied about, and the foundation of trust you'll have painstakingly built will collapse entirely, and he'll be worthless as a source. Whereas, if you had just ordered a glass of wine, none of that would have ever happened."

I was silent for the rest of the drive, brooding over this. She didn't speak anymore either. After a few minutes she pulled her tablet out and I could hear her tap-tap-tapping away as I stared out the window, watching the streets slip away behind us.

We pulled up to the Bureau several minutes later. Moulson pulled the car around to the back VIP entrance where my mother entered — I, a mere peon, was forced to line up at the front door security station every morning with the rest of the rabble, but department directors and up could pull their chauffeured cars into a secured private entrance with a password-protected elevator for their use only.

This was a safety measure; anyone coming in the office either had to brave the main lobby, with its endlessly invasive full-body examinations and retinal scans for unaccredited visitors, or have access to a director's password.

I'm a cynic, so any time the Bureau installs another pointlessly expensive security tool as part of their ongoing waste-of-taxpayer-money contract with United Enterprises, my first step is always to annoy my mother by explaining to her how it can be hacked. The elevator had just gone in three months ago and this was the first time I'd seen how it worked.

"What if I had a contact in Human Resources with access to the security database that holds the list of passwords?" I said as Moulson piled my suitcases inside.

"We each choose our own password, they're not shared with anyone, and there is no list. Transport Lab, please, Moulson, floor seven. They don't live on any server. The elevator itself is the computer." I had to admit this was pretty cool.

"What if I worked for United Enterprises and programmed the initial passwords into the elevator in the first place?"

"We change our passwords every fourteen days."

"What if I came in with you once legitimately, like for a meeting or something, and then tried to sneak back later on my own?"

"The visual recognition software would catch you. If you weren't a Bureau employee whose vitals were stored in the personnel database, it just wouldn't open the doors."

"What if I set off an explosive to blow the doors open?"

"Metal walls as thick as an old-time bank vault would slam down all around the lobby and you'd be trapped until security arrived."

"What if I held a gun to your head?" I said.

"I'd rather you didn't."

"No, I mean what if I held a gun to your head and made you put in your password to let me in?"

"We each have two passwords for that exact reason," she said. "One takes me to my floor and opens the door. The other takes me to my floor and opens the door, where we'll find an entire squadron of armed guards waiting for us."

"All right," I admitted grudgingly. "Not bad."

"I'll be sure to pass along your compliments to the rep from U.E."

"Although it's a lot of high security for a building that just has a bunch of desks and computers in it," I said. I was deliberately being a pain in the ass but she didn't take the bait.

"It has nothing to do with our security," she said, "and

everything to do with appearances and profit. You don't want to know how many taxpayer dollars went into purchasing this shiny metal box just so the Director can make the Committee feel important."

"It's all connected, do you see?" she went on, and I suddenly had the sense that she was trying to tell me something important that she didn't have the words for. "If we had lost Grove — if you hadn't caught the Chronomaly when you did — if the Director couldn't bring presidents and prime ministers in for a tour to show off his shiny high-class technology — if things keep going wrong..."

"What things?" I asked. She shook her head.

"I don't even know. I just have a sense. Something feels off. But that's why all this matters, you see. We're constantly battling for our own legitimacy. Snagging a fat corporate contract helps, flashy technology helps, lobbying politicians helps. But underneath all of that is the real, unglamorous, person-to-person work that gets things done."

She glanced at me. "You believe in computers more than you believe in people, Regina, and that's your fatal flaw. You believe that history is that big, lit-up screen in the server room with the endlessly scrolling lines moving up and down, points of light flashing on and off any time agents enter or leave the field."

She shook her head. "But that's not history. History isn't *made* by that lit-up screen, it's just *recorded* there. It is still now, as it has always been, made by people. And despite their complexities and contradictions, in the long run people are a far safer bet."

I looked at her for a long time, still standing outside the elevator, arms folded. We were alone — Moulson had long since driven away — and in the hush of that small elevator lobby I felt a sudden primitive jolt of fear. Not the ordinary, sensible fear of screwing up an important job that had been plaguing me ever since I got this assignment less than a week ago, but a bigger, darker fear of something I couldn't quite name.

I looked at my mother and tried to see her as a stranger might — thick dark hair pulled back to perfectly accentuate the whisper of gray at her temples, jaw set, a flawlessly-tailored gray suit on a body that had lost the taut angles and hard surfaces of her athletic youth after having two children but had lost none of its power and strength.

She looked like what she was — a member of the governmental ruling class with whom one did not screw around.

But suddenly, just for a second, I saw a flash of a different Katie Bellows inside her eyes, a worried parent whose face was drawn and tired. Then it was gone, as quickly as it came, and as we stepped inside the elevator she was so brisk and no-nonsense I thought I'd imagined it.

She placed her hand on a sleek metal panel, and a screen above it cycled through the database of Bureau employees until it found a match.

"PASSWORD RESET REQUIRED," said the blinking red letters over the picture of her face onscreen, and she sighed, exasperated. "This is the most annoying part," she said. "Exactly five characters, letters and numbers, no spaces, at least one special symbol every time, never the same combination twice."

I don't know what it was about this morning, this weird fear that something terrible might happen and I might never see her again, that was making me behave like an obnoxious teenager, but I couldn't stop myself. Before she could stop me, I leaned into the keypad and typed, lightning fast, then hit the button marked "CONFIRM."

She gave me the look. "Are you kidding me?" I giggled like a twelve-year-old. "Are you kidding me with this, Regina? You're going to make me type that in twice a day for two weeks?"

"So you'll remember me when I'm gone," I said.

She sighed. "This was a terrible idea."

"I told you! I told you that! It's not too late to change your mind and not send me."

"You're going, Regina."

I wasn't sure when I would next get an opportunity to heave a childishly dramatic and exasperated sigh at my mother, so I was careful to make this one count. She arched one flawless eyebrow at me but said nothing.

It's funny how things hit you; there was a part of me that didn't fully and completely digest the fact that this was really, truly, actually happening until that elevator door whooshed noiselessly open (God, even the elevator door noises were fancier in Mom's wing of the building) and I saw the Director solemnly waiting for me. As an aide with a cart collected my bags and zoomed away with them, he and my mother shepherded me with an almost funereal ceremonial formality down the hall to the transport bay. I swallowed hard and fought the urge to run.

I'm not a politician, I wanted to say, *I'm not a military general, I'm a twenty-five-year-old with a good math brain and a famous mother, where the hell do you get off sending me to save millions of lives when all I wanted to do today was sit at my desk and stare at numbers? I can't do this. I can't do this.*

I must have whispered it out loud — or she could see it on my face — because as we entered the bay and I looked around that the gleaming whiteness of it I took a sharp breath, and suddenly, in a very un-Katie-Bellows-like gesture, my mother reached down and squeezed my hand.

My suitcases were piled on the transport platform already. Mark was there with a garment bag and pulled me into the changing room to put on my traveling outfit.

I stood there mechanically and let him dress me like I was a doll. All I was doing was trying to keep breathing, to keep from having a panic attack. He smiled at me warmly and patted my cheek. "You're gonna be fine, kiddo," he whispered. "You're Katie Bellows' daughter."

"God, don't remind me," I whispered back, and he laughed. Mrs. Graham was there when we stepped out of the changing room, to put the final touches on my makeup and hair, and give me a few last-minute etiquette and deportment reminders that I immediately forgot.

Calliope held out a large burgundy leather handbag.

"Don't let this out of your sight," she said. "There's a pocket sewn into the lining with a handheld in it. All your mission briefing files are there, for reference, and it's wired for two-way communication so you can ring in if you need me."

I nodded. She could tell — I'm sure everyone could — that I was starting to freak out a little bit, so she stepped onto the platform and gave me a reassuring hug.

"They're sending you because you're the best," she said. "This is what you do all day long. You're just doing it from there instead of here. But you've got this, Reggie. You breeze in, you poke around, you track the Chronomaly, you breeze out." She smiled at me and stepped down off the platform and went over to the console.

"Good hunting, Agent Bellows," said the Director, as he, Mark and Mrs. Graham put their hands over their hearts in the old-fashioned department salute. After a moment, my mother did too. She smiled at me and nodded. Calliope keyed in the coordinates.

"It's just a math problem, Reggie," she trilled cheerfully as I felt the familiar tingling sensation close in around me. "You'll be home by the weekend!"

I wasn't.

PART II

PAST IMPERFECT

"How very near us stand the two vast gulfs of time, the past and the future, in which all things disappear."

—MARCUS AURELIUS, *Meditations*

CHAPTER ONE

WE'D LIKE TO KNOW
A LITTLE BIT ABOUT YOU
FOR OUR FILES

Washington D.C. — May 25th, 1972. 11:26 p.m.

"Excuse me," I said politely. There was no response. I tapped on the plastic divider separating me from the front seat. "Excuse me," I said again, a little louder and a little less politely.

"Zip it, lady," came the gruff voice from the passenger seat.

"I just thought you might like to know," I told him helpfully, "that he didn't read me my Miranda rights. And neither did you."

"What'd she say?" said Passenger Seat to Driver's Seat.

"Dunno. Wasn't listening."

I tapped on the plastic again. "Stop doing that," Driver's Seat said.

"I said, nobody ever read me my rights," I repeated, louder

this time. "You're already going to be in just an *insane* amount of trouble and I wouldn't make it worse by—"

Passenger Seat whirled around and smacked his fist ferociously against the plastic divider, scaring the daylights out of me. "*Shut up!*" he barked.

I shut up.

"Drive faster," he snapped to Driver's Seat. "I want this mouthy broad out of my damn car."

"Whatever," I grumbled under my breath, sinking down in my seat, irritated. "Just trying to save you both from totally screwing this up."

"That don't sound like shutting up to me," said Driver's Seat, and I glared at him in the rearview mirror as hard as I could.

"This is just *classic* Reggie Bellows," snapped Calliope's voice in my ear. "I mean it. This is one for the record books."

"Don't start with me, Calliope," I mumbled.

"Don't start with you? Don't *start* with you?"

"I'm sorry, I didn't mean that."

"I have half a mind to—"

"I said I was sorry," I whispered through gritted teeth. "Just get me out of this."

"It's 1972, you moron. I can't just click my computer screen three times and erase your arrest record. Everything's on paper."

"Well, you better think of something. I'm supposed to start work on Monday."

"Oh, no problem. I'll just call Human Resources at the White House and tell them to push back your new hire date until after your *bail hearing*."

"I don't know how many more times you want me to admit I screwed up, Calliope."

"Well, a couple more at least."

"I can't tell if you're genuinely pissed at me or if you're enjoying this."

"No reason it can't be both."

I groaned.

"I did tell your mother this was not a good idea," she said. "Just for the record. I was on your side here. You weren't ready."

"I know. I told her that too. Clearly she doesn't listen to us. Can you just, please, please, please – I'll owe you one forever – figure out some way to get me out of this mess without her finding out?"

"I'm doing the best I can," she said tightly. "Just . . . try not to make it worse." And she rang off.

I sighed again, and turned my head to look out the window, watching the night skyline of D.C. speed by, idly wondering exactly how many veins in my mother's forehead would pop out once she found out I was about to spend my first night in 1972 in jail on solicitation charges.

~

Less than twenty-four hours ago, it was the year 2112 and I was Regina Bellows, United States Time Travel Bureau Apprentice. Now I was suddenly Field Agent Bellows, and it was 1972.

One day forward, 140 years back.

Six hours before finding myself in the back of a squad car, I had stepped out of the Slipstream and into a private train compartment on the way from Kansas City ("home", according to my fake cover story) to Washington D.C.

Sense of smell comes back to you first, so I followed the sharp acrid tang of black coffee out of the foggy darkness of the Slipstream into a world of shrieking, rumbling chaos.

Good God, 20th century trains were loud. Every single motion of the train reverberated up into my bones. The cacophony of clatters and whistles and hisses, with the dull roar of human voices in the backdrop, made my head throb. How did people live like this?

I checked my wrist Comm. HIO level 0. I had landed with no impact whatsoever on the General Timeline. Flawless.

I sent Calliope a silent prayer of thanks. While I had spent four days learning about everything from bras to espionage, she had not been idle. Prep work was her specialty. Long-haul drops are nothing like last week's reckless headlong charge into chaos in Ohio; the level of detail that goes into the planning would astonish you. Regina Bellows, aspiring Republican secretary, didn't just have a wardrobe. She had a history too.

There was an entire department assigned to this part of the process, staffed with specialists operating a dazzling spectrum of antiquated technology and communications. They were there for any field agent who might require a telegram or a wire transfer or a video message or a voice at the other end of the phone.

On specific instructions from Calliope, they had arranged my apartment and a bank account. Should anyone at the White House decide to check my references, the phone numbers they dialed in 1972 would connect them to one of the three agents with my case file and they would get the whole carefully-crafted story of my previous life in Kansas City.

Very, very carefully, I edged my way to the door of the train car – bracing myself against its constant jarring movement, trying to look like I knew how to walk in these high-heeled shoes – and moved gingerly down the hall to the ladies' room.

Omitting the inappropriate personal details, let me just say that unless you have attempted to do your business while strapped, corseted and buttoned into absurdly restrictive 20th century women's clothes (in a stall so small that you can touch both walls with your elbows, *in a moving train car, no less*) then you have not known suffering. I hoped that whatever monster had invented pantyhose was eventually strangled with them.

As I washed my hands, I looked at my new, 1970s face, and hardly recognized myself. Mrs. Graham, the Time Travel Bureau's customs and etiquette specialist, and Mark the wardrobe supervisor had clearly never met such a human disaster and their pitying looks had grown harder and harder for me to politely ignore, but I could not deny that they had done excellent work on my hair, makeup and clothes. Even my eyebrows looked different.

"You'll want to touch up your face on the train," said Mrs. Graham, as though I knew what that meant, but Mark had packed a small bag of supplies in my handbag for this purpose, along with a patronizingly detailed manual ("STEP ONE: REMOVE CAP FROM LIPSTICK. SET ASIDE"). I knew nothing about hair or makeup, but I did have a degree in Chrono-Engineering. So if nothing else, I could follow a diagram.

Hoping to God no one else entered the ladies' room to see me carefully studying a giant paper schematic of a human head covered in notes and arrows, I refreshed my lipstick and did things to my hair per Mark's instructions, then staggered like a drunk baby deer down the rapidly-whipsawing train hallway, clutching the walls for support, until I returned to my train car and sank gratefully into my seat.

I watched out the train window as the 20th century rushed by my windows – houses, cars, telephone poles and a blue sky that was just faintly warming into purple as the sun began to think about setting. I felt a sudden ache of longing just to stay on this noisy train forever, to let myself be pulled along with it to wherever it was going next.

I closed my eyes for a long, long time, trying to block out the rest of the world for a little while longer. Just as I began to think that throwing my Comm out the window and staying in this train compartment for the rest of my life wasn't such a terrible plan after all, I felt the engine slow. The noises grow louder, and I looked out the window to see the grand white bulk of Union Station suddenly right in front of me.

It was too late. I was here.

"Break's over," I muttered to myself as I stepped off the train and followed the crowd into the station. It was somehow awe-inspiring and distressing at the same time, its soaring white ceilings and teeming sea of human life making me feel very alone and very small.

My HIO meter ticked softly in my pocket, causing me to jump and wince involuntarily. It was only at 2, which could be caused by any number of inadvertent things – had I disembarked the train the wrong way? Was my demeanor off?

Or was I fine, and my meter was picking up somebody else?

The hairs on the back of my neck prickled very suddenly. As I looked around at the endless crowd of 20th-century people, just walking around and living their 1972 lives, the 50% of my genetic code that belonged to Katie Bellows suddenly whirred to life and I knew – without knowing how I knew – that I was being watched. I craned my neck, making an elaborate show of looking around for the luggage room and pantomiming an "Ah! There it is!" expression as I walked towards it, scanning the room as I went.

The problem, of course, was that it could be *anyone* – the man in a dark suit over by the coffee stand, reading the *Washington Post*, nothing visible of his face except a cowlick of very blond hair over the top of the newspaper; the elderly woman seated in the waiting area, clutching a brown paper parcel; the family with two small children in line for their luggage right in front of me.

Under the right circumstances, any one of them could be suspicious. "*Is it you? Is it you? Is it you?*" My brain whispered to each of them in turn. I didn't know. But somebody from my time was in this room with me, I was sure of it. Friend or foe, I couldn't tell.

In the luggage line, waiting behind the young family, my mind drifted to the Embed – the deep cover agent on the ground in 1972 – whom I had been told would soon make contact with me. He occupied some highly-sensitive position in the administration, so I was relegated to knowing virtually nothing about him until he was ready to reveal himself. Mom had called him a "he," so that was my lone concrete fact. But who he was, what he did, why he was so secretive, what he looked like – all of these were mysteries I couldn't solve until he decided to contact me.

I was pulled out of my thoughts by an argument between the two children in line in front of me. Bigger Child was attempting to convince Smaller Child that they were going to see the Statue of Liberty. Smaller Child, either through a more-solid grasp of geography or hard-wired sibling distrust, remained skeptical.

"Mom, are we going to see the Statue of Liberty today?" he asked dubiously, and his mother laughed.

"That's New York, Charlie, that's next week," she said. "We're in Washington now. Remember? The museums and all the monuments for the presidents, like you learned about in school?"

I stared at her for a moment – she was young and pretty and pregnant, with a shiny blonde ponytail and a pink dress and very rosy cheeks – and I wondered if the enemy agent who caused the Chronomaly was here in 1972, watching my every move. I thought about fake pregnancy stomachs and how traveling with children was the perfect cover and whether anyone really had teeth that white.

She intercepted, and misinterpreted, my look. "We're not much on geography," she said apologetically, shrugging in the direction of the children with a grin, and I found myself unable to resist smiling back, hating myself a little for my suspicious mind. She was normal. Her big cheerful husband, negotiating with the man behind the counter for their heap of suitcases, was normal. The kids were normal too (though my partiality was all with Smaller Child).

Everything was normal.

Get it together, I ordered myself.

I stuck my tongue out at Bigger Child, who responded in kind, as the family moved away and I stepped up to the counter and handed over my ticket. Just as I was reproaching myself for my nonsensical paranoia, I felt the prickle at the back of my neck again. My HIO meter hadn't ticked up, but it hadn't gone back down either.

I scanned my periphery but nobody in the luggage area seemed to be paying that much attention to me. As the clerk took my ticket and disappeared to collect my bags (cargo-dropped by Calliope into the luggage car), I dropped my handbag deliberately. As I knelt to pick it up, I turned slightly, making a casual slow scan of the room as I stood.

There he was.

Leaning against a pillar, just outside the entrance to the luggage room, there was a nondescript man in a nondescript gray suit with a hat pulled low over his face. Our eyes met as I stood up, clutching my handbag, and we sized each other up for a long moment. He was youngish, probably in his late thirties, with sandy brown hair. His eyes didn't match the rest of him. There was a studied casualness in his nonchalant posture and a vagueness that must have been deliberate about his physical appearance.

But his eyes were sharp, quick and piercing; eyes that would miss nothing; eyes that were currently looking at me with great interest. I was reassured by this. No enemy agent would allow themselves to be spotted so easily. But as an introduction from an undercover ally, it wasn't bad.

"Your luggage, ma'am," said the clerk, and a young man stepped out from behind the counter pushing a cart full of my bags.

"Thank you," I said, reaching out to take the cart from him, thinking he meant me to steer it myself, but he shook his head.

"I got it, Miss."

"No, no," I said. "It's really okay. Thank you. But really, don't worry about it."

"Wouldn't be right, Miss," he said firmly, and pushed the cart on. My HIO meter ticked twice, warningly, and I sighed and gave up and let him take the cart. "Taxi stand?"

"Yes," I said. "Thank you." And I followed him towards the exit.

"You don't have to thank them every time," said the man in the suit, and I stopped short. The young man with the luggage cart didn't see, and kept going.

"I'm sorry?"

"The kid with your bags," he said. "You thanked him three times. You don't have to do that. People don't need to be thanked three times for doing their job."

"It's good manners," I said. "There's nothing wrong with good manners."

He shrugged.

"Up to you," he said. "But you might be giving off the wrong impression." And he looked at me pointedly, as if trying to tell me something. After a short moment, it clicked.

"You can tell I'm not ... from around here," I said, remembering the HIO meter. A rich Midwestern businessman's daughter would never be hauling her own pile of suitcases if there was someone to do it for her. I was already breaking character.

He nodded.

"Were you waiting for me?" I asked. "I mean, did you come here to meet me?"

"What do you think?" he said. I could see the baggage clerk up ahead realizing he had outpaced me. He turned the cart around and was headed back in my direction.

"Look," I said. "I have to go. He's waiting with my bags. I have to get to my apartment. Can we meet later?"

"You just tell me where and when."

"Fine. It's, what, five-thirty now? Okay, meet me at eleven at the Lincoln Memorial," I said as I waved at the baggage clerk to let him know I was coming. "You're terrible at this, by the way," I called over my shoulder. "I spotted you immediately."

"I picked you out pretty quickly too," he said. "So maybe we're even." And he winked at me in a way I wasn't sure I liked as I scurried off to catch up with my suitcases.

$\sim$

When I got up to the front of the taxi line, where three or four cabs were lined up waiting, I stepped up to the front door of the one nearest the curb, mimicked the diagram from Mrs. Graham's guidebook and raised my hand in the gesture she had described. The driver stared at me.

"The hell you doin'?"

"I'm . . . hailing a cab?"

"I'm right here."

"I know."

"What, you think I can't see you standing here with your twelve suitcases? My eyes work. I can see you."

"She tryin' to hail you from right in front of your face?" the driver of the cab behind us shouted out his window. "The hell you from, girl?"

And they both hooted with laughter until their pink beer-bloated faces turned red, as I irritably climbed into the back seat. Adding insult to my injury, I felt my HIO meter tick up to 5. Thank God I didn't have Calliope – or worse – in my ear for this. My Microcam was packed ("We're assuming you can handle getting yourself from the train to your apartment without the entire team on call" had been my mother's oh-so-supportive way of putting it).

"Where to, sweetheart?" said the driver. Even under the best of circumstances, that "sweetheart" would have set me off, but I couldn't risk another increase in HIO levels by punching him in the teeth, so I gritted my teeth and gave him my address. Seeing that I was not feeling particularly chatty, he turned on the radio.

"No, I would not give you false hope/On this strange and mournful day . . . "

"'Mother and Child Reunion,' Paul Simon, 1972," I said aloud without thinking.

"Yeah. You like Paul Simon?"

"I do," I said truthfully, feeling an irrational surge of pride and confidence as I heard my HIO meter tick back down.

See, you can do this. You know this stuff. Look, you're talking to a cab driver about music like a totally normal person.

I had taken two semesters of "Music and Film of the 1970s" at the Academy and could identify all of the "Billboard Year-End Hot 100" singles from 1965-1980 in sixteen bars or less, a skill which had come in handy far more often as a parlor trick at drunk college parties than it ever had at work. (My mother had protested mightily, insisting that that time be better spent on another year of Advanced Social Skills & Customs – yet another reason to be glad she wasn't in my ear right now – but she had never appreciated *Blazing Saddles* like I did.) I started to say more, but then stopped as my heart caught in my throat at a sight out the car window.

The U.S. Capitol Building.

I knew the silhouette of that iconic white domed roof like the back of my hand, but only as a symbol of things lost during the war. I'd never seen it with my own two eyes. As the car turned down Louisiana Avenue – and the building loomed into view in front of me, so real, so alive, teeming with human bodies flowing in and out of it – I wasn't sure whether to laugh or cry. I felt a fierce joy at seeing it standing there, tall and proud and majestic.

But that joy was tempered by wondering how many of the men and women I could see right now walking up and down its steps would be dead in ten years, crushed by falling masonry at their desks when the first bombs fell.

"And the course of a lifetime runs over and over again," sang Paul Simon as the taxi rolled past all those people whose lives I had been sent here to save, and I closed my eyes tightly, unable to look at it anymore.

~

Calliope had mapped the circumference of the Chronomaly range and found me an apartment conveniently located right in the center of it. The cab driver transferred my luggage to the bellhop outside the lobby as I clip-clopped in my uncomfortable shoes over to the concierge desk. "First time in D.C.?" said the chirpy young woman as I signed the stack of forms she placed in front of me.

"Well, yes and no," I said honestly. "It's . . . very different from what I remember."

"Well, I hope you enjoy your time with us. Here are your keys," she said with a bright smile. "Welcome to The Watergate."

The bellhop carried my bags into the apartment and set them down in the hallway. The 1970s were widely reputed to be a fairly dismal era, interior design-wise, but I was relieved to see that the place was not as bad as I'd feared. One full wall of the living room contained a set of sliding doors leading out to a concrete balcony which, I soon saw, spanned the width of the apartment (my bedroom connected to it as well.) It was mostly one airy, open space with the kitchen separated by a half-wall from the living and dining area.

The furniture, though bearing the unmistakable curves and angles of the mid-20th century, was mostly pale wood, glass and soft gray fabric, with a few potted plants and some discreet accents of yellow. But there were no glaring patterns of orange and brown, no garish flocked wallpaper. It was remarkably un-horrible, and I made a mental note to tell Calliope so.

Then I stepped into the bedroom.

And changed my mind.

It was the most appalling room I had ever seen, papered top-to-bottom with a blindingly-bright tropical floral pattern, a tangle of hideous flowers and vines snaking their way up the walls and even across the ceiling. The bedding and the furniture were varied hues of grass-green, giving the impression that you were trapped at the bottom of some monstrous jungle cage.

Just looking at it all made me tired. Or rather, it made me more tired, since the exhaustion of Chrono-Jumping 140 years and navigating 20th century travel had already worn me out.

I "unpacked" by tossing all the suitcases into the closet in my bedroom and decided that, with nothing left to do today except show up at eleven for the meet, I was allowed a nap. I sent a brief message to Calliope letting her know that I had arrived safely and that her taste in wallpaper was deplorable; then curled up on the hideous but comfortable green bed and closed my eyes.

Thanks to the distressing scenery around me, my dreams that evening incorporated masses of writhing jungle snakes as a prominent stylistic feature. So when I opened my eyes a few hours later and beheld the grotesque wallpaper once more, it took me a moment to realize I was awake.

I had missed my first two alarms – or, rather, it appeared my subconscious had turned their sounds into the squawking of the massive tropical birds that had been chasing me through the Amazon – so there was no time for more than a half-hearted attempt to straighten my sleep-rumpled clothes and hair, and add a bit more makeup, before I put my earpiece in and dashed out the door to meet the Embed.

～

It was a pleasant walk of about twenty minutes along the water to the Lincoln Memorial, one of the D.C. landmarks I most wanted a chance to see. The path was largely deserted this late at night, and I felt occasional flickers of apprehension at any shadowy figure who passed me. It occurred to me that it was possible this hadn't been a very good idea. I wasn't combat-trained, after all, and I didn't know if the Embed was. It was a risk to meet at night, even in a public place.

But if it was really all that dangerous, he wouldn't have agreed to it, said one voice in my head.

He would if he's the agency mole, said another.

You're a woman in a public place, said a third. *If this goes haywire, you can call for a policeman.*

I froze as a cluster of loud, laughing men came around the corner and towards me. Their faces were invisible, the angle of the street lamp over the brims of their hats casting dark shadows. I tried to shrink back, make myself invisible. They saw me, and I braced myself, but nothing happened. One of them nodded at me, but then they passed on.

You're a woman out at night alone, said one of the voices. *Not a good idea . . .*

I shook my head to clear the worried thoughts out.

Nothing happened, said another voice. *You didn't do anything wrong. You're safe. But if it makes you feel better, you can call Calliope.*

That thought helped somewhat, so I tapped my Comm and paged her. It buzzed in my ear, but she didn't pick up. I was trying to decide whether to hang up and try again later, or just let it keep buzzing, when a figure separated itself from the shadows and the man in the suit was suddenly standing beside me.

"Well hello there, girl from the train station," he said with a smile – a smile that felt wrong somehow, although I didn't know why – but still I dropped my hand away from my earpiece and let it buzz silently.

"It's Reggie," I said. "What's your name?"

"Call me John Smith," he said.

"Oh," I said, feeling awkward. "I'm sorry. I'm new. Do we not use real names? Is that safer?"

"Yes," he said, nodding. "Much."

"Well, that's fine then. I didn't know. You can call me . . . " I cast around desperately, thinking of an appropriate alias *(why hadn't Calliope prepped me for this?)* before the lights of the monuments in the distance gave me an idea. "Mary Todd," I said. He looked at me very strangely, but finally shrugged in acceptance.

"If that's what works for you," he said, "then it works for me. Miss Todd."

"Great, then. Mr. Smith."

"You were very forward at the train station."

"You spoke to me first," I said, a little defensively. I didn't think I was quite as bad at this as he was making me out to be.

"Yes, but you were staring first," he pointed out.

"I was staring because *you* were staring," I said, feeling for the first time like maybe this wasn't going the way it was supposed to go. "Never mind. It doesn't matter. We're here now."

I checked over my shoulder, but there was no one within earshot – just a few clusters of people on the path, a man reading a newspaper on the next bench over, but that was all. I decided it was safe. I motioned John towards a nearby park bench. I sat down, and after a moment, he sat down next to me. "So, what now?" I asked.

"Meaning what?"

"Well, look, I'm new. I just got here. I've never done one of these before."

"You're doing all right for your first time," he said, and I felt a little better.

"That's reassuring," I said, and he smiled. "Really, I'm just trying not to screw up so bad that I get a lecture from my mother." This made him start visibly for some reason.

"Your mother knows you're doing this?"

"She's the one who sent me," I said in surprise. 'I thought you knew."

"I didn't."

"Oh, yeah," I said. "This whole stupid job was her idea. So, if I seem bad-tempered about it, I promise it's not you, it's just . . . you know, this was always *her* thing. This was *never* what I wanted to do." I sighed. "Sorry," I said. "I'm blathering. That's not what I came here for. Should we get started?"

In hindsight, the sheer scope of my obliviousness should have been obvious long before. But in the moment, I was completely unprepared when he whipped a pair of handcuffs out of his pocket and slapped them on my wrist.

"Goddammit, Reggie!" shouted Calliope, who I hadn't even realized was there. "What the *hell* have you done?"

"I don't know," I hissed, then turned to the man in the suit. "Hi, um, what exactly is happening here?"

"You know exactly what's happening here. I don't know where you got off the train from, lady," he said coldly, "but prostitution is illegal in the District of Columbia. You're coming with me."

～

I had seen enough old 20th-century films and television shows about life in prison to instill a high level of panic about my fate. But once we got to the station, Driver's Seat and Passenger Seat just tossed me into a large cell with one other woman in it and left me alone. Nobody frisked me, or took my clothes. I hadn't brought anything with me except the apartment keys in my pocket. So as long as nobody checked inside my left ear for 22nd-century Chrono-Technology, I was safe, and Calliope could shriek at me with impunity.

Calliope was apparently working on a plan, though she wasn't sure how long it would take and had informed me that I was likely to be stuck there until she could arrange for the right phone calls to the right people. I could not shake the sneaking suspicion that she was enjoying holding this over my head, since several hours had gone by and she had not, as of yet, informed my mother. I suspected this would continue to pay off as a blackmail opportunity for some time to come.

I leaned my head back against the cold cement block wall and heaved the dramatic sigh of the wrongfully imprisoned.

"First time?" said the woman on the bench next to me.

"Yep."

"Don't worry," she said. "It's almost always just for the night. They'll toss you out in the morning. With a fine. It's really the money they want. Cigarette?" She held out a pack.

"They let you have those in here?"

"Big Jim offered," she said, nodding at the beefy guard sitting outside the cell, who heard his name and gave us both a friendly wave. "These are his, but he doesn't mind sharing. Want one?"

"I'm good, thank you. I don't smoke."

"Oh, should I not? I don't mind."

"No, no. Go ahead. It's okay." She smiled at me, then pulled a cigarette out and stood up from the bench, dusting off her dress, to hold the cigarette out for Big Jim to light.

"Kitty," she said politely as she returned, holding out her hand.

"Reggie," I said, and shook it. She was probably about my age, and very pretty, with a heart-shaped face and a passing resemblance to the movie star Dorothy Dandridge. She was the first person I'd met since I landed that I found myself able to talk with normally, so of course I liked her immediately.

"Do you mind if I ask," said Kitty, "where they picked you up?"

"Rock Creek Trail," I said. "There was . . . a slight misunderstanding."

"I don't know their names, the two that brought you in," she said. "I've seen them around. We call them Bugs and Daffy. But I wondered if there was a white guy, good-looking, gray suit, kind of light brown hair—"

"That's the one," I said. "He handed me off to the other two."

"That's Barlow," she told me, "and he's awful."

"Pompous jackass," Big Jim agreed from across the room.

"He's an undercover guy from Vice," said Kitty. "He pockets the fines, we think. If you get picked up by Barlow, the fine's always in cash. No paperwork, see."

She arched one perfect eyebrow meaningfully, then went on. "He hangs out all over town in public places, hunting for girls at work. The train station, the airport, the parks – any place people tend to go and bring their kids. It's part of some big clean-up-the-city crusade."

That brought a chuckle from Big Jim.

"You have to be careful around the Mall in particular," Kitty went on. "There're always cops lurking around. You'll learn to pick them out eventually. They dress like normal people, but a little *too* normal, you know? Like something's not quite right? And their shoes are always wrong. No matter how sleek the suit is, they always wearing these clunky cop shoes."

"That's good to know."

"Yes, these are very helpful D.C. survival tips," said the voice in my ear. "Don't worry, I'm writing this all down." I waited until Kitty turned her back to politely blow smoke away from me, then tapped my earpiece to spell "BITE ME" in Morse code, which made Calliope laugh.

The hours ticked by. Kitty and I mostly sat in amicable silence. She smoked thoughtfully and I listened to the noises of the Time Travel Bureau through Calliope's desk Comm – beeps and buzzing from her computer, occasional voices in the background.

Calliope could jump me back, I suddenly thought with a pang of homesickness. *She could just pull me out of here. It would all be over. I could just go home. I want to go home.*

And then I remembered that an emergency jump in front of two civilians would send my HIO meter straight into the red zone, triggering an automatic alarm to Director Gray and my mother. I pictured the look on their faces when I stepped off the platform and decided that would be a fate far, far worse than one measly night in a quiet city jail.

"Are you cold?" Kitty asked suddenly, startling me back to reality. "Big Jim can get you some coffee if you want."

"I'm good. But thank you." I looked at her suddenly, as a thought popped into my mind.

"Hey, Kitty?"

"Yeah?"

"How long have you lived here?"

"Born and raised," she said, exhaling a stream of smoke into the unoccupied corner of the cell.

"Then you might be able to help me," I said. "I'm looking for information."

I could see her stiffen, and the friendly light went out of her eyes. "I'm not asking you for names," I went on hastily, "I totally respect your professional boundaries. You don't have to tell me anything you don't want to. But if I asked you general questions, could you give me general answers?"

"I don't know," she said cautiously. "We'll see."

"I'm not a prostitute," I told her. "I'm . . . investigating.

Undercover. I thought Barlow was my contact, but it was a big mix up, and he arrested me instead."

"You a girl spy or something?" said Kitty with great interest.

"Yes," I said. "Something like that. Have you ever – and obviously you don't have to tell me who – but have you ever met anyone who worked at—" I lowered my voice, "the White House?" That made her laugh out loud.

"Reggie, you're adorable," she said. "Men from the White House are how every girl I know pays her rent."

"Even the Nixon White House?" I asked, a little surprised. "They always seemed so . . . I don't know. Strait-laced. Law and order. Family values."

"Of course they are," she said reasonably. "In public. But if you think the things a man says into a microphone on national television and the things he does in the dark when nobody's looking are the same, you don't know men very well. The things these guys get up to . . . " She shook her head.

"Like what?" I asked, trying not to sound eager. She looked at me appraisingly for a long moment, then nodded.

"What the hell. I'm gonna trust you," she said. "You have a trustworthy face. So, you want to hear a crazy story?"

Calliope had been silent for so long and I was so bored that I would have consented to letting Kitty read me the warning label on a jug of industrial cleaning solvents, and told her so. She laughed.

"You're funny, Spy Girl. I like you."

She folded her legs underneath her and I watched her settle in, as it were, in that universal way all great storytellers do before they begin, and I wondered how many times she had been in this cell before, who she went home to, whether her family had cut her off or whether there was a screeching mob of aunts at family Christmas critiquing her outfits and life choices.

"I don't mind telling you this story," she said, "because she never heard from the guy again anyway. And it was real fishy. You'll see what I mean."

I nodded at her to proceed.

"I heard this story from a friend of my roommate," she began. "A couple months ago, one of her regulars, this big-shot attorney, calls her up and says he's in town for the weekend and is she free for a drink, he's got a business proposition for her. A big one."

"So she says sure, and he takes her to some real posh hotel bar, and he asks her, does she ever take jobs where she has to travel? So she says, you know, if the guy's paying for the travel expenses on top of the regular rate, sure, she'd love the chance to get out of town for a few days."

"Then she says, 'So where are you taking me?' And he laughs and he says no, no, it's not for him, but he ran into an old college friend at a party and they got to talking and the guy says he needs to hire a girl for a really sensitive client out-of-state and does the lawyer know any he likes and trusts. And the lawyer says for him to call—"

She stopped herself just then and looked at me.

"Let's call her Jane," I said, and she nodded gratefully.

"Right. So the lawyer tells Jane to expect a phone call from this guy. And sure enough, he rings her up the next day and says, 'My friend recommended you, are you free the second week in July for a three-day job?' Well, Jane's not stupid, she trusts her friend but she doesn't know *this* guy at all, so she decides she needs a lot more information before she's willing to commit to going off with him somewhere for three days."

"So she says she'll check her schedule, and he asks how much, and she gives him the base rate, and he says 'Does that include travel?' And she says no, he has to cover that, airfare and everything, and he says not to worry about that, that she'd be going on the private plane."

"Well, that gets her attention, obviously. So he says it's an easy gig, three days on a boat in Florida with some of his business associates, and he quotes her a price."

Kitty leaned forward. "And Spy Girl, when she told me, I about fell on the floor. I'm talking three months' pay in three days, that's how big. And he says it like it's nothing. Jane was beside herself. So then he asks, does she know anybody in Miami. She says, sure, her *abuelita* lives there, and he laughs and says that's not what he meant, he means does she know any *girls* in Miami."

"She says no, but she can find some, and then she asks what he can tell her about his business associates – you know, so to figure out what kind of girls they like – and then he says he's never met the guys and can't tell her anything, but as long as the girls are English-speaking, clean and extra discreet he's sure it's fine."

Kitty paused to take a drag and let out another long stream of smoke.

"So Jane tells him, okay, but if he wants her to hire all the girls herself then the rate goes up. Really, all she was thinking about was a couple bucks' extra for a finder's fee – cover the cost of her time to make phone calls, things like that – but just as casual as you like, he says, 'Fine, no problem, you find me five other girls and I'll pay them the same I offered you, cash, and I'll double your fee if you take care of the whole thing.' And then Jane . . . now, you might think this sounds crazy, but as soon as he said that—"

"She turned it down," I said, realizing. "Because of the money."

"Exactly," she said, relieved. "It was just *way* too much money. Jane's smart – never been arrested, never gotten mixed up in something shady, never gotten in trouble. She's just a nice white girl that rich politicians take on their arm to the opera. She's never gotten involved with anything that wasn't straightforward business."

She shook her head. "But this was fishy. It didn't add up. See, rich people hate talking about money. They don't ask how much anything costs. They just tell you what they want and then there's a discreet little envelope waiting for you later and nobody ever mentions it out loud. But Jane said this guy didn't talk like someone who had ever had money – real money, I mean. He's throwing around cash like it grows on trees but he talks like a used-car salesman."

"So the question, then, is – whose private plane is it?" I asked.

"Exactly," she said.

"What did Jane tell him?"

"Well, she thanked him very politely and pretended to walk over and check her appointment book, flipped through the pages real loud so he could hear it through the phone, you know, to make it sound real, and then she told him she was so sorry but she was away the first two weeks of July and not back until the 18th. And then, get this, he offers double *again* if she could change her plans and get to Miami by the 10th. She said no, it was for a family trip, she couldn't reschedule, and he fussed and fumed for a few minutes and then hung up. And she never heard from him again."

"You were right," I said, "that is fishy."

"You don't know the half of it," she says. "There's more. Two weeks later Jane was having drinks with her friend Lacey, and get this – Lacey got the exact same job offer."

"From the same guy?"

"No. That's the weird part. From a totally different guy. Or the same guy using a different voice and a fake name, which is equally suspicious."

"What?"

"I told you it was a crazy story," she said. "The same thing that happened to Jane happened to Lacey. A regular client referred her to a friend (someone he didn't know very well and hadn't seen in years) – a law school buddy, I think that was the story Lacey got – and the friend called her and offered her the same deal. Private plane, all travel expenses covered, three days on a yacht in Miami, double fee bonus if she rounds up five other girls. Well, Lacey was dazzled by dollar signs, so she told him yes and asked for the exact dates, and he tells her, get this, it's July 10th through the 13th."

It was clear that this meant something to Kitty, but nothing to me.

"July 10-13 in Miami," she said again, impatiently. "The Democratic National Convention."

"Oh," I said. "Well, that solves that. These guys work for the DNC and they're arranging entertainment for visiting fat cats. That all sounds pretty standard."

She shook her head.

"Jane told me all the men's names," she said, "and every one of them is a Nixon Republican."

"*What?*"

I stared at her in amazement, wheels turning in my head, and I could tell she was pleased to have gotten a reaction out of me.

"So the question is," she said, "why is there a group of

Republicans offering an absolutely staggering sum of money to fill a yacht with hand-selected call girls in Miami during the Democratic convention?"

"I don't know," I said.

"I do," said Kitty, coolly exhaling a plume of smoke. "I've seen this kind of thing before. You know what that kind of money buys? *Discretion.* I think the girls were there to get the men to talk, and I think the boat would have been wired to the gills with listening devices."

"*Would* have been?"

"Oh, right," she said, "I forgot that part. A week later, Lacey's guy calls her back and says the plan is off. Never explains why, just says something about how the money didn't come through. She hasn't heard from him since."

"Good Lord."

"Politics is a strange business," she said. "There's more going on in this town than the newspapers will ever tell you."

"I'm beginning to believe it," I said.

"Get her to talk about the White House," said Calliope in my ear.

I did.

"What kinds of stories do you hear about the men who work for the President?" I said. "No names, I'm not going to get you in trouble. I just want a sense of what the place is like."

"It's the worst fraternity you've ever seen," she said frankly. "I met a guy once who told me that to get into the inner circle, you know, the new boys have hazing rituals. I mean actual hazing. You have to screw over an enemy of the Nixon White House and then you have to show how you did it. I know a guy who knows a guy who had a reporter's office secretly wiretapped."

I stared. She nodded and went on, "Another guy did all this

goofy stuff like, he would call and order a hundred pizzas to be sent to some Democratic Party event and then the truck shows up with all the pizzas and somebody there has to pay for it. Kid stuff like that, mostly, but sometimes really vile. That's what made the boat thing stick in my mind, you know?"

"How does the President put up with that?" I asked incredulously. "How have these assholes not lost their jobs?"

"Where do you think they learned it from?" said Kitty, yawning. "He can go on television and talk about his working-man values and his sainted Quaker mama all he wants to, but behind closed doors, he's a drunk with a nasty temper." And with that, she stretched out on the bench and closed her eyes.

"Wake me up if anything interesting happens," she said.

"You should get some sleep too," said Calliope. "It's going to be another couple of hours before I have anything more for you."

I obediently stretched out on my bench too, opposite from Kitty, and closed my eyes, but I couldn't fall asleep. It was a relief to have someone else's puzzle to solve, to take myself out of myself for a little while. The Chronomaly forgotten, I kept thinking back over Kitty's story and hearing the same five words cycling through my brain over and over and over.

The money didn't come through.

The money didn't come through.

The money didn't come through.

Jane's gut instinct had been right. The guy who called her wasn't wealthy. He was throwing around money he didn't have. He was waiting on it, or had requested it, and hadn't gotten it. Whose money was it? What had he claimed it was for? Was it really a second man who had called Lacey, or the same man under a different name? What was he really after?

I lay there staring up at the dingy concrete ceiling for a

long time – I didn't know how long, hours, probably – before I finally heard the telltale click that signified that Calliope was back online.

"Miss me?"

"Please tell me you've figured out how to get me out of here."

"You're *so* lucky I like you," she said. "And that Detective Barlow's commanding officer was still awake. There's an extraction plan in place. I went with the story you just gave Kitty. You're an undercover agent and you thought the Vice cop was your contact. Just roll with it and try not to ruin everything."

"Your faith in me is touching," I murmured.

"Oh, no no no," said Calliope. "I will have no sarcasm from the agent who got locked up in a jail cell her very first day in the field. I am saving your ass *so hard* right now."

That was hard to argue with.

Barlow came into view just then and said something quietly to Big Jim, who looked at him in surprise, but nodded and opened the door.

"Calliope Burns?" he said, looking at me. The sound of his voice woke Kitty, who stirred sleepily and sat up.

"Oh. Um. Yes," I said. "That is – I guess you mean me."

"You're free to go," he said.

"You mean, you've finally figured out what I told you from the very beginning, which was that this was a colossal mistake?"

Kitty chuckled.

"You shut up," he snapped at her. She rolled her eyes, unfazed.

"It was nice to meet you," she said.

"You too," I said, meaning it. "You were very helpful. Take care of yourself."

"You too, Spy Girl." She winked at me. So did Big Jim. I followed Barlow out the door and down the hall.

"How was I supposed to know?" was the first thing he said once we were out of earshot.

"That's not a very promising start for an apology," I said.

"You were alone in the train station, you were staring at me, look at how much makeup you were wearing! What was I supposed to think?"

"You're basing this on *how much makeup I was wearing*?"

"Well—"

"First of all," I said, irritated into defensiveness, "makeup diagrams are harder than they look."

"What?"

"And second of all, I *told* you that you were making a mistake, and I told the other cops, and none of you listened."

"You should have told me you were FBI."

"You're a Vice cop, Barlow," I said coldly, and I could see that he was startled and uncomfortable that I knew his name. "You think I owe you classified intel?"

"I wasn't trying to interfere with a federal investigation." I could not help but notice that he still had not actually said he was sorry, so I shot him one magnificently withering stare but said nothing, maintaining a grand air of lofty, patronizing silence as he pressed on.

"In my defense, I didn't even know that the FBI had lady agents. I've never heard of one before. You can hardly blame me for—" I turned to him just then and summoned my most Katie Bellows glower, and he shut right up. "It's been scrubbed from the records," he said uncomfortably. "Nobody here will talk."

"Good," was all I said, and I filled it with as much frosty condescension as I could muster.

"I'll drive you home."

"The hell you will," I said. "I'll walk."

"Look," he said. "Is there anything I can do to persuade you not to call Hanson tomorrow and have me fired?"

"Use him," said Calliope. "A police source might come in handy." I pretended to think for a minute, then nodded.

"Outside," I said, and he followed me out of the station's front door, down the steps and around the corner where I fervently hoped there were no security cameras.

"All right," I said. "Here's how this is going to go. I need three things. Say yes to all of them, and Hanson (*like I even know who that is*) never has to know about this."

He nodded his agreement.

"First of all," I said, *"apologize."*

He looked at me, startled, then stared down at the ground and mumbled something.

"I didn't catch a word of that."

"I'm sorry," he mumbled a little louder.

"Like you mean it."

"I'm sorry! I should have listened to you, I made a stupid mistake, I'm an idiot, I'm sorry."

"That will do," I said benevolently. "Now, here's the second thing. It may turn out that at some point during my investigation I need to get my hands on police information without anyone knowing that I'm asking for it. You understand what I'm saying here?"

He swallowed hard.

"So I'm going to need the direct line to your desk and I'm going to need your word of honor that you'll help me out if I ask."

"Like what kind of information?" he said uncomfortably.

How the hell should I know, I'm making this up as I go along!

"You'll know when I know," I said, rather vaguely, but in

a portentous, dramatic tone, and he nodded his agreement. "And, the last thing," I continued. "Let Kitty out too."

"What?"

"Kitty. The woman who was in the cell with me. Let her out, apologize to her, waive the fine, and have someone drive her anywhere she wants to go."

"I can't do that, ma'am," he said. "She's a criminal."

"Oh, is she?"

"Yes ma'am. She's a prostitute. She broke the law."

"She broke the law tonight, specifically?"

"What do you mean?" he asked, shifting his weight uncomfortably.

"Did *you* pick her up tonight?" I said.

"Yes."

"And what crime exactly did you catch her in the middle of committing?"

"She was – I saw her loitering—"

"Oh, *loitering*, well, that's different, we can't have that. What's the fine for loitering?"

"I'm sorry?"

"Is it, by any chance, *less* than the fine for solicitation? Which I assume is what you charged her with?"

"She's a known prostitute," he said defensively.

"That's not what I asked. I asked what she was picked up for *tonight*." He was sullenly silent.

"She knows who you are," I said. "She's not stupid enough to solicit an undercover vice cop. I think you saw her minding her own business in a public place and decided you could rack up another arrest and a fat little fine. A fine that's very unlikely to make it out of your pockets and into the official police accounts, I suspect." He turned white at that, and couldn't look at me.

"Well played," said Calliope, and I beamed with pride.

"And besides, Kitty works for me," I said. He stared at me.

"Too far," Calliope sighed in my ear.

"She . . . what?" stammered Barlow.

"That's right," I said. "Kitty works for me. Doing . . . FBI stuff. Secret stuff."

"How come this is the first I'm hearing about it, then?" he said. "C.O. just told us to let *you* out. Didn't mention anything about Kitty."

"Maybe because none of us ever know what's going to happen when Reggie Bellows decides to ad lib," snapped Calliope. "Tell him, I don't know, tell him she's a covert asset."

"Yes!" I exclaimed triumphantly. "She is a *covert asset*! That totally works! You're a genius!"

Calliope groaned, and Barlow looked at me oddly. "It's . . . important to congratulate yourself on a job well done," I fumbled by way of explanation.

Clearly not satisfied with this, but unwilling to press me further, Barlow let it drop. "Well, I'm going to be on my way," I said, desperate to be gone. He extended his hand to me. I almost took it, but stopped myself. Katie Bellows would not shake this man's hand, I thought to myself, and I gave him my steeliest glare.

"You screwed up, Barlow," I said coldly. "I'm going to be watching you. If you don't want to run into me again, I'd advise that you leave Kitty and her colleagues alone for the foreseeable future. Put your time to better use. Stick to crimes you actually see happening in front of you."

"I will," he said. "I promise."

"Good. Now go away, I'm done with you." I summoned all the regal grandeur I could muster and swept grandly down the steps and around the corner, until I was out of his line of sight and could walk normally again.

"Well, that was . . . I'm not sure what that was, but it was something," said the voice in my ear. "You're welcome, by the way."

"Shut up, Calliope."

CHAPTER TWO

HELLO DARKNESS, MY OLD FRIEND

With very little hard information available about the actual moment the Chronomaly would hit, Calliope had spent a significant portion of her prep time over the past week attempting to determine where within the monstrous bureaucracy of the federal government I would be best placed, in order to maximize my potential for information-gathering while minimizing what she, rather unflatteringly, described as my "total inability to stay out of trouble."

"You have no specialized skills," she had pointed out during my mission brief.

"Stop. I'm blushing."

"I mean we can't very well send you over to the budget department to do math all day."

"That's what I do *here*," I snapped, gesturing rather dramatically at my computer screen. "What do you think this is?"

"Yes, I'm sure your Chrono-Engineering degree will come in very handy in cutting $7.8 million from the fiscal year 1973 budget of the Bureau of Land Management," she said. "I can't believe I didn't think of that."

In the end, after a resigned sigh, she decided that while she fully believed in my ability to screw this mission up from absolutely anywhere, she wanted to keep me within the walls of the White House if possible, and stuck me in the counsel's office. This seemed, initially, a promising notion. After all, at some point, every government conspiracy involves lawyers.

On principle, I am rarely an advocate of nepotism, but in practice, I was very grateful that my fictional parents had contributed such a sizable sum to Nixon's re-election campaign that I was spared the hassle of any kind of a job interview.

I arrived on Monday morning and was surprised to find that the new hire process in Nixon's White House – at least for those of us fortunate enough to have wealthy imaginary fathers in Kansas City – was much less paperwork than my Bureau apprenticeship had been.

A bored-looking woman gave me some forms to sign and asked me some perfunctory questions. Then I was given an identification pass and shown to my desk on the ground floor of the West Wing, in the outer office of White House Counsel John Dean.

The White House Counsel is, essentially, the President's lawyer. I assumed there was no shortage of legal business to attend to on the President's behalf, but was surprised to find that Dean also provided a wide range of services that took him all over the building.

I was "Dean's new girl," which was a free ticket into every wing of the White House. Everyone from the press secretary to the Executive Chef had business with our office, which meant that I spent half the day dashing around the building to either drop off or collect files that Dean didn't trust in the hands of the White House pages, while sending silent mental curses to Mark and Mrs. Graham for forcing me to do it in high heels.

I began to doubt whether Calliope had placed me in the right office, since nothing even remotely relating to a possible war with China ever came anywhere near John Dean's desk; but as an education in the White House's inner workings, it was invaluable.

Kitty wasn't lying about the frat-boy atmosphere. I wasn't even halfway through my first day before I had to physically remove a junior aide's hand from my ass. The building reeked of testosterone. The most powerful women in the building were the President's wife and his secretary; every other woman I met was about thirty rungs down the ladder. Knowing these things as abstractions – and living them day to day as workplace realities – was startlingly different.

Fortunately, I liked Dean. He was not, as far as I could tell, one of the assholes. He was young and funny and charming and drove a sports car, and if he flirted, it was with such a light touch that it didn't bother me. He didn't seem to have the inflated sense of his own importance that characterized so many of the men who buzzed in and out of our office. It was certainly possible that he too was an asshole, deep down, but as a boss he was perfectly fine. If the two of us had had the office to ourselves, the job would have been a snap.

Unfortunately, we did not.

Beth Rutherford had been Head Secretary for the White House Counsel's Office for longer than John Dean had been White House Counsel; she had worked for his predecessor as well. She was abrasive, demanding and ruthlessly efficient, and she visibly could not stand me, which perversely made her my absolute favorite person in the whole building.

Surely, if she had been my boss in real life and I knew I'd be stuck with her for years, I would have quickly tired of being treated like a moron and given the most hopelessly tedious tasks coming in and out of the Counsel's office. But as it was, I found her vastly entertaining.

Beth was one of those commanding women who had probably looked a brisk forty years old when she was in high school and would probably still look a brisk forty years old when she was seventy. She was born to wear impeccable suits and stare disapprovingly over the rims of her glasses (a move which visibly unsettled Dean).

As I sat at my desk, typing the day's four millionth staff memo about the new financial disclosure policies, I concocted elaborate backstories for the life I imagined Beth Rutherford leading. I liked to imagine her in another era as a medieval abbess, ruling with an iron fist. I pictured her at the center of an elite circle of lesbian intellectuals, women with bespoke suits and leather armchairs and degrees in French Literature from East Coast women's colleges, who kept purebred dogs and doe-eyed young mistresses, who would one day rise up and turn Washington into a matriarchal paradise.

These daydreams were partly a way to pass the time, and partly wish fulfillment; it made me sad to dwell for too long on how Beth Rutherford's first-class legal brain was wasted on typing and filing because it had been born in 1927 into a woman's body and not a man's. She knew she could do Dean's job better than he did. Dean knew it too, and treated her with an elaborate politeness that both she and I recognized as patronizing.

And I knew what she saw when she looked at me – another

social-climbing young Future Mrs. So-and-So on the hunt. How I wished I could tell her the truth and ask what she knew. How I wished *she* were the Embed; her level head and phenomenal memory would have been a perfect partner in espionage.

Calliope had sent me in three weeks ahead of the Chronomaly – or as close as she could get, given the interference – so I'd have time to get my feet under me and take a look around first. But the truth was that I didn't actually know what I was looking for. I wasn't convinced I was going to find anything. And none of us had ever discussed what would happen if I didn't.

What if the Chronomaly hit and I couldn't stop it? What if it was right there in front of me and I still missed it? What if I blinked and the moment passed me by and all those millions of people still died and it was my fault? These were the thoughts that kept me up at night in my ridiculous tropical bedroom, lying awake and watching the thick green vines snake their way up the walls and wishing I were anywhere else but here.

The closest Calliope could pin down the crisis point – that is, the specific moment in time where someone did something they were not originally meant to do and set off the series of reverberations that would coalesce into a Chronomaly – was between midnight on the night of Friday, June 16th and noon the following day. I had a twelve-hour window and a roughly one-mile radius where it would hit. There was just one problem: If Calliope's calculations were correct, that circle did not contain the White House.

We had quibbled about this when I called in the day before. "If this apartment really is at the center of the circle, then the White House is outside of it," I had told her. "The map says 1.1 miles."

"It's one-ish miles. That's the best I can do with the data I have."

"But it's going to hit on a Saturday," I argued. "Do I need to figure out a way to somehow sneak into the most secure building in the world outside of business hours, or not?"

"I'm sorry. That's as accurate as I can get about the map. The Chronomaly's boundaries are fluctuating all the time. I can't pin it down any further than what I gave you already."

"But what do I *do*? Just wander around the target area, hoping to spot something weird happening? Do I try to get into the building?"

"I don't *know*, Reggie!" she finally snapped. "I'm not the field agent here. I can't do your job for you."

That silenced me. Calliope's refusal to apply for advanced training, on the grounds that she was perfectly content where she was and Grove needed her, was a longstanding bone of contention between her and my mother, who thought she was wasting her potential. Calliope was fairly sensitive about it, largely because of her fanatical loyalty to Grove, who had been her mentor since she was fresh out of the Academy. I didn't press further; I was frustrated, but not at her, and it wasn't worth picking a fight with the best ally I had.

I arrived home that Friday night around seven, takeout burger and fries in hand. I didn't have much of a plan for that night except maybe just wandering around the streets taking HIO level readings, hoping to God that the Chronomaly would be something dramatic like a spaceship landing on the National Mall and I'd be able to spot it.

I still hadn't thought of a plausible reason for the security guards to let me into the building on a Saturday when they knew Dean wouldn't be there, but I had some time to kill in the hopes that something would come to me.

I breathed a sigh of relief as I kicked off my shoes, stepped out of my tailored skirt and blouse, leaving them in a heap on the floor, and unclasped the murderous torture device bra-from-hell.

Mark and Mrs. Graham had made a tactical error in leaving the suitcases at my house after they had packed them, so I had taken the liberty of adding in a few anachronistic necessities of my own. Buried in the middle drawer of the jungle-green lacquered dresser, underneath the pajamas I never wore, I had concealed my favorite threadbare cotton pants and a feathery-soft faded t-shirt. I pulled these out of the drawer and put them on.

I would strap myself into their tailored, waist-pinching Republican heiress costume in public, to keep my HIO levels down. But dammit, in the privacy of my own apartment, I intended to be comfortable.

I took the bag of takeout and a bottle of beer from the refrigerator and slid open the balcony door, stepping outside into the warm night. Washington in 1972 was already plenty urbanized, but still, the air had an open green scent keeping the sour concrete tang at bay, a fresh clearness where the smell of the trees met the smell of the water that was entirely new to me. I drank it in.

There was no furniture on the balcony, and the view was not stellar – my balcony opened straight out to the adjoining Watergate Hotel next door – so my scenic vista was a wall of unlit office windows. Many floors above me, on the other side of the building, the pricey upper units of Watergate West looked out on the Potomac. But the combination of night breezes, salty French fries, good beer and loose cotton against my skin was so pleasant that I didn't care much about the view.

Tomorrow was coming. Tomorrow the world would change,

and I was supposed to stop it. It was a big job. It was a lot for me not to screw up. But for now – for the next few hours – I was okay. I could take a minute to just be with myself. Just me, alone, with my beer and my burger and the warm June night.

I sat down on the cool concrete balcony floor and leaned back against the wall, staring out through the iron rails at the lights of the city, as though I were trapped in some prison in the sky.

Lulled into a warm, summer-evening complacency, I stared out into the dark stillness for a long, long time. I'm not sure how long I sat there before I became aware of a flicker of movement just at the corner of my vision. When I turned my head to look, it was gone. A feeling of uneasiness stole over me, and I set down my beer and moved closer to the balcony railing. I watched and waited, waited and watched, until suddenly there it was again. A pinprick of light flickered through the darkness in front of me for a few moments and then vanished.

A flashlight.

In an office building.

In the middle of the night.

I went back into the living room and grabbed my handheld, turning off the lamps inside in order to see better (and remain unseen myself). Half of my brain was telling me to ignore the light and go back to bed, reminding me of the potential HIO impact of intervening.

So what, I thought. *There's probably a robbery in progress. Sometimes this job means standing by and letting terrible things happen.*

Grove had said those very words to me once, trying to explain the incalculably complex potential consequences anytime an agent interfered with the justice system. He had just come back from a jump to New York in the 1970s, where a minor patch on the Bronx borough president had crossed paths with a rash of vandalism against African-American-owned businesses. He had seen a white man set fire to a black barbershop and had not called the police, even though he knew that if he didn't, nobody would, and the man would go free.

I had been furious at him.

"You have to take a step back and look at the whole field," he had said. "You have to think about the drunk driver who wasn't pulled over because the cop who was meant to arrest him was here arresting the arsonist. You have to think about the lawyer who gets called to defend the arsonist, and what other case he didn't take instead. You have to think about the criminal, too; and his family. Plus all the people around him whose lives would be changed forever if he were arrested. There are too many variables, Agent Bellows. It touches too many lives. This isn't about right and wrong; this is about accurate and inaccurate. Sometimes this job means standing by and letting terrible things happen."

Grove had been right about the arsonist. I discovered later that his wife had learned about the fires and left him, and I felt a small cruel pleasure that he had been punished by at least one person. I knew if Grove were here, he would tell me not to call the police, and he would be right about that too.

But still, I wanted to know.

I took a 3-D image of the building with my handheld, marking where the light was coming from. It was an office on the sixth floor. I pulled up the property manager's files to cross-reference. When I found the sixth floor, my heart stopped. I stared at the screen in shock.

"*Jesus Christ*," I said aloud, to no one.

"FLOOR SIX," read the building plans in big block letters on my handheld screen. "DNC HEADQUARTERS."

Someone with a flashlight was walking around inside the main office of the Democratic National Committee, looking for something in the middle of the night.

I had a sudden desperate yearning for advice from Grove, but he was still out on medical leave. So I rang Calliope at her desk, but there was no answer. I allowed myself one bone-deep sigh of pre-emptive exasperation, leaning my head back against the wall, before I bit the bullet. It connected immediately, and a face I was decidedly un-thrilled to see popped up on my screen.

"Oh God, Regina, what did you do?" she said, panic in her eyes.

"Hi to you too, Mom."

"Yes. Fine. Hello. What's wrong? What did you do?"

"Is that Reggie?" I heard in the background. "Oh God, what did she do?"

"Et tu, Calliope?" I said peevishly as she came around from behind the monitor and pulled up a chair next to my mother so they were both visible onscreen. "Seriously, guys, can you give me a little credit? I didn't screw anything up, I just need Calliope to run a search for me. I tried you on the Comm, but you didn't pick up."

"Well, I'm here now," she said. "What do you need?"

"Anything you can get me on a break-in at the Watergate. Not my apartment, the building across from mine. The hotel and office complex. Sixth floor. DNC headquarters."

"Sure. Date and time of the break-in?"

"Um, right now."

"What?" they both screeched in my ear.

"I'm on the balcony and I can see flashlights in the windows, but the whole floor is dark. It's the middle of the night here."

"There's nothing in the file," said Calliope.

"So you're saying the break-in isn't significant?"

"I'm saying the break-in doesn't *exist*."

"So this is it, then," I said. "It's after midnight here. This is the Chronomaly."

"Or it's a robbery that was never reported," my mother pointed out. "It's possible that this is playing out the way it's supposed to."

"I don't know," said Calliope. "It could be either. There's no record in the media, in the Watergate security office's files, nor in any criminal records. Nothing in the DNC's security files either."

"Then what do I do?"

"You wait and watch," said Calliope. "If in the next 24 hours we detect a heightened level of interference in the Timeline, we'll know this is the Chronomaly."

"But then I'll have missed it!"

"If it is the Chronomaly, we can pull you out for a Rewind," she snapped, "and send you in again, now that we know where and when it is."

"I can't just stand here," I said.

"You have to."

"No," I said. "I'm going over there to take an HIO reading."

"Are you crazy?" snapped Calliope, very much like my mother just moments ago. "You want to go stop a possible robbery in progress? *You?* You're a desk agent, Reggie, you're not combat-trained. Someone might have a gun. Don't be an idiot."

"Regina is right," said my mother unexpectedly. "We gave her a one-mile radius and a twelve-hour window to look for unusual activity that could be related to the Chronomaly. This could be the crisis point we couldn't pin down. We need eyes inside that building. If she can get within 50 feet to do a full scan on whoever is holding that flashlight—"

"At the very least, Calliope, I can rule out whether the

burglar has had recent contact with a time agent," I said. "The HIO meter will catch traces of Slipstream radiation if he was exposed within the last few days."

"I cannot believe I'm going along with this," she snapped again, but with less conviction. "But fine. I will call you back in twenty minutes from my desk with a mission plan. And all you are going to do – I mean it, Reggie – is sneak in, run a scan and then get the hell out. That is all. Just one scan."

"Just one scan," I repeated. "You're a saint."

"Whatever. Dark clothes, cover your hair, no shoes. Go get ready. I'll be back in 20 minutes."

"Did you pack me a Microcam?"

"Check the Bible in your big suitcase. Microcam is in Second Timothy. Earpiece is in Ruth."

"This is a weird job."

"Just go get dressed," she tapped on the screen and it went black.

I had done a fairly half-assed job of unpacking; my work clothes were neatly hung up in the closet (even in 1972 I feared Mark's wrath) but everything else was piled in a heap on the floor of the bedroom closet. One of the cases, which I hadn't opened, contained a small pile of books, carefully curated by Mrs. Graham and surgically modified by Calliope to hold a modest collection of tech equipment.

I pulled out the heavy black King James Bible (apparently my alter ego was Protestant, a wise move on Calliope's part; post-Kennedy, Catholics weren't popular in the Nixon White House) and flipped it open.

Midway through the Old Testament I found the first of two small, flat, square hollows carved neatly out of the center of the book and holding a small metal box, the case for a new earpiece. This one was multi-channel, so I could communicate with up to three different Comms at a time, unlike the standard-issue one I had been using. Apparently being a field agent came with a significant tech upgrade. The second hollow was towards the end of the New Testament and held the Microcam.

On a whim, after I had removed both, I turned the book upside down and shook it to see if Calliope had hidden anything else inside. Nothing.

I hadn't looked in any of the rest ("standard field agent kit" was all Calliope had told me during my mission brief) so I reached for the next book, a small leatherbound volume labeled *The Collected Writings of Abraham Lincoln,* and opened it to find a larger square hollow, about the size of the palm of my hand – inside was a Short-Hop, which would allow me to make smaller jumps (six months or shorter) from here without having to transport back home and re-set coordinates from the lab. It was pre-loaded with five round-trip jumps, charged and ready.

I didn't have a weapon, as such, but there was a low-impact stun pistol inside *Peyton Place* in case of emergencies and a really good scanner, way better than the tiny one on my wrist Comm, in *Great American Poetry Volume III.*

I flipped the scanner on to test it – I hadn't gotten the chance to use a Mark-10 Chrono-Scanner since the Academy and I had a little crush on it. I switched it to stealth mode to dim the screen and turn off all the sound, then scanned my bedroom top to bottom. Instantly the black screen on the scanner lit up with thousands of tiny little blinking red dots. It was picking up traces of Slipstream radiation from everything in the room I had touched, which was pretty much everything in the room. I turned it around to scan myself and adjusted the settings so it would filter out all radiation coming from me. Instantly the red dots all disappeared.

I pinned the Microcam in my hair and put in the earpiece, stuck the scanner in my pocket and rummaged through the top drawer of the jungle-green dresser, where I had dumped everything in the small suitcase which Mark, waving a vague hand, had indicated contained something called "accessories." ("Like, to a crime?" I had asked, as he looked at me with a deep and pitying sadness.) The best I could do was a square of navy blue satin, which I tied around my head like an old Polish grandmother, hoping that the sheen of the heavy fabric was dull enough not to catch the light. Then I slipped my apartment key into my pocket and crept out the door.

Calliope rang in right on schedule, buzzing me from channel 1 of my shiny new earpiece. Channel 2 clicked on shortly after, but my mother knew better than to interrupt while a tech was doing her job. "There's a night guard in the lobby," Calliope said, "and no through-way from the apartments to the office building, except through the parking garage."

"Okay, but once I get to the parking garage, how do I actually get inside the building and up to the sixth floor, if everything is locked?" I asked as I stepped into the elevator and closed the door.

"One step at a time," she said. "Right now, just get to the parking garage."

"I'm just saying... You know I can't pick a non-computerized lock, right?"

"I know."

"Because if you're expecting me to figure out how to break into a building—"

"This will go a lot more smoothly if you stop talking."

The elevator slowly made its way down to the underground garage. When the door opened and I stepped out onto the concrete floor, everything was still and silent. The garage lights somehow made everything more sinister, casting heavy shadows in corners and making an ominous buzzing sound. I suddenly felt very exposed, and caught myself nervously eyeing each car I passed to make sure nobody was watching me from inside it.

"Stop," said Calliope sharply. "Duck." I dropped behind a dark sedan just three or four cars from the door that led from the parking garage to the stairwell. "Someone's coming," she said. "Just one. Security guard making his rounds. He's going to exit from the door to the stairwell and is probably going to enter the door next to it, which leads to the lobby. You're okay. Stay where you are until he's gone."

Heart pounding, I crouched as low as I could, praying I wouldn't make a noise. I heard the door clang open and then close behind him, and waited for him to do what I hoped would be a perfunctory check and then go back inside.

Nothing happened.

"Calliope?" I murmured as softly as I could.

"He's still here," she said. "Don't move. I can't tell what he's doing."

"Are there cameras?" asked my mother, who I had forgotten was there. "Any feeds you can tap into?"

"No cameras," she said, "and I couldn't get at them anyway. It's 1972, nothing's networked. Reggie, I need you to see if you can get a look at him through the car windows. He should be in your Microcam's line of sight."

I rose very, very slowly from a low crouch until my eyes – and the camera in my hair – could see through the windows of the car to the door a few dozen feet away. The security guard stood there, with the door open, and he appeared to be scraping at something on the door latch with his fingernail. He was totally occupied with this task and was paying no attention to me, so I decided to get a closer look. I ducked as low as I could and crept from car to car until there was only one Volkswagen and about six feet of garage floor between me and the security guard.

"It's tape," said my mother quietly. "The burglar taped down the catch."

"Why?" asked Calliope. "To keep the door from locking behind them?"

"Or," she said, "to let someone else in."

I felt a chill at this, and looked around me nervously.

"No life signs besides you and the guard," said Calliope, reading my mind. "Well, now we know how the burglar got in, but if he pulls off that tape—"

She never got a chance to finish her sentence. The guard pulled off the tape and I saw him flick it off his fingers onto the ground, then open the adjacent door – the one leading to the lobby – and disappear inside. Faster than I'd ever run in my life, I bolted over to the stairwell door and caught it just before it closed all the way.

"That was impressive," Calliope admitted.

"Eh. It's just a really slow door," I shrugged. Then, before I really knew what I was doing, I had picked up the small X of white tape the guard had dropped on the ground, and I neatly replaced it over the catch.

"What the hell are you doing?" asked Calliope incredulously.

"If you were planning a break-in, and you had hired help, you'd send him in first, wouldn't you?" I said. "I think whoever is already in the building is the little guy, and whoever this tape is for, that's the one we want. I want him in the building. I want to get a look at his face."

I climbed stair after stair, tiptoeing in my stocking feet. As

I passed the door leading to the third floor, my heart froze at the sound of loud voices on the other side of it. The stairwell was brightly lit, I was dressed exactly like a burglar, and there was nowhere to hide. I sprinted up the next flight and paused for breath on the fourth floor, looking down below me to see if I had been spotted.

But the door never opened, and the voices faded away.

Safe.

I exhaled deeply and pressed on.

When I reached the door labeled "6th Floor," I stopped in front of it, heart pounding.

"Okay, open the door, and then hard left," said Calliope. "There's an unoccupied corner office with no vital signs. It should be unlocked."

"And then what?"

"Just get out of the stairwell first, Reggie, there's nowhere to hide. *Go.*"

I took a deep breath and silently pushed open the door just enough to quickly shimmy through it, praying that the shaft of light it let in with me couldn't be seen. Then I gently pushed it closed, and stepped into darkness.

My eyes took a second to adjust, and my first stab at a "hard left" sent me face-first into a file cabinet with a loud *thunk*.

"Goddammit, Reggie," Calliope hissed in my ear. I stood frozen in place for a long, terrifying moment, but it seemed no one had heard anything. I clung to the wall for safety and crept alongside it until I located the doorway Calliope had mentioned.

The office was indeed unlocked. The door was about half ajar, so I slipped behind it where I could peer out through the gap between the hinges to get the lay of the land.

"Okay," said Calliope. "Take a breather. No life signs within

100 feet. I've got them all on screen and they're not moving. Let's decide what you're going to do next."

"Okay," I whispered.

"I'm inside the property manager's files," she continued. "This whole floor is leased to the DNC. That means whatever they're looking for could be anywhere. You're going to have to be quiet and quick. I can guide you towards the life signs and get you close enough to do a scan while you're still mostly hidden, and then the second it's done you run. Got it?"

"Got it."

"This is where it gets real, Reggie."

"I know."

"All right," she said. "Duck low so you've got the cubicle walls for shelter. Go right, then left, then right."

I followed her instructions and found myself in a long hallway full of offices with closed doors. I could see, at the far end, flickers of light coming from the one open door.

"Don't speak," said Calliope in my ear. "Just tap your earpiece once for yes and twice for no. Can you see the room they're in, over there at the end of the hall to the left?"

I tapped YES.

"Okay. They're six doors down from you, on the left. The door to the office across from them is open. On your right-hand side, four doors down is an unlocked office. Can you get in there without being seen?"

I tapped YES again, and then crept silently to the fourth door.

"Stop," said my mother. "Don't touch it. Fingerprints."

Dammit.

"She's already touched the stairwell doors and the cubicle walls," said Calliope.

"Then she'll have to go back the way she came and scrub them as she goes."

"That could mean destroying evidence. Erasing the real burglar's fingerprints. Isn't it better to leave them? Hers will just come up as unidentifiable."

"It's risky."

"Oh my God, just make a decision," I hissed. "I'm literally just standing in the hallway."

"Go inside. Use your sleeve to touch the handle. Just get out of the hall."

I turned the handle as slowly and gently as I could, praying it wouldn't creak or rattle. It opened smoothly and I stepped inside, closing it silently behind me.

"Okay," said Calliope briskly. "To your left is a door that connects to the adjoining office, which connects to the one next to that. You should be able to get to the room right across from where the burglars are, scan, and then get back here in about 30 seconds. Can you do that?"

I tapped YES as I moved through the two consecutive doorways and found myself in an empty office with an open door. Through the space between the door and the wall, the men in the room across from me were clearly visible. And I could hear them now, too.

"Where's Jimmy?"

"He didn't say."

"He's coming, though, right?"

"Yeah, he's supposed to be coming."

"Good, because I don't know what the hell we're supposed to be looking for."

"Just help me with this, would you?"

I heard a scraping noise and squinted into the crack in the door, trying to see.

"Reggie, don't move, life signs approaching," said Calliope.

"Hang on, I want to get a closer look."

"No, don't move, someone's coming. Just wait until the coast is clear, then do your scan and get out."

I shook my head. Something about this felt wrong. Why break into a building if you didn't know what you were supposed to be looking for? Why didn't he know what he was here to steal? Why would you rob an administrative office? What could they possibly have inside these cubicles worth all this trouble?

Information, a voice in my head told me, and I suddenly remembered Kitty's story. My blood ran cold. This wasn't a run-of-the-mill burglary. They weren't here for money or computer equipment or to pinch the high-end whiskey from the private stash in the corner offices. They weren't robbers. They were *spies*.

"Stay still," Calliope ordered me. "He's coming." And sure enough, I heard footsteps approaching down the hall. A tall man in a business suit, wearing a pair of surgical gloves, rounded the corner. I felt the men in the office freeze, and the flashlights switched off.

"Cool it," said the new voice, "it's just me."

"Hey, Jimmy," said one.

"Man, where you been?" said another irritably.

"I got held up. You guys aren't done yet?" said Jimmy.

"The ceiling panels were a pain," said one of the other voices.

Ceiling panels? I thought. *What the hell?* What possible use could the ceiling panels be? I crept slowly around the half-opened door to get a better angle, praying that none of them would step out into the hall where I'd be instantly spotted.

"Use the goddamn scanner already," hissed Calliope.

I pulled the scanner out of my pocket, checking that it was still on stealth mode, synced it to Calliope so she could see it on her handheld, and carefully scanned the room top to bottom.

The screen flashed full of red dots, startling me so badly that I almost dropped it.

"Holy shit," said Calliope, who never said "shit."

"How is this possible?" I whispered.

"What?" asked my mother.

"Look," said Calliope, and I knew she was showing her handheld screen to my mother. I heard her breath catch in her throat and then there was a long, tense silence.

"Can anyone explain to me," my mother finally said in a strange, unreadable voice, "how a group of burglars from the 1970s got their hands on 22nd-century Chrono-Technology?"

The scanner's black screen roughly mapped out the layout of the room, just as it had back in my apartment, and was filtering out all radiation coming from me. None of the vital signs were red – that is, none of the men in the room had come through the Slipstream themselves or had direct contact with somebody who had – but there were at least a dozen hot spots all over the room.

They appeared to be tiny objects, composed mostly of plastic and metal, with some electronic function that my scanner couldn't identify. Some moved as the vital signs did – as though attached to the men – while others were scattered around with no clear pattern.

"The readings are weird," I whispered. "They're not actual Chrono-Technology – they're some kind of antiquated device the scanner can't identify, but they definitely came through the Slipstream."

"Someone in the 22nd century is manufacturing 20th-century electronic devices?" asked Calliope. "Why?"

"You know why, Calliope," said my mother. "You do it all the time."

"It's a field mission," I said softly.

"An off-the-books one," said my mother. "There's no registered agent activity anywhere nearby."

Unlicensed time travelers with their own secret transport and prop shop? The thought made my blood run cold. This wasn't just one rogue agent. This was something big.

"Regina, we need eyes in that room," said my mother. "We have to know what those things are."

"I'm on it," I said, and looked around desperately, willing a brilliant idea to come to me, when I spotted a pencil cup and tape dispenser on the desk nearby. I unpinned the Microcam from my hair, grabbed a pencil, tore off a small piece of tape (wincing at the tiny tearing noise, which thankfully went unheard) and taped it to the end of the pencil.

"You're going to have to tell me what you see," I murmured as I knelt down on the floor and slowly, slowly reached a hand out to set the pencil down square in the middle of the hallway.

"Carpet," said Calliope. "Fix the angle."

I turned the pencil a quarter turn to give the Microcam a better view.

"Got it," she said. "Five men, well, we knew that already. They're all wearing suits and ties and rubber gloves."

"Can you get their faces?" asked my mother, but Calliope shook her head. "Nobody's facing out this direction. I'm capturing side-profile of a couple of them, but that's it. I'll run it through the database later and see what I can find."

"What are they doing right now?" I murmured. She watched in silence for a few moments before she spoke.

"Somebody's at the desk," she said, "doing something with the telephone. One of them has a file cabinet open. It may be Jimmy. I can't see, but I think he's maybe photographing documents. He's flipping through the file drawers and pulling stuff out, but he isn't actually taking anything."

"That would explain why the burglary was never reported," Mom pointed out. "If they only broke in to take photos and nothing was stolen, maybe no one ever knew."

"That's only two," I said. "Where are the other three?"

"They're doing something weird with the ceiling," she said. "Two of them are standing on chairs and they're taking down ceiling panels and handing them to a third guy. I don't understand."

"I think I do," said my mother grimly. "Look at the building plans again."

"What am I looking at?" said Calliope.

"Look at whose office that is."

"It's the secretary's office."

"No, not that one. Not the office they're in now. Look whose office is next door."

"Who's next door?" I whispered.

"Lawrence O'Brien," said Calliope. "Chairman of the Democratic National Committee."

"Oh my God," I whispered as it all clicked into place. "Mom. Mom. They're *wiretaps*."

"They're putting bugs in the ceiling," said Calliope. "They're eavesdropping on the DNC chairman next door. Reggie, it's just like Kitty said."

"Kitty who?"

"Never mind, Mom. Look, this is it. This is the crisis point. Somebody from our time is spying on the Democrats. They're trying to steal the election. If Nixon loses then Reagan isn't president and if Reagan isn't president then there's no war with China. This is how it happened, Mom, *this is how they did it*."

"We were right," she said softly. "God help us, Regina, we were right."

There was a heavy silence, broken by a sharp inhalation from Calliope.

"Goddammit," she said. "Goddammit, Reggie, you idiot."

"What? What did I do?"

"The security guard just came back through the garage," she said. "The same one as before. He's stopped at the stairwell door."

"Oh no," I whispered.

"Reggie, *he's going to see the tape.*"

Shit. The *tape.*

"We need to get you out of there," said Calliope sharply. "He's coming up the stairs. And there are three more life signs moving in from the lobby."

"I need to get my hands on one of those wiretaps," I said.

"No, you need to get out of here before you're arrested," said my mother. *Again,* I could feel Calliope silently adding.

"I *told* you guys you should have sent someone else," I snapped defensively. "I told you."

"Yeah, well—" Calliope started to respond but my mother cut her off.

"Later," she said briskly. "No time for that now. We need to get you out of the building. Calliope, options."

"Stairwell is blocked," she said. "No fire escape. No way out through the windows. She's going to have to take her chances with the elevator."

"That's clear on the other side of the bullpen," my mom said.

"Yeah. She's going to have to run."

I grabbed the pencil and pulled the Microcam off it, pinning it back into my hair and tiptoed out back through the interconnected offices the same way I had come. The burglars, who had no idea the guards were closing in, were absorbed in their work and didn't notice me. Once I had reached the last door, I heard thunderous footsteps and bolted for cover, finding myself inside a maze of cubicles.

"Left, then left," said Calliope. I got on my knees and crawled, following her instructions. "Right. Left. Left. Right."

Then the stairwell door crashed open.

"Police! Come out with your hands up!"

"Goddammit," said one of the voices, and a lazy drawl followed it with, "All right, you caught us", in a surprisingly calm, somewhat amused tone.

"For God's sake, keep moving," said Calliope. "Left, then right, then you're there." I reached the end of the cubicle maze, but there were twenty feet of open ground between me and the elevator. "You'll just have to chance it," said Calliope, reading my mind. "They've got all five men. They're distracted. Go low, and fast. *Go.*"

I melted into the shadows along the wall, pressing my body up against it and trying to disappear as I bent low and moved as fast as I could towards the elevator. I pounded the DOWN button over and over and over again, looking desperately behind me as it crawled with excruciating slowness up to the 6th floor. Finally it arrived, with a soft ding, and I dove in without waiting to see if the police or the burglars had heard it.

"Parking garage. Now," snapped Calliope. I pushed the button marked P and then endured the most excruciatingly slow elevator ride of my life. I was jumping out of my skin by the time the door opened.

"No life signs," she said. "You're clear. Now send the elevator back up to the lobby. Hopefully no one will notice it was gone." I pushed the button marked L and stepped out. The garage was empty, but it felt even more sinister then it had before.

I abandoned all subtlety and caution, sprinting like a crazy person to the apartment building entrance on the other side.

They were nice enough to give me a few minutes' grace period, and as I stepped out of the elevator in front of my apartment – sending it back down to the lobby too, just in case – and then closed and bolted my door behind me with shaking fingers, I had a brief interlude of silence to collect myself.

A *very* brief interlude.

"Regina Theresa Bellows, *what in the name of God were you thinking*?"

They had apparently decided between the two of them that my mother would go first, and she had clearly been working on some new material as I was scampering through the parking garage picturing security guards on my heels. It was some of her finest work, and even though I pulled out my earpiece and set it down on the bedside table while I took off my clothes and sank into the soft green depths of the bed, I could still hear every word with crystal clarity.

". . . the *first thing* you learned on your *first day* at the Academy, you *don't touch anything* if you don't know what it is," she was saying. "The security guard would never have known the burglars were in the building if you hadn't replaced the tape. Now the readings over here are going crazy and five men have been arrested and we have absolutely no idea what's going to happen next. All you had to do, Regina, *all you had to do,* was go inside that building and do one scan and then leave. This is so typical. You never think about the consequences of anything. You just float along, expecting everything to turn out all right, and you never stop to *think.*"

"Ma'am, it's very late over there," said Calliope in her best soothing-the-raging-beast voice, the one she saved for Grove when he was in a particularly grumpy mood in the mornings. "She needs sleep. Why don't we give her a break until tomorrow morning and then she can call in when we have more information on what the fallout of this is going to be, and in the meantime she can get some rest. We can't do anything right now, and neither can she."

I turned out the lamp and the snaky jungle vines melted into darkness. Dimly, I could hear that Calliope and my mother had stepped away from the Comm to bicker privately, and I could make out a line here and there – the higher-pitched voice, Calliope's, saying "Yes, well, what's done is done" and the lower-pitched (and much angrier) voice barking something about interference levels and "still no closer to knowing who commissioned those wiretaps."

I had long since stopped caring. I closed my eyes and felt the coiled-up tension in my body release. My mother was right — I had screwed up, and badly. But Calliope was also right – I could do nothing about it now. Right now, the only thing I wanted was to disappear into the darkness and put this night behind me. Drained and exhausted, I snuggled deeply into my satiny green pillows and let the comforting sound of Calliope and my mother shouting at each other through my earpiece lull me to sleep.

CHAPTER THREE

I SAID BE CAREFUL, HIS BOW TIE IS REALLY A CAMERA

I slept away most of Saturday, ignoring multiple calls from my mother, before finally dragging myself out of bed in the late afternoon. Attempting to put off the inevitable as long as possible, I rang Calliope first instead.

"Good morning, sunshine," she said dryly as the screen blinked to life, and I was irritated to see that even though she was in the same clothes she was wearing yesterday and could hardly have gotten any more sleep than I had, she was as bright-eyed and peppy as always. Her hair was still perfect, and she hardly even looked rumpled. I hated her a little bit and grumbled a cranky greeting as I put grounds in the coffee maker.

(This was another of my particular specialties, which Katie Bellows disdained as an utter waste of time. I can make coffee in any decade of the 20th and 21st centuries. The Academy's prop shop had a whole closet of coffee makers, all different shapes and sizes, from percolators to pour-overs, and I taught myself how to use them all. This was the only part of my job Leo had ever been genuinely interested in.)

"Are you making coffee in your underwear?" she asked, raising an eyebrow.

"It was a long night," I said. "Clothes make me tired."

"You know your mother's been trying to reach you for the last five hours, right?"

"Oh, believe me, I know."

"We can talk for five minutes," she said. "And then I'm going to have to ring her and tell her that I have you on Comm."

"Ten minutes."

"This isn't a negotiation," she said. "I don't have a second offer. Five minutes is the offer. And you're wasting them."

"Fine."

"You know you have to tell her what Kitty told you," she said.

"I know."

"Nobody else is going to make the connection between a burglary gone wrong in Washington and a Miami yacht party that never actually happened."

"I know."

"We have no idea how far back this plan to sabotage the Democrats goes, and we might be the only people who know that this wasn't an isolated incident."

"I know, Calliope."

"And if there's a greater conspiracy to sabotage the Democrats and steal the election—"

"I said *I know*."

"I'm sorry," she said. "I assumed you'd be more difficult than this and I put a lot of effort into my speech."

"It was a good speech."

"Thank you."

"And we're on the same page."

"Good."

"Except—"

"Uh-oh."

"I'm just wondering if there's *any* way for me to tell her about Kitty while leaving out the part where I got arrested for accidentally propositioning a cop."

"There is not."

"Damn."

"Think of it this way," she said. "For the rest of your life, this is the absolute worst that breaking bad news to your mother is *ever* going to get."

"Challenge accepted."

"Okay, time's up," she said. "I'm calling her." The screen on my handheld split from one image to two, and my mother's face appeared next to Calliope's.

"Are you in your underwear?" she said with a horrified expression, and I noted that she too looked fresh as a daisy despite also still wearing last night's clothes. Apparently I was the only one on the team who actually needed *sleep*.

"Hello, Mom."

"I've been trying to call you for—"

"I know, Mom."

"Because we have a lot of—"

"I got arrested," I said, and was pleased to see how thoroughly that silenced her. I took a deep breath and poured the whole rest of the story out in a rush. "There was a guy at the train station when I first got here and I thought he was the Embed, but he obviously wasn't, and in the course of trying to set up a meet with him, I said some stuff that he interpreted as being, well, suggestive, so he basically thought I was a prostitute—"

"He *what?*"

". . . which to be clear, I was *totally* not propositioning him, but anyway, so I was in jail for a couple of hours—"

"You were *where?*"

"I swear this will go so much faster if you just let me finish. Anyway, so I'm in this jail cell with this girl named Kitty; she actually *is* a prostitute. She got picked up by the same cop, and we got to talking, and I told her I was working undercover for the FBI—"

"You said *what?*"

"Mom!"

"Just let her finish," said Calliope.

"Fine," said my mother, through clenched teeth, and remained silent for the duration of the story.

So I told her all about my conversation with Kitty, about Jane and the Republican lawyer and the yacht in Miami and Lacey and the second lawyer who said the money didn't come through.

And I told her about the cover story Calliope had concocted for me, and about my conversation with Detective Barlow and the promise of future help I had exacted from him.

After I finished, my mother was silent for a long time. Her face on the screen was expressionless. I swallowed hard, and braced for impact.

Then she burst out laughing.

She laughed and she laughed and she laughed. Calliope and I stared at her in utter bafflement as her whole face turned red and tears ran down her cheeks.

"What is happening?" I said to Calliope.

"I'm . . . not exactly sure. Ma'am, are you feeling all right?" This set off fresh peals of laughter as Mom desperately attempted to collect herself.

"Oh God," she said, wiping tears from her eyes. "I'm sorry. I don't know what came over me. It's just . . . we had dozens of specialists working around the clock for a week to prep this mission, you have hundreds of pages of background documents, you went through eight hours of field drills, and *in the first ten minutes* you hit on a cop and get arrested."

"It was more than ten minutes, Mom," I said irritably.

"But he was basically the first person you talked to," Calliope pointed out, the flicker of a smile on her face, which sent my mother into further paroxysms of laughter.

"*He was the first person she talked to,*" she howled with laughter. "And he *arrested* her."

"Look at it this way. There's nowhere to go but up from here," said Calliope. Now they were both laughing.

"Listen," I snapped. "I made two incredibly valuable contacts and I got you a piece of information you would never have gotten otherwise."

"And you did it while smoking prison cigarettes with a man named Big Jim."

"I didn't smoke, Mom."

"Well, thank God you weren't giving yourself lung cancer while you were *spending the night in jail*—"

"All right, that's enough," said Calliope. "We've had our fun at Reggie's expense—"

"You certainly have—"

"But the truth is that we know a lot now that we didn't know 24 hours ago and it's all solid."

"The good news," said my mother, "is that there's significantly escalating chaos in the General Timeline around the crisis point."

"Why is that good news?"

"Because there wasn't before," she said. "It's new. The

break-in was clearly *a* Chronomaly – if not *the* Chronomaly – and it's sending this Timestream into a tailspin. That's a positive sign. That means something is changing."

"Did it work?" I asked, hardly daring to hope. "Is the war fading out of the General Timeline?"

"No," she said. "Not yet. There are ripples in the pond from this Chronomaly but they don't reach that far yet. You're going to have to throw in another rock."

"What's next, then?"

She thought for a moment. "All right," she said. "What do we know? We're fairly sure what we're looking at is a carefully-orchestrated plan to tamper with a national election. We know there are multiple parties involved, working from multiple angles, and the common thread seems to be gathering information on the Democrats."

"But we don't know if it's the party as a whole or the 1972 campaign specifically," said Calliope. "Or how long it's been going on."

"And we don't know if it's someone looking for dirt on the Democrats," I pointed out, "or if someone is afraid the Democrats have dirt on *them*."

"We also don't know if Kitty is on the level," said my mother. "It's possible she was a plant. You didn't see her get arrested. She was already in the cell when you got there. She could have been feeding you deliberate misinformation."

"I don't think she was," I said.

"I don't think she was either," she replied, "but we can't rule it out."

"Still," said Calliope, "even if we don't trust the story about Miami, we know what we saw last night with our own eyes. There's definitely something going on here."

"And we know at least one 22nd-century chrono-agent is

involved," said my mother. "Probably the same person who's been manually reconfiguring the Timeline. It's bigger than just 1972."

"So, kind of like a conspiracy," I said.

"No, *not* like a conspiracy," she said sharply.

"Right. Because you don't believe in government conspiracies."

"I do not."

"But, like, hypothetically, if you *did* believe in government conspiracies, you might be forced to admit that this looks an awful lot like one."

"Well, I don't know. Let's get a second opinion from your new boyfriend, Big Jim."

"Don't be jealous. I'll give you his number. He's closer to your age anyway."

"Both of you, knock it off," Calliope interrupted. "What's our next move? Should Reggie come home?"

I thought about it for a long moment – I could see my mother was thinking about it too – before I realized with surprise that I didn't actually want to. Against all probability, I wanted to stay here and see this through. "No," I said. "I'm staying put." Calliope looked worried, but didn't argue. My mother's face was harder to read, but in her eyes I thought I saw something like pride.

"All right," said Calliope. "Reggie's mission was to find the Chronomaly, and she's done that. What's next?"

"The mission isn't over," I said. "We're no closer to figuring out who we're up against. Who's pulling the strings here? We know what they did but not who they are, or why."

"Well," said my mother, "if you were hunting for a likely suspect to execute a massive espionage campaign against a Democratic candidate, what's the most obvious place to start?"

"Probably with the Republican candidate," I said, and she nodded with approval.

"That's what I think too," she said. "So you're going to need to stick around the White House a little bit longer. We need to get inside the Committee to Re-Elect the President."

~

Mom gave me Sunday off ("There's nothing you can really do until you're back in the office anyway," she said, "except go get yourself arrested again"), so I spent the rest of my weekend lying around in my underwear with beer, take-out hamburgers from the diner across the street, and piles of research on Nixon's re-election campaign.

The most perplexing aspect of this theoretical conspiracy was that I couldn't see any reason for it. Nixon won the election in a landslide, and the polls showed it early. Even his most psychotically paranoid political operatives couldn't *possibly* have thought they needed that much extra ammo against George McGovern, his Democrat opponent.

Wiretaps? Eavesdropping prostitutes? It was like swatting a fly with a wrecking ball. So *why*, then? I didn't know. I needed to talk to somebody on the inside.

I had been in 1972 for weeks already, and it was starting to weigh on me a little that the Embed hadn't yet contacted me. I pressed Mom yet again for more information, and again she refused.

"He's a deep-cover agent," she said. "Only two people in the entire Bureau – Director Gray and me – know who he is or what he does or who he really works for. He'll contact you when *he* decides it's safe enough. I can't have you accidentally propositioning him on a park bench or something."

So the answer is, no, she did *not* let that go. But I did know she was briefing him regularly, so I just waited and hoped he would make himself visible soon.

The Sunday edition of the *Washington Post* ran an article about the break-in, which was excellent news for several reasons – both because its sudden appearance in Calliope's press archives was a sign that the Timestream was continuing to slowly shift, and because it contained two very important facts about the man called Jimmy that none of us had known.

His real name was James McCord, and he used to work for the C.I.A.

When I arrived at the office on Monday morning, Dean's door was closed but I could hear raised voices on the other side of it. Beth was in a terrible mood, which I took to mean that Dean was; she bore the brunt of it when he had a bad day, and in turn, generally took it out on me. She had clearly been called in early and had already been at her desk for hours when I arrived at nine (9:02, actually, as Beth pointed out, rather more forcefully than I thought necessary).

"Who's in there?" I asked, gesturing to the closed door as I hung up my coat on the rack.

"That's not your concern, Regina."

I peered over her shoulder at Dean's calendar, which was lying open on her desk. The entire day's schedule had been erased (Beth wrote everything in pencil just in case) and in its place was a line going from 8 a.m. to 6 p.m. that was marked only "G.L."

"G.L.," I said. "Green Lantern?"

She was magnificently unamused.

"Back to your desk, Miss Bellows. That stack of files all need signatures by noon."

"Gaston Leroux?" I tried again. "Gypsy Rose Lee?"

"Miss Bellows—"

"Why is Mr. Dean in an all-day meeting with Green Lantern?" I said. "He had the Vice President this morning, and a lunch with the Chief of Staff."

"He canceled all of that."

"He canceled on the Vice President?" I asked incredulously. "Why?"

"Because he's a sensible man," she said, not looking up from her paperwork. "And in a fight between Vice President Spiro Agnew and Green Lantern—"

I never got to find out the end of the only joke Beth Rutherford ever made in my presence, because the door banged open just then and Dean stuck his head out.

"Beth," he barked, "I need you in here."

She nodded obediently, gathered her steno pad and a pen, and followed him into the office. "Back on my desk, with signatures, by noon," she snapped at me, gesturing to the two-foot-high stack of files she had unceremoniously dumped on my desk before my arrival, then disappeared and closed the door behind her.

Normally I hated being "John Dean's errand girl," but today I welcomed it as a chance to see what was going on in the rest of the building.

Everyone was in a tizzy. The White House press office had of course disavowed any knowledge of the break-in – Jimmy McCord was an outside consultant, not "one of us", they asserted – but it felt sinister, and the involvement of a former C.I.A. agent gave everybody a case of the shivers.

I went into office after office, handing files to harried secretaries and whispering, "Beth needs this signed by noon!" and seeing them nod and wave me away without ever pausing in their phone conversation. Every senior staff member's office door was closed. Every secretary looked frazzled and snappish. Whatever was going on, John Dean wasn't the only one worried.

"I don't see how we could have had anything to do with it," I overheard one secretary say to another as I took a break from my rounds to stop by the coffee cart.

"I don't see how we *couldn't* have," said the other.

"Did you hear he used to be a spy?" said the first. "Ex-CIA. And you don't just put away all those skills when you retire, you know. Once a spy, always a spy. Sometimes even when they say they're retired or quit, they haven't really."

"So it's kind of like *anyone you meet* could be a spy," said the second in awe.

"Anyone," I agreed, chiming in. "Me, for example. I could be a spy sent here as part of a far-reaching investigation about why people just stand in front of the coffee cart talking and blocking the way even after they have their coffee in hand and other people are waiting in line."

They both stared at me, completely incredulous, before moving away, whispering. "That was *rude*," I heard the second one say to the first. I rolled my eyes as I filled up my coffee cup.

"Is it just me," I asked Billy, the coffee cart attendant, "or is everyone in this building acting weird today?"

"Not just you," he said. "You hear about the burglary?"

"The one in the papers?" I said.

Billy nodded.

"Mark my words, Miss Bellows," he said. "I've worked in this building for thirty-one years, and I can feel when something ain't right. And something ain't right."

"I think so too," I said.

"So you better take an extra cherry Danish," he said, handing me two of them wrapped in a napkin. "When things go wrong in the White House, sooner or later all hell breaks loose in the Counsel's Office."

I thanked him and wolfed down both the pastries, carefully avoiding any contact between legal government paperwork and my sticky cherry fingers, and continued on my rounds.

It will probably not surprise you to learn that I had a significantly easier time getting along with Billy the coffee cart attendant than with the secretaries. I was not popular with the secretaries. Or, in all honesty, with anyone. I had made no friends at the White House, so the mess hall was a hurdle for which Mrs. Graham had failed to prepare me.

I had finally mastered Mark's make-up diagrams, I was wearing the clothes correctly, I was a competent worker, and I had memorized a breathtaking volume of information on the customs and social mores of 1972. But nobody had told me I would have to decide whose table to eat at in the cafeteria.

I solved this mostly by taking my lunch break at strange hours, when the mess was least likely to be crowded, and always having a book in my hands. For that, though, I'd had to pay a visit to the library, since all the books in my luggage had chunks carved out of the middle for storage compartments.

So I was sitting alone with my turkey on rye and Mark Twain's *Roughing It* – which possessed the dual virtues of fitting my wealthy Midwestern Republican backstory while also being incredibly funny – when Beth plunked herself down at my table and took the book out of my hands.

"You can borrow it when I'm done, Beth."

"Don't be cute."

"Literally no one in my entire life has ever accused me of that."

She glared at me.

"Listen to me, Regina," she said sternly. "There's a pair of reporters sniffing around this burglary and I want to make sure you're clear on the procedure."

"I would assume the procedure is 'Don't talk to reporters.' Is there more to it than that?"

"Mr. Dean has a very sensitive position," she said. "An enormous amount of confidential information, much of it financial, flows in and out of our office. Obviously, all our staff is expected to comply with questions from the federal investigators but we owe no such obligation to the press. So you will respond with 'No comment' or refer them directly to Mr. Dean. Is that clear?"

I set down my sandwich, book forgotten. "What federal investigators?"

"I'm sure it's nothing," she said, and I could see on her face that she realized she'd already given away too much.

"The government is investigating the break-in at the Watergate?"

"There was talk of a potential situation involving the FBI, but it's nothing. But most importantly, the reporters—"

"Screw the reporters," I said impatiently, and I swear to God she almost, *almost,* smiled. "Is there something going on here that I don't know about?"

"My dear, you are a junior secretary to the White House Counsel. The things going on in this building that you don't know about—"

"Don't pretend like you don't know exactly what I mean," I said impatiently. "This can't be what you signed on for either, can it? Sneaking around, spying on the Democrats, planting bugs in ceil—"

I stopped short, suddenly afraid of giving away more than the newspaper had mentioned.

"It's nothing to do with us," she said crisply. "It's nothing to do with the White House."

"Well, clearly the FBI doesn't think so," I retorted, "if you're here to warn me about how to proceed when they start asking me questions."

"Listen to me, Regina," she said, her voice hard and cold. "You know nothing. You have seen nothing. And when asked, you will say you know nothing, and you have seen nothing. Do we understand each other?"

I looked at her for a long moment. I *didn't* understand her, not really, but I nodded anyway, and she handed my book back to me and left.

As the afternoon dragged on, I became more and more curious about Dean's mystery meeting. Beth did not re-emerge from his office, but either her presence quelled the rage or whoever was shouting in there had worn himself out; although I could still hear voices through the wall, they never rose above a murmur.

An hour or two after I returned from my lunch, a waiter from the kitchens arrived pushing a cart, covered in white linen and containing a tray of sandwiches under a glass dome, along with the seltzer water Dean liked and a glass pitcher of orange juice. He was about to knock when I jumped up and stopped him.

"Better let me," I said in a conspiratorial voice. "They've been shouting all morning. I'll be your human shield; you come in behind me."

"Thanks," said the waiter gratefully, and I stepped in front of him and knocked on the door.

Beth opened it, and her initial expression of utter horror at my presumption faded only slightly when I stepped aside and she saw the uniformed waiter behind me.

"So sorry to disturb you, Mr. Dean, but your lunch has arrived," I said, in my sweetest voice, trying to dig up every last drop of what little feminine charm I could muster, and used the pretext of carrying the orange juice and bottled water over to Dean's sideboard to scan the room.

Dean's office was less flashy and ostentatious than most of the senior staff's. He didn't have a sofa in there, like some of the other guys did, no art on the walls, nor even a plant. It was spare, tidy and just big enough for his desk, his private files, a small sideboard where his coffee and water and whiskey sat on trays, and a small table with two chairs, where the man with the raised voice was currently seated.

I recognized him immediately, though I didn't know his name (privately I had nicknamed him "Moustache", as his was particularly ostentatious). I had seen him in the office two or three times since I started.

When I entered, Dean was standing near the door, and Moustache sat at the table with a glass of Scotch in his hand. I noticed a few things as I carried the orange juice and water over to the sideboard as slowly as I could without looking suspicious.

I noticed that Dean was sweating a little, though he was a young, fit guy who swam and played tennis and couldn't have been doing anything more physically demanding than pacing back and forth. I noticed that both men had their sleeves rolled up. I noticed that as I neared the sideboard, Dean moved immediately to pour a glass of water from the tray, putting his body directly between me and the desk – even though the glass of water on his desk wasn't even half empty yet.

"Your new girl's a looker, Dean," said Moustache in a jovial voice. Dean didn't appear to hear him, but I saw Beth flinch just as I did. We looked at each other, and something passed between us at that moment that might, just might, have been solidarity. Then it was gone.

"What's your name, little lady?" he said.

"Regina Bellows," I said, smiling sweetly through gritted teeth.

He stuck out his hand. "Gordon Liddy. Nice to meet you."

Well, that solved the mystery of G.L. at least. The name was faintly familiar to me from my mission briefing; he worked in the building somewhere, I was fairly sure. I shook his hand politely and retreated to the door as the waiter set their lunch on the table where Liddy sat.

"You know how to make a screwdriver?" said Liddy. It wasn't clear to anyone in the room which of us he was talking to.

"Gordon, you have a drink in your hand," said Dean impatiently.

"There wasn't orange juice before," he said. "Now we have orange juice. You can go," he said, waving a hand at the waiter, who beat a hasty retreat. "Peggy, can you make me a screwdriver?"

"Her name is Beth," said Dean.

"No, not the old one, the pretty one," said Liddy, and I was almost, almost grateful to him for saying it, for the way it made temporary but decisive allies between Beth and me. I marveled at her calm collectedness. She didn't even dignify Gordon's response by acknowledging it, but returned to the chair across from Dean's desk at which she had clearly been sitting, and sat down with marvelous poise, whispering "Vodka and orange juice" into my ear as she passed me.

"You! Pretty girl," said Gordon, which apparently meant me. "You know how to make a screwdriver? There's vodka in there."

"You know your way around Mr. Dean's liquor cabinet pretty

well," I said before I could stop myself. Dean looked annoyed, though not at me, while Beth was carefully expressionless and Liddy laughed uproariously.

"That I do," he said. "That I do. Dean can't hide anything from me." A flicker of tension passed over Dean's face, and our eyes met then. And that's when I saw what I had been missing.

Dean was afraid. And Beth knew it.

My eyes asked Dean a silent question, and his shrug and half-smile was all the answer I would get.

"Left cupboard, bottom shelf," said Dean, resignedly. "There are glasses—"

"Don't need a glass," said Liddy, knocking back the two fingers of Scotch remaining in his glass and handing it to me. "Anyway. Back to what I was saying before, about the—"

"You must be hungry, Mr. Liddy," said Beth politely but firmly, as I pulled the vodka out of the cupboard, my back to the room, pretending not to hear. "Why don't you both take a break for a little while and enjoy your sandwiches?"

"All right, all right," he said. "I can take a hint. Loose lips sink ships."

"For Christ's sake, Gordon, don't be dramatic," Dean said wearily, taking a sandwich from the tray and returning to his desk with it. "All she means is that we've been at this for six hours, let's take a break."

I was almost exclusively a beer drinker and had never made a mixed drink before, but I was certain it couldn't be that hard. I could just see Beth out of my peripherals. I reached my hand for the ice bucket and then hesitated. She nodded imperceptibly. I plunked two ice cubes into Liddy's empty glass. I reached for the orange juice. She shook her head. I reached for the vodka. She nodded. So, alcohol first, juice second. Got it.

Behind me, Liddy was fully occupied with noisily eating his sandwich, but I could see Dean watching our little pantomime, highly amused. I began to pour the vodka. Math, and logic, decreed that if this drink had two ingredients, that the proportion should be fifty/fifty, so I poured vodka until it just about cleared the halfway mark of the glass, ignorant of Beth's desperate "Stop pouring!" gestures and Dean's barely-concealed laughter until it was too late. I mimed a question to Beth – "Should I dump it out?"

"How long does a screwdriver take around here?" Liddy bellowed from the other side of the room, and Beth threw up her hands in resignation. Dean winked at me. I added a splash more vodka. Beth buried her head in her hands. Dean coughed to conceal a laughing fit. I filled the glass to the top with orange juice and carried it carefully over to Liddy so it wouldn't spill.

"Old family recipe," I trilled girlishly. He took a long swig, spluttered and choked and almost spit it out. Dean, Beth and I watched to see what would happen next. But he burst out laughing, and took another long, hearty swig.

"This one's a keeper, John," he said to Dean, and went back to his sandwich.

"Thank you, Miss Bellows," said Beth in her most formal voice. "That will be all." And she stood and walked me back to my desk. She closed the inner door behind her and hesitated, as though about to say something.

"Who is that creep?" I asked.

"Nobody," she said. "He works for the campaign. And don't call him a creep."

"What have they been doing in there all day?"

"Budgets," she said. "Liddy's involved with the campaign's finances and Dean had some questions about the reports. That's all."

"But—"

"That's all, Regina."

She looked worried, and I was feeling more warmly towards her than I had in a long time, so I did something very unlike me.

"I could help," I said.

"What?"

"You have a stack of messages to return," I said, pointing to her desk. "Let me go in there and take notes for awhile and give you a break from Liddy and his elevator eyes."

"Elevator eyes?" she said in puzzlement, and I wondered if it wasn't a slang term that existed yet.

"Yeah, you know, when a guy's eyes go up and down, like this?" I demonstrated for her, perfectly imitating Liddy's hungry leer, and I swear to God, she almost laughed.

"No," she said. "But thank you."

"Really, I don't mind," I said, and I moved back towards the door slightly. Instantly our camaraderie vanished and she was chilly Beth Rutherford again.

"Back to your desk, Miss Bellows," she said. "Your help isn't needed."

"I wasn't trying to—"

"Stay out of that office," she said. "I mean it. Don't barge in there again." And she swept back inside, closing Dean's door behind her.

I didn't see any of them for the rest of the day; they were all still in there with the door closed when I left at five. As I typed up memos on Dean's behalf to a trio of presidential aides who were caught accepting pricey Omaha porterhouse steaks from a beef industry lobbyist, I ran Beth's words from earlier that day over and over in my head, trying to puzzle them out.

On the one hand, of course, they were perfectly true. I

did know nothing. I *had* seen nothing. She had very neatly silenced Liddy in the office, when he had tried to start talking again while I was still in there. And her description of their meeting as "something about budgets" was vague enough to cover any number of things. Every task Beth assigned me was as dull and trivial as this one was.

Was that to punish me – or to protect me? It suddenly occurred to me that there were all kinds of reasons she might want me sitting out here typing up beef memos while Dean and Moustache argued on the other side of the wall.

I wondered what the notes in her steno pad said.

I wondered what she knew that I didn't.

I wondered why Dean was sweating and nervous.

And I wondered what our office was involved in that nobody wanted the new girl accidentally mentioning to the FBI.

~

As puzzled as I was by it, though, I was grateful for Beth's heads-up. It was only a week or so later when my name came up on the reporters' list.

They were very cautious. They waited until I had turned onto G Street and melted into the end-of-day pedestrian traffic several blocks from the White House. I was grateful for this courtesy, until it occurred to me that there was little comfort to be found in their assumption that I was being watched. Still, I thought it best to act natural. When I heard a male voice say my name behind me, I swallowed my anxiety and turned around as with as much casual nonchalance as I could muster.

Everything I knew about 20th-century journalists I had learned from 20th-century films. I think I was expecting a pair of grizzled old newsmen chomping cigars and thrusting their notepads in my face while calling me "sweetheart" in thick New York accents. So I was startled beyond reason to find myself face-to-face with two perfectly ordinary guys, not that much older than me.

"You're young," I said, startled into rudeness, and the one on the left grinned widely. He had the kind of country-club handsomeness that would age well, with brown hair that curled just a little in the back and unexpectedly warm eyes.

"Let me guess," he said. "You were warned off us."

"No comment," I said.

"I'm Bob Woodward from the *Washington Post*," he said. "This is Carl Bernstein."

As partners, they didn't match. Carl had dark hair that he wore very long, and where Bob had a kind of easy grace, Carl looked a little rumpled. Still, quite unexpectedly, I found that there was something about them both that I liked immediately.

"I'm sorry," I said. "I can't talk to you."

"We won't take up much of your time, I promise," said Bob.

"I'm on my way home," I said.

"Walking?"

"Yes."

"Can we buy you coffee?" said Woodward, "And then maybe give you a lift? I'm just parked a few blocks away."

"*No comment*," said Beth's sharp voice in my head.

"*Don't make it worse*," said Calliope's.

"*You never think about the consequences*," said my mother's.

Tick, tick, tick, said the HIO meter in my pocket.

But they found out McCord worked for the C.I.A., said a voice in my head that belonged entirely to me. *They might know lots of things you don't know yet. They could be useful friends to have.*

"You can talk to me right here," I said, quietly praying this wasn't a terrible idea. "I don't want to be seen getting into your car. I could get fired for that."

"That's fine," said Bob.

"Although I don't know what I can tell you," I said. "I'm brand-new. I've only been here a few weeks."

"We were told you were a straight-shooter," said Bob. "You have a reputation for being honest."

"According to who, exactly?" I said. "That's remarkably charitable."

"We were given to understand that you're the kind of person who would speak candidly if you had something to say," Bob said, deftly dodging my question.

"Ah," I said. "Because I'm new. I haven't been here long enough to form any loyalties and I'm more likely to spill because I have so much less to lose."

"Not at all," said Carl reassuringly.

"Yes," said Bob at the same time.

There was a silence.

"You should rehearse better beforehand," I said.

"We won't use your name if you'd like us not to," Carl said. "This is all background."

"And we won't print anything that isn't verified by multiple sources," Bob added. "We're not going to hang you out to dry."

"No, you won't," I said, "because I can't tell you anything." I turned and started to walk away.

"We just wanted to ask you a few questions about Gordon Liddy," Bob called after me, which stopped me in my tracks. I turned.

"So you do know him," said Carl.

Shit.

"I don't work for him," I said. "I work for John Dean."

"You won't be telling us anything we don't already know," said Bob. "We're just looking for confirmation. If that makes you feel more comfortable. We're not asking you to rat out your boss."

"What do you want to know, then?" I said cautiously, heart racing. If they were hoping I would be a confirmation source, then they were probably about to tell me something that their editor had deemed too explosive to print without independent verification. I considered turning on my Comm to let Calliope hear, then decided against it.

"We already know about the slush fund," said Carl. "And that Liddy had oversight of it." I kept my face carefully expressionless and waited for him to go on.

"And we know the burglars were paid in cash from that fund," said Bob. "So what we're trying to confirm is whether Liddy has been seen since the burglary in any meetings with the President's senior staff."

"Why would that matter?" I said, voice neutral.

"It matters whether Liddy was acting on his own or not. Given that he's on the payroll of the Committee to Re-Elect the President."

"We're not asking you to tell us anything we don't already know," Carl said again. "We have reason to believe that Liddy came in recently to meet with John Dean." He looked at me for a long moment, waiting for me to speak. I didn't. Bob tried again.

"Say we were putting together a story that said Liddy had met with John Dean since the burglary," he said, "can you give us any reason why we *shouldn't* run it?"

I almost told them everything then and there, but something stopped me. Not loyalty to Dean, certainly. Not fear of exposing my real mission. No, what stopped me was remembering the way Beth had looked at me when I offered to go take notes and she blocked my way to the door. She had kept me out of that office for a reason, and I didn't know whether she was hiding something from me – or trying to keep me safe.

"I'm sorry," I said. "There's nothing I can tell you." Carl looked disappointed, but Bob just nodded, like I had given him exactly the answer he expected.

"Here's my phone number," he said. "In case anything changes, or you want to talk."

"That's very unlikely," I said, but I could feel all three of us wondering if it really was.

~

"What did you do with the State Dinner purchase order files?" said Beth the second I walked in the door the next day.

"Good morning to you too, Beth," I said as I hung up my coat on the rack behind my desk.

"Good morning. What did you do with the State Dinner purchase order files?"

"I dropped them off with the Head Chef's office yesterday morning for a signature," I said. "Like you asked me to."

"No, you didn't," she said. "He just called. He didn't get them."

"Well, I don't know what to tell you," I said. "I put them right in Lillian's hand."

"We need that file today," she said. "Mr. Dean needs to get it to the State Department's budget office."

"I know."

"Expenses for state dinners can't be billed to the regular kitchen accounts."

"I know that, Beth. You told me. And I took care of it."

"Check on your desk again," she said.

"It's not *here*," I said. She glared at me until I finally threw up my hands and gave up. "Fine," I said, half-heartedly rifling through my files. "Not here, not here, not here, not—"

And then I stopped short. Because even though I knew I hadn't left it on my desk, even though I knew beyond a shadow of a doubt that I had delivered it to the correct office and put it directly into the hands of the Head Chef's assistant, there it was, staring up at me. I picked it up and stared at it, too absorbed in my own puzzlement to notice Beth's look of triumph.

"What are you waiting for?" she said. "Go deliver the file."

"Fine," I said. "Tell Lillian I'm on my way."

"Lillian's out today," she said. "Just hand it off to the first person you see in a service uniform and tell them it's urgent. Go."

I went.

The White House was divided roughly into thirds. The part you think of when you think of the White House is the Residence, with the West Wing on one side, where the President and his staff work, and the East Wing on the other side, which houses the First Lady's office and many of the public reception rooms.

The lower floors of the Residence are a labyrinth of oddities, with everything from a florist to a bowling alley. I was headed towards the kitchens when I passed the Flatware Room and noticed that the door was open and someone in a uniform was inside. How weird would it be, I thought, to live in a house that had a *flatware room?* I decided to take advantage of the opportunity and sneak a peek.

"Excuse me," I said to the back of someone's head, and he turned around. It was a young African-American man, probably around my age or a little older, tall and lanky and, I noticed with relief, wearing the formal uniform of one of the White House butlers.

"Oh, good," I said. "I hope you can help me. I need to get this file to—"

"Close the door," he snapped at me. I was too startled to respond, but looked behind me to see if he was talking to someone else. "*Close the door*," he repeated. "People *work* in this hallway."

"Good Lord. Fine," I said, not even bothering to hide the irritation in my voice. "So sorry to have bothered you." I stepped back into the hall and began to close the door behind me.

"With you on *this* side of it, Agent Bellows," he said, exasperated.

I froze, with my hand on the doorknob.

I looked at him.

He looked at me.

I stepped back inside and closed the door.

"You," I said.

"Yes."

I sized him up again, with different eyes, wondering if I would have spotted that he was from my time if he had never said anything. But I knew it never would have happened. He might have passed me in the hall a hundred times and I would have missed it.

I had been looking for someone who looked like Detective Barlow – someone in a suit, someone who wore authority comfortably.

But in 1972, in the White House, who was better positioned for deep-cover espionage than a butler? It was brilliant. He could move invisibly in and out of rooms with the First Family, with heads of state. Nobody would even notice he was there, because he was a black man in a uniform and nobody would be looking at his face.

Which is too bad, because it was a handsome one, in a boy-next-door way, with sharp eyes that I could tell would miss nothing. Even though we still hadn't quite decided if we liked each other yet, it eased something inside me, just a little, to know there was somebody else in this building on my side.

"You got me in big trouble with Beth Rutherford," I said.

"I didn't mean to."

"You couldn't think of *any* way to set up a meet that didn't make me look incompetent?"

"Well, I'm sorry," he retorted. "I've never had to do this before. I'm a historian, not a super-spy."

"You're a butler."

"I'm a butler for the White House. I'm a historian for the Bureau."

"Great. So neither of us knows what we're doing. What's your name?"

"Agent Carter Hughes," he said. "Listen. I don't have long, but I need you to tell me what you said to the reporters."

"Have you been following me? Oh my God, is everyone in 1972 following me?"

"What did you tell them, Agent Bellows?"

"Nothing," I said. "I didn't tell them anything." He seemed to relax at this somewhat.

"Okay. Good. That's good."

"Don't you want to know what *they* told *me*?" I asked him. "About the burglars being paid out of a secret slush fund that the President's re-election committee controls?" I was pleased to see that he was astonished by this, pleased that I had obtained information he had not known.

"You saw the papers, right?" I said. "That ex-CIA guy they nabbed at the break-in, James McCord, he was working for the re-election committee too. The committee washed their hands of him and said they didn't have any idea what he was up to in his free time."

"Really."

"Yeah, but I don't think the reporters believe that," I said. "They've found out that this secret pile of cash exists which they think Gordon Liddy controls, and what they're trying to figure out is how many other people would have known where that money was going. And, I suspect, whether it's just people at the campaign or people at the White House too. That's why they wanted to talk to me. They wanted to know if, after the break-in, Liddy came in to meet with Dean."

"Did he?"

"Yes," I said. "Right away. First thing that Monday. They were holed up in Dean's office all day, shouting at each other. I think Dean can't stand him. He was afraid of something, and I think Beth was too. But I didn't tell the reporters that."

"Good," he said. "We don't want them snooping around and interfering with our own investigation. They'll just get in the way."

"But what do I do if the FBI asks?" I said. "Beth said to answer 'no comment' to the reporters but that I was supposed to be honest with the FBI. What do you think? Should I tell them?"

He stared at me.

"What do you mean?"

"The FBI is questioning staff in the West Wing," I said. "Beth told me. You didn't know?"

"No," he said. "I didn't know."

"Agent Hughes—"

"Carter."

"Carter. What the hell is going on?"

"I don't know," he said. "The President is tense. So is the senior staff. Everyone is acting strange."

"Here too?" I said. "Because the junior staff in the West Wing is going crazy. There's something in the air. Everyone's walking around wondering what everyone else knows."

"So what's our next move?" he asked.

"Can you go anywhere," I asked him. "Or do you just work in the Residence?"

"Just the Residence," he said. "But I can get to you."

"How?"

"There's a tunnel through the subbasements that connects all three wings together. If you can get to the West Wing's ground floor stairwell, next to the men's room, I can find you."

"You want me to just lurk around outside the men's toilets all day?" I said. "Right down the hall from the goddamn Situation Room?"

"Oh God," he said. "You're hopeless. Go back to your desk, act normal, and see if you can get anything from Beth's files about Dean's conversation with Liddy. Maybe she took notes."

"What are you going to do?"

"The President doesn't handle election-related business in the Oval Office," he said. "It's frowned upon. He usually saves campaign calls for the evening and does them from the Residence. I'm going to see if I can find anything out from the phone logs. We can meet tomorrow. Stairwell. 9:15 a.m."

"Fine," I said. "I'm glad you finally decided to show up, by the way. I've been flying blind without you."

"You've been doing fine without me," he said. "I've been getting the Deputy Director's reports. That was good work with the girl in the jail. And with the burglars. You're doing really well." I was irrationally pleased to hear this.

"See you tomorrow," I said as he opened the door to let me out. "Oh, and by the way, you better get this file to the Head Chef. You owe me."

"I promise," he said, smiling.

"All those boxes on the shelves – it's really all just silverware? This whole room?"

"The whole room."

"Man, this is a weird place," I said, shaking my head as I stepped out into the hallway.

"You don't even know the half of it," said Carter, and he closed the door behind me.

CHAPTER FOUR

IF I COULD,
I SURELY WOULD

I had barely been home that evening long enough to take my shoes off when there was a knock at the door. Perplexed, I opened it and saw Carter Hughes standing outside.

"What are you doing here?"

"Nice to see you too."

"I couldn't find Beth's notes," I said apologetically. "I'll try again tomorrow. She has a steno pad for meetings and she locks it in her desk at the end of the day. There's nothing filed under 'Liddy' in her file cabinet, that's all I can tell you today."

"That's all right," he said cheerfully. "That's not why I came by. Get your coat, we're going for a walk."

"A walk? Now?"

"Yes. Now."

"Why?"

"You don't get out enough."

"I get out the regular amount."

"You go to your office and then you come home," he said. "And then you go back to the office, and then you come back home."

"That's what people *do*," I said. "That's *normal*."

"You need to get some fresh air. Clear your head."

"I can't. I have plans."

"Plans to drink beer in your underwear while staring at the screen of your handheld for five hours while your brain slowly melts?"

"Are you a *wizard*?"

"Just get your coat, Reggie."

"Fine," I sighed dramatically. "I will come with you for a stupid walk in the stupid outdoors and look at stupid nature—"

"For Christ's sake, we're not going to the *woods*—"

"Just give me a minute to change my clothes," I said. "This dress is for work. Mrs. Graham would kill me if she caught me wearing it near anything that grows in dirt."

"Okay, but hurry," he said. "We don't want to miss the sunset."

"Oh no. You're one of *those* people."

"It's gonna be fun," he said breezily. "You'll see."

"I think we have different definitions of fun," I called over my shoulder as I closed the bedroom door behind me to change, and from the other room I could hear him laughing.

∼

You may recall that I had been on my way towards the National Mall when Detective Barlow had picked me up. After that, for some reason I couldn't quite name – superstition, maybe? – I hadn't dared to go back there. I had walked to and from work very near those white marble landmarks but had never ventured inside the green park to look at them up close.

But Carter made it a delight. He wasn't a Realignment Agent like Grove or my mother, bouncing around through different Timestreams to fix errors when the General Timeline went wrong. He was a historian.

I was a specialist in a particular era, but he was a specialist in this city. He had been here four years now and knew everything there was to know about Washington, D.C., so he was full of stories. He told me about every building we passed, swooning over architectural details and using words like "cornice" and "finial."

I was tempted to dismiss him as a hopeless nerd before I learned that his initial drop had been scheduled for June 1968, but he had filed a request for an earlier drop so he could be here in April, when Dr. Martin Luther King Jr. would be assassinated. The liability attorneys had refused his initial request, but he had appealed and won.

"The risk assessment for a black male agent in April 1968 would have been well outside recommended mission parameters," I said.

"Yes, that's exactly what they told me."

"It could have been dangerous."

"It was."

"Then why risk it?"

"Because I had to know," he said. "I didn't want to read about it. I wanted to *feel* it. To feel it like a real person."

This puzzled me. In fact, nearly everything about Carter puzzled me. I could tell that he saw, just as I did, that everywhere we walked, suspicious eyes followed us, full of questions or judgment or patronizing concern, making it impossible to forget that interracial marriage had only been decriminalized here five years ago – but it didn't seem to infuriate him the way it did me.

I didn't understand it. I didn't understand his whole life. The federal government paid him a depressingly tiny sum to move unobtrusively through the White House all day, invisible in plain sight, head subserviently lowered, being called "boy" (or worse) by cocky men in suits, while the Time Travel Bureau paid him a lavish one to report back on the things that he heard and saw while he did so. I wondered if his loyalties were ever conflicted.

I wondered how he felt about the people he worked with. I wondered if he looked around at these 20th-century people and felt like I did – as if he were a traveler from far more civilized shores shipwrecked on a barbarian island.

I wondered if he had made friends here, if there was anyone he went home to at night, or if it was simply too dark and sad to let himself grow close to anyone who might be killed in ten years when the first bombs would strike.

We walked and talked for a long time. The sun set over the water, and night fell, sweeping away the crowds and noise and most of the scampering children, leaving warm breezes and a mellow green hush.

He showed me the path along the Tidal Basin where the cherry trees would bloom in the spring. He let me take as long as I wanted to stand in front of the Washington Monument, trying to forget about the dark crater that sat in its place back in the time we had come from. And then we followed the long, glossy bulk of the Reflecting Pool, gleaming at night like a dark mirror, towards the place I had wanted to visit since I was five years old.

"The best way to see the Lincoln Memorial is at night," he said as I stepped up onto the low concrete ledge so I could be a head taller as I walked alongside him. "Always at night. And you have to come at it from this side, walking along the water. You have to ease into it. You have to take it in a little bit at a time. He was a force of nature, Abraham Lincoln. You have to enter his temple with respect."

It was a beautiful night, and I was having a lovely time. I couldn't remember the last time I'd enjoyed myself so effortlessly. And Carter's feelings about Lincoln were so exactly my own feelings about the man that I felt myself loosening up, growing dangerously close to comfortable in his presence.

It was the only explanation I can think of, when I look back, for doing what I did next.

I decided to pick a fight.

"You do know that his attitudes on racial equality were very problematic," I said, carefully placing one foot in front of the other on the ledge, arms outstretched like I was walking a tightrope. "Many of the leaders of the Abolitionist movement viewed his positions as too moderate."

"He *was* moderate. Moderate is what gets you elected. Fire and brimstone is how you survive the primary; playing to undecided voters is how you win."

"I'm just saying, the children's history book Lincoln – the moral crusader, the American saint – isn't necessarily supported by the whole picture of his life," I shrugged.

"You take the fun out of everything," said Carter.

"'I have no purpose to introduce political and social equality between the white and black races.' That's a direct quote."

"Yeah, thanks, White Girl, I've heard that one before."

"You might not know this, but—"

He stopped walking. "Why do you have to win every conversation?" he said. His voice wasn't harsh or accusatory – he sounded more curious than anything else – but his question was so excruciatingly *true* that I deflated entirely. "We were having a nice time," he said. "We were just talking. And then suddenly we were in a contest, playing 'Who-Knows-The-Most-About-Lincoln.'"

"I just don't understand it," I said. "A cab driver calls me 'sweetheart' and I want to break his kneecaps. Beth Rutherford could be a CEO – hell, Beth Rutherford could be *President* – and she's stuck as a lawyer's secretary. It isn't *like* this where we're from, Carter, I'm off by a hundred and fifty years and I'm aware of it every second of every day. We keep passing people on the street who look at me like they're trying to get me to signal them if I'm in some kind of danger, just because I'm out after dark with a black man."

"Yeah," said Carter. "It's 1972."

"That's my *point*," I said, frustrated. "You're from the same place I am. We both grew up in the 22nd century. We both have degrees from the Academy. Back there, we're the same. But this place . . . How do you stand it? How can you *like* it here?"

"What did you get on your Academy final exams, Reggie?"

"What does that have to do with anything?"

"Just answer the question."

"95%."

"And what level did you get placed at?"

"Level 2."

"I got the exact same score as you," he said. "And I'm a Level 6. You know what the difference is?"

"Your professors weren't all colleagues of your mother?"

"Besides that," he said.

"It's because you're black," I said. "Because there are higher security restrictions on where agents of color can go."

"You *picked* Nixon," he said. "You chose your field. This is your area. This was the posting you wanted. I didn't. So don't tell me that back home, you and I are the same."

I looked away. "Look," he went on, "everything you know about what it's like to be a black man in America is theoretical. Nothing you learned in an Academy textbook is going to teach you what it's like to walk through a nice neighborhood and see white women clutch their purses and cross to the other side of the street. Nothing you learned sitting in a classroom, studying the words of Malcolm X and Dr. King and parsing them for layers of meaning, as though they're dead works of rhetoric and literature, will ever convey to you what those words really *meant*. The way they changed people. The way they changed America."

He looked at me. "So don't come to me with your out-of-context quotes from the Lincoln/Douglas debates and your superior attitude, like I'm not allowed to respect a man whose racial attitudes were problematic. You know who else's racial attitudes are problematic? *America.* And everybody in it."

He turned away from me then, and started walking. I hopped down from the ledge and followed, but a few paces behind, cheeks flushed hot with shame. We walked in silence for a while, watching the looming white bulk of the temple columns rise up before us. When we reached the base of the steps, he stopped to let me catch up.

"The funny thing is, I bet Lincoln is your favorite president too," he said to me. "I bet this was the thing you most wanted to see from the minute you set foot in Washington."

"He is," I said, embarrassed again. "It was. I was just—"

"Showing off," he said.

"Yes."

Carter sighed. "You're in the field now, Reggie," he said. "You're not looking at the General Timeline from a screen, you're *inside* it. And sometimes in here, good people do bad things and bad people do good things. Nobody is a monster and nobody is a saint."

I looked down at the ground as he went on. "You're used to sitting at a computer watching human lives like they're lines on a screen," he said, "while all the rest of us live down here in the muck and the mess. Here, a man says during a presidential campaign that he believes white people are the master race and then signs the Emancipation Proclamation after he's elected. Because Lincoln was a *real person*, and real people are complicated. They're motivated by incomprehensible things, they're shaped by forces they're not even aware of, they're products of their times, they grow and change their minds, they achieve greatness and then make terrible mistakes that undo all the good they've done, and then they start from scratch and build it all back up again. There are no rules. There are no straight lines."

He looked at me then, really looked at me, his gaze so steady and so serious that I found myself shifting uncomfortably and staring down at the ground to avoid looking back. "You don't have to try so hard," he said. "You don't have to be the smartest kid in the class. You don't have to prove anything to me."

"I'm sorry," I said, and meant it more than I had ever meant anything in my life. He grinned at me, and the tension was broken.

"Good," he said.

"Are we okay?"

"Yeah," he said. "We're okay. Just maybe, you know, next time how about not trying to teach a black person about racism like you're the first person who's discovered it."

"That's fair," I said, and he followed me up the white marble steps.

The evening crowds at the monument were dissipating as we arrived, with more people going than coming, so that we found ourselves pushing through a crush of bodies at the bottom (as my HIO meter ticked reprovingly in my pocket, reminding me not to shove so much) and nearly alone at the top.

A shape in the corner of my eye caught my attention, but I only had a split second to wonder why a man would sit on the steps of the Lincoln Memorial to read a newspaper when there were plenty of benches nearby, before I looked up and found myself in the presence of Abraham Lincoln with a startling suddenness, as though he had somehow snuck up on me.

It took my breath away a little, and I entered the hushed white sanctum with shy reverence, like I was in church. There were a smattering of other visitors who clearly felt it too; everyone seemed to have agreed through collective osmosis to speak only in low voices, if they spoke at all.

I had seen pictures of the memorial, of course. I knew it was a wide rectangular space separated into three chambers by row of Ionic columns. I knew that Lincoln's two most famous speeches were engraved on the walls, one on each side, that the statue in the middle was carved of Tennessee marble and that if he stood up from that white chair he would be twenty-eight feet tall.

I knew which step Dr. Martin Luther King had stood on when he made his famous "I have a dream" speech, and that there was an urban legend that Lincoln's hands were carved to form the initials "A.L." in American Sign Language. I could have told all these facts and dozens more to Carter, to show him how much I knew.

But I didn't want to. I just wanted to stand there in silence and look up at Abraham Lincoln's face.

Carter sensed that I wanted to be alone, and drifted tactfully away, leaving me in front of the statue. I don't know how long I stood there, looking into those white marble eyes for answers I would never find, before I looked over and found Carter reading the Second Inaugural Address. The crowds were beginning to dissipate, and we had the space mostly to ourselves.

"'*Neither party expected for the war the magnitude or the duration which it has already attained,*'" I read in a soft voice, as Carter turned to see me coming up behind him. "'*Each looked for an easier triumph, and a result less fundamental and astounding. Both read the same Bible and pray to the same God, and each invokes His aid against the other.*'"

"'*The prayers of both could not be answered,*'" was his response. "'*That of neither has been answered fully.*'"

"This," I said, suddenly comprehending. "*This* was the field posting you wanted. But you were a Level 6 so they wouldn't send you."

"Civil War era is basically off-limits for black agents, without assassin-level self-defense and firearms training." he said, "And that's not me. That's not what I wanted. I just wanted to work for Lincoln."

I watched him quietly for a long moment as he read the words on the wall. "'The prayers of both could not be answered,'" he said again. "I think that's the truest thing anyone's ever said about war."

"All these people are going to be dead in ten years, Carter," I said, unable to tear my eyes from the clusters of tourists making their way up and down the steps.

"You don't know that."

"I do know that. Everyone knows that."

"Why do we do what we do, then," he asked me, "if not for the belief that the future can be changed?"

"You're looking at this sideways," I said. "I'm not here to stop the war because it was terrible. I'm here to stop it because it's *historically inaccurate*. I don't approve of the Vietnam War either, but I have to leave it alone. Vietnam stays. The Civil War stays. The Trail of Tears, the Ku Klux Klan and the World War II internment camps all stay. Every other atrocity in our history stays. We're not *him*," I said, gesturing angrily at Lincoln. "We're not *heroes*, we're *editors*. It's not a moral victory."

"You say that, but you don't believe it," he said. "You can't tell me that those millions of lives don't weigh on you."

"They do. Of course they do."

"Right. And why is that?"

"Because it was genocide," I said. "Because it was horrific. All those lives. Twenty-two million Americans and thirty-four million Chinese. Gone. Just like that."

"Right," he said earnestly. "But you knew that *before*. You always knew that. You grew up knowing that. What's different now? The only thing that's changed is you. Your responsibility. Before, they were just dead people from history. Just another war. The perpetual story of the human race, played out over and over."

I moved away from him, towards the steps, and he followed me. "They were innocent, even then," he went on. "Nobody who gets killed when a bomb drops onto a park they're visiting with their children is a combatant. Nobody *enlisted* for World War III, Regina. They were *always* innocent. They *always* should have been permitted to live. It only feels different because now there's a chance to save them."

"Hope is dangerous, Carter."

"Giving up is worse."

We stood there at the top of the steps for a long time, gazing out over the National Mall, Lincoln rising up like a Greek god behind us.

"You don't hate it here because this era is primitive compared to yours," he said. "You think that's why, but it's not. Not really. You hate it here because you can't look at these people without picturing what might happen to them."

"I'm afraid of them," I said. "I'm afraid of what's coming."

"I know."

"Kitty," I said. "Where's Kitty going to be in ten years? Or Beth Rutherford? Or Billy the coffee guy? Or Bob Woodward? Or even stupid Detective Barlow? The President's going to get hustled off to a bunker. The President's going to be fine. The important people are always fine. But nobody will care what happens to the secretaries and the bellboys. That's not how war works. That's not how *anything* works."

"*You* care," he said. "That's what matters. You're right. Nobody on the National Security Council is going to leave any room in that underground bunker for Beth Rutherford. And whoever started this war, they didn't care how many Kittys and Billys and Beths were lost, on both sides. But they're not the ones calling the shots anymore, Reggie. Beth doesn't know it, Bob Woodward doesn't know it, and John Dean doesn't know it but . . . "

He paused for a moment, took a breath and looked at me. "Right now the most important person in the whole world is you."

CHAPTER FIVE

THE MOTHER AND CHILD REUNION IS ONLY A MOMENT AWAY

Beth kept her steno pad in plain sight when she was at her desk and in her hand when she was in Dean's office. She left the office exactly three times per day – coffee breaks at 10:30 and 3:30 for ten minutes, and lunch for half an hour at 1:00 – and in her absence, the pad was locked in the top middle drawer of her desk. I presumed those were also the times when she went to the bathroom. She seemed like the kind of person who scheduled her bathroom breaks.

Carter and I had considered a number of possibilities, from the elaborate (Carter spilling a pot of coffee on her in the hallway and stealing the desk drawer key from her pocket in the ensuing chaos) to the straightforward ("Can't I just *ask* her to borrow her steno pad?") before we settled on a plan that was somewhere in the middle.

The phone rang at 10:45, right on schedule. She was just

back from her coffee break and wouldn't leave the desk again until lunch.

"Mr. Dean's office," she said in her crisp, clipped telephone voice, and I saw her face darken almost immediately. "For the State Dinner?" she said. "From yesterday?"

There was a pause while she listened to the voice on the other end of the phone and shot me a poisonous look. I smiled back politely and kept typing. "Certainly," she said to the voice on the phone. "I'm so sorry. I'll get that to you right away." Pause. "Of course, I'll bring them myself. I'll be right there."

She hung up the phone and stormed over to my desk.

"Hey, what kind of Danish do they have today?" I asked her, not looking up from my typewriter as she tore through the files on my desk.

"Where are they, you stupid girl?"

"If it's cherry again, I might skip it, but if they have the cream cheese ones they had on Monday I might—"

"You gave them an *empty folder*, you utter nitwit," she snapped at me. "I cannot imagine how you have managed to fail so utterly at such a simple task *three days in a row*, but the State Department budget office just called the Executive Chef and his office just called me and nobody knows where the file with the signed purchase orders is."

"I took it over yesterday, remember?" I said, as she flipped through the pile of folders on my desk frantically.

"You took them the file folder," she said. "Apparently you didn't stop to see if there was actually anything *inside* it before you went ahead and – *aha!*" she exclaimed, thrusting a sheaf of papers in my face.

"Huh," I said nonchalantly. "What are those doing there?" She was too enraged to respond, and I was delighted to see steam practically coming out of her ears.

"Want me to run those down to the chef's office?" I asked sweetly, reaching for the papers, and she yanked them away as though my touch would turn them to stone.

"You stay right where you are," she said icily. "Don't touch these papers or come anywhere near them. I am taking these down there myself because apparently I can't trust you with one simple—"

My phone rang, and I waved her into silence as I answered it. She was as close to apoplectic as I'd ever seen her, and I was enjoying myself tremendously.

"White House Counsel's Office," I said formally.

"How's it going?" said Carter. "She seemed pretty pissed at you."

"Yes indeed, sir," I said in my most correct and proper telephone voice. "Miss Rutherford has located the paperwork."

"You better find something in that steno pad worth the tongue-lashing you're going to get when she comes back upstairs."

"On her way right now, sir. She'll be there in two minutes," I said, and hung up. "They're waiting," I said helpfully. She turned on her heel and stormed out, papers in hand.

We had pegged Beth correctly. Annoyance at me had superseded every single other thought, and the precious steno pad was just lying right there in the open, on her desk. With elaborate casualness, in case Dean should come out of his office suddenly, I bent over her desk and flipped through the notepad, hunting for any mention of Liddy.

But Beth Rutherford was a perfect secretary – she wrote in shorthand. I couldn't read any of her notes. Fortunately, the handheld back at my apartment could translate it. I leaned over to give my Microcam a clear shot and hastily flipped through the entire notepad, beginning to end, capturing each page onscreen.

On a whim, I opened up the drawer in her desk to see if there was anything else helpful inside, but there was nothing. It was as Spartan and unhelpful as I could have expected her desk drawer to be, just a sea of pens and pencils and stamps in impeccable rows.

I took a picture of the inside of the desk drawer – and the surface of the desk, too, for good measure – before darting back to my seat. When Beth returned, still seething, I was seated at my desk, tap-tap-tapping away as though I'd never left.

Carter and I were scheduled to meet after I finished my lunch. He was waiting in the stairwell, tapping his foot with impatience, when I came out of the mess and around the corner.

"Anything?"

"She writes in shorthand," I said. "I don't know why I didn't see that coming."

"Damn."

"I got every page on camera, at least," I said, more optimistically than I felt. "We can translate it tonight and look it over."

"Anything helpful in her desk?"

"Nope," I said.

"I hope you didn't get yelled at for nothing," he said glumly.

"I didn't mind," I said. "It was fun to watch her get that mad."

"I'll bet."

"What's going on here?" boomed a voice behind me, and I turned to see a cluster of gray-haired men coming out of the Situation Room. Carter and I looked at each other, neither sure how to respond.

"Boy, what the hell you doing in the West Wing?" barked

one of them. I flinched a little at the "boy," but Carter didn't. Instead, something strange happened. Right before my eyes, I watched him transform. Agent Carter Hughes disappeared entirely and he *became* his uniform. I don't know how else to explain it.

"Beg your pardon, sir," he said, and I was so irritated that he was being forced to apologize, that I didn't realize, until the pause grew painfully long that neither of us had prepared any kind of a cover story.

"It's my fault," I said, "I needed . . . the purchase order files for the State Dinner. And I didn't have time to run over to the kitchens to pick them up, so the Steward's office sent him to bring me the files on my way back from lunch."

You could drive a tractor through the plot holes in this story – starting with the fact that neither one of us had any files in our hands – but the man who had spoken appeared satisfied.

"Hope to hell you didn't saunter through the lobby in that getup," muttered another. "Christ."

"No sir, I came through the basements."

"Good," said the first. "He ain't been bothering you, has he? You just say the word and I'll get on the phone to the Steward's office and—"

"He's fine. It's fine. Everything's fine," I said, desperately attempting to sound polite despite my gritted teeth and itchy punching fist.

"Good, then. Well, you give out a holler if he bothers you again," he said. "This can't be what your mama had in mind when she sent you off on the train to the big city."

"Actually—" I began, but Carter was too quick for me.

"Pleasant afternoon to you, Miss Bellows," he said, with a deferential bow. "Sorry for taking up so much of your time."

And then he disappeared down the stairwell, leaving me no choice but to go back to my office. I could feel the cluster of old men staring at my ass as I walked away.

Beth was in a gleeful mood when I returned from lunch, never a good sign, and I spotted a mammoth stack of files on my chair.

"What's this?"

"Your project," she said, aglow with evil delight. "For the next month."

"What's in these files?" I asked her, heart sinking.

"Congratulations," she trilled. "You are now responsible for processing every case of potentially illegal usage of the Presidential seal."

I could hear her laughing all the way to the coffee cart, from which she returned with the very last cheese Danish.

This was hardly what I would deem a proportional response. I prayed to God there was something in that steno pad that would make the brain-melting tedium of my punishment worth it.

~

Six of the one hundred and eighty-two files later, with the will to live drained out of me entirely, I shuffled home from work and went straight into my bedroom. I gave myself exactly ten minutes to lie on the bed and groan and fantasize about ways to murder Beth Rutherford before forcing myself to get to work.

First things first. I kicked off my shoes, unpinned my hair, and changed into my illegal 22nd-century cotton shirt and pants, sighing with relief once I was finally barefoot and comfortable. Then I opened my handbag and pulled out the items I had discreetly pilfered from the supply closet on my way out of the office – a fistful of colorful highlighter pens and a plastic box of thumbtacks.

I delicately removed the Microcam from my hair, sent its image files to the handheld's translator, and pulled out the tiny instant printer Calliope had concealed inside *The Great Gatsby*. I turned on the radio as the printer hummed away and pulled the messy sheaf of papers out of the drawer in my dragon-green nightstand.

It wasn't much yet – a handful of news clippings about the burglary and paper printouts of my notes on the break-in – but as the printer spat out translated copies of Beth Rutherford's steno pad, I carefully pinned everything up over the garish jungle wallpaper, creating a calming oasis of white space.

I've always felt strangely comforted in the midst of huge amounts of paperwork – maybe it's the side effect of being a bureaucrat's child – and this primitive version of the Bureau's digital evidence walls soothed me somehow, with its promise of order amidst chaos. I knew I would sleep better with it in the room.

Once everything was pinned in place, I stood in front of it, taking it all in. If I had hoped for an obvious solution to be found in Beth's notes, I was disappointed. She had taken notes in the Liddy meeting – and in two other meetings with him over the previous month – but her notes weren't meant to be read by strangers; they were for Dean and her.

Merely decrypting the shorthand didn't help me decipher what "ASK HALDEMAN TV INTERVIEW" or "VPOTUS GOLF PAPERWORK" meant. It was discouraging. Still, there were answers here, I told myself. There were connections hidden in plain sight. All I had to do was find them.

I opened the glass door leading out to the bedroom end of

the balcony, to let in the warm summer air, and then sat down on the edge of the bed, staring at the wall. I stared at it for a long, long time.

Outside my window the sun set over Washington, bathing the white marble landscape in gold, rose and violet before finally sinking behind the horizon and spreading a dark blue quilt full of stars across the city. I sat there for hours and hours as the light changed around me, until I was sitting in the dark, until the wall was no longer visible except in my mind's eye, every detail burned into my memory.

I sat in silence, staring and waiting. Waiting for the answer to come. I walked around inside my own mind, like it was room full of file cabinets that a tornado had swept through. If I picked up each thought and filed it back in its proper place, then eventually the one I wanted – the one with the right answer – would make itself quietly known to me, and everything would click into place.

It had to. Millions of lives were at stake.

It had to.

It had to.

So what did I know? What did I have to go on? I knew who the burglars were, but they weren't important. I knew Gordon Liddy was somehow linked to them through the money, but I wasn't sure he was so important either.

No, the thing I was beginning to clearly see – and which I suspected both the reporters and the FBI could see as well – was that Jimmy McCord and the burglars were just the hands. They weren't the *mind*. Maybe even they didn't know who it was. But someone bigger than Jimmy, even bigger than Liddy, was backstage, hiding, pulling the strings.

And whoever he was, he was here. He wasn't back in the 22nd century, monitoring his plan's progress through the Hive.

No, he would understand, just as we had, that he needed eyes on the ground. He was here.

And he was watching.

Waiting to see what I would do next.

But how, with millions of people in this city and hundreds of them working in the White House alone, was I ever supposed to find him?

It's too much, a voice in my head whispered. *You have no idea what you're doing. It's too much to ask you to figure this all out on your own.*

And that was when I remembered, for the first time, that I didn't have to.

I picked up the phone and dialed.

"Hello?" I heard Carter's voice at the other end of the line.

"Come over," I said. "I need help."

"I'll be right there," he said, and hung up before I could say anything else.

In just over twenty minutes he was there, pounding at my door. I opened it. He stared at me.

"Are you okay?" he asked.

"Fine."

"What's the emergency?"

"No emergency," I said.

"You said you needed help."

"I do," I said. "I'm stumped. I need a fresh brain." Then I looked at him and realized for the first time that he was wearing a coat and sweater over his pajamas. He hadn't even stopped to dress. His pajamas were striped blue-and-white cotton, like a little boy's.

"You were asleep," I said.

"Well, yes."

"It's only nine-thirty."

"Yes."

"You were asleep at nine-thirty?"

"Do you want my help or not?"

"You're in your pajamas," I said.

"So are you."

"Yes, but I live here."

"I thought you were in trouble," he said.

"And you rushed over to rescue me. In your pajamas."

"Are you actually going to let me in?"

I stepped aside to let him through. As he took off his coat and carefully folded it and set it on the chair, there was a strange awkwardness to his movements, and I wondered if it was because he was uncomfortable being in my apartment with us both in our night clothes.

I hadn't changed out of my thin cotton shirt and suddenly found myself acutely aware that I wasn't wearing a bra. Hastily pulling a sweater off the back of the sofa and wrapping it around me, I led him into the bedroom. I could feel his discomfort palpably rising, until I opened the door and he saw the evidence wall.

"This is *amazing*," he whispered. I shuffled my feet a little awkwardly, embarrassed by his obvious delight. "Really. This is seriously the coolest thing I've ever seen."

"I need your help," I said. "I've been staring at this for so long I can hardly even see it anymore. And what I really want is just to talk through the whole thing, top to bottom, and see what you spot that I didn't. What do you think?"

He looked at me for a long moment, his face serious, then nodded. "I think we need coffee," he finally said, and I beamed at him with relief.

It was about an hour later, as he reviewed the transcripts of my Microcam footage from the burglary while I highlighted references to Liddy in Beth's notes, that he spotted the first clue I hadn't.

"Who's Opal?" he said.

"Who's what?"

"Opal," he repeated. "It's in the transcript, right here. It's James McCord. 'You better not [unintelligible] 'another chance with Opal to [unintelligible] get it right.'"

"I think it was 'hopefully' instead of 'with Opal to,'" I said. "The Microcam was taped to a pencil buried in carpet, and whole chunks of that transcript are useless. The carpet muffled the sound and threw off the auto-transcription."

"Well, did you ever actually look to see if there are any women named Opal working at the White House or for the campaign?"

I was forced to admit I hadn't.

"I'm not saying it means anything, necessarily," he said. "I'm just saying, it's an unusual name. It would probably be fairly easy for Calliope to check."

"Should we call in?"

"What do you think?" he asked.

"I think I'm starving," I said, realizing as I said it out loud how true it was. "Did you eat dinner?"

"Well, yes, I did," he said. "Three hours ago, at a normal human being's dinner time. Have you not eaten anything yet?"

"I didn't have time to eat, I've been doing *this* all night."

"Okay," he said. "I can tell you're getting cranky, so how about this – I'm going to go get food, because I think we're going to be up all night and we're going to need sustenance. You page Calliope, see if she can dig up anything on Opal, and have her call us in an hour with whatever she finds."

"Got it."

"We're going to crack this," he said, and there was something so reassuring in his voice that just for a moment, I believed him.

~

He returned about half an hour later with a giant brown paper bag. "What's in there?" I asked.

"Food. As promised. Do you have beer?"

I made a vague gesture in the approximate direction of the refrigerator, then made a loop through the apartment closing all the curtains, so I could project Calliope onto the wall where we could both see her instead of huddling over my handheld.

I could hear Carter clattering around in the kitchen; when I returned I saw he had neatly set out a cluster of white paper boxes and put two tidy place settings on the kitchen counter, with plates and napkins and silverware. The food had come with chopsticks in paper wrappers and little packets of sauce, which were lined up in the center between us. He had even opened a beer for me and set it, label perfectly centered, to the left of my plate.

"It is clear from this kitchen that you prefer to eat standing up," he said. "I prefer a bit more formality. This is my compromise. Okay?"

"Okay," I grinned. "I can meet you halfway."

He opened the boxes one by one. "Now remember," he cautioned. "This is midcentury American Chinese food. You're going to need to appreciate it, or not, on its own merits, but don't get hung up on historical accuracy, okay?"

"This is not my first rodeo, pal," I said as I speared a rosy slice of barbecued pork with my chopstick and popped it into my mouth. "I know about the cultural bonds between Jewish communities and Chinese-owned restaurants in early 20th-century New York and how Chinatowns sprang up throughout the Western U.S. as the railroad boomed and how Chinese food became a cultural signifier for urban living in 20th-century popular culture. Don't try to tell me about – oh my God, what am I eating?"

"That's chop suey."

"The hell is chop suey? This is not Chinese food."

"That's what I'm trying to tell you."

"No food from the actual country of China tastes like this."

"You don't have to eat it."

"More like chop *gluey*."

"Just put it back."

"No, I'm good. I'm on a roll. Chop suey? More like – More like—"

"Take as long as you need."

"I should *chop sue* you for making me eat this!"

"There it is."

"That was my last one," I said, my mouth full. "This chicken's pretty good, though."

"Two Advanced Time Travel degrees between us," he said, "and I bet neither of us could answer the question of who General Tso was and why he gets a chicken named after him."

"Yeah, because there was no pre-1982 Asia on our exams," I pointed out. "It's a little difficult to get U.S. agents excited about the rich tapestry of Chinese culture when their office looks out over the dead pit where the White House used to be."

"Yeah, but that's not real," he said, passing me the egg rolls. I pulled one out and chomped it in half, immediately burning the roof of my mouth. "None of that is supposed to happen. That's what you have to remember. Are you listening?"

"Sorry. This egg roll just tried to kill me."

"You eat like a wolverine."

"You come into my house, you call me names—"

"I brought you food—"

"You did bring me food. That is true."

"See, this is what's called a partnership," he said. "I provide a veneer of respectability and manners, you contribute the serial-killer wall of newspaper clippings. I think this is gonna work out, Bellows, I really do."

Before I could come up with a sufficiently scathing retort to this, I heard the Comm in the living room buzz.

"Brace yourself," I told him. "That's Calliope calling back, and she said she'd have my mother with her. Are you ready to meet Deputy Director Katharine Bellows? Do you want to pee first so you don't wet your pants in fear?"

"I'm not the one that got arrested my first day on the job. What do I have to worry about?"

"Famous last words, pal," I said, and he followed me into the living room.

"Agent Hughes," said my mother. "Pleased to meet you face to face. This is Calliope Burns, Agent Bellows' tech."

"Nice to meet you," said Carter, and Calliope smiled and nodded back at him, then made a mortifyingly unsubtle *"He's cute!"* face at me, which Carter wisely chose not to see.

We caught them both up on our progress so far, which hadn't been much, though Mom was interested in what the atmosphere was like on his side of the White House after the break-in.

I was pleased to see how easily she and Carter conversed with each other; he was deferential to her as a senior agent but not at all intimidated, and she peppered him with the kind of detailed, seemingly irrelevant questions – *How is the First Lady's mood? Is the President ordering different food for dinner? Who comes to meet with him after hours in the Residence?* – that showed she trusted his powers of observation.

"Oh, by the way," said Calliope. "I ran that word search and came up dry. No female employees in the White House by that name. When I widened the circle, all I got was a former housekeeper and the wife of one of the press aides. Either of those the woman you're looking for?"

"I don't think so," I said. "But thanks for checking."

"What woman?" Mom asked.

"It might be nothing," I hastened to explain. "Carter and I are having a difference of opinion as to whether the auto-transcription of the Microcam footage might have made an error."

"No, I think you're right," said Carter glumly. "I think it was 'hopefully.' Or something like that. It was a long shot."

"You were hoping Opal was going to be, like, the finance director of the re-election campaign, weren't you?" said Calliope. "I'm sorry. It would have been so convenient."

"What name did you just say?" said my mother, very quietly, but with a strange tone in her voice that caused the three of us to look at her in puzzlement.

"Opal," I said. "Why?"

"Calliope, is this a secure line?"

"It's the standard director-level frequency, ma'am, security clearance 8 and up. Is something wrong?"

"Listen to me," she said urgently. "*Nobody say another word.* Calliope, scrub this call from the records. Reggie, stay right where you are."

"Mom, what the hell –"

The screen went dark. Carter and I stared at each other in bewilderment.

"Well, that was . . . I'm not sure what that was," I said.

"Where did she run off to in such a hurry?" said Carter.

"I have no idea."

And then, out of nowhere, I heard a soft *ping!* from my Comm, and we no longer had to wonder where my mother had gone.

She was standing right there.

CHAPTER SIX

I GOT THE PARANOIA BLUES

"It was called Operation Gemstone," my mother said as she handed me a large paper cup of coffee from the all-night deli. She had decided, after submitting Carter, me and my apartment to aggressively thorough scans for hidden electronic devices ("Mom, you *really* think someone snuck a bug into my pocket without me noticing it?" "Please. How many times have you come to work wearing mismatched shoes?") that it was safer for us to have this conversation in a public place, and preferably moving.

So she had left Carter keeping watch at my apartment while we took a stroll around the Tidal Basin, which at this hour was just busy enough for decent camouflage but not busy enough to run the risk of eavesdroppers. Any time a pedestrian neared us, she slowed our pace to let them pass and waited to speak again until she had put some distance between us and them.

"It was treated, for the most part, as an old wives' tale," she went on. "Kidnappings, black bag operations, a houseboat full of prostitutes to ensnare politicians. Cheap spy novel stuff. Most of the Bureau agents didn't really believe it had ever existed. The rumors were too crazy. The plan cost an insane amount of money, for one thing. Upwards of a million dollars. Nearly every element of the plan was a felony – miles beyond standard opposition research."

She went on, "It was pitched in a White House meeting by some unnamed aide, and of course Nixon's campaign manager threw it out. Presumably whoever was crazy enough to propose it with a straight face was fired on the spot. But the point is, of course, that Operation Gemstone never happened."

She took a long drink of her coffee. "It's a pity we're too late in the season for the cherry trees," she said absently. "They only bloom in April. I haven't gotten to see the cherry trees in six years."

"Mom."

"Right. Anyway. Well, first of all, from your reports on the break-in it seems reasonably likely to suppose, if there was an Operation Gemstone, that Gordon Liddy and his secret re-election campaign slush fund were behind it. Second of all—"

"You could have told me all of this over the Comm," I said impatiently, and she looked away. "Mom, *why are you here*?"

She stopped walking, then, and stood for a long moment looking out over the water. My heart began to thump in my chest. Finally she collected herself and gave a little shake of her head as though returning back to earth from somewhere very far away.

"I'm sorry," she said. "This is . . . you'll understand. This is very difficult."

"Mom, you're scaring me."

"I first read about Operation Gemstone nearly thirty years ago," she said, "in the files of a fellow agent. He had formed a somewhat colorful hypothesis which he shared with me – he had very little to back it up, just an endless succession of wild hunches, but the few hunches he *could* check were disturbingly accurate."

She took a long sip of her coffee before continuing. Her voice was clear and focused, but her eyes weren't, as though part of her was somewhere else entirely.

"He had a theory that perhaps the campaign *hadn't* killed Operation Gemstone after all," she went on, "but simply whittled it down. Slice out the most egregiously over-the-top elements – the kidnappings, the prostitutes – and what remained would have been a tidy, affordable and tremendously thorough campaign of espionage, smears, misinformation and illegal data-gathering to sabotage the Democrats. Not just to secure the 1972 election, but over several years."

"The agent was ordered, none too gently, to stop wasting company time investigating it. But the obsession never left him, not until the day he—" She stopped, swallowed hard and collected herself.

"Mom," I said urgently. "Mom."

I didn't want it to be true. It was too hard already, I thought to myself. All of this was too hard. She didn't want to say it. I didn't want to hear her say it. We stood there, miserably, looking out at the water, until I couldn't take it anymore.

"It was him, wasn't it?" I said, but it wasn't a question. "The other agent was Dad."

"Let's sit for a moment," she said, motioning us over to a park bench. I sat down with a hard thunk and flopped back against the cold, hard slats. She sat down next to me, but distantly. We shared the bench like a pair of strangers.

"He found something," she said finally, breaking the long silence. "That's what I came to tell you. He was digging through some documents for a routine patch in Reagan's first term and ran across a fragmented, heavily redacted FBI memo which seemed to describe a two-part electronic surveillance plan to be carried out both at the campaign office of George McGovern, the 1972 Democratic candidate, and a second location that was never specified."

She looked at me seriously. "It had been given a code name," she said. "Reagan referred to it as 'Opal.'"

I felt my blood run cold. "The Watergate was the second location," I said. "DNC headquarters."

"Yes."

"And they were never caught. Nobody ever knew."

"That's right."

"And Kitty's friend—"

"That was Sapphire," she said. "Just as you described it. The boat in Miami and the call girls and everything."

"What happened at the McGovern office?" I asked. "Did they plant wiretaps there? Was it part of the same plan? Did they steal the election?"

"He never found out," she said, her voice flat. "He called Daisey to ask for permission to set up a McGovern campaign task force. Daisey said no. And then three days later—"

(*No, don't say it, don't say it—*)

"...he was sent to Sharpeville. And never came back."

I couldn't speak. My throat had closed up, tight with repressed sobs. I could hardly breathe. I became strangely aware of the heat of my coffee seeping from the cup through to my hand, heavy, warm and comforting. The rest of my body was made of ice. The hand wrapped around the coffee cup was the only thing that was warm.

It all made so much sense, suddenly. Such a bleak, horrific kind of sense. I felt that my life had been composed of a dizzying kaleidoscope of questions that had suddenly, neatly clicked into place and resolved into one dark answer.

"They killed him," I said. "Because he knew about Gemstone."

"Yes," said my mother. "I believe they did."

She leaned back against the bench and closed her eyes, and I scooted closer, pressing myself into the side of her body, not affectionately, but just wanting to feel her physical presence attached to me in some way. To keep her from disappearing too.

"I didn't ever really believe him," she said. "The whole thing was so crazy; you wouldn't have believed it even in a third-rate spy thriller. I was angry at Daisey – my God, was I ever angry at Daisey; for negligence, for ignorance, for refusing to listen – but in my wildest dreams it would never have occurred to me that Carstairs' death was deliberate. Even when you told me about Kitty, even after the break-in. I hadn't thought about Operation Gemstone in decades. It wasn't until you mentioned Opal that I finally put the pieces together."

She pulled a small portable data drive out of her pocket and handed it to me.

"What is this?" I asked.

"I was pregnant when your father died," she began.

"Yeah, I know."

"My first trimester was very difficult," she went on, "and I was sick nearly every morning for several months. Carstairs made arrangements with Human Resources so we could work from home in the mornings and come in together at noon."

"Is this going somewhere or are you trying to get me to apologize for my half of all that vomiting?"

"Listen to me, Regina. HR gave us security clearance for our home network so we could work from there unrestricted. Log into the Hive, share files, everything. After Daisey slapped Carstairs down about wasting time on Operation Gemstone, he told Carstairs to delete the whole file from his computer." My eyes widened as I realized where she was going with this.

"He didn't delete it," she whispered, incandescent with triumph, and suddenly she was twenty years younger; she was the legendary Katie Bellows again, and I saw her for the first time as she must have been before Carstairs died, all bright-eyed and fiery and alive with the joy of the hunt.

"I had forgotten. But he didn't delete it. He just took it home. Now you have all of your father's research on Operation Gemstone. And, most importantly, *the Bureau doesn't.*"

I wanted to share in her delight, but something in the way she was looking at me felt strange. "Embeds have cargo drops," I said. "Even if you were afraid the Comm link wasn't secure and you didn't want to send the files remotely, you could have cargo-dropped this drive right to Carter's apartment. But instead you came here yourself and put it right in my hands."

"It's the safest way."

"It's also the most conspicuous," I said. "Katie Bellows doesn't accidentally tip her hand." We looked at each other for a long moment. "You're not going back, are you?" I asked, desperately hoping to see a denial in her eyes. But she just nodded calmly, entirely unfazed, as though we were discussing the weather.

"I masked my coordinates," she said. "Or rather, Calliope did. It looks like she sent me to Ireland in the 80's."

"How did she do that?"

"By sending me to Ireland in the 80's," she said, smiling. "That's where I went first. I left my Comm and all my equipment there. I took nine different Short-Hops with me to get here and then destroyed them as I went."

"Yeah, but all they'll have to do is run a search in the Hive for your vital signs and they'll see that you're here," I pointed out. She did not respond, but unbuttoned the top three buttons of her blouse and pushed it back, revealing an ugly scar on her shoulder.

"You dug your own tracker out?" I shrieked. "Oh my God, *who are you*?" I poked at the scar a little and she winced.

"Wait a minute," I said suddenly. "This isn't new."

"No," she said.

"The scar tissue is already healing."

"Yes."

"Mom."

"Two months," she said. "It took me two months to get here."

"Holy shit, Mom, you're a fugitive."

"Yes, I am," she said seriously, "and I need you to listen to me very carefully, Reggie, because this is about to get very dangerous. There is somebody in the Bureau who wanted so badly for Operation Gemstone to disappear that they killed your father."

"What do you mean, 'somebody?' You mean Daisey." She shook her head.

"Daisey was a suit," she said dismissively. "No, somebody somewhere is pulling strings that go in every direction – Congress, the FBI, the CIA, Homeland Security, the White House – and they've been doing it for a hundred and forty years at least."

I shivered a little, and not from cold.

"So it's one of us," she continued. "Maybe more than one. But somebody wanted Operation Gemstone hushed up. We found the Chronomaly, so we know *when* it all went wrong. And now we know *why*. We went to war over Gemstone and someone in the Bureau will kill to keep it quiet. But what we still don't know is who."

She sipped her coffee thoughtfully. "And I don't mean the Colin Daiseys and the Gordon Liddys," she went on, "I mean the *brain*. It's someone with very, very high security clearance, pulling the strings from the Time Travel Bureau, manipulating events like they're moving pieces around on a chess board. And we're going to smoke him out."

"Mom, this is – I don't even – this doesn't sound like you at all."

"It's *not* me," she said, and there was something sad behind her eyes even though she was smiling cheerfully. "That's the *point*. These people know me. They can predict my every move. So I only have one choice."

"What's that?"

"To stop being me," she said with a reckless grin, "and start being someone else. I'm doing what Carstairs would do."

"Carstairs was *murdered*."

"I didn't say it was a perfect plan. Do you trust Carter Hughes?" she said suddenly.

"I do. I do trust him."

"Good. Because you're going to need an ally. With a cargo drop. The long-term Embeds fly below the radar. Only Calliope and I know you've even made contact with him. With a little luck, he won't come under suspicion for a long time. You, however, are going to be watched. You will be followed."

"How much danger am I in, exactly?"

"You're protected as long as you stay in 1972," she said, and there was something in her voice I didn't quite understand. "I can promise you that."

"How?"

"I can't tell you, Reggie, I just need you to trust me."

"What am I supposed to do?"

"They threw a rock in the pond," she said, "and the ripples extended either direction, for years and years. So you're going to stay here, where the rock went in. You're going to keep hunting for the agent on the ground here, and keep trying to patch the Chronomaly."

"And what about you?"

"I'm going after the ripples," she said.

"What does that mean? Where are you going?"

She shook her head. "The less you know, the safer you are."

"Does Leo know?"

"He knows I'm gone," she said. "He doesn't know where. But he's safe. He's going to be okay."

She stood up, threw her empty coffee cup in a nearby trash can, and suddenly there it was, crystal clear and real and true and right in front of me, the possibility that I might never see her again. I suddenly felt very young and very frightened. "How will I find you again?" I asked in a very small voice and unexpectedly, she pulled me into her arms.

"Listen to me," she said. "We'll find each other again. I promise."

"How can you promise that?"

"You have to trust me," she said.

"Mom—"

"There's an emergency plan in place," she said. "In case things go wrong. The less you and I know about it the better. The only person who knows is Calliope."

I had forgotten about Calliope. I pushed the button on my wrist Comm, but nothing happened. It didn't even ring. Mom looked at me sadly.

"Mom," I said, swallowing rising panic, "where's Calliope?"

"She's alive," she said. "But she can't help you now. We're on our own."

She reached into her pocket just then and pulled out a small object, which she pressed into my hand. "Do not lose this," she said, and there was a desperate urgency in her voice that I had never heard before. "Whatever happens. Whatever you do."

I looked down at my open palm, where I saw an impossibly delicate filigree chain, gleaming silver in the moonlight, with two small round silver pendants attached. I looked closer. One pendant was carved like the face of an old-fashioned clock with Roman numerals, with the hands pointing at just shy of a quarter after three. On the other I could just make out, in the dim light, the outline of a tree with words carved inside it. I squinted to try and read them.

"Time is a tree/this life one leaf/but love is the sky/and I am for you," she said. "e.e. Cummings. Your father gave me that. The clock is for you."

I looked at her for a long moment, cold fear clenching at my heart. Katie Bellows was not sentimental. For twenty-five years I had endured birthdays and Christmases of ruthlessly practical gifts. She had never done anything like this before.

"No," I said. "Give it to me when we're done."

"Put it on, Reggie," she said. "Keep it with you. Promise me you'll keep it with you."

"Mom, we're going to see each other again," I said desperately. "You don't have to –"

"Just promise me," she said, her voice firm. I swallowed hard and nodded.

"I promise," I said. She fastened the chain around my neck, then stepped back to look around, checking for pedestrians. "I don't have an HIO meter on me," she said. "I'm flying blind."

I did a quick scan. "HIO 2.3," I said. "You're good." She nodded briskly, all traces of sentimentality gone, and she was Deputy Director Bellows again.

"It's just you and me," she said. "It's all on us now. I'm counting on you."

"I know."

She gave me a long look, opened her mouth as if she were about to say something, then closed it again. She pulled out her Short-Hop, tapped it twice, and then she was gone.

~

I didn't walk home right away. I kept walking around the water for a little while longer, reflecting on everything my mother had said.

Questions kept floating through my head, nagging little questions that wouldn't go away. If the reporters were right, and Liddy had access to a safe full of cash to fund Gemstone, where had the cash come from? Beth had nearly lost her mind over the thought of misplacing one set of forms about one State Dinner to make sure the cost of the food was billed to the right department. These people were *fanatical* about budget tracking.

So unless the annual White House budget had a convenient line item labeled "Burglars," the cash must have been quietly hidden in some other account where nobody would notice it had gone missing. But where? By whom?

And what had happened in that first meeting? Had the campaign really shot down Gemstone, or just pretended to? Did someone go back to Liddy on the sly and give him the go-ahead later? Had the campaign director ever even known? Had the President?

All these questions, and dozens more, flapped around my mind like a swarm of bats. But the big question, the truly terrifying one, boomed in my mind over and over, silencing the clamor of all the others, until finally I dared to whisper it.

Who killed Leo Carstairs?

The second the words had been said out loud, it was so staggeringly obvious that I was shocked it had never occurred to me before. A messy stack of disconnected facts crystallized into this one perfectly clear truth which contained my entire life inside it. The mysterious rock-thrower inside the crowd in Sharpeville, who startled the police into firing blindly but who nobody afterwards remembered seeing. Daisey's peculiar insistence, never really explained, about benching my mother on a technicality that week. A massive patch on Nelson Mandela, where no massive patch had ever been needed before, pulling every black agent in the whole department out of rotation.

As a field mission, none of it made sense.

As an assassination, it was flawless.

But if that were true, that meant there was a murderer still out there, who hadn't flinched at killing my father and wouldn't hesitate to kill anyone in their way. *"You're protected as long as you stay in 1972,"* she had insisted. I couldn't worry about Mom, or Leo, or Calliope and Grove. Right now, Carter and I were all we had to keep each other safe. That meant we had to work fast.

I turned away from the water towards home but stopped short when I saw movement out of the corner of my eye. A shadowy figure in a trench coat was rising from a park bench about a hundred feet away from me. I could see him folding up a newspaper. His back was to me, but could see the street lamp above him lighting up his blond hair. The same blond hair I had seen behind the same newspaper at the train station, and at the Lincoln Memorial with Carter.

"Hey!" I shouted at him, suddenly too angry to be afraid. "Hey! Why are you following me? Who are you?" He didn't turn around, but kept walking. I took off at a run towards him, feeling my HIO meter tick up to 4. "Who are you?" I yelled again. "Show me your face! Why are you following me?"

He never turned around. I never saw his face. He simply stepped out of the light and melted into the shadows, and by the time I reached the place where he had been, he was gone.

I walked as fast as I could back to the apartment, taking only the busiest streets, and found Carter anxiously waiting for me. He opened the door to let me in and I walked right past him, scarcely registering his presence. In my absence he had cleaned the kitchen and made a fresh pot of coffee.

I pulled off all my tech devices – Comm, HIO meter, Microcam and receiver – and placed them, for lack of any better ideas, inside the refrigerator. Then I turned the television on and walked outside to the balcony. Carter, who was quick, removed his own Comm and followed me outside, closing the door behind him.

"My dad was murdered," I said without preamble. "He was killed by a fellow agent. They made it look like an accident but it wasn't; it was murder. And if they killed Carstairs, and they're after my mother, they won't hesitate at taking me out, since by family badass-ness standards I'm the weakest gazelle – even Leo's better off than I am, he went to chef school, he's got all those knife skills – so I'm a sitting duck. I'm a weak, sitting gazelle-duck. That's not a thing. But you see what I'm saying."

I turned to him and looked him right in the eye. "So what I need to know right now, Carter Hughes, is if you're the one who was sent to kill me. Because if you are, you son of a bitch, I'm telling you this right now, you will pay for it. She will make you pay. You will not be able to hide. There is nowhere in all of time where you could run that Katherine Bellows would not find you. She will not give up. She will not stop. So I'm asking you right now, no, don't come any closer, stay where you are, *look at me*. Tell me the truth. *Is it you*?"

He reached out a hand for me. I pulled away, shaking, pressing my back against the wall of the balcony, trying to make as much space between us as I could. He looked at me in silence for a long moment, then ducked back inside and returned with his handheld. He tapped on it a few times, then held it out to me.

"I was never supposed to tell you this," he said. "Director Gray asked me not to. I don't even think your mother knows." I looked down at the screen and saw the Bureau registry dossier for an agent I didn't recognize, a black man in his late fifties with a scar running down his cheek. "WILLIAM PAUL HUGHES," said the white lettering above his picture. "AGENT #14165. STATUS: RETIRED."

"Who is this?"

"That's my father," he said.

"Your father worked for the Bureau too?" I asked. He nodded. "Why are you showing this to me?"

He tapped on the screen again.

"The only way I can think of to prove I didn't kill your father," he said, "is to tell you something important about mine." He clicked a few times and then pulled up a field report. It was a grid view, just dots and lines and text on a black background. I could see a scattering of blue dots moving around the screen in a cluster of agents, surrounded by yellow dots representing civilians.

"What am I looking at, Carter?"

"Just watch," he said. I squinted at the screen, trying to figure out what I was supposed to be seeing, when I spotted a blue dot labeled "14165-WPH."

"WPH. Your dad?" I said. "Why are we watching one of your dad's old field missions?" As I watched the blue dot zipped around the screen (he was replaying it for me at high speed) I noticed that it tended to move in concert with another blue dot, this one marked "14493-CEJ."

14493 . . . Why was that familiar?

Still uncertain, but curious now, I watched WPH and CEJ move through the vast mob of yellow dots. Then, abruptly, CEJ disappeared. Carter paused the screen and tapped the green button in the upper right corner marked "SHOW COORDINATES," and I suddenly saw where – and, more importantly, *when* – they were.

"CEJ," I said softly. "Carl Evan Jenkins. He was his partner."

"Yes."

"He was on the Mandela task force with Jenkins. He was there when Jenkins got pulled out to go to Sharpeville and rescue my dad."

"More than that," he said soberly. "My father was the agent your father requested. But he had gotten close to Mandela, he thought it was more important for him to stay where he was. So the commander sent Jenkins. But Jenkins was new."

"That's right," I said, remembering. "The Mandela patch was Jenkins' first mission."

Carter nodded. "That's why the commander was willing to spare him. She didn't think he'd be missed. But then, when it all went wrong—" He stopped.

"My dad retired early," he said finally. "He's a fourth-grade teacher now, back in Alabama where our family's from. He couldn't take it. It haunted him. 'Jenkins was too young,' he would say. 'Jenkins wasn't fast enough. I should have gone instead.' And every night, for the last twenty-five years, he goes to bed wondering if Leo Carstairs would still be alive if he had gone back instead."

"No," I said, my voice hollow, because I so deeply knew that it was true. "You just would have lost *your* dad too. Leo Carstairs was going to die in Sharpeville, no matter what. When we get home, tell him. He should know that."

I suddenly felt tears welling up in my eyes, threatening to spill over. I gritted my teeth, swallowing them back. "He was going to die there, no matter what," I said again, choking on sobs. "My dad was *always* going to die."

And then I couldn't hold it back anymore. Carter took two long steps and wrapped his arms around me, and I collapsed into him gratefully, resting my head on his strong shoulder and burying my face in his cool white shirt. We stood there on the balcony as warm June breezes swirled around us, and there in Carter's arms, held close like a child, I cried for my dead father for the very first time in my life.

CHAPTER SEVEN

I DON'T KNOW WHERE I'M GOING, BUT I'M ON MY WAY

I am not one of those women who looks lovely and tragic while weeping. I sniffle and snort and make hideous noises and my face turns into a wet red mess. After I was tired and spent and all sobbed out, I pulled away from Carter and we stood there awkwardly for a few minutes, me all blotchy and snot-nosed, him uncomfortable and serious and sad.

"I'm getting cold," I finally said, though it wasn't remotely true. "I'm going in."

He led the way back inside and closed the balcony door behind us, switching off the blaring television I had left on, then followed me into the kitchen.

It wasn't until I had opened the refrigerator to see if there were any leftover dumplings and spotted my Comm sitting there next to the food cartons that I remembered the data drive my mother had given me. I whirled around, startling Carter, who I hadn't realized was standing quite so close behind me.

"I forgot," I said. "I forgot to tell you." I pulled the device out of my pocket and handed it to him.

"What is this?" he said. "Is this your mom's?"

"Even better," I said. "It's my dad's."

Two pots of coffee, all the cold dumplings and half a box of chow mein later (I left the chop suey to Carter, despite his earnest assurances that "you get used to the texture!"), I had read every document in the Gemstone files. Then I had paced back and forth impatiently while Carter read them. Now I was lying on the bed listening to the radio and crunching on fried wontons while he used the instant printer to add Carstairs' notes to our evidence wall.

"'TURQUOISE: commando raid to destroy the air conditioning at the site of the Democratic National Convention,'" he read as he pinned the list of the Gemstone operations onto the wall. "Good Lord. Your wallpaper is terrifying, by the way."

"You're telling me. And look," I added. "Sapphire, like Mom said. The yacht in Miami. Kitty was right."

"Thank God for Kitty."

"Thank God for Kitty," I echoed fervently. "Ooh, and the one to sow discord among Democrats by funneling huge chunks of money to Shirley Chisholm's campaign, on the grounds that a black woman candidate would make everyone lose their minds."

"Oh, you mean Operation *Coal*?" he said dryly. "Hard to believe African-Americans don't believe the Nixon Administration has their best interests at heart. What's *his* role in all this, I wonder?"

"Nixon's?"

"Yeah."

"Well, I don't think he *ordered* the break-in," I said, crunching thoughtfully. "Not specifically, anyway. But he knew he had people doing all kinds of unsavory things to sabotage the Democrats and throw the election. He knew there were criminals on his payroll. His hands aren't clean here."

"But did he sign off on Gemstone?"

"'But did he sign off on Gemstone . . .' That's the question."

"This whole thing gets a lot messier if you're trying to take down the President," he said.

"No kidding."

Finished with the wall, he stepped back to give me a clear view. I stood, dusting wonton crumbs off my shirt, and went to stand in front of it, hearing my mother's voice in my head. *Think simply, Regina. Go back to square one. Strip away everything you don't need.*

I stared at the wall, thickly covered with photos and clippings and case documents. So many disconnected fragments. A sea of faces and words and names. The redacted FBI memo on Project Opal that had launched my father's investigation. The transcripts of the Sharpeville hearings. The faces of the five Watergate burglars. An outline of Project Diamond, where muggers and kidnappers would be hired to target anti-war protesters.

And right in the center, pinned there at eye level so I wouldn't forget, a photo of the World War III Memorial – the bombed-out crater where the Washington Monument used to be.

"I'm on my way/ I don't know where I'm going, but I'm on my way," sang Paul Simon unhelpfully as I let it all wash over me, trying to clear my head and let the answer I needed bubble up to the surface. What was the thread that connected all those things together? How was it possible that a rinky-dink

burglary could be the seed that blossomed ten years later into a war costing millions of lives?

And then I knew.

It couldn't.

"Carter," I whispered hoarsely. "Carter. I've got it."

Instantly he was at my side.

"What? What is it? What do you see?"

"If my dad was investigating all this decades ago," I said, words pouring out in a rush of excitement, "and then he was killed by somebody who didn't want anyone to know about it, then Gemstone *itself* can't be the Chronomaly. Gemstone must really have existed. So what if we've been looking at everything backwards?"

"Oh my God," he whispered. "Gemstone wasn't the Chronomaly. The Chronomaly was that *nobody ever found out about it.*"

"Exactly!" I said triumphantly. "Calliope couldn't pin down the crisis point because there *wasn't* just one crisis point. It was the whole cover-up, stretching a hundred and forty years. *That's* the Chronomaly. It's not one tiny moment, it's *everywhere.*"

Suddenly everything made sense. It wasn't a rock thrown in a pond, not at all. It was a hailstorm. There were crisis points all over the place. It was a cloak of secrecy, coming from two different times and from multiple sources, inside the White House and out. Whose guiding hand was behind it all, whose brain was shaping and forming the plan, I still didn't know. But I felt something stirring inside me, the beginnings of something you might call hope.

Because if the crisis point wasn't one single moment in time, then *I hadn't missed it.*

I hadn't run out of chances. Even a small rip could cause the whole thing to unravel. There was still time.

And maybe, just maybe, we could stop the war.

"So you're saying it doesn't matter that we didn't stop the break-in," he said. "If the Chronomaly is the cover-up, then all that matters is that the cover-up needs to fail."

"Exactly," I said.

"How do we do it?"

I stared at the wall, willing an answer to come to me. The five burglars' two-dimensional, black-and-white faces stared back at me from a *Washington Post* clipping, and I suddenly felt a satisfying mechanical click inside my brain as the answer revealed itself. I pulled the clipping from the wall and handed it to him. He looked down at the paper and then up at me. Then suddenly, unaccountably, he burst out laughing.

"You're kidding," he said. "It was staring right at us."

I nodded, finding myself smiling too. "We need the voting public to get their hands on as many of the Nixon White House's dirty little secrets as possible," I said. "If you and I can't stop this war, maybe Woodward and Bernstein can."

"I like it," he said, grinning. "It works. It *fits*. Nixon the revered elder statesman with decades of foreign affairs experience, or Nixon the petty thug who kidnaps protesters and plants wiretaps? Which one of those two guys can stand at Reagan's right hand and sell the U.S. on a war with China?"

"We don't even know if there's supposed to *be* a Reagan," I pointed out. "If Nixon doesn't serve a second term, the floor is wide open. The next president could be *anyone*."

"So . . . it could be someone worse."

"Well, yes," I admitted. "But it won't be someone who bombs the shit out of China. One thing at a time."

"Okay," he said. "So how do we start? How do we get the reporters? You can't show them Carstairs' files; half the stuff in his notes hasn't happened yet."

"We need to give them a target," I said. "We need to point them in a direction that gives them the story they want and us the story *we* want. Someone connected to Gemstone, and to the break-in cover-up, but also someone who benefits from the war."

"Liddy?" he asked. I thought for a moment, staring at the wall. Then I shook my head.

"No," I said.

"Why not?"

"First of all, we've seen the first draft of Liddy's plan," I said, "and it was bonkers. Somebody edited it. Made it efficient. That's who we're looking for. It's a totally different kind of brain."

I pointed to a page from Carstairs' notes. "And second of all," I said, "Liddy dies."

"*What?* Let me see that."

"He was in D.C. that day," I said. "Look. Here. He was killed in the bombing. So it's not just that he doesn't benefit from the war. He's a casualty of it. Maybe a deliberate one. Maybe *he* knew too much, too. He's not our guy."

I went back and sat down on the bed, crunching another wonton and trying to clear my head. Then I heard an exclamation of delight from Carter.

"What?" I asked him, and he turned to me with an ear-to-ear grin on his face. "Hey, here's a nifty piece of White House trivia for you," he said. "Name the current senior Nixon aide who was *both* present at the meeting when Gordon Liddy first proposed Operation Gemstone *and also* gets promoted to Deputy Chief of Staff under President Reagan two weeks after the first bomb drops on Washington."

"What? Who?" I exclaimed, and rushed over to see what he was looking at. He pointed at the page pinned to the wall and I stared at it in amazement.

"I'll be damned," I said. "Right underneath my nose."

"Poor Calliope," said Carter. "She was trying to keep you out of trouble and she stuck you right inside the lion's den."

"It does look that way, doesn't it?" I said. "It appears all roads lead to John Dean."

~

The night sky was beginning to lighten into dawn by the time we both found ourselves too bleary-eyed, dull-witted and full of cold chow mein to get any more work done. I was hit with a sudden, violent bout of yawning, and drew the blinds closed against the impending sunshine, then climbed into my bed, flapping one arm at Carter in a vague gesture towards the living room.

"Couch," I said, closing my eyes. Nothing happened. When I opened them again a minute later, he was still standing there, looking from my bed to the door and from the door back to me in deep discomfort.

"Couch," I said again.

"But—"

"Blankets in the closet," I said, too tired for verbs.

"I don't know if this is appropriate—"

"Don't care," I mumbled. "I'm bed." And I closed my eyes, pointedly.

When I finally woke, many hours later, the light was hard and sharp on the other side of the blinds. I heard sounds of movement in the living room and bolted out of bed in a panic, the shadowy man with the newspaper rising up before me like a specter, before I realized how unlikely it was for an intruder to be running the sink and whistling "Me and Julio Down By the Schoolyard."

I came out of the bedroom, rubbing my eyes, staggering a little under the full force of broad daylight pouring in through the balcony doors, and saw Carter in the kitchen. The detritus of coffee and leftovers from last night was long gone. There was a fresh pot of coffee brewing – I could smell it all the way down the hall – and two place settings on the kitchen island, where we had eaten last night.

"You know, I do have a dining room," I said blearily by way of greeting. He handed me a glass of orange juice.

"Oh, are you referring to the Central Branch of the National Coats and Stacks of Paperwork Depository?" he said, pointing at the table which was buried under piles of crap. I shrugged, conceding defeat. "How do you like your eggs?" he asked, which was the first time I realized he was standing over a hot skillet I did not recognize, deftly cracking fresh eggs into a glass bowl while wearing a cheery red-and-white striped apron I didn't know I owned.

"What is happening? Where did you get that pan? Where did you get that apron? Where did you get *eggs*? There was nothing in this kitchen last night except beer and Chinese food."

"And your HIO meter and Microcam," he said, pointing them out on the counter. "Left to chill overnight but none the worse for wear. I went to the store while you were sleeping."

"And bought a French chef's apron?"

"The apron's yours, it came with the kitchen."

"It did?"

"Serious question," he said, sprinkling some herbs and black pepper into the glass bowl and whisking it in with the eggs, "have you opened any of the drawers or cupboards in this kitchen since you moved into this apartment?"

"Serious answer, yes I have," I said, pouring myself a cup of coffee. "When I was looking for the bottle opener."

"Well, while you were snoring like a warthog—"

"I do not snore like a warthog."

"Fine, while you were snoring like a dainty and elegant lady—"

"Thank you."

"*—driving a herd of buffalo—*"

I kicked him in the shins, but gently, so as not to cause him to mess up my eggs.

"Anyway, while you were sleeping the restless sleep of the late-night leftover Chinese food eater, I went to the grocery store and home for a change of clothes—"

"Oh," I said, noticing for the first time. "You *are* wearing different clothes."

"The fate of the nation is in excellent hands."

"Shut up and feed me. So, blah blah, I was sleeping, you were being a productive member of society . . . "

"*And,*" he said with dramatic emphasis, "I think I have a plan."

"Oh, goody."

"Shut up. Here's what I'm thinking. So, remember that time you got arrested for being the world's least subtle prostitute and Calliope saved your – wait for it, wait for it . . . " He pulled on a pair of oven mitts (*since when did I own oven mitts?*) and pulled a pan of sizzling bacon out of the oven, which he presented to me with a flourish. I buried my head in my hands.

"I'm barely awake, Carter, I can't deal with puns right now."

"It was ready anyway, it would have been a missed opportunity. Anyway, so remember—"

"Yes, yes, I remember, it was excruciating, let's all have a good laugh at Reggie's expense."

"I'm not making fun of you. Well, I *am* making fun of you, but I also have a point." He plunked a plate of bacon and eggs in front of me, then served himself. "My point is, wouldn't it be helpful if we could get our hands on the crime scene photos of the Watergate break-in? And ideally, a closer look at that wiretap?"

"Well, sure, in a magical world where I could just steal things from police storage, that would be very helpful."

"Okay, I know you're not really awake yet but I need you to meet me halfway here."

I made a face at him and took a huge hungry bite of bacon before I figured out what he was talking about.

"Oh. You want me to call Detective Barlow," I said, realizing.

"I want you to go *meet* Detective Barlow," he said. "I just called him."

"That was very foresightful of you. Foresightish. Foresight-having."

"Farseeing, I think is the word you're looking for."

"No, that doesn't sound right."

"He can meet you at five at the diner across the street from the police station."

"Did you tell him you were an FBI agent too?" I asked around a mouthful of eggs.

"I told him I was your assistant. I tried to make you sound impressive and fancy."

"That's a big job."

"I'll say."

"It's the wiretap that could unravel the whole thing," he said thoughtfully. "We know it's 22nd century, or at the very least we know that it's been through the Slipstream. If we're lucky, it might tell us something about whoever manufactured it on our end. If we're very, very lucky, it might give us something that can tie it to the White House."

"Hopefully, that something would be John Dean."

"Hopefully," he agreed. "And I was thinking afterwards you could pass along whatever you get from Barlow to the reporters. Maybe this is all it will take. Maybe we point them towards Dean, they start digging, they find what we hope they'll find, and the whole house of cards comes tumbling down."

"Cheers to that," I said, taking a big swig of orange juice. "So what are you going to be doing with your day while I'm off scaring cops and wooing reporters?" He looked away.

"I don't want to say," he said. "You'll want to come with me, and it's too risky."

"Fine, I'll drop it."

"Really?"

"No! Tell me where the hell you're going!" He sighed and pulled his Short-Hop out of his pocket.

"Election Day," he said.

"Oh, that's smart," I said approvingly. "That's a really good idea."

"You think so?"

"I do," I said. "All we really know for certain is that we need to keep Nixon from completing a second term. The first, most basic tactic should be to see if using the *Post* means the voters will do it for us. So we need to know if outing Gemstone on the front page has any effect on the actual election."

"Exactly."

"It might not, you know," I pointed out. "The polls are solidly in Nixon's favor. The election is set to be a landslide. It may not be this easy."

"I know. But it's a place to start, at least."

"Yeah. It's a place to start," I agreed. Then added, "Why shouldn't I come with you?"

"Because your Short-Hop is probably being tracked," he

said somberly, and I suddenly felt cold all over. "I'm an Embed, I use my Short-Hop all the time, and I'm deep-cover. No one but the Director and Deputy Director can access my files. But your mission parameters had no internal transport. Yours is just for emergencies. The second you're detected in a hot zone – like Election Day – they'll red-flag your device and shut it down."

I swallowed hard. "You're probably being watched from the Bureau, but it's possible you're not being watched from here," he went on. "That's good. That means scanners, GC coordinates, HIO readings, but no eyes and ears. So if you stay within the coordinates you were sent to, you can move around freely. Like your mom said. You're safe in 1972. But the second you switch that thing on, they'll know."

I wanted to argue with him, more out of habit than anything else, but I didn't. I knew he was right. If I had to, I could do what my mother had done. I could dig my tracker out of my shoulder and go on the run in 1972.

It was so easy, in this pre-computer era, to hide. There were no networks. Nothing to hack into. It had taken Calliope hours and hours of paperwork and phone calls to break me out of jail, and she had known exactly where I was.

Yes, I could hide out here if I had to, I thought, swallowing nervous thoughts about the man hiding his face behind a newspaper who seemed, somehow to be everywhere I went. But until the mission was completed, Carter was right. I couldn't leave.

We parted ways after breakfast and Carter went home to shower and pack for his jump. After the weird intimacy of the previous night, I could feel as I walked him to the door that we were both debating whether or not we should hug as we said goodbye.

"I'm not good at this," I said finally, as I opened the door and he stepped out into the hallway.

"At what?"

"This. People."

"What does that mean, you're not good at people?"

"You know what I mean."

"Honest to God, Reggie, I really don't."

He stood there, framed in the doorway, and he watched me, patiently waiting for me to untangle my thoughts and explain what I meant, and I felt an entirely unexpected wave of reassuring comfort wash over me. I somehow knew, without knowing how I knew, that here was someone with whom I couldn't put a foot wrong, that whatever I said to him, however fumblingly and incomprehensibly I said it, he would listen and understand.

I didn't answer him immediately, just looked at him for a long moment and tried to figure out what this thing was that made me feel so strangely at ease with him, and as it dawned on me I was so startled by the truth of it that I blurted the words out loud.

"You don't know my mother."

"What?"

"That's what it is. That's why you're different. You don't know my mother. I mean, you *know* her, obviously, but when you met me, I wasn't Katie Bellows' daughter."

I saw comprehension dawn in his eyes, and blessed him for it.

"Oh. I see," he said. "No, you weren't. If anything, you were Leo Carstairs' daughter. But that's completely different, isn't it?"

"Yes," I said. "That's what it is. Yes. You get it."

He leaned his tall lanky frame against the doorjamb and looked at me appraisingly.

"It's like you think you're not allowed to make mistakes," he said. "You're used to everyone watching to see how you measure up to your mother. That's why you didn't want this mission, why you're so afraid of it. Because if you think you're going to fail, you just don't try."

He did hug me then, and his arms were as comforting and steady as they had been last night when I cried into his starched white collar. "Can I give you one piece of advice?" he said, as he pulled away. "I think instead of being Katie Bellows' daughter, or Leo Carstairs' daughter, you should see what it's like to be Reggie for a while."

I didn't say anything to this, and he didn't look as if he expected me to. I just watched him walk away. "See you on Monday," he said over his shoulder, and I gave him a small wave.

CHAPTER EIGHT

EVERYTHING PUT TOGETHER SOONER OR LATER FALLS APART

Barlow was already there when I arrived at the diner, and his expression was difficult to read. He plainly wasn't happy to see me, but I suspected that there was something a little thrilling in the idea that he was in on a secret FBI scheme that the rest of his colleagues – even his supervisors – had no part in. He wasn't friendly, but he had come.

"Agent Burns," he said coolly, and I stared blankly for a second before remembering why he thought that was my name.

"Detective Barlow," I said, with a curt nod, slipping comfortably into the caricatured impression of my mother that had been my best party trick while I was at the Academy. (The trick is pretending like you're about ten feet taller than you are, and never, ever smiling.)

"I don't want to offend you," he said. "But if all you needed was the photos I'm not sure why we had to meet in person."

"I missed your handsome face," I said. "And I thought I might have some questions for you after I saw the photos."

"Sure," he said, and then there was a pause. I waited for him to pull out the photos. He didn't. "Did you have a question?"

"Well, I don't know," I said. "I haven't seen the photos yet."

"That's hardly my fault," he said. "Your assistant must not be very reliable, then."

"My what?" I said quietly, feeling my blood run cold.

"Your assistant," he said. "The one you sent to pick up the photos?"

"A young black guy?"

"No," he said. "An old white guy."

"What name did he give you?"

"He didn't," said Barlow. "He just came to the front desk and said he was here to pick up an item for Agent Calliope Burns."

"Oh, for Christ's sake, Barlow, how stupid are you?" I snapped, standing up from the table so rapidly that I almost knocked my chair over. "You goddamn idiot. You complete and utter boneheaded shitbag. Why the hell do you think I set up a meeting to come pick up those photos from you myself?"

"So . . . that guy doesn't work for you."

"No, Sherlock, he doesn't. I have no idea who he is. But now he has the crime scene photos, and I don't, so you've done a terrific day's work."

"I can have another set made," he said hastily. "Those weren't the originals."

"That's not the *point*," I said. "It's not just that I don't have them. It's that *somebody else does*. That was the one lead I had, and now it's useless. You stupid, stupid man."

"I'll get you another set by the end of the day."

"Fine," I said. "I'm going." And I stormed out. I was so furious I was shaking – and not just at Barlow. How had I failed to see this coming? Carter had called Detective Barlow from my house while he was making me breakfast. If I was very, very lucky, they might have done no more than tap my phone. If I was not so lucky . . .

I hailed a cab. "Watergate," I said, "fast as you can." We sped down the streets as I felt my heart pounding. *Oh please*, I thought. *Oh please, oh please, oh please . . .*

I flung a wad of cash at the driver, bolted out the door and through the lobby, pounded on the elevator button, then crawled with agonizing slowness up each floor – ding, one, ding, two, ding, three, ding, four, ding, five, ding, six – before sprinting out the elevator door, keys already in hand, and bursting into my apartment, headed straight for my bedroom.

The evidence wall was gone.

I stood there, staring at the jungle vines snaking up the ceiling, suddenly visible again where a sea of white paper used to be.

They're pros, I thought, a tiny distant part of my mind almost impressed. They had heard Carter's phone call, telling them not just that I was investigating the burglary but the exact time I would be out of the house. And now they didn't just have the crime scene photos. They had everything. My press clippings, my field reports, the notes I'd stolen from Beth, and Carstairs' files on Gemstone.

Gemstone.

I froze in my tracks, and turned around, very, very slowly, hardly daring to hope, and saw the jungle-green dresser with its neat pile of books on top.

They hadn't touched the books.

I ran over and opened them all. Everything was still there. My Microcam and my Short-Hop and my scanner – and, most importantly, there inside the Book of Ruth where I had casually tossed it with my earpiece before going to bed, was the Gemstone drive.

I reached out a trembling finger to touch it, to reassure myself that it was real, and read for the first time the words just above the carved-out hollow – Ruth, chapter three, verse eleven.

"And now, my daughter, fear not. I will do for you all that you require, for all the people in the city know that you are a woman of great courage."

Struck by a sudden thought, I tugged at the filigree chain around my neck and looked again at the clock pendant my mother had given me.

The hands were set at 3:11.

I slipped the necklace back inside my collar and felt the cool metal against my skin. My faceless enemy might have had a head start, but I had something better. I had Carstairs and Bellows.

Now, I thought to myself grimly, it was a race.

$\sim$

I shoved every single piece of my tech equipment into my handbag and changed out of my dress into clothes I could move in. I folded up my contraband cotton pants and shirt as small as they would go and threw them, along with a toothbrush and some other necessities, into the purse as well, blessing Mark for how roomy it was. Then I took the hollowed-out books, dumped them in the hallway chute that led to the trash incinerator, and left the Watergate.

I crossed the plaza from the apartment to the hotel, where a bank of taxis stood waiting, and directed the driver to a large, busy hotel. Once inside, I found a telephone booth and dialed the number on the card I had pulled out of my purse.

He answered on the first ring.

"*Washington Post.* Bob Woodward speaking."

"It's Regina Bellows," I said. "From the other day. I work for John Dean."

"Miss Bellows!" he said. "I'm glad you called."

"I need to talk," I said. "I'm in trouble."

"Where are you?" he said immediately.

"The lobby of the Shoreham."

"Regina, were you followed?"

"I don't know," I said. "I don't *know.* I keep thinking – I don't know." The frustration inside me finally snapped. "I'm a *desk* worker," I said. "I'm not a spy. I have no idea what I'm doing. I'm just a girl who sits at a desk all day. But my apartment has been ransacked and my phone has been tapped and this is *insane,* Bob, all of this is *completely insane.*"

"Stay where you are, Regina," he said. "We're coming to get you."

"Fast," I said, scanning the room, pulse pounding, for fair-haired men with newspapers.

"Get out of the lobby," he said. "You're too visible there. Go wait in the ladies' room. Come out in fifteen minutes. I'll meet you out front."

"Okay," I said. "Hurry." And then I hung up.

I followed the signs to the public ladies' room and stepped inside the stall farthest from the door, clutching my handbag close to me and staring at the clock on my wrist Comm, willing it to move faster. Twice somebody entered and my heart stopped beating, but both times they simply did their business, washed their hands, and left, leaving me faint with relief.

When the clock finally hit fifteen minutes, I bolted out of the restroom and through the lobby, just as a car pulled up to the curb. I could see Carl step out of the passenger seat, holding the door open for me. I dove in.

"Get me out of here," I said to Bob as Carl closed the door behind me. Bob nodded. His calm was reassuring, and I felt safer in their car than I had since Carter left.

"You hungry?" he said, as he pulled away into the late-night traffic.

"Starving," I said. And in just a few minutes we pulled up in front of a gleaming black façade with an enormous neon sign over the door that read YENCHING PALACE. Carl held the door open for me and the proprietor, nodding when he saw us, beckoned us towards an empty round booth towards the back of the room.

By an unspoken agreement, we all waited to begin until the waitress, an artificial *chinoiserie* work of art with impeccably-penciled eyebrows and a red cheongsam covered in golden dragons, had taken our order. Carl's shaggy hair had led me, incorrectly, to assume that he would be a vegetarian, but he dove into the barbecued pork with gusto. They both liked lots of hot mustard in the red sauce for their spring rolls, which I found enormously endearing.

I felt safe with them. I liked them. I hadn't really expected to. They had been dead for centuries in my real world, after all. Everyone here had. The world had felt curiously unreal when I first entered it, everyone scurrying about like little animatronic dolls, following the paths programmed for them.

But there was something about the reporters that felt real. Warm and alive and unpredictable. Maybe it was because they weren't historical celebrities. It wasn't like being in the White House, craning my neck as I walked down the hall, wondering if I'd ever catch a glimpse of the President. Bob and Carl were just people doing their jobs.

I suddenly felt a pang in my chest, wondering if I'd done the right thing dragging them into this. But I was here already. So I might as well get on with it.

"The burglary was only part of it," I began slowly. "It goes much deeper than anyone thought. It was called Operation Gemstone, and Gordon Liddy was its architect." Carl pulled out his notepad and pencil, looking at me for permission. I nodded. Bob didn't take notes, just watched me as I spoke and piped in from time to time with questions. I told them everything I knew and I watched their eyes widen in disbelief.

"And Dean was in on it?"

"I think so, yes," I said. "I wasn't straight with you before. Liddy did come visit Dean. The Monday after the break-in. They were in there for hours. I didn't know about Gemstone then. I found out later. But Dean was there, in the room, when Liddy first pitched it. At first they made a joke out of it. The story was that Liddy was sort of a nutjob and had proposed this cracked-out million-dollar pulp spy novel plan, and it was shot down."

"But it wasn't."

"No, it wasn't. The best I can figure out is that afterwards, somebody – maybe someone from the campaign, or maybe Dean – quietly went back to Liddy and basically told him that if he whittled it down to a more manageable, practical size, they could funnel him the money to execute it. I don't know how many of the different elements were actually executed, but I know Project Opal was clandestine surveillance of the DNC offices and Project Sapphire was a wiretapped yacht full of call girls in Miami at the Democratic Convention. There may have been more."

"Holy shit," said Carl.

"I know," I said.

Then the waiter approached, depositing several plates of food in front of us, and we all stopped talking. Bob thanked him, and they chatted casually about the weather for a moment as I dug into my food.

And almost choked on it as I felt the HIO meter in my pocket: *tick, tick, tick, tick, tick, tick.*

I hadn't done anything. Or rather, I had done a great many things, but the meter hadn't reacted when I had called Bob, or gotten into his car, or started talking about Gemstone. In fact, I had taken its continued amicable silence as a kind of encouragement, a sign that I was on the right track. I certainly hadn't done anything, besides take a possibly too-large-to-be-entirely-ladylike bite of orange chicken, that would cause the HIO meter to tick up to 6.

Then 7.

Then 8.

And then I knew.

It wasn't measuring interference from me.

The other agent was here.

I looked around, attempting to be discreet, and saw that the restaurant was about half-full. Nobody I recognized, of course, they weren't that stupid, although several people who could have fit Barlow's frustratingly vague "old white guy" description.

9.

10.

Something in this room was very, very wrong.

I turned back and saw Bob watching me curiously.

"What is it?" he said.

"I just . . . " I swallowed hard. "I have a bad feeling."

"Like you're being watched?"

I nodded.

"Okay," he said quietly. "Carl, stay here." Then he raised his voice so as to make sure he was overheard. "We're going to go have a cigarette. We'll be right back."

I grabbed my purse and coat and followed him out, attempting to look nonchalant. Bob walked perfectly normally, and made a show of reaching into his inside jacket pocket to pull out a pack of cigarettes as we walked. As soon as we were outside, he turned to me.

"Who was it?"

"I don't know," I said. "Honestly, I don't."

"But someone inside the restaurant."

"Yes."

"Okay," he said. "You stay right here. I'm going to go get Carl and we're taking you to the *Post*. There's a couch in the editor's office you can sleep on, and most importantly, there are night security guards. We need to get you somewhere out of sight. Stay here. Don't move. I'll be right back." I nodded obediently and watched him dash back inside.

"Reggie!"

I turned, startled, to see Carter leap out of a taxi and sprint across the street, through the traffic, towards me.

"I tracked your Comm!" he shouted, not caring as both our HIO meters ticked up and up and up. "I went to Election Day and then I went to the bombing raids—"

"You went to the *bombing raids*?" I shouted at him. "Are you insane? You could have been killed!"

"Later," he shouted back. "Reggie, listen to me, you can't go home, it's not safe." He leaped up onto the sidewalk and came running towards me. "Reggie, listen, I was there, the day of the bombing, I was there, they knew, Reggie, they *knew*—"

"Slow down, Carter, what are you talking about?"

"You have to get out of here," he said, looking over his shoulder at something, I didn't know what. "We have to go."

"Carter—"

"You have to get out of here," he said again, wild-eyed, closer to panic than I'd ever seen him, then grabbed my hand and pulled me away. "Reggie, *run*."

But I didn't get the chance to run. Or to find out what Carter meant by "they knew."

Because by the time Woodward and Bernstein came back out to the sidewalk, Carter and I were gone.

~

I had never been force-jumped before, and the impact as we hit the Slipstream was startling. One minute we were standing outside the Yenching Palace, the next we had been pulled, against our will, out of 1972 and into nothingness.

There were only three reasons that an agent would ever be pulled back to the lab without their own authorization and ready signal – without even having done the most cursory HIO scan.

One, some amateur with no idea what they were doing was at the Comm.

Two, it was a Rewind – meaning, I was about to get killed and someone jumped me back to reboot the mission and start over.

Or three . . . *I was being abducted.*

I closed my eyes and gritted my teeth, bracing myself to land on my feet. But I didn't land. The Slipstream continued to stretch out around me, long past the point where I should have arrived back at the lab, and I felt a slow, cold fear clench around my heart. I didn't feel the telltale atmospheric pressure of an Incongruity, but something was wrong.

Instead of feeling the reassuringly solid weight of the transport platform under my feet, I floated, unmoored to anything, for what could have been hours, minutes or even days. The red-black darkness around me lightened in places, and I began to see a gap open up.

But then it closed again. Then another opened up somewhere else. Then another. It was as though the veil was thinning in places, taunting me, making me think I could reach through to the real world, before slamming shut again.

I floated, watching, waiting. Idly, I wondered if I had died, if the transport had gone wrong and killed me, if this was the afterlife. Good Lord, an eternity of this?

Just as I had convinced myself that this was Purgatory and begun attempting a rough mental tally of my history of sins to estimate how many eons of penance I could realistically expect, I heard Carter calling my name. His voice was muffled, as though he were underwater, and with a shock I realized that at some point we had let go of each other.

I fumbled around in the darkness, limbs heavy and slow like I was moving through molasses, desperately trying to reach out for Carter's hand. But I couldn't find him.

Panic set in. Somehow, inside the Slipstream, Carter and I had become separated. I screamed out his name, once, twice, three times, and waited for a response, but heard only a thick silence.

Then out of nowhere I felt a brutal jolt, like a steel cable wrapped around my waist had been tied to the back of an airplane that suddenly took off at thousands of miles per hour.

It knocked the wind out of me, so that when I finally crashed through the Slipstream and felt solid ground beneath my feet, I doubled over, breathing heavily for several moments before I looked around to see where I was.

My relief at surviving whatever the hell had just happened inside the Slipstream and emerging unscathed was short-lived. I was, as I had anticipated, standing in the Bureau transport lab, on the same platform where I had stood what felt like a lifetime ago to jump into 1972. But this was not the place I had left. Something was very, very wrong.

The room was clearly the same room. I had grown up here, I knew it like the back of my hand. But the control panels were covered with a thick layer of grimy dust. Chairs were overturned. The curtains around the wardrobe changing station had been pulled down.

Two of the four central consoles had been completely smashed in. And inexplicably – even though the equipment had somehow functioned well enough to transport me in – the machinery was dark and silent. No lights flashed. No servers hummed. Not even the telltale red blinking of the "TRANSPORT COMPLETED" light above the door. It was a ghost town. But the worst was yet to come, as I looked all around me and realized with a sinking heart that Carter was missing.

I was standing in the silent, lifeless remains of the Time Travel Bureau, and I was completely alone.

PART III

THE WAYWARD TRAVELER

"*The time is out of joint. O cursèd spite,*
That ever I was born to set it right!"

—WILLIAM SHAKESPEARE, *Hamlet*

CHAPTER ONE

GHOST TOWN

Silence.

Something was wrong.

I stepped down from the transport platform gingerly, with only the smallest of movements. The heavy, dusty hush of the deserted room frightened me in a way that I didn't want to disturb, and I suddenly realized it was a room in which I had never before experienced silence.

If there is personality in a room, then the lab's personality included noise. Lots of noise. The climate controls, lights, transport equipment, elevators – they should all hum constantly, the way they always have, to say nothing of the bustle of the building's seven thousand inhabitants walking, talking, and breathing.

The Bureau is alive twenty-four hours a day. To arrive on the platform and find the lab – not merely empty, but utterly still – meant that something was very, *very* wrong.

The impossibility of the emptiness baffled me as I walked slowly around the room, stepping over broken equipment and shattered glass covered thickly in dust, straining to understand how I could have been brought back here.

Somebody had stood at these controls.

Somebody locked onto my vitals.

Somebody jumped me.

Yet whoever that person was, they were long gone. Which was not possible.

My heart sank as I completed my inspection of the room and realized there was still no sign of Carter. Whatever had happened to me inside the Slipstream, Carter hadn't come through with me. I was alone in the abandoned transport lab. No Carter. No Calliope. No Mom.

Just me.

I swallowed hard and took a deep breath. "Okay, Reggie," I said to myself in a soft voice. "Don't panic. You're okay. You just need to make a plan." I didn't have a partner anymore. I was going to have to figure this out on my own.

What would Katie Bellows do?

"GC coordinates," I said aloud. "You know *where* you are, but not *when*." I cleared the dust off the console's controls in order to pull up the home coordinates, but the equipment stayed dark, no matter what I did. "Okay," I said, "we'll do it old school. Get out of the lab, into the office, and find anything that will help narrow down the date." I swallowed hard, took a deep breath, and pushed open the door.

Everything was deserted.

The sinister hush from inside the lab extended out here too, and I floated through the 20th-century department like a ghost, afraid to touch anything or make a sound. The hallway stretched from the transport lab to the main elevator bay. To my left were rows of senior agents' private offices, and to my right a sea of cubicles for apprentices and techs.

All were entirely abandoned. Computers were missing and file cabinets empty, their drawers jutting out haphazardly like mouths with missing teeth. Office doors hung open, revealing empty desks. Nobody had worked here in a very long time.

I wandered from hall to hall, from office to office, hoping against hope that some sign of human life would reveal itself. But everywhere I went was the same. The building was a ghost town.

I stopped short at the desk in front of me and reached a trembling hand out to pick up the coffee mug sitting on top of it, next to the empty space where a computer screen had once been. A standard office mug with the Bureau logo printed on it in dark blue. The bottom of the cup was thick with the dark, hard, glossy crust of what had once been coffee.

My coffee.

The coffee Calliope had pressed into my hands the night I went to Ohio to search for Grove.

I had set this cup down when we ran to the transport lab, and I had gone from the transport lab to Ohio, from Ohio to sickbay, from sickbay to my mother's office – then office to home, home to 1972, and from 1972 to here – without ever being back at this desk long enough to make coffee again and remember to wash out the mug.

It was still right where I had left it.

Which meant that whatever had happened here, it had happened so soon after I left for 1972 that nobody had touched my coffee cup. And that was when I realized the thing that I had missed.

Everyone's personal effects were still here.

Sweaters. Picture frames. Potted plants, now long dead. All of it, still in place. From my desk I could see into Calliope's cubicle, where her private stash of expensive loose-leaf Darjeeling and little yellow teapot still sat neatly on their glass tray. Across the hall, Grove's office door was open, and I could see his framed diplomas all hanging on the wall, dusty but untouched.

Every single piece of equipment was gone, from computers and Comms to files and documents – everything, in short, that was technically the property of the U.S. Time Travel Bureau – but everyone's personal possessions were right where they'd left them, including mine.

If you ignored the missing computers, and the layers of dust on every surface, it looked as though everyone had just stepped away from their desks for a minute and would be right back.

"What happened here?" I murmured aloud, running a fingertip over the layer of dust on Calliope's desk. What made her leave in such a hurry that she wouldn't – or couldn't – take her coat with her? Who came in afterwards to take her computer away?

And, more importantly, *why*?

I fought down rising panic. "Plan B," I said, keeping my voice quiet, pretending like Carter was standing next to me – *where the hell was Carter?* – and that I was speaking to him. "We need to get out of this building."

And then I realized, with dread, what that meant – what the first step was to getting out of here undetected implied. I swallowed hard, turned left, and pushed open the door to the bathrooms.

I set my bag down on the counter in front of the mirror and rifled through it, praying I hadn't misremembered, then breathed a triumphant sigh of relief when my fingers brushed against it: the travel cosmetic case Mark and Mrs. Graham had sent with me to 1972, packed in this bag so I could fix my makeup on the train.

But this time, I didn't need the lipstick.

I needed something sharp.

I pulled off my shirt and tossed it aside, then ripped off a strip from the bottom of my camisole, knowing I'd need it shortly. I opened the cosmetic case and pulled out the thing that would maybe, just maybe, save my life.

The metal nail file.

Which I was about to plunge, unsterilized and without anesthetic, into my own skin, to dig out my tracker.

I held it in my hand for a long moment, stalling, willing any other possible solution to come to me. But none did. I had to get out of this building. And in order to do that safely, I had to be untraceable. Subdermal trackers couldn't be turned off except from sickbay, and even then they could easily be switched back on again.

No, I had to get it out of my body and leave it here. That way, if by some chance it were detected – if anyone was even watching this godforsaken deserted building – they'd think I was still here.

"For Christ's sake, just *do* it," I snapped at myself, and gritted my teeth. "Just get it over with." I took one last deep breath, swallowed hard, and plunged.

It was all I could do not to scream. Even under the best of circumstances, I have a pretty low pain threshold – my mother says I used to cry as a kid when she tried to brush my hair – and as painful as I ever imagined it might be to stick a piece of metal into my shoulder blade, reality was a thousand times worse.

The edges of the file were rough and ridged, turning every attempt at a gentle prod into a sawing motion. Tears stung my eyes. I couldn't breathe, couldn't see, and had to continue on nearly blind from the pain.

I let go of the file – its length sticking horribly out of my flesh – and palpated the open wound to try and coax the tracker closer to the opening. It moved just a fraction of an inch, but it was enough. I shifted the angle of the file, felt it clink against the tracker, and slowly levered it out, soaked in blood.

The second it was out, I felt my knees give way beneath me, dizzy and faint from pain. Blood smeared everywhere. I reached for the water faucet, and to my utter astonishment, hot water poured out. What had happened here, I wondered, where every human being had disappeared and every piece of technology had gone with them, but somebody – somewhere – was still paying the water bill?

I washed my hands and cleaned out the wound as best I could – wincing at the stinging pain as hot water touched open flesh – then tied the makeshift bandage around it. It wasn't enough. The blood soaked through it almost immediately. I needed gauze or cotton, something soft and clean that would soak up the excess blood while the wound scabbed over.

On a whim, I dashed back out to the hall and into Grove's office, whose door was wide open. *Oh please oh please,* I prayed, as I pulled open the drawers one by one until my gamble finally paid off.

They had left behind everything that wasn't Bureau property. Which meant that in the small upper left drawer of Grove's desk, his private stash of monogrammed, old-fashioned linen handkerchiefs were still there. I sent him a silent apology, grabbed the whole pile, and ran back to the bathroom to retie the strip of silk as best I could, pressing the stack of small white squares against the wound.

It worked.

I mopped up the blood all over the bathroom as best I could, pulled my sweater back on, and left. I debated flushing the tracker down the toilet, but then decided that if it survived the trip and they tracked it to the sewage system, they'd know what I had done. Better to leave them thinking I was still in the building, and get myself out as fast as I could.

I returned to my desk and placed the tracker inside one of the drawers, then made my way to the elevator bay, where a wall of floor-to-ceiling windows opened out onto the city below. Seven stories down, the streets spread out beneath me.

Washington itself looked the same. If I wasn't back in the Timestream I had left, I was at least close enough that I recognized my own city. There were birds in the sky, cars on the street, and lights in the surrounding buildings. The view from these windows was the view I remembered. I was so comforted by this fact that it took me a minute or two to catch the thing I should have noticed immediately.

The building was deserted on the outside too.

There were no people nearby. Nobody hurried in and out of the lobby doors, nobody relaxed outside on the plaza benches in the sun, no cars or trucks idled out front in the short-term parking zone, no one even strolled down the street on this side. The city was full of people – I could see them from up here – but they were all giving the Time Travel Bureau a remarkably wide berth.

All of them, that is, except for the heavily-armed guards that were blocking my only way out of this building.

So, I couldn't transport out the way I'd come because the equipment was dead and I had no way of setting my own coordinates without knowing my location. Plus, there were at least four guns between me and walking out the front door. I was just about to try and figure out what Plan C might be when a sudden gentle whirring sound cut through the deep hush.

There was a soft "ding!" behind me. My blood ran cold and I watched as the black screen over the middle elevator door ticked from "L" to "1."

Somebody was coming.

Call it panic, call it intuition, call it being a total chickenshit. Call it anything you like. But the fact remained that as the elevator slowly ticked its way up from the lobby, I felt the cold chill of impending danger close around me. Whoever was on the other side of those metal doors was unlikely to be an ally, and I did not imagine they would be pleased to see me in this place where I so clearly didn't belong.

So I did the only thing I could think of.

I ran.

I flew like a bat out of hell back down the hall – shoulder screaming in pain – bypassing the transport lab (the most logical place I would go to look for me, if I were them) and veered left, down the corridor that led to my mother's office. It was too much to hope that I'd find some sign of her presence; but if fate were on my side, I might at least find a better place to hide.

The door to the executive wing was wide open, another disconcerting sign. I slipped inside, past the anteroom containing the desk of my mother's tech Yasmina, her computer missing like all the others – and into the lush, carpeted corridor behind it where four mahogany doors with brass plates faced each other. On my right were the office of the Director and the adjoining Council Chambers; on my left, my mom's office and the private executive elevator – which, without a password, was as useless to me as a cardboard box.

Mom's office door was open, and I slipped inside. The curtains were drawn and the lights off, leaving the room midnight-dark even though the sun blazed outside, so it took me a second for my eyes to adjust and realize what I was seeing.

While outside, in the agent cubicles, there were coats on coat hooks and framed photos on walls and other signs of former life, my mother's office had been stripped completely. There was a desk, and a chair, and nothing else. Every other trace of Katherine Bellows was gone. Had she done it herself? Or had *they* done it when she went on the run? Either way, I felt a chill prickle the back of my neck. It certainly did not look as though, no matter what I did, Deputy Director Bellows was ever coming back.

Footsteps thudded, the sound dull, muffled, and there was a low murmur of voices in the distance – still far away, but jarring in that heavy dusty silence – and I realized that I was exposed. I couldn't close the door without running the risk of someone noticing it. There was only one place to hide – behind the desk – and it was risky, both because it was so obvious (the first and only place they'd look if they knew I had come through this way) and because I wouldn't be able to see what was going on.

And it was then, as I crawled into the roomy cave of the desk's kickspace, surrounded on three sides by solid antique wood, wondering how long I'd have to hide here and wait for the coast to clear, that I remembered there was more in this bag than just my cosmetic kit. I had all my tech with me.

Just a few weeks (and technically a hundred-odd years) ago, hiding in another office building, I had spied on the Watergate burglars with my Microcam. If I could hook it up to transmit on a closed circuit to my own handheld, instead of syncing back to Calliope's screen, I could monitor the hallway from the safety of this desk, without being spotted.

The footsteps moved at a leisurely pace, which reassured

me. It didn't sound like I was being chased. It didn't appear, in fact, as though anyone had flagged my tracker yet. I rifled through the bag until I found my handheld, pulled it out and set it to the Microcam's channel, then synced it to my earpiece so only I could hear. I didn't have a pencil to tape the Microcam to this time, so I took my chance and – slowly, gently – tossed it across the carpet as close as I could get it towards the door.

It would have been a brilliant plan if I had a better pitching arm, but unfortunately the Microcam landed wrong way up, so the screen on my handheld showed nothing but a dramatic close-up of some carpet fibers. But I did have sound.

I ducked back down beneath the desk just as I heard the footsteps getting closer. The muffled distant sounds I had overheard now resolved into two male voices, in the middle of an unhurried conversation. ". . . so then the waiter leaves again and then she turns to me and she says, this is what she says, she says 'I just don't think I can see myself with a man with so little ambition.'"

"She said that?"

"She said that. She was all, 'What are they even paying you for, you just spend all day wandering around an empty building doing a job any low-rent minimum wage security guard could do?'"

"It's a temporary assignment!"

"That's what I *told* her. I was like, 'Look, this isn't going to be my life forever, this is a good job with steady pay and a lot of room for advancement—'"

"And the training program – you told her you're in the training program? You told her you were the only person in the class to score 100 on the final exam for Advanced Interrogation Techniques? Tell her *that*."

"I did. She just rolled her eyes. She didn't believe me."

"She didn't *believe* you?"

"No. She got all patronizing, and then I started getting super defensive, so finally I just changed the subject. But it pissed me off. I feel like she just doesn't respect my accomplishments at *all*."

"This is why you don't date people from work, Charlie, I *told* you. Everyone above Floor Twenty-Five thinks they're so goddamn cool and we're just schmucks who walk around holding guns and doing nothing."

"Right? Like, whatever, I know I don't have three degrees in Chrono-Engineering, but it's not like *she* could do *my* job either. She won't even kill a spider."

"Look. I didn't want to say anything before because you guys seemed super happy and whatever, and that's great, but I feel like Zoey is walking all over you here. This is what I was telling you before. In the morning briefing. When Mars asked about the daily agent tracker reports and you had the answer and you didn't raise your hand until I made you. Remember? You need to learn how to like *assert* yourself."

"Ugh, I know. I know. I just get tired of getting shot down."

"You know what this is? This is about you and your dad."

"Don't start with me, Mike."

"No, this is about you and your dad, and how you feel like your dad never listened to you—"

"For the last time, I am not going to go see your therapist. . . Wait, hang on, that's my Comm." He paused for a second, as though listening through an earpiece.

"Yes, sir. Seventh floor executive wing. . . No, sir. . . Just a minute, sir, let me ask Mike, he was in there last."

"Ask me what?" said Mike.

"They flagged something on the tracker reports he wants to

show us. Is the Comm screen inside the Council Chamber still working or should we go back down to three?"

"No, it's powered off, but it's still connected."

"Okay," said Charlie into his Comm. "Mike says it's still hooked up. Go ahead and send the report over. Just give us a second to turn it on."

There was the sound of movement, and then their voices dimmed slightly.

"Yeah, no, we're there now. Go ahead and send up the report."

It was silent for a moment or so while Charlie and Mike switched on the console for the Comm screen, leaving me with a dilemma. On the one hand, I was safely concealed where I was and unlikely to be spotted unless somebody came all the way into the room looking for me. On the other hand, I was suddenly very interested in the "tracker reports," which had now been mentioned twice, and wondered who this "Mars" person was, for whom they presumably worked.

The only smart thing to do was to stay exactly where I was.

So, obviously, I took off my shoes, picked up the Microcam, tiptoed into the hallway, checked to see that the coast was clear, then very, very slowly edged myself around the door leading down into the Council Chambers.

Charlie and Mike had their backs to me, fiddling with the projection screen. There was a brass hinge on the door about midway up, facing directly into the room. I set the Microcam on top of it, then scurried back behind the desk before I could be seen.

The front of the desk was a solid wall of mahogany (the thing took six people to move, Mom had discovered several years ago when they came in to replace her carpet) which mercifully shielded the light from my handheld screen from being visible out in the hallway. But it lit up the dark little cave beneath the desk like a lamp, and it showed me something I hadn't seen before.

Leo and I used to come to the office with Mom all the time as kids, and we each had our own favorite hiding spots. His had been underneath a large potted ficus that sat in the corner (now gone) and mine had been under the desk. I spent years of my childhood curled up in this little cave, listening to my mother work, watching her feet tap impatiently as she waited for reports to come in and popping my head out in the middle of meetings to startle visitors.

I had spent hundreds, maybe thousands, of hours over the years sitting in this exact spot – which was why it took me a moment to realize that on the roof of the little cave, on the direct underside of the surface of the desk, were two etched words that I had never seen there before.

"YOURS BACKWARDS."

I stared at them for a long time, running my finger over the letters. They had been hacked into the wood, edges rough and messy, as though done in a hurry. I hadn't been underneath this desk in at least a decade, but it had sat all that time right here in my mother's office, untouched by anyone but her and locked securely in her absence. Either whoever had cleaned out her office and taken away everyone's equipment had decided to engage in a very specific form of vandalism . . .

Or my mother had left me a message.

Yours backwards. What the hell did that mean? S-R-U-O-Y? Was that supposed to mean something? The babble of voices in the Council Chambers became soothing white noise as I leaned my head back against the dark wood and tried to think like Katherine Bellows.

My mother wasn't a cryptic person – on the contrary, she

was irritatingly blunt – so if she had left a coded message it was for a reason. I thought hard. Why would this place, underneath her desk, be the place she left the clue?

Because she foresaw this exact scenario, I realized. *Because she knew if I were on-the-run inside this building, this is the place I would go to hide. She knew it even before I knew it.*

The Comm screen came to life just then, perfectly visible through the Microcam on my handheld screen, and a row of three faces lined up side-by-side flashed onto the screen.

My father, my mother, and me.

Two of the faces were slightly dimmed, framed in black, calmly labeled "TRACKER DEACTIVATED. NO AGENT ACTIVITY." But the face belonging to one Apprentice Agent Regina Bellows was brightly illuminated, framed in blinking red, with huge red block letters beneath it:

"SIGNAL DETECTED."

In a surprising moment of solidarity, Charlie and I had the same thought at the same time.

"*Shit.*"

Charlie tapped his earpiece, "We're looking at it now, sir. I'm sorry, I don't understand how – Wait, *inside* the building?"

Mike turned to him, startled. "She's in the building?" Mike whispered.

"He says that's what the report says," Charlie whispered back, then went back to his call. "Yes sir, sorry sir. We're here. No, I was just telling Mike… Yes sir, right away. We're on Seven now, it's clear. How close can you narrow down the signal?" He turned back to Mike. "He says somewhere between floors 5 and 9."

"Put him on speaker," said Mike, who was doing something with the console. I heard another male voice pop in, midsentence out of nowhere.

". . . teams blocking the stairwells, so that shouldn't be a problem, and we already have teams in the lobby if she tries to come down through the central elevators."

"He should run a geofilter," said Charlie, almost to himself. Mike elbowed him, pointing at the headset, and mouthed, "Tell him." Charlie shook his head. Mike sighed.

"Sir, you're on speaker, this is Mike. If you run the tracker's signal through a Class C-12 geofilter, you should be able to narrow down the location to within a fifty foot radius. It only takes about seven minutes."

"Good thinking," said the voice on the other end approvingly. "We'll do that right away. In the meantime, stay where you are, sweep Seven again starting with the transport lab, and we'll page you back when we have geofiltered coordinates."

"Yes, sir," they both said.

"No stone unturned," said the voice sternly. "I do not want to report back to Mars and Saturn that we had her and she got away."

"She won't, sir," said Mike. "She's got no way out of the building."

"See that she doesn't," said the voice. "We've already lost the mother. Mars wants this one alive."

My heart stopped. What did he mean, *lost her?*

I swallowed hard, gritted my teeth and pushed the rising swell of fear down, out of my chest, as Mike and Charlie switched off the Comm screen and came back out into the hall.

"That," said Mike, as they walked back towards the transport lab. "Right there. With the geofilter. This is exactly what I was talking about."

"Drop it, Mike."

"I'm telling you. I blame your dad."

The second they had turned down the hallway, I dashed

out to retrieve my Microcam, dizzy with panic. There were fingerprints and footprints in the transport lab. The thick dust would rat me out. If they went into the bathroom they'd still see wet counters.

In seven minutes they would trace my tracker to the desk, realize I had dug it out, and then the whole floor would be crawling with armed guards, hunting me down to deliver to two shadowy enemies with stupid planetary code names.

And Mike was right. Even if I'd had home coordinates, the transport lab was now useless to me, and it was clear that the guards with guns blocking the front door were on the side of whoever was hunting for me.

It was a dead end.

I stood in the hallway for a long moment, leaned my head back against the wall behind me, shooting death glares at the Council Chamber, and sighed.

It wasn't until my head hit the wall with a hollow thunk that I remembered that that wall wasn't a wall. It was a door.

And then it clicked.

My mother had left me – and only me – a way out of the building.

I ran back to her office, grabbed my bag, carefully replaced the chair so the desk looked undisturbed and, without a sound, eased open the door next to hers.

Mike and Charlie had come up through the central elevator bay from the lobby, which their boss had told them was guarded. So were the stairwells.

Nobody had mentioned the private executive elevator.

The elevator was installed by the Bureau with the express purpose of giving department directors and visiting VIPs an elegant and high-security entrance of their own so they could avoid the main lobby's annoying retinal scans.

The elevator's most prized feature was that it was not hackable, because its controls weren't networked to anything else.

"The elevator itself is the computer," I heard my mother's voice say. At the time, I had thought it to be a clever security measure. Now, however, it was the thing that was going to save my life. Because it meant I had a foolproof way out of the building that nobody else could track.

If I could get it to let me in.

I placed my thumb gingerly on the small black screen in the elevator door. This was step one. If it recognized my vital signs from the Bureau database, it would open. I waited for what felt like an eternity before the screen flashed green and the doors slid noiselessly apart. I had cleared the first hurdle. I was in.

Inside the elevator, I placed my hand on a flat metal panel and waited, as the doors whooshed closed behind me. The Bureau didn't want to force members of Congress or visiting dignitaries to undergo invasive personal scans, so the elevator's primary security was in the password system.

But there were only a small group of people permitted to operate the elevator, all of whose genetic information was stored inside the database. The question was, how sophisticated was the scan? Would it read my vitals, identify me as Regina Bellows, and refuse to budge because I didn't have security clearance? Or was half my mother's DNA enough to confuse it?

The screen above the metal scan panel cycled through its roster of faces one after the other. When it got to my mother's face it stopped. Then the screen went dark. My heart sank. Then it flashed back on again and scanned again. The same thing happened. After the fifth cycle, it paused on my mother's face, blinked in and out several times, then flashed a message on the screen.

"SCAN COULD NOT COMPLETE. PLEASE CONFIRM IDENTITY WITH PASSWORD."

Yours backwards, I thought to myself, unable to resist grinning as I punched in the security code. I had set her password for her that day, as she took me in this elevator up to the transport lab, and because I was annoyed at her, I had picked something she would hate being forced to type twice a day, every day, for two weeks until it was time to reset it again. *Yours backwards*. She had set the password before she left and left me a clue in case I needed it.

I typed five characters in a row.

$-1-n-e-P.

Or, reversed, the way I had made her enter it all those weeks ago: P-e-n-1-$.

(Don't ever let anyone tell you that purposely annoying your parents serves no purpose.)

"PASSWORD RESET REQUIRED," said the screen. She had been gone long enough that it was past time to reset her password, but the computer had recognized it.

I typed in a new password – "0-P-a-l-*", so I'd remember it in case I needed it again – and hit CONFIRM. With a silent whoosh, the elevator started down, and I let out a sigh of relief so deep that I felt my whole body go shaky.

I was free.

I had no idea where Carter was, nor what had happened to my mom. I had nowhere to go, and only about six minutes until the entire block was crawling with armed guards hunting for me, but I was no longer trapped inside that ghost town of a building.

I stepped gingerly out of the elevator into the small foyer that led to the VIP parking garage. It was silent and still and empty.

Correction. It was *nearly* empty.

If nobody inside the building had a password for the elevator, then nobody should be parked in the executive garage. So then whose lone black car with tinted windows and no license plates was that, sitting quietly on the far end of the lot?

Suddenly, as if it could feel me looking at it, the car came alive. The headlights switched on and the engine turned over. Someone was inside it. Someone who wasn't supposed to be here.

I ran.

The car gave chase as I sprinted as hard as I could, the wound on my arm tearing open again as I made a mad dash across the garage to the emergency exit that led to the sidewalk outside. It was wired with an alarm, so I was screwed either way, but at least it gave me a fighting chance.

I cut through the center of the lot, leaping over the low concrete dividers between rows, as the car behind me made an abrupt turn, tires squealing, as it wheeled around and barreled through the garage in the wrong direction to cut me off at the pass.

Oh please oh please, I thought. I was so close. I could see the door.

It. Was. Right. There.

I was no more than twenty feet away.

And then it was blocked from sight as the black car screeched to a halt right in front of me and the window on the passenger side rolled down. I spun away, one foot raised, arms ready to pump, already leaning into a sprint in a new direction, when I was stopped short by a voice I had wondered if I'd ever hear again.

"For Christ's sake, get in," said my brother Leo.

CHAPTER TWO

BAILEY'S CROSSROADS

I stood motionless, staring at him, seeing him, yet not quite believing it.

"Get in the car," he said again, this time through clenched teeth, voice rising. "The building's about to go into lockdown and in sixty seconds these garage doors seal. Reggie, *get in*."

I got in.

"On the floor," he said by way of greeting. "Can't let anyone see you."

Still too astonished to even form words, I obediently curled up as tiny as I could on the floor of the car, and Leo tossed a dark coat at me to cover myself with.

"Not a sound," he hissed as the car pulled away. I breathed as quietly as I could, buried under Leo's good winter coat. It smelled like pine and rosemary and home, and I felt absurdly comforted by it.

He wheeled the car around and headed for what I assumed

was the VIP exit. Sure enough, he soon slowed to a standstill and there was the telltale beeping of the keypad on the parking garage's security door.

"You can't get into the building from here without a password or proper clearance," he said without turning around, as the security door opened and he pulled out into the street, "so they've long since stopped caring about security in and around the garages. They're useless to anyone who might try to use them as a way to break inside."

"Though," he continued, chuckling as he drove, the sound remarkably dry, humorless and ultimately more terrifying than outright screaming would have been, "as it turns out, they're fairly handy if you're trying to break someone *out*."

A moment of silence, then, "Now stay down, don't move, don't breathe. We're about to drive past the front door and the guards are going to stop us. The patrol out front just got paged on their Comms and moved to defensive positions two minutes ago. They know you're here, but they're only watching the front door. Nobody knows about the other elevator. Don't make a sound or we're both dead."

I curled up as tight as I could, adjusted the coat so my bag and I were completely concealed, and held my breath. The car stopped and I heard the windows roll down.

"Hey Bruce," said Leo.

"Kid, you can't be here today," said a gruff but not unfriendly voice. "There's some weird security thing going on. You better scoot on home."

"I'm sorry," said Leo, "I hate to bother you." He was so good I almost applauded. There was just the faintest hint of a waver in his dejected voice, like he was holding back tears. "I don't suppose there's any news?"

"Nothing," said Bruce. "Building's deserted."

"Huh," said Leo. "I thought I saw people moving around in the lobby."

"Oh, that," said Bruce. "Somebody tripped an alarm on the seventh floor and they sent the team in for a routine sweep. Nothing to do with the investigation."

Leo sighed.

"I'm sorry you got your hopes up," said Bruce. "You're in a tough spot. But you got Callahan on your case, he's the best there is. The second he finds anything he'll call you, you can take that to the bank."

"Yeah. I know. He's been great. It's just hard feeling like . . . there's nothing I can *do*, you know? I'm just waiting."

"Kid, you've got to stop torturing yourself," said Bruce. "You've got to start thinking about moving on. You still have your whole life ahead of you. You ain't heard any good news by this point, time to grit your teeth and face the worst. Nobody likes it but we all got to do it."

"I just keep thinking," said Leo, in a tone of masterfully understated tragedy, "that one of these days I'll be sitting there and I'll just see them walk out that door like none of this ever happened."

"I know, buddy, I know," said Bruce.

Leo sighed again.

"Well, I better get going," he said. "I don't want to be in the way if you have to go deal with a security thing. I know how busy you are." They chortled like this was some kind of long-running inside joke.

"Yeah, guarding a deserted building really takes it out of you," said Bruce. "I'm wiped out by the end of every day."

"Well, I'll get out of here and leave you to it," said Leo. "Say hi to Martha and the kids for me."

"Will do," said Bruce.

"And tell her next time I'll bring over some more of that risotto. Maybe no prawns this time if she's still having morning sickness."

"You're a real pal, Leo."

"It's the least I can do," he said. "I'll see you soon."

"You take care," said Bruce.

Then the window rolled up and we drove away.

"Stay down," said Leo quietly, without turning around. "I'll tell you when it's clear."

I waited obediently in silence for what felt like an eternity but realistically was probably three minutes before he gave me the all-clear, and I sat up in time to see that we were about to cross the river.

"Okay," he said, "we're good. You can get up off the floor."

I maneuvered myself to a seated position, shoulder screaming in pain, and looked at him in the rearview mirror.

"Hi," I said.

"Hi," he said back.

"What in the holy name of Jesus Christ our Lord is happening right now?"

"I'm rescuing you."

"Yes, I see that. Where are we going?"

"Bailey's Crossroads, Virginia," he said. "By the way, there's a bag on the seat back there with water and a sandwich for you. I thought you might be hungry."

The memory of the orange chicken I had only gotten two bites of before I fled shimmered before me, and I realized just how long ago that was. I took the bag gratefully.

"Okay," I said to Leo around a mouthful of sandwich, "I'm gonna eat and you're gonna talk. How the hell did you get here? Why aren't you in Croatia? Mom said you were in hiding. How did you know how to find me? How did you get into the building? Did Mom tell you? Where's Mom?"

"Oh my God," said Leo. "If I'd known you were going to be like this I would have sent Calliope."

"Calliope?"

"She's really the best person to answer most of the five hundred questions you just asked me, and we'll be there in a few minutes, but in the meantime I'll do my best. One at a time."

"Where's Mom?"

"I don't know," he said. "She hasn't come back. You saw her more recently than I did."

"She said you were in hiding."

"I was. In a manner of speaking."

"What does that mean?"

"It means that the best way to demonstrate that I (an innocent civilian with Croatian citizenship and no security clearance) was no threat and could be safely ignored altogether," said Leo, "was for me to come home to D.C. for a surprise visit, find you both missing and call the police."

"What?"

"It was my idea," he said proudly. "I filed a missing persons' report and everything. See, the FBI knew that if I was working *with* you, bringing in the cops and the media and drawing attention to your absence would be the absolute last thing you would want. Detectives sniffing around the house, treating it like a crime scene. Access to all Mom's files, even the private ones. Everything."

He went on, "But of course the FBI couldn't have the D.C. police accidentally stumble across anything classified, so they 'took over' the investigation themselves. Out of respect for the family, they said."

"So I'm here, living at Mom's condo, and once a week I get a call from a friendly agent telling me they haven't discovered anything new, but they're still hard at work, and they ask if I've heard from either my mother or my sister and I say no in a very sad voice, and they tell me to call if anything changes, and then they hang up and forget about me until the next week."

"So nobody's watching you?" I said incredulously. He shook his head.

"They were at first," he said. "I tried some things out, just to see. I would drive to the Bureau a lot, at weird times of the day or night. I'd just sit out front, in the car, and then go drive around the city. After the first time, I got a call the minute I got back. 'Just checking in,' he said. I think he was testing me to see if I'd lie about where I'd been. I told him nothing had changed, but that I had driven to the Bureau and sat there for a long time, trying to think of anything I could remember that would help the investigation, but nothing came of it."

"And I kept doing it. Sometimes during the day, sometimes at night. Sometimes I'd stay in the car. Sometimes I'd get out and walk around and chat with the security guards. After the twentieth or thirtieth time, a guy in a suit came to talk to me and said having a suspicious car loitering in front of a building that was closed pending investigation was a security risk and I couldn't park out front anymore. So then I switched to doing very, very slow drive-bys of the front. They didn't like that either."

"After another couple dozen visits, when they realized I didn't mean any harm but I also wasn't going to stop, they gave up, and the security guards told me that if I had to keep coming to the office, that I had to park the car somewhere out of sight so I didn't worry the neighbors. I said my mom's driver still had a pass code to the executive garage, and asked if I could be allowed to sit in there."

"They said they weren't sure how sitting alone in a dark, empty parking garage for hours on end was productive to dealing with grief, but it was easier on them than having me lurking around where everyone could see me, so they just gave in."

Leo grinned. "They're all private security, not FBI or cops or anything, and I think they're all pretty far down the ladder. It's not a very exciting job; the building has been dead so long that they're all a little half-assed about it. They're bored out of their minds and I bring a little occasional interest to their week. Also food. I show up with lunch once a week or so and we sit in the plaza and make small talk. They think I'm a sad, pathetic weirdo, but they definitely don't think I have any idea where my sister and mother are. I've cooperated fully with the investigation for so long that they've totally lost interest in me as a suspect."

"That's . . . actually brilliant," I said in astonishment, the thousand other things I wanted to ask him temporarily forgotten. Leo and Calliope, hatching plans together? What the hell kind of crazy world had I come back to?

Small-town Virginia rolled past. "Nearly there," said Leo, and turned down a dead-end gravel road full of nondescript houses. The last house on the block, before the street dead-ended into a large, swampy ditch surrounded by bracken and raspberry bushes, was a two-story brick-front with a dingy old truck parked outside and a sign reading "BEWARE OF DOG" on the metal fence in front of it.

He stopped the car about half a block away from this house and tapped the Comm on his wrist, which was the first time I noticed that *Leo was wearing a Bureau Comm on his wrist*, and then—

"Clear," said Calliope's voice, and a web of crackling

blue electricity blinked into view right in front of us, then disappeared again.

"What the—"

"Invisible security fencing," said Leo. "Around the whole perimeter."

"That can't be much fun for the neighbors," I said as he pulled into the driveway.

"There are no neighbors," he said. "We own the whole block. All these houses are empty." Me and Leo got out of the car and went towards the dingy house. I grabbed my bag and followed.

"Hey," I said to Leo. "Wait." He stopped and turned to me, and I threw my one good arm around his neck and hugged him harder than I'd ever hugged him in all of our lives.

"I didn't think I'd ever see you again," I said into the shoulder of his soft sweater.

"Same here," he said back, holding me tight and kissing the top of my head.

"This is all very adorable, but some of the rest of us would also like a turn," said a voice behind me. I turned to see that the front door was open. "About goddamn time," said Carter, who was standing there in the doorway with a huge grin on his face, and the knot of panic I had been desperately trying to swallow since I had lost his hand in the Slipstream finally dissolved.

"You're here," I said in wonderment. "How are you here?"

"It's a long story," he said. "Come in, we'll tell you everything."

"I lost you in the Slipstream."

"I know."

"When I landed at the Bureau and you weren't there, I thought—"

"I know. Come in, we'll explain everything."

"I thought you—I didn't think I'd—"

"Don't you go getting sentimental on me, Bellows," he said, and wrapped me in a crushing embrace, hugging me so hard my feet lifted off the ground. This was the last straw for my bruised and bloodied shoulder, and I gave a howl of pain. Carter pulled away, horrified and confused.

"For Christ's sake," snapped an irritable voice from the doorway behind him, "can neither of you idiots see that she's *bleeding*?"

Carter and Leo stared at me. At some point on the car trip, the blood had soaked through all the handkerchiefs and a dark wet patch had spread over my black sweater. It was barely noticeable on me, from a distance, but Carter's crisp white shirt had a murderous red stain on the left breast where my shoulder had touched him.

"Oh my God," said Carter in horror. "She *is* bleeding."

"Nothing gets past you," said Calliope. "Get her inside, for God's sake. Reggie, can you walk?"

"I can walk," I said. She put her arm around my waist, very carefully, and helped me inside.

Carter closed the door behind us and hit a small button on the wall, and I realized that the small dingy kitchen and oak hallway paneling I was looking at were false, like theatre scenery; they folded up and vanished and revealed a much larger, open-plan great room behind them.

I didn't get much of a look at it at first, as Calliope led me over to a dining table in the corner, pulled out a chair and sat me down.

"Rags, hot water and the med kit," she barked. "Reggie, take off your shirt."

"I missed you too," I said. She snorted.

"Take off your shirt so we can look at your shoulder."

"Oh, is that what the kids are calling it?"

"Just do it, Reggie, you can be hilarious later." I obeyed her, attempting to shrug out of my sweater, but every movement of my shoulder caused more excruciating pain. Calliope watched me struggle for a few seconds before sighing and taking over.

"How much do you like this sweater?"

"Not that much, now that it's got blood all over it."

"Good." She grabbed a paring knife from the kitchen counter and slit the sweater down the middle, then slit the sleeve of my bad arm and gently peeled the fabric away to reveal a bloody pile of linen handkerchiefs tied half-assed to my arm with a strip of silk from my now-ragged camisole.

"Christ Almighty," said Leo, horrified. "What the hell happened to you?"

"What happened is, she's her mother's daughter," said Calliope. "You know, Carter and I did each other's, with ice and sterilized tools, like civilized people."

"Did what? What happened?"

"I had to dig out my tracker," I said.

"What do you mean, 'dig it out?'" asked Leo, a flicker of dread in his voice.

"They embed it in the skin underneath your shoulder," I explained. "Every agent has one. It's so they can lock onto you for transport and measure your vital signs. Like if something happens to you in the field and you're injured and you need to be pulled out. Or if the personal transport devices you're carrying stop working. It's a safety valve. But it's also how they track the location of every agent. Mom dug hers out before she came to find me."

"Where's yours now?"

"I left it at the Bureau," I said. "In my desk. I wanted them to think I was still in the building in the hopes that they might waste some time hunting for me and give me a little head start."

"That was good thinking," said Carter approvingly, bringing over a bowl of ice and a bowl of warm water with a cloth as Calliope opened a cupboard and pulled out a med kit.

"It didn't last quite as long as I hoped," I said. "They flagged it while I was still inside. But it took them long enough to run a geofilter that it bought me a couple minutes to get out of the building."

"And you dug it out of your own skin yourself?" said Leo, face very pale.

"Well, yeah," I said. "I had to."

"How?"

"You don't want to know," said Calliope, delicately untying the makeshift bandage. "Trust me."

"How?" Leo repeated.

"Nail file," I said. He swallowed hard, blanched and looked a little sick.

"Christ, no wonder you're a mess," said Calliope.

"You're in good hands," said Carter. "She did mine, and it healed up like magic."

"All techs get basic emergency care training," she said, gently stripping away the handkerchiefs one by one. "In case an agent transports back with an injury and you have to wait for the med team."

"She wanted to do her own," said Carter. "She didn't trust me."

"You did okay," she admitted.

"All of you are insane," said Leo.

"You know," I said, wincing as Calliope took the warm wet cloth from the bowl on the table and began carefully cleaning the blood away from the gash in my shoulder, "I think I have been heroically patient with all three of you so far, but while Calliope is poking at my open wound over here it might be a really excellent time for somebody to tell me *what the ever-loving hell has been going on.*"

"What did Leo tell you in the car?" said Calliope.

"I got a very impressive rundown of his ploy to get inside the executive garage," I said. "But I'm still missing, you know, literally every other part of the story."

"Oh, I see how it is," said Carter to Leo. "You just told the part where you come off looking really cool. And nothing else."

"We were short on time. What do you want from me?" Leo retorted.

"So, he didn't tell you, for instance," said Carter, "anything about the Chrono-Splice."

"What Chrono-Splice?" I asked.

"For Christ's sake, Leo," said Calliope irritably.

"I decided it would be better coming from you," he said defensively. "I'm still bad at explaining it."

"For the love of God," I said, "if somebody doesn't start talking right now—"

Carter pulled up a chair right across from me and took my hand.

"Reggie, when you landed in the transport lab, what did you see?"

"It was deserted," I said. "Everything was smashed and broken and the computers were missing, but it was all dusty, like it had been that way for a long time."

"And you must have wondered how that was possible, given that somebody must have been there at some point to jump you back."

"Right."

"I planted a Chrono-Splice," said Calliope. "I placed an

untraceable glitch in the system that would trigger a time delay automatically if you were ever jumped back to the lab without doing an HIO scan first."

"Why was I jumped? Who did it?"

"I don't know," she said. "I wasn't there. It was long after I was gone. It was your mother's idea to hide you – and the Gemstone file – in the Slipstream for long enough that any active investigation would have died down. To give you some cover."

"How long was I in the Slipstream?" I asked. Nobody answered immediately, and that was the first time I looked around and actually noticed the room.

The whole bottom floor of the house was one vast, open space with exposed beams and white walls, a big brick fireplace on one end and an open-plan kitchen on the other, with an island facing into the rest of the room. The furniture was comfortable, faded brown leather and dark wood, but the abundant natural light let in by a series of skylights and windows (all covered, I noted, with digital illusion panels to prevent anyone from getting a look inside) kept it from feeling gloomy. It was warm and inviting and lovely.

It was also *aggressively* decorated for Christmas.

"It was summer when I left," I said.

"Yes," said Carter gently. "You were in the Slipstream for eighteen months."

"Eighteen months?" I shrieked, struggling to my feet as Calliope forced me back down into the chair.

"Yes."

"Eighteen. Months."

"Yes."

"A year and a half. A whole year and a half of my life, just gone."

"It was the only thing we could think of," said Calliope. "The Slipstream was the only place no scan could find you."

"But it's all moot now, since my tracker was live today," I said.

"Yes," she said. "Now they know you're back. We suspected this might happen. Granted, we thought you might have a little more time, but Leo was ready from the moment you landed, just in case."

"Wait a minute," I said. "So a year and a half ago, when my mom hatched this plan, you guys picked this exact date to set the Chrono-Splice and bring me through."

"That's right," she said.

I turned to Leo.

"You," I said. "Driving around the building every day, playing the sad weirdo – you spent *eighteen months* running a long con on a team of armed men just so that when this day came you'd be able to get a car into and out of that garage."

"That was the idea."

"My God, that was a gamble," I said. "Did Mom know?"

"Not about that part, no," said Leo. "We were hoping she'd be back by now, or at least in contact."

"But she hasn't been?"

"No," said Calliope. "I can track her vitals, so I know she's still alive, but I don't know where she is. But in the meantime, until we hear from her, we're all carrying on and trying to investigate from this end as best we can."

"The last time I saw you was on the video Comm," I said, "when Carter and I told you and Mom about Opal."

"Yes," she said. "She had me scrub the call from the records and told me to never, ever mention what you had said to anybody. Then she disappeared for a couple of days, and I didn't see her until the week afterwards when she came to me and asked about the security protocols around cargo-dropping – could I send a small object through the cargo-drop to Carter's apartment without the central transport logs cataloging it?"

"I said no, you have to scan the item first and report its contents, then get approval, then scan it again before sending to make sure it matches. It's how we keep terrorists from cargo-dropping chemical agents and explosives. There's no way to drop something secretly using Bureau equipment."

"That was when she told me about the Gemstone drive, and the files Agent Carstairs had found. She told me the whole story, and swore me to secrecy. She said she suspected a mole inside the Bureau, and that until we knew who it was, nobody was safe. That was when the rumors started."

"What rumors?" I started to say, then yelped in pain as I felt the raw metallic burn of alcohol on the cut in my shoulder.

"Son of a *bitch*, Calliope," I snapped.

"You perform surgery on yourself with a nail file, you get the best antiseptic money can buy," she said. "You'll thank me later when you don't die of blood poisoning."

"Keep talking," Leo said to Calliope. "Distract her."

"Eyes on me, Reggie," said Carter firmly. "Don't look at Calliope, look at me. Squeeze my hand if you need to." And he took my hand in his. It was warm and strong and comforting, and I remembered how he had held me on the balcony of the Watergate while I cried about my father.

"Reggie, I need you to stay very still," said Calliope. "I have ice, but no anesthetic."

"Work fast, then," I said. "The rumors. Keep going."

"Your mother told me that Director Gray had told you that there was a possibility that Agent Carstairs might have – that your father—"

"That's right," I said. "I'd forgotten. Gray said there was a chance that the Chronomaly in Ohio could have been caused by a Ghost."

"A Ghost?" asked Leo.

"A dead agent," I said. "Agent Carstairs had a field mission that put him within Short-Hop distance of the place where Grove and I got caught in the Slipstream. He said there was a possibility we had to consider that Carstairs was the one behind it."

"It's technically possible," said Calliope. "We don't know how long the Chronomaly of the war was hidden in the system. Carstairs could have done it thirty years ago. But it would have taken a massive amount of data manipulation to keep it camouflaged as a natural occurrence, which means somebody would have had to keep it going after he died. Gray was clearly not the only one who spotted that as a possibility. Somebody else thought so too."

I stared at her.

"Please don't be saying what I think you're saying," I said. Calliope's needle pierced my skin but I hardly felt any pain. I was too horrified by what she had just said.

"I don't know where it started," she said. "Nobody does. But within weeks, everyone in the building was talking about how Agent Carstairs had planted a Chronomaly in the General Timeline to create a war that never should have happened, that Deputy Director Bellows had been covering his tracks since he died, and that when Director Gray discovered it, she arranged that the agent sent back to investigate should be her daughter, to ensure that the truth never got out."

"You're kidding me."

"I wish I was," she said.

"That's *treason*."

"Yes."

"They think we did this?"

"Director Gray doesn't," she said. "And nobody who knows you or your parents really believes it. But the story was leaked to the press. The outcry was huge. The idea that Leo Carstairs, national hero, tragically dead in the line of duty, was a traitor to his country the whole time? That story is too juicy to pass up."

"That's why she went on the run," I said. "She was about to be arrested for treason. She knew we had to find the real traitor to clear her name. And Dad's."

"And ours," said Leo.

"What happened after that?"

"Well, there was an epic investigation," said Calliope. "Every senior agent and tech with high enough security clearance to have planted the Chronomaly was placed under house arrest. Some of them still are. Gray is, Yasmina is, and I think a few others that were known to have worked closely with your parents in the past."

"Everyone else was let go but placed under heavy surveillance. Support staff and apprentices were interrogated and then released, and the building was closed down. The investigation is still technically going on, and they won't reopen the Bureau until it's completed. Which might be never. Very convenient, if you're an enemy agent who doesn't want a Chronomaly repaired."

"Why aren't you under house arrest?"

"On paper, I don't report to Katie Bellows," she said. "I report to Harold Grove. And Grove was out on medical leave when all of this happened."

"They asked me some questions about you, and the mission Gray and your mother sent you on. I said exactly what your mom told me to say – that you were on an administrative research mission as punishment for jumping to Ohio to rescue Grove without filling out the requisite paperwork, and that if you were doing anything else while you were there, I didn't know about it. They pushed me around a little, but they couldn't get me to say anything else, so I think they finally gave up and decided I didn't know anything."

"What do you mean, they pushed you around a little?" I said sharply, and Calliope looked away. I had never seen her embarrassed before, and it made me deeply uneasy.

"Just show her," said Leo gently, putting his hand on her shoulder, and something indefinable passed between them that I didn't understand.

"Show me what?"

Calliope set down her med kit, stood from her chair, and wordlessly turned around. Very gently, Leo lifted up her sweater, and I drew in my breath sharply, fighting back waves of nausea.

Calliope's back was a mess of ugly red welts, laid out in a precise, tidy symmetry of criss-crossing lines. It was the most horrifying thing I'd ever seen. The scars running one direction – at an angle from her left side towards her spine – looked different from the ones running the other direction, and I realized it was because they were newer. She had been tortured twice.

"Stun rods," I said softly, and she nodded. "Somebody flogged you. And *enjoyed* it."

"It's not so bad," she said gruffly. "I got off easy. Yasmina's are worse."

"Who did this to you?"

"I don't know," she said. "I don't know who they were. I was told I was being questioned by the FBI, but these men looked like private security."

"Black uniforms, high-end body armor, no visible badges?"

"Yes."

"Then they're the same people that are guarding the Bureau right now," I said. "Whoever we're up against has their own private militia, apparently."

"Well, whatever they're paying them, they earned it," she said, pulling her sweater back down and busying herself once more with stitching up my shoulder. "They seemed to demonstrate very high rates of employee satisfaction."

"Calliope—"

"It's true. I bet their personnel files are full of glowing reports from their supervisors. 'Mr. Blah Blah continues to impress us with his commitment to going the extra mile for a job well done.'"

"Calliope, I—"

"Don't," she said sharply. "*Don't.* Don't apologize."

"This is my fault."

"No, it's not."

"This was because of me. Because they were trying to find out what you knew about me. If I hadn't—"

"You stop that right now," she said. "I mean it. I don't ever want to hear that from you again. I chose this job. I chose to help your mother. I chose to help you. I *chose* this. Katie Bellows told me that fifty-six million civilians were killed in a war that should never have happened and asked for my help to stop it. If a web of scars on my back is the cost of that, I'll pay it. Happily. And I'd do it again."

"We've all made choices," said Carter quietly. "We all had a chance to run, and we didn't take it. We're in this together."

I looked at him suddenly.

"Wait a minute," I said. "You. Last time I saw you was outside the Chinese restaurant. You said you'd just come from the bombing raids."

"Yes," he said. "Or, no, not exactly. I wasn't at the site of the bombings. I was there just before they hit. I went to the White House."

"How did you get in?"

"I didn't," he said. "That's the thing I wanted to tell you. I signed up for a spot on the free tour, but when I arrived that day – the afternoon of the bombing raids – I was told that the building wasn't open to the public that day."

"What?"

"Yes," he said. "No tours, not even any meetings. I asked why, and the tour guide said it wouldn't be very interesting anyway, since there were no staff in the West Wing that day."

"No staff at all?"

"Right."

"At, what, like noon on a Tuesday?"

"Yep."

"Did you ask why?"

"She said they were redoing the floors."

"Holy shit," I said. "They knew. They knew the bombs were coming. Somebody *knew*."

"I came back to tell you," he said. "I went to the apartment first, and saw that the evidence wall was missing."

"They got the police photos too," I said. "That moron Detective Barlow gave them to somebody else claiming to be there on my behalf. And the printouts of Gemstone. But I have the drive."

"Oh, thank God," said Calliope.

"So I tracked you to the restaurant," Carter went on, "to tell you not to go home, that it wasn't safe. Just as the cab pulled up, I saw a car stop right in front with two men in it, with hats pulled down low over their faces. I didn't get a good look at them, but they were watching the restaurant. There was a third man, too, standing on the corner – a blond-haired man pretending to read a newspaper." I felt my blood run cold.

"Yes," I said, "I've seen him before. I've never seen his face, but he seems to turn up everywhere I go."

"I saw you come out of the restaurant," he said, "and all three men looked at you like you were the person they'd been waiting for. The two men started to get out of the car, and the blond man dropped his newspaper and started coming towards them, which was when I ran across the street. I thought if I made a scene, it might scare them away. And then the second I touched you, boom. Slipstream."

"How did we get separated?"

"That was my fault," said Calliope. "Carter wasn't under suspicion then. Nobody was watching him. I didn't think he'd need an evac, I assumed he would just stay in 1972. I only set the Chrono-Splice for you."

"So I arrived back on the transport platform to find a small army of our uniformed friends with the stun guns, waiting for you," he said. "They were more than a little surprised to lock onto you and get me instead. I got a little bit of a shakedown – very light, nothing like Calliope's," he hastened to explain as he saw the look on my face.

"I'm fine. I'm really fine. They didn't even use stun rods, just fists. A broken nose was the worst of it. I finally convinced them that I was who I said I was – a high-level research Embed who had been given the same cover story about your mission in 1972 that everyone else got. I said that Agent Bellows was there on a research mission about the evolving roles of women at the White House, that I had been tasked with briefing her on domestic service, and that when I had arrived at the Chinese restaurant where she had asked to meet me, I was force-jumped with her the moment we shook hands"

"And believe me, my surprise at you not landing right next to me was very real. They eventually realized I had no idea where you were. So they slapped me around a little bit, revoked my security credentials, told me the Bureau was closed pending investigation, and sent me home. Calliope came to my parents' house and found me, and then we tracked down Leo."

"All done," said Calliope, and I looked down at my shoulder. I was relieved to see, now that it was all cleaned up, that the gash wasn't nearly as huge as it had seemed when it was covered in blood. There was nothing left but a neat row of precise, tiny stitches, only about three inches long.

"I owe you one," I said.

"Just be careful with it," she said. "It will be sore for awhile."

"Fortunately, we have a few days of downtime," said Leo. I rose and went over to the far corner of the room where there was a huge, real Christmas tree, festooned with a hodgepodge of ornaments I recognized from my childhood, along with some decidedly amateurish strands of fresh cranberries and paper garland and other handmade ornaments. I went to inspect the tree more closely, then turned back to Leo.

"You made glitter pinecones," I said, my tone slightly accusatory.

"Well, yes."

"Glitter. Pinecones."

"It was Carter's idea."

"I was running from my life from armed guards and you were just hanging out here, drinking apple cider and *making glitter pinecones.*"

Leo and Carter looked at each other.

"We ran through many different scenarios where you might be mad at us about something," said Leo. "We didn't cover pinecones."

"Everyone stop yelling about pinecones," said Calliope. "Reggie, where's the Gemstone file?"

"In my bag," I said, gesturing. "Help yourself." She rifled through my purse until she found it, then pulled it out and kissed it fervently.

"Hello gorgeous," she said. "I'm so happy to see you." She took it over to a digital projection port near the wall, plugged it in, and instantly an air-screen materialized in front of the fireplace, projecting Carstairs' Gemstone files in front of her.

"She'll be dead to the world for the next four hours," said Leo. "I'm going to go start on dinner." He made his way over to a marble-topped kitchen island that faced out into the rest of the great room and began pulling out pots and pans, leaving me alone with Carter.

"Why isn't this place being watched?" I asked him. "Gray, Yasmina, somebody would have known where my mom's safe house was. Or been able to trace it. There'd be real estate sales records, she'd have driven out here before, they could find it through her tracker. How is it possible nobody's found it in all this time?"

"Because her tracker's never been here," said Carter. "That's the brilliant part."

"What do you mean?"

"This wasn't her safe house," said Carter. "It was his. Leo Carstairs built this place thirty years ago. Nobody ever knew about it but the two of them. And after the Bureau switched from wrist Comm trackers – which could be removed – to subdermal ones, she never came back."

"Carstairs never had a subdermal tracker," I said, realizing. "They implemented those after he died."

Nice work, Mom, I thought approvingly. I had learned about all of this in school and completely forgotten it. One of the security measures implemented in the aftermath of my dad's death was the costly (and painful) embedded tracking system, based on the supposition that Carstairs might have survived the Sharpeville Massacre if his equipment hadn't failed.

Mom had received the information with disdain – "A subdermal tracker wouldn't have made Colin Daisey good at his job" had been her response – but the fact remained that during the entirety of my father's career, he had never been assigned a tracker that could not be removed at will. If no registered agent had been in this house for twenty-five years, then it meant nobody in the Bureau knew it was here.

Which meant those guards with guns hunting for me didn't either. It was the perfect hideout.

"This is insane, I hope you all realize that," I said to Carter. "You've been holed up in this house for a year and a half. I saw you like two hours ago or something, we went into the Slipstream at the same time, and you beat me home by *a year and a half.*"

"That's about the size of it, yes."

I wasn't sure why I felt so guilty – it wasn't like I had known about the Chrono-Splice, obviously, and I could hardly be upset about it when it had clearly saved my life – but they had all been busy keeping the Gemstone investigation alive, hiding from the authorities and even being tortured, while I was stuck in the Slipstream for what felt like five minutes. Thank God I was bringing them helpful information or I would have felt completely useless.

"You're reproaching yourself for something, aren't you?" he said, smiling.

"I feel badly," I said. "I can't believe you sat in this house for a year and a half just waiting for the Gemstone file."

"You idiot," he said. "I've been in this house for a year and a half, waiting for you."

There was something in the way he said "I" and not "we" that I wasn't quite sure how to respond to. So I took the safe route and just said "oh, shut up" and walked away to join Calliope in front of the screen where she was taking notes. I heard both Carter and Leo laughing as I walked away.

CHAPTER THREE

BOUGHS OF HOLLY

Our family Christmases tended to be fairly low-key affairs. Usually Mom and I went to visit Leo, who would cook us a big dinner on Christmas Eve and a big brunch the next day – while attempting to prevent us from arguing – and then we'd be back at our desks on the 26th.

But Carter came from a big family who took Christmas very seriously, and had appointed himself the master of ceremonies for the occasion. The tree had been his idea, he told me, and on one of Leo's many secret trips out here, hauling documents and equipment from Mom's condo, Carter made him dig out the Christmas stuff too.

There were four stockings hanging up by the fire – mine and Leo's, made decades ago by our grandmother on the Carstairs side, and two crocheted ones which Carter had apparently made for himself and Calliope.

"He's been driving me insane," said Calliope, nodding towards Carter as she scrolled through the Gemstone documents on the projector screen. "We made cranberry garlands. We sang carols. Did you notice that the whole room smells like a grandma's house? He did a thing with a pot of water and some cinnamon sticks and sliced apple."

"It smells good," I said.

"That's not the point," she said. "The point is that I've been trapped in this house with Santa Claus and Julia Child for a month now with no escape. It's so – *festive*," she shuddered.

"A little Christmas cheer will do your cold dead heart some good, Calliope."

"I like Christmas!" she said defensively. "I have no problem with Christmas! But I draw the line at trying to work in a house that's a hundred and seven degrees inside because Carter's teaching Leo how to make quince jam."

"What the hell is a quince?"

"*This is what I'm saying*," she exclaimed. "God, I'm glad you're here."

"I'm glad I'm here too," I said. "Thank you."

"Anytime."

"No, I mean it," I said, and she turned to me, looking me in the eye for the first time since I had walked into the house earlier that day. "Thank you," I said again. "You saved my life. And you risked your own to do it. What they did to you—"

"It's okay," she said. "It was a long time ago."

"What does Grove think about what happened?" I said. "About you being hurt, I mean. He must have seen it."

"Grove never came back," she said.

"What do you mean, he never came back?"

"He was still on medical leave when your mom went missing," she said. "There was a thing with his heart. Something to do with the long-term effects of the Incongruity. They wouldn't take him back on active duty. I don't know if he's formally retired, exactly, but he never came back to the office after you brought him back from Ohio. I was warned never to contact him again."

"So you haven't seen him since the investigation?"

She shook her head, and blinked back tears, which she attempted to conceal by turning her attention back to the screen. I felt sad, and angry.

Calliope had done nothing wrong except work hard and be excellent at her job for years, and the Bureau had rewarded her for it by treating her like a criminal, torturing her, taking her job away, and – the part I knew she felt the most keenly, even more than the flogging – keeping her from the side of the man she had devoted her entire career to. Grove wasn't just her boss, he was her mentor and her North Star. That she was prevented from even visiting him in the hospital felt like the cruelest blow of all.

"We're going to fix this," I said. "We're going to make it right."

"I know," she said. "I know."

Carter bounded down the stairs just then, carrying an armful of boxes wrapped in shiny paper, and that was the first time I noticed that the tree in the corner had piles of presents underneath it.

"Did you really all get each other presents?"

"There're presents for you here too," said Carter.

"But I didn't get you guys anything. Although, in my defense, that's because yesterday I was in the middle of July."

"You brought the Gemstone file," he said. "That's the best gift in the whole bunch. But if it makes you feel better, you can put it under the tree when Calliope's done with it. I think I have some ribbon left over."

"You are ridiculous."

"He's making up for lost time," said Calliope absently. "Last Christmas pretty much sucked." Then she stopped short, realizing what she had said. Leo looked up from the stove. Carter paused halfway down the stairs. It took me a second to piece together why they were all acting so strange.

It had been August in my time when Mom sent me back to 1972. When she came to give me the Gemstone file, she had already been gone for two months, so it was sometime in late October or early November. It wasn't hard to imagine why none of them felt particularly festive last Christmas – with me stuck in the Slipstream for another year, Mom newly missing, the investigation at its height.

Leo was being watched; Calliope was being flogged; Carter was in hiding. They would have been frightened. They would have been alone.

"It's not fair," I said to them all. "It's not fair that all these things happened to you, and I wasn't there to stop it."

"There was never anything you could have done," said Leo. "You would have been arrested. You know that. You'd be in jail for treason right now and we'd never see you again. You can't protect us from this. Neither could Mom. That's not a failure on your part. That's just reality."

"I know that," I said, "but I still feel—"

"Look," said Calliope. "You can choose, if you want, to keep feeling guilty about the things that happened to us, as though they were all somehow your fault. You can do that, if you feel like it. Or you can do what the rest of us have done and let it make you stronger."

"These scars," she said, indicating her back, "that's what keeps me going when I get frustrated and tired. I know the face of the man who did this to me. But I don't know the face of the person who made him do it, the person whose orders he was following."

"And I know, without a shadow of a doubt, that when we find out who orchestrated Gemstone and who planted the Chronomaly that started the war, we will also know who manipulated the Congressional Committee into shutting down the Bureau to keep from getting caught. And I am very, very interested in finding out who that person is. That's the meaning I give these scars. If you need to feel something about them, feel anger, not guilt."

"Go easy on her," said Carter gently. "Don't forget, she only found out about Gemstone twenty-four hours ago."

And I realized with a shock that he was right. It hadn't even been a full day. Mom had arrived in the middle of the night, then the next morning we had split up, Carter to Short-Hop to Election Day and me to go see Detective Barlow. Then that evening I had gone to meet with Woodward and Bernstein, and been force-jumped away the second their backs were turned.

There's a big difference between spending years studying the intricate complexities of Chrono-Interference and experiencing a rift in the Timeline of your own life. One day had passed for me, including a period of just a few minutes that I had been stuck inside the Slipstream. When I emerged on the other side, everything in my world was eighteen months older.

I had seen my mother twenty-four hours ago. She had not seen me for a year and a half. Both of these things were simultaneously true.

I leaned my head against the back of the couch and closed my eyes.

"Let her sleep a little," I heard Carter say. "Dinner won't be ready for a few hours anyway. She needs a break."

"We don't have a lot of time, Carter," said Calliope.

"We have time for this," he said firmly. "We're going to have dinner tonight. We're going to have Christmas tomorrow. Gemstone can wait. And in the meantime, Reggie has lost a ton of blood and has just found out that a year has been taken out of her life, so I think she's earned a nap, don't you?"

I wanted to thank him, but I found that opening my eyes or sitting up had suddenly become impossible, as had forming coherent sounds. So I simply mumbled something unintelligible and curled my feet up on the sofa underneath me. Someone, I don't know who, spread a soft thick blanket over me, and that was the last thing I remembered.

∼

I slept heavily, and dreamed strange dark dreams of being trapped inside the Slipstream. Sometimes I was reaching out for Carter, sometimes Grove, sometimes my father.

I dreamed of Saturn, crashing down from the sky towards me, spinning a million miles an hour, its rings transformed into murderous whirling blades. I dreamed of Mars, staring down at me with its angry red eye. I heard my mother's voice and frantically tried to run through the thick darkness towards her, but it was like swimming through molasses. My limbs were drowsy and I wasn't strong enough to push through to find her.

I heard Leo's voice suddenly – not calling my name, like my mother was, but speaking in a normal voice, and I followed it like a beacon back into the light.

As I eased back into wakefulness, eyes still closed, I smelled rosemary and roasted meats and the comforting, ancient scent of a wood fire in a brick fireplace. At some point, Calliope had vacated the couch and I had stretched out my legs into the space she had left; I heard her behind me, in the kitchen, talking to Leo. They weren't talking about anything in particular – he seemed to have recruited her assistance with stirring something on the stove and was criticizing her technique – but the very ordinariness of their conversation was the most wonderful thing I had experienced in ages.

This was all a temporary reprieve, I knew; a way to keep me out of the city while those black-uniformed guards with guns hunted high and low for the fugitive who had snuck through the Slipstream right under their noses. We were all on borrowed time. But for now, for this moment – lying on the couch and breathing in the woodsy scents of fireplace and Christmas tree – I felt entirely at peace.

Footsteps came down the stairs and I heard Carter's voice. "Is she awake yet?"

"No," said Calliope.

"Yes," I said.

"Welcome back, Sleeping Beauty," called Leo from the kitchen. "Come set the table."

"I'm too comfortable," I murmured sleepily. "It's nice here."

"Dinner's almost ready," he said. "Get off your ass and come help."

I dragged myself up from the couch, moving as slowly as possible to proclaim that I was only doing this under duress. They were all busy in the kitchen, however, and nobody noticed.

There was a stack of plates, silverware and real cloth napkins sitting on the kitchen counter, along with glasses for wine and water. Someone – presumably Carter, the Sugarplum Fairy –

had placed small pine boughs in a ring on the surface of the table, with little white candles in little glass cups interspersed around them, like a deconstructed modernist Advent wreath. It was lovely against the gleaming dark wood of the table, and I took extra care in setting the plates and napkins with perfect symmetry to do it justice.

Carter passed by me with two bottles of wine he'd retrieved from some other room, and nodded approvingly at my handiwork.

"I'm so glad we have a professional chef and butler on hand," said Calliope, carrying a pitcher of water to the table and setting it on an intricately carved wooden trivet. "This is much classier than my usual style."

"This is just a regular Wednesday for Carter," I said dryly, watching him open the wine and pour a precisely even amount in each glass.

"Even I can't roast a chicken like your brother can roast a chicken," said Carter.

"You're coming along," said Leo encouragingly. "Carter made all the sides."

"No he did *not*," snapped Calliope. "He did not make *all* the sides. There were three of us in that kitchen this morning, Leo Christopher Bellows."

"I'm so sorry," said Leo. "Carter made all the sides except for the rolls, which Calliope took out of the packaging and put into that lovely bowl herself."

"Thank you," said Calliope, mollified, and they grinned at each other.

There was a small part of me – I was ashamed of it, I admit, but it was there – that felt a pang of jealousy at the easy rapport the three of them had built without me. I felt guilty about it, because I knew what the last eighteen months had cost them, and I was glad they had all found each other. But the three of them had become a family in some way that didn't quite feel like it included me.

And besides that, there was something in the air from time to time between Leo and Calliope that made me cognizant for the first time that Calliope was very attractive and Leo was very attractive and they were both single and very close to the same age. There was something about this collision of my worlds that was comforting and disorienting at the same time; there were no circumstances in which it would ever have occurred to me that Leo and Calliope would have become friends – or that I would ever see Carter and Leo cooking dinner together. And yet here they were, a cozy little family with their own private jokes.

Then Carter motioned for me to sit, and took the seat next to me, and smiled at me with such joyous delight – that I was here, that we were all together, that Leo was bringing a gorgeous roast chicken surrounded by potatoes to the table on an elegant silver tray, and that the others had clearly allowed him to have his way on every single matter pertaining to the proper observation of the Christmas holidays – that all jealousy was forgotten.

How could I resent them for bonding together like this? How could I feel left out when the thing that connected them was that they were all waiting for me?

Leo set down the chicken with a dramatic flourish as Calliope followed him with a heavy stoneware casserole dish of crispy Brussel sprouts flecked with almonds and bacon, and a plate of sliced blood oranges with shaved fennel. He pulled out a carving knife but Carter stopped him.

"Wait," he said. "Before we eat—"

"Oh my God," I said to him. "If you make us all go around

the table and say one thing we're grateful for I will literally murder you with this spoon."

"Before we eat," he continued, ignoring me, "let's all go around the table and say one thing we're grateful for."

"It's not Thanksgiving," said Calliope.

"Reggie wasn't here for Thanksgiving," said Carter.

"Fine," I said irritably. "I'm grateful Calliope has secret powers and fixed my shoulder, I'm grateful for naps, I'm grateful not to be eating protein bars, and I'm grateful I'm not dead. Pass the rolls please."

"I'm grateful you're safe," said Calliope, entirely unexpectedly, without a trace of sarcasm in her voice, and I stopped short in the middle of reaching across her to grab the bread. "There was only about a 56% chance that the Chrono-Splice would work and for all we knew there would be armed guards with guns pointed at you the second you landed."

"I'm grateful I get to be with my sister on Christmas," said Leo. "I didn't know if I'd ever see you again."

"I'm grateful for your tracker," said Carter. "Without it, I would never have found you at that restaurant. I would never have been pulled back here. I would still be stuck in 1972 in your ransacked apartment with no idea whether you were alive or dead."

I cleared my throat. "May I have another turn?" I asked, suitably chastened, and Carter smiled at me. "I'm grateful for—" I stopped, and thought for a moment. I wanted to find something true to say. I wanted to make it count.

"I'm grateful to be alive," I said finally. "And that I don't have to do this alone."

Calliope raised her wineglass. "To Carstairs and Bellows," she said, "and to finishing the work they started."

"To Carstairs and Bellows," echoed Carter, toasting her.

"To Mom and Dad," said Leo, reaching over and clinking his glass against mine, and I could see through the tears in my eyes that his were glistening too.

~

After we had stuffed ourselves with chicken and potatoes, recovered a little, then stuffed ourselves again with a sugared-cranberry pie and glasses of brandy, Carter bid everyone goodnight and disappeared off to his room with the four stockings from the fireplace. Calliope departed soon after, taking her handheld, a second glass of brandy and the Gemstone drive to bed with her, which was probably her idea of the perfect night. I helped Leo with the dishes for awhile in amiable silence until he told me he and Carter could finish the rest in the morning.

"Are you going to bed?" I asked him.

"Not for a while, yet," he said. "I thought I'd wait up. The weather report said it might snow tonight."

"Really?"

"Really. There's a cold front moving in around midnight. Want to wait up with me?"

Staying up late at night in our pajamas to see if it would snow overnight was a grand family tradition in the Bellows household. It didn't snow very much in D.C. anymore, and it had always been a cause of great rejoicing (and freedom from school) when it did.

"Let me go put my pajamas on," I said. "I'll be back down."

"I'll come to your room," he said. "There's a balcony. We can watch from there."

"Which room is mine?" I said, grabbing my bag from the dining room table where I'd left it during Calliope's operation.

"Second on the left," he said. "Calliope is next door to you, and Carter and I are across the hall next to the bathroom."

He followed me up the stairs to my room (helpfully labeled with a sign hanging from the doorknob that said "REGGIE'S ROOM!" in Carter's handwriting, surrounded by drawings of candy canes) and watched as I opened the door.

The room was huge and white and airy, with a wall of windows to the left and French doors to the right that opened out onto a balcony with two comfortable-looking chairs. There was a big, soft-looking bed, an antique dresser and a plush, cozy carpet underfoot. But I didn't notice any of those things until much later, because I was transfixed by the sight right in front of me.

It was my evidence wall.

"We did the best we could," said Leo behind me, apologetically, as I ran my fingers in wonderment over the neatly-organized collection of documents with which they had covered the entire wall opposite the door. "Carter told me that you liked things on paper because it helped you to think. We found some stuff at Mom's house, and Calliope had your field notes on her handheld with all your reports. And then Carter rewrote everything he remembered. It's only about half of it, maybe three-quarters, but we thought it might help."

"This is incredible," I said. "Thank you. I was beginning to feel naked without it."

He watched me in silence for a few moments as I immersed myself in the wall, feeling a little more grounded, a little more confident of myself, now that I had it back.

"I helped them hang everything," he said after a moment. "They talked me through the whole thing. They were very patient with me. Calliope told me all about your job at the Bureau, how you saved your boss, how you were the one who spotted the Chronomaly before anyone else. And Carter told me all about Gemstone."

"I spent the past year following your mission. I read every piece of paper on this wall a hundred times – I would come up here and sit on the bed and just stare at it. I just kept thinking, 'That's your sister. Running from enemy agents, going undercover in the White House, spying on burglars, trying to stop a war and save fifty-six million people. That's your *sister*.' And it made me feel like I don't even really know you at all."

I put my arms around him and buried my face in shoulder.

"Come on," I said. "You know me. We shared a uterus."

"That's a good point," he kissed the top of my head. "I'm proud of you, sis," he said.

"Thank you for my evidence wall," I said. "I love it."

He left me alone to change my clothes then, and returned a few minutes later with two glasses and a bottle of brandy.

"I don't know why you always waste the good stuff on me," I said. "You remember the Chrono-Imported whiskey incident."

"I keep telling myself that someday I'll train your barbarian palate to tell the difference," he said, opening the French doors to the balcony and ushering me outside. "But for now, we're just getting drunk."

"Excellent," I said, following him outside and closing the door behind me.

We sat in silence for awhile, sipping our brandy and looking out. The balcony faced away from the street over a marshy, bracken-filled old swamp. "The security fence runs a scan every ninety seconds for vital signs and surveillance equipment," said Leo, answering my question. "Yes, we're safe out here."

"Twenty-four hours ago, my brother was making scallop risotto in Croatia," I said. "I guess I don't know you that well either. I would never have guessed that the person who showed up to rescue me from that building would have been my brother, the chef."

"Your job's a lot more dramatic than mine."

"I know," I said. "I miss when it used to be boring."

I looked over at him and felt my heart contract a little at seeing so much of Leo Carstairs in his profile. "Mom would be proud of you," I said. "So would Dad."

"You talk about him like he was a real person," he said. "I mean, like a person that you knew. You always have. I never had that. I know nothing about him."

"Yes, you do. You know everything that I know."

"He's not real to me though, not in the same way he's real to you. Like, just now, what you said. That Dad would be proud of me. You said it like you knew it was true. I couldn't say something like that. It's – I don't know – it's hard to explain."

"Try," I said. "We have all night."

"It's like history class," he said. "Or, it's like history class is for the rest of us who don't actually go inside of history. I feel like . . . I believe in Leo Carstairs the way I believe in Abraham Lincoln. Does that make sense? I know he existed, I know he was important, I know about the things that he did because I've heard about them and read about them, but I don't have a *relationship* with Leo Carstairs. We were never in the world at the same time. He was gone before we were even born. But it's not like that for you."

"No," I said, "it's not. Because every day I go to work and I'm a celebrity's kid. Everywhere I go, everyone knows that my mother is Her Majesty the famous Katie Bellows, and everyone knows that my father's death was a national tragedy, and nobody can separate me from those things. You just get to go to work and be you, Leo Bellows, a person with a job and a life. I'm Katie Bellows' daughter. That's my whole identity. And Carstairs is tied up in it too."

"You call him Carstairs as much as you call him Dad," Leo said.

"Because 'Carstairs' is how I know him," I said. "Everyone I work with, they also worked with him. I know more about what his life must have been like than you do. Everywhere I go I'm Leo Carstairs and Katie Bellows' daughter. But that's as much a burden as it is a gift, don't you see that? I'm constantly tripping over his work, Mom's work, every day. All I have to do is click on my computer screen a couple of times and there he is, all over the 20th century. I can't separate him from my life."

"Still," said Leo, "you knew. When they told you he might have been a traitor, that there was a chance he had been the one that caused all this, you knew it was wrong. You knew he would never have done that. You knew him well enough to be absolutely sure. I don't know that. I have only your word, and Mom's, that our dad wasn't a traitor. It's not like I don't trust you," he added. "But it would be nice. It would be nice to be *sure*."

"I'm sure enough for both of us," I said. "I promise."

"You're always sure enough for both of us, Reggie," he said. "That doesn't guarantee you're right."

"I'm right about this," I said, and we sat in silence for a long time, wrapped in our own thoughts, both thinking about Leo Carstairs.

"There's something I've been meaning to ask you," he said finally. "We learned a little bit in school about the founding of the Time Travel Bureau. I've been trying to remember. The scientists, the ones who invented it – what were their names?"

"Li Chidong and Martina Garcia Lopez," I said. "The first scientists to successfully master Chrono-Transit."

"Right," he said. "And they met in college. In New Washington."

"That's right," I said. New Washington was an American outpost built on the site of what had once been the northeastern corner of Beijing. It was one of the many towns in postwar China that began life as a hastily-cobbled-together heap of concrete bunkers to house the American defense contractors the government hired to rebuild the country once we annexed it.

"And without World War III," he said, "New Washington wouldn't exist. Which means they'd never meet."

"Not necessarily."

"Hang on – because if they never meet," he said, "and they never invent time travel, then there's no Time Travel Bureau. Which means no Carstairs and Bellows. Which means—"

"No us," I said slowly.

"Exactly," he said. "Aren't we, maybe, fighting to save a world where we don't even exist?"

"We might be," I said. "There's no way to know."

"How can you be so calm about that?"

"Because that's what we do," I said. "That's our job. We don't fix the Timeline to make it the way we want it. We fix it to make it *right*. The war isn't supposed to happen, which means I have to stop it."

"Even if what's really supposed to happen is worse?"

"Yeah," I said. "Even so."

"Even if it means you don't exist?"

"I mean, I definitely want to keep existing," I said. "I'm really holding out for that to be part of the plan. And I'd also very much like for *you* to keep existing."

"What if I don't?" he said. "What if after everything gets fixed, there's still a you but there isn't a me?"

"You'll still be my brother," I said.

"You won't even know I existed," he said.

"I promise you," I said to him firmly, with more confidence than I actually possessed. "We're going to stick together. We're going to get through this and we're going to find Mom. I promise, Leo. It's going to be okay."

"Look," said Leo suddenly, pointing out at the night sky. "It's snowing."

It was.

I took his hand.

~

I slept like the dead, and woke ten hours later feeling almost human again. Calliope's stitches had worked like magic; they itched, and if I wasn't careful in moving my shoulder they pulled tight, causing me to wince, but the wound was healing clean, with no redness or swelling.

I pulled on the only clean clothes I had – my favorite cotton pants and shirt that I had illegally smuggled back to 1972 with me against Mark and Mrs. Graham's wardrobe regulations – and followed the smell of nutmeg downstairs to find that everyone else was already awake. Calliope was curled up on the sofa with coffee and her handheld, while Leo and Carter made breakfast.

"She's up!" said Carter triumphantly as soon as I came into view. "You have to put it away now."

"You said I could work until breakfast," protested Calliope.

"Breakfast is ready," said Leo.

"Coffee," I mumbled at him, and he waved a hand towards the counter behind him where a fresh, steaming carafe of coffee was waiting next to a bowl of sugar and a pitcher of real cream. I poured myself a huge cup and held it up to my nose, inhaling the magical smell, and watched Carter and Leo.

They had clearly established a familiar chef/sous-chef routine, and moved comfortably around each other in the kitchen like people who were used to sharing space. It was like choreography, watching Leo pour pancake batter onto the griddle in perfect circles, move aside to let Carter move in underneath him and pull a tray of sausages out of the oven, then step back to the griddle in time to flip the pancakes.

"Calliope, put the computer away," said Carter, and she sighed, but obeyed. We sat down at the table, coffee in hand, while Leo and Carter served us gingerbread pancakes, apple-sage sausage, and berries with cream. We ate in contented silence for awhile. Carter was the only one of us who was particularly convivial in the mornings, but he respectfully restrained himself until the last dish was cleared before he forcibly shoved us over to the couch.

"Presents!" he announced, handing each of us our stockings.

"I feel like a jerk, I didn't get you guys anything," I said, but Carter waved me into silence.

"Don't be silly," he said. "You're the guest of honor. You owe us nothing."

I felt around in my stocking and pulled out three small bundles, wrapped in colorful paper. The first was from Leo, a small paper box of madeleines he'd made himself.

"These are my favorite!" I said.

"I know," he said.

"I got oatmeal walnut," said Carter happily.

"Whose favorite cookie is oatmeal walnut?" I said, staring at him.

"Don't," said Calliope, "don't get him started, for the love of God."

"What did Leo make you?" I asked her.

"Pfeffernüsse," she said, and she smiled at him. "My grandmother used to make these for me."

"Do Calliope's next!" exclaimed Carter.

"Well, they're not as exciting as oatmeal walnut cookies," she said dryly. "But I generally prefer to give practical gifts."

We each pulled out a small tissue paper bundle.

"You might as well do it at the same time," she said. "They're all the same."

"It's a key," said Carter, who had torn through his first.

"What's this for?" Leo asked curiously, looking down at his key, and she pointed to the corner of the room, where a large, ornately-carved *chinoiserie* sideboard stood.

"It's for all of us," she said, "but let Reggie have the honors."

I took my key over to the iron lock, and turned it until I heard its heavy click, then gently pulled open the double doors.

Inside the cupboard were four shelves, stacked high with neat rows of the Bureau-issue disaster-proof metal boxes agents stored tech devices in. There were boxes of all shapes and sizes.

"Your dad was a hoarder," she said. "This place was full of good stuff. We have weapons, emergency rations, Comms, Microcams, Short-Hops, scanners, everything. It's all a couple decades out of date and needed the Calliope touch, but it works."

"All of it," I said. "All of this works."

"Yep."

I turned back to her. "Just so we're clear," I said in a low voice. "When you say it needed 'the Calliope touch,' are you saying you took an entire arsenal of thirty-year-old Bureau equipment and retrofitted *every single piece* so we could use it?"

"Merry Christmas," she said.

"I can't believe you did all this," I said in wonderment. She shrugged.

"I got bored stuck in the house with these two all day, I needed something to do."

"Calliope—"

"Don't get all squishy on me," she said. "I just did my job."

"I love you, Calliope."

"Shut up."

"My turn! My turn!" exclaimed Carter, who had obviously saved himself for last on purpose. Calliope pulled a sparkling, misshapen bundle out of her stocking and Leo and I watched her open it. She delicately peeled back layers of paper to reveal a wooden square, painted white, about the size of the palm of her hand, with a ribbon running through the top of it.

"I found some wood in the basement that was still usable," he said. "I made Christmas ornaments. That's for the tree."

Leo and I peered over Calliope's shoulder and saw a delicate, remarkably skillful drawing of the Golden Gate Bridge.

"Did you draw that?" said Leo, awestruck. "That's amazing."

"She's from San Francisco," said Carter, pleased with himself. "I wanted to give everybody a little piece of home."

Calliope hugged him, quickly and fiercely and almost as though she was as surprised at it as we were, but Carter beamed. Leo opened his next, and I saw him tear up a little.

"It's the Old Harbour in Dubrovnik," he said. "This is like three streets from my apartment. Carter, thank you. This is incredible."

"Now you, Reggie," Carter said, and he watched me intently as I untied the ribbon and lifted the layers of paper away.

It was the Lincoln Memorial.

I looked at Carter.

Carter looked at me.

"To remind you," he said. "When you get scared. When you lose faith. This is so that you remember who you are."

"And who am I?" I said softly.

"You're a hero," he said. "You just don't know it yet."

CHAPTER FOUR

OMELETTES, AMONG OTHER THINGS

After much negotiation, Calliope convinced Carter to waive the no-work rule for the rest of the day, and we had our first meeting of what Leo dubbed the Un-War Council. They all knew each other's stories, of course – but I didn't know theirs and they didn't know mine.

Sitting around the dining room table with a pot of coffee and our handhelds, we began the process of filling in all the rest of the blanks. I told every detail of my sojourn through the eerily desolate Bureau, and they told me everything they had learned in my absence. Carter's powers of observation and Calliope's meticulous research were gold mines of information, but it didn't get us any closer to formulating a real plan.

"All right," I said, after we'd been discussing for hours and our brains were beginning to melt. "Let's lay our facts out. What are the things that we know?"

"We know that Gemstone was real," said Carter, "and that

all or some parts of it really occurred in the General Timeline. But it was covered up, artificially, to protect Richard Nixon and ensure that he served two full terms and ended on a high note."

"So that he could hand the reins to Reagan, and that the two of them could get us into a war with China," I added. "And that, if not Reagan, somebody high up in the White House knew those first bombs were coming long before they dropped."

"John Dean?" said Leo.

"That's my guess," I said. "But we can't be sure of that yet. He's top of my list of suspects, though."

"We also know that whoever planted the Chronomaly is either still alive and has access to the General Timeline," said Calliope, "or they have a partner who is. Not just because of the cover-up in the system, but because that rumor was calculated and deliberate. It didn't just take the whole Bureau out of commission; it discredited everyone with any knowledge of Gemstone as a traitor."

"All right," I said, as Leo poured me the last of the coffee and then took the pot back to the kitchen to refill it. "What do we *not* know? The identities of our planetary friends, obviously."

"Is there anything helpful in the code names?" asked Carter. "I mean anything about Mars and Saturn that could lead to their identities? Maybe they're not just random planets, maybe they mean something."

"I never took astronomy in school," I said.

"Neither did I. One has rings and one has an eye – I know that much, but that's it."

Calliope pulled out her handheld and tapped away.

"Mars is the second smallest and fourth from the sun," she said. "Terrestrial. Saturn is a gas giant; sixth from the sun and second largest."

"Okay, so in order from the sun they're 4 and 6," said

Carter, "and in order of size they're . . . 2 and 7? Does that mean anything?"

"Badge numbers?" suggested Calliope. "Chain of command? Ranking order?"

"Ring and eye," I said, more to myself than anyone else, turning the words over and over in my mind. "Two and seven. Four and six."

"War and time," said Leo absently as he set the coffee down in front of us, and we all stared at him. "Mars and Saturn," he explained. "The Roman gods."

"Holy shit," I said. "The names aren't planets."

"Saturn is the Roman name for Chronos," said Leo. "The god of time. And Mars was Ares."

"God of war," I said softly, feeling a chill down the back of my spine.

"That's it," said Calliope. "That's what the names mean. Mars is the ringleader, the one who started the war in the first place. Saturn is the one manipulating time to cover it up."

"That means—" Carter began, then stopped.

"No," I said. "Say it. We need to get used to saying it."

"I really want to be wrong," he said.

"I know," I said. "But I don't think you are. Saturn works for the Time Travel Bureau. Saturn is one of us."

Calliope and Carter looked uncomfortable. The room was suddenly full of things nobody wanted to say.

"The Sharpeville transcripts," I said suddenly. "He said it. Carstairs said it. He tried to tell her."

"What are you talking about?" asked Leo.

"Carstairs lost his signal in Sharpeville," I said, "but his Comm still worked. He couldn't connect to the Slipstream, but he could still record. He left an emergency transmission for Mom. She saved a copy for herself, without telling the

Bureau, before she returned all of his tech. The Bureau classified it."

"How do you know about it, then?"

"She showed it to me," I said. "I asked her once why she hated Congressman Holmes so much. She told me that there was evidence – clear evidence – that something serious had gone wrong in Sharpeville and that instead of doing his job, Holmes had let Daisey get away with murder."

Calliope tapped on her handheld screen a few times to pull up the hearing transcripts.

"She does say the word 'sabotage,'" she said. "She says that's what Carstairs thought happened."

"I don't think I ever took it that seriously," I said. "When I read the hearing transcripts for the first time, I just thought – you know, she was grieving, she was pregnant, the special prosecutor was kind of a dick—"

"You thought she kind of just went Katie Bellows on him," Leo said.

"Yeah," I said, "but what if she didn't? Jenkins mentions the trucks – Carstairs was looking at the trucks, he said there was something not right about them. He mentions it in the transmission. Something felt off to him about the second wave of police officers."

"Give me that," said Carter suddenly. He reached over to Calliope and grabbed her handheld.

"Don't get fingerprints all over the screen," she snapped. Calliope hated it when people touched her stuff. Carter ignored her.

"Here," he said. "This is what I was looking for."

"What?"

"CARSTAIRS: 'Sir, someone did this. This was deliberate. These people were manipulated,'" he read. My blood went cold.

"CARSTAIRS: 'I think there's another agent in the field, sir.'"

"CARSTAIRS: 'Due respect, sir, something is off here. I'm in a Flexible Timeline and somebody is messing with it. Someone is trying to turn a peaceable protest into a mob and I want to know who, and why.'"

"Another agent," said Calliope softly. "Leo Carstairs was killed by someone from the Bureau."

I got up to pour myself a glass of water, suddenly unable to keep still or to bear their eyes on me. The room was silent for a long time.

"What about Mars?" asked Calliope suddenly. "If we follow the same logic, that Saturn is someone inside the Bureau manipulating time, then the question is: Who's the one manipulating the war?"

"Well, who benefited the most from the war?" asked Carter. "Who gained from it? That's the part I can't quite put my finger on. It doesn't make any sense."

"There's a lot about this war that doesn't make sense," said Calliope gloomily.

"Like why they didn't use nukes," said Leo absently, reaching across the table for the sugar bowl.

I stared at him.

"Say that again," I said quietly.

"What?"

"What you just said."

"Oh," he said. "It's not anything important. It's just one of those things they never teach you in regular-person history class, and I always wondered. Do you know?"

"Know what?" asked Calliope.

"Why neither side used nuclear weapons. It always seemed weird to me. We both had them, for Christ's sake, why not use them? Or threaten to, at the very least? Isn't that way easier? I mean, either side could have sent over a couple fighter jets loaded with nukes, then called the other one and said, 'Hey, look up in the sky! See that? All right, let's talk.' They'd get anything they wanted, no bloodshed required. But fifty-six million people? All those cities firebombed and leveled to the ground? I mean, it's not just sick and sad, it's . . . *bad strategy*."

Finally he noticed us staring at him. "What?" he asked, in genuine bafflement. "What did I say?"

"Hang on," I said. "Nobody say anything. Nobody move. It's coming to me." I closed my eyes. *Breathe, Reggie,* I told myself sternly. *Think. Don't push. The answer will come.*

I repeated it over and over in my head.

Why didn't *they use nuclear weapons?*

Why had I never asked myself this before?

Mars, god of war, I said to myself. *Who is the god of war? Not in Greece, not in Rome, but here. 22ⁿᵈ-century America. Who is Mars here?*

And then I knew.

"What's the biggest difference," I said slowly, "between a city that's been bombed by nuclear weapons and a city that's been bombed by regular explosives?"

"Given the same blast radius, same degree of force?" asked Carter.

"Yes."

"Radiation, obviously," said Calliope. "If City A is mined and City B is nuked, they'll both be crushed to rubble but City A won't be poisoned."

"So why would you destroy a city, and kill all the inhabitants, the slow and tedious way, just to prevent irradiating the area? Who gains by that?" asked Leo.

"Whoever rebuilds the city," I said, and the others stared at me. "I know who started this war," I said. "I know who flogged Calliope and I know who planted the Chronomaly and I know who is guarding the Bureau and I know why they didn't use nuclear weapons,"

I was breathless with excitement. "I don't know how we'll ever prove it," I said. "I don't know if this helps at all. I still don't know their faces. But I'm right. I know I'm right."

"For God's sake, Reggie, just tell us."

"It's so simple," I said. "Who built the new cities in China on top of the ruins of the old ones after we annexed the country? Who owns half the members of the Congressional Time Travel Committee and a third of the Senate besides? Who has access to every piece of security equipment owned by the Bureau and runs their own under-the-table, unregulated private militia? Who sold us all those subdermal trackers, for Christ's sake?"

"Oh my God," said Carter.

"Oh no," whispered Calliope. "No, no, no."

"Yes," I said. "The person with the most to gain by artificially creating this war wasn't a person at all. It was *United Enterprises.*"

～

Once we knew what we were looking for, suddenly we could spot signposts everywhere. United Enterprises was founded in the mid-20th century as a small Georgetown family business that ostensibly specialized in electronics repair but actually did a brisk side business in manufacturing surveillance equipment.

They were notoriously secretive, and public records on the company were vague and difficult to find, but Calliope was the best in the business for a reason. She sat us down an hour and a half later and took us to school on the origins of the U.E. corporate empire.

"They started out running the manufacturing end out of a back room, dealing mostly with private investigators, criminals and the kind of clients who tended to pay in cash," she said, reading to us from her piles of notes.

She went on. "Then in the seventies, there's some inference that they may have come to the attention of somebody in the federal government, and the company just exploded, seemingly overnight. They billed themselves as sort of an all-purpose security service for high-end private clients, providing everything from personal guards with military-grade training to sophisticated alarm systems to wiretaps."

"And, eventually, weapons. Not manufacturing, not to start out with, but sales. And they just kept growing. By the end of Nixon's second term, they were juggling multi-million-dollar government contracts, handling everything from eavesdropping devices for the CIA to security personnel for embassies."

"What about after the war?" asked Carter.

"They took a hit financially," said Calliope, "like everyone did – but it was a remarkably small one, considering. They were an odd choice for the Chinese rebuilding projects. They didn't have any real expertise in construction – I imagine they subcontracted most of it out – but the funding went through them, and they managed it."

"So within like thirty-odd years," I said, "these guys went from building wiretaps out of tinfoil to basically owning every building in occupied China."

"And it just kept growing from there," she said. "They invested early in helping build the Time Travel Bureau, and they've always got at least one retired agent on their Board of

Directors. It's a symbiotic relationship at this point. Practically every piece of tech you own was made by them. Which means much of it is, or can be, *controlled* by them."

"If we can prove that United Enterprises was connected to the Watergate break-in," I said, "It links them to Gemstone and to the cover-up, which links them to the war."

"A war they profited from to an alarming degree," said Leo.

"Exactly," I said. "Saturn is the Bureau. Mars is United Enterprises."

"We have to get our hands on those police photos," Carter said. "If we could prove that U.E. manufactured wiretaps and provided them to the Watergate burglars for the purposes of sabotaging the 1972 election, that's the ballgame. We win."

"But prove it to *who*?" I said. "Who would believe us? U.E. has taken over that whole building. They've shut the Bureau down. The Director is gone, the agents are gone. They're all under house arrest and being investigated as criminals."

"Not all of them," said Calliope, a sudden realization dawning on her face. We all stopped and stared at her.

"You said every agent in the building was arrested," I reminded her, puzzled. She grinned at me.

"Every agent in the building *was*," she said, and I stared at her for a second before the penny dropped, and I laughed in delight.

"Of course," I said. *"Grove."*

"He was out on medical leave the whole time," she said, "so he was in the clear. They may have asked him some questions about your parents as part of the investigation, but they knew he could never have been in contact with you or your mother because he never came back to the office. That means he's the only agent who was never a suspect. If Harold Grove went public with proof that the war was a Chronomaly started by United Enterprises, everyone would believe him."

"I can't believe I didn't think of that," I said.

Calliope laughed. "I can't believe *I* didn't," she said. "I was warned not to make contact with him, so I stayed away. He was at Sweethaven when your mom went on the run, and as far as I know, he's still there."

"What's Sweethaven?" asked Leo.

"It's a very posh sort of convalescent facility for Bureau agents," I said. "Like a combination rest home, hospital and retirement center. They specialize in time travel-related illness and injuries –Slipstream radiation poisoning, that kind of thing."

"It has two very strong points in its favor," said Calliope. "One, it's only a few hours' drive from here. And two—"

"Oh my God," I said, realizing what she was about to say before she said it. "Sweethaven has its own transport lab."

"That's right," she said. "If we can get in to see Grove, we can get back to 1972 to get the proof we need."

"But for who?" said Carter. "The Congressional Time Travel Committee was disbanded when the Bureau was. They're all under suspicion too."

"Benjamin Holmes," I said suddenly, and they all stared at me.

"As in Congressman Benjamin Holmes of the Sharpeville Hearings?" said Carter incredulously. "*That* Benjamin Holmes? The one who let Colin Daisey get away with the death of your dad?"

"He was there," I said. "He was in the meeting with Mom and Gray, when we realized the war was a Chronomaly. He believed it. I don't think he and Mom like each other at all, but I think he trusts her. And, most importantly, he was never on the Time Travel Committee. He's House Intelligence."

"And anyway, we know now that the results of that hearing

weren't his fault. Of course he didn't find anything on Daisey. U.E. made sure that he wouldn't. No, I think if we went to Congressman Holmes with the truth about what really happened to Leo Carstairs – if we had Grove's backing, if we could *prove* it – I think he'd be more than happy to take the case on. Hell, I think he'd shut down United Enterprises himself."

"So let me get this straight," said Leo. "We need to break into a highly-secured government medical facility, convince the only agent who hasn't been dragged into this investigation to dive into it voluntarily, then hack into their transport lab to send one of you back to 1972 to pick up some police evidence that you hope – but don't know – will implicate the largest and most powerful corporation in the world, and pray that Grove can get it in front of the House of Representatives before they find him and have him shot."

I looked at Carter. Carter looked at Calliope. Calliope looked at me. We all nodded.

"Oh," said Leo, "well, if *that's* all . . ." And he looked like he might have been about to pass out.

"First things first," I said to him. "We'll figure out a plan for all of this, but breakfast was hours ago and I'm starving. Leo, you'll feel calmer after you've cooked something. Carter, keep him from losing it, will you? Calliope, we need a Comm link. I have to be able to contact Detective Barlow from here."

"What are you going to do?"

"I'm going to make another pot of coffee," I said, "and figure out how I'm going to get into Sweethaven without, you know, getting shot on sight."

"Good plan," said Carter. "Come on, Leo, let's make omelettes. You'll feel better after we make omelette." He put his arm around Leo and led him to the kitchen.

After half an hour or so, bored with watching Calliope tinker around on her handheld, I made my way over to the kitchen where the boys were cooking and watched them work while I drank my five hundredth cup of coffee.

Carter minced shallots with a brisk gracefulness, then passed the cutting board to Leo so he could scrape them into a sizzling pan. There was bacon in another pan, chopped up small and cooked to dark crunchy bits, and as I watched, Carter pulled a bowl of pale green rings out of the sink, where it had been draining, and passed it to Leo.

"What's that?"

"They're leeks," said Leo. "For omelettes."

"Leeks?" I said. "When did we become fancy people who eat leeks?"

"Fancy? You mean *civilized*?"

"Where the hell did you even *find*—"

"What the hell is your problem with leeks?"

"Where the hell did you even find leeks in Bailey's Crossroads, Virginia?"

"I'm sorry, I know you'd be happier if we were all just standing around in our underwear eating protein bars over the sink, but *some* of us —"

"Everybody shut up, I got it," called Calliope from the living room, and we all shut up.

"Got what?" I asked, moving over closer to the couch so I could see her handheld screen over her shoulder.

"A Chrono-Spliced Comm link," she said. "Undetectable from within the system, on both sides."

I kissed the top of her head.

"You're a miracle worker," I said. "I adore you."

"What does that mean?" asked Leo from the kitchen, still sautéing away.

"It means we can make a 20th-century telephone call through Calliope's computer," said Carter. "An untraceable one. It means we can set up a meet with Barlow and make sure he still has the photos. Nice work, Calliope."

"Oh, this is gonna be fun," I said, climbing up next to Calliope on the couch.

"I've set it for two hours after you left the meet with him," she said. "You're going to tell him you're coming in tomorrow for the photos."

"Got it," I said. "I'm ready when you are."

"You're live in ten," she said. "The rest of you shut up. Reggie has to do her Katie Bellows impression and she can't screw this up."

I heard a click and the voice of a switchboard operator.

"Detective Barlow, please," I said sweetly.

"Detective Barlow is unavailable at the moment, may I ask who's calling?"

"It's Calliope Burns," I said. "And believe me, he's going to want to take this call."

"Will he know what this is in reference to?"

"Oh yes," I said. "He most emphatically will. Go get him, please."

"But he asked us not to—"

"*Now*," I said, as sternly as I could muster, averting my eyes from the sight of Carter and Leo in the kitchen, collapsed in helpless, silent giggles. I heard her set down the receiver and walk away.

"Shut it," Calliope hissed at the boys. "No cackling in the background."

"Sorry!" whispered Leo. I waved him into silence as I heard footsteps in the background. I took a deep breath and thought about my mother. What would Katie Bellows do?

"Agent Burns," said Detective Barlow's voice, polite but annoyed. "So sorry to keep you waiting."

"Then next time, don't," I said frostily, and Carter nodded approvingly.

"I wanted to apologize again for—"

"Save it," I said. "I'm not interested in your excuses. What I need to know is, when I come back tomorrow to pick up another set of those photos, will they actually be there waiting for me, or will yet another enemy agent be strolling around town with classified information that the Bureau somehow can't manage to get its hands on?"

"Tomorrow?" he said.

"Yes. I'm assuming you have the ability to reproduce a set of photos given an entire twenty-four hours to do so. Or should I just take the originals down to the Fotomat and hand over confidential evidence to the teenager in a polo shirt behind the counter and see if he can do your job better than you can?"

"I . . . there's no need for . . . Agent Burns, I assure you, I . . . there's—"

"Yes, that's very well put," I said in a lofty voice, turning my back away from the kitchen, where Carter and Leo were doubled over in soundless laughter. "But be that as it may, what I need from you is your assurance that you will have a set of photos ready to place in my hand – mine only, Detective Barlow, absolutely no one else's – and that you will tell no one else about this conversation. Can I trust you with those two extremely simple tasks?"

There was a sullen, grumbly silence before he finally muttered, "Of course, ma'am."

"Good," I said. "I'll see you tomorrow."

"What time should I expect you?" he said.

I looked at Calliope. Calliope looked at me. We hadn't

figured that part of it out yet. *What should I tell him?* I mouthed to her. She shrugged, *I don't know, make something up.*

"I don't know," I said, then caught myself. "I mean . . . my schedule is exceptionally crowded and I can't possibly make any guarantees. It could be any time."

"You're asking me to sit around the police station with an envelope all day long and you can't even tell me when you might possibly be coming by to get it?"

"Yes," I said. "That is what I'm telling you. And unless you want me to tell . . ." (I paused, thinking; *Hanson,* Calliope mouthed at me, and I nodded gratefully) ". . . *Hanson* about your little scam with falsely arresting my friend Kitty to pocket an extra fine in cash, you'll do it."

"Tomorrow, then," he said irritably.

"Tomorrow. Don't screw this up, Barlow."

And then I nodded at Calliope, who clicked twice and the line disconnected.

Free of the encumbering restraints of silence, Carter and Leo burst into hysterical peals of laughter.

"Oh man," said Leo. "Oh man. That was a badass Mom impression."

"I could have listened to him fumble around for like nine more hours," said Carter. "I really could. It was glorious."

"Nice work," said Calliope. "You're really getting into character. A masterful performance."

"So we did it," said Leo. "The photos will be there."

"Yeah," said Carter, "now we just need a way into Sweethaven so we can actually send Reggie back to get them. Any brilliant ideas yet?" he said, turning to me.

"Well," I began slowly, looking at the boys as the traces of a plan clicked together in my head.

"It's not as easy as all that," Calliope jumped in. "Unless

you've forgotten about the part where she's a fugitive on the run from a global corporation with eyes on the ground in two different centuries looking for her. And me. And you. She can't just waltz in there and say, 'Hello boys, I'm here for your transporter.' We need to assume that U.E. has access to the Bureau's entire personnel database. Any one of us could be spotted."

"So how do we get in unrecognized?" asked Leo, sliding a spatula under the flawless bacon-and-leek omelette in his pan and gently setting it on a plate before looking up to realize I was staring at him.

"I do have a way in," I said, and suddenly I had Carter and Calliope's attention too, "but I'm pretty sure you're not going to like it."

"What is it?" he asked.

"Send in the only person in this room who *isn't* in the Bureau's personnel database," I said, and the spatula clattered out of Leo's hand and onto the counter.

"Why don't I finish this one," said Carter, gently shoving Leo out of the way and into the living room towards me and picking up the omelette pan. Leo's face was still expressionless.

"You can't be serious, Reggie," he said finally. "I mean you can't actually be serious."

"Give me another option, then," I said, and he was silent. "Leo, this is the only way."

"I'm not *you*, Reggie, I can't do this."

"You've done it already," I said. "You did it for a year and a half. You got me out of that building. I'd still be trapped there if it weren't for you. You're on the team. You're in this."

"That was different," he said. "I wasn't actually lying. I mean I wasn't hiding anything. I told them I didn't know where you were because I *didn't* know where you were. I would park outside the Bureau and they'd search me and I'd tell them there was nothing in the car because there *was* nothing in the car. I told the truth for so long that they just stopped asking, so by the time I had to actually smuggle you out of that building underneath my coat, they didn't even look in the back seat."

"That was different." He paused, then went on. "That, I could do. This is, what, marching up to an armed guard in front of a medical facility and lying to his face to get let in? And then somehow convincing Grove to trust me? Who, by the way, I don't think I've seen since we were like ten years old and used to come to the office with Mom after school, so how the hell does *Grove* know I'm one of the good guys?"

"You'll have a Comm with you," I said, "and as soon as you're inside, you'll turn it on and Calliope and I will explain everything. All we need you to do, Leo, is get the Comm to Grove."

"Oh, that's it?" he snapped. "That's *all*?"

"Leo—"

"God, you say that like it's so easy," he said, frustrated. "It's not easy for the rest of us. Our mom went missing and left me some cryptic instructions I could barely understand, and then these two show up and say, 'Oh, by the way, your sister is stuck in a time warp, you need to figure out a way to get inside the building, but not until *next Christmas,* and by the way we don't know if Reggie is alive or dead but we're in charge of erasing an entire war from history to save fifty-six million people,' and there are spies chasing you in two different centuries, and to top it all off, apparently they *murdered our dad*."

Carter, behind him, picked up the two plated omelettes, gave Calliope a look, and left the room. She followed him wordlessly upstairs. I held out my hand to Leo, and he came over to sit down on the couch next to me. I pulled my feet up underneath me and curled into the side of his body. He put his arm around me and I rested my head on his shoulder. We sat like that for a few minutes in silence.

"Our mom is missing," he said. "Our dad is dead. Me and you, we're all we have."

"I know."

"No part of this is normal. You can't be pissed at me for not being ready to turn into a government super-spy at a moment's notice. I didn't go to school for this, like you did. I went to public school, with the regular kids. I learned everything that regular kids learn about the 20th century – about Nixon, about Reagan, about World War III."

"You're all experts. I'm not. Calliope, she just has to *look* at a piece of computer equipment and it does her bidding. Carter is an encyclopedia of knowledge about the presidency. You and Mom, you spent years of your lives becoming experts on Richard Nixon."

He sighed. "I didn't do any of that. I wait tables and clean fish and sign purchase orders and manage bar staff. Do you need me to do that? Do you need me to make goulash? Do you need me to hire and fire employees? If you need an informational lecture on Old Town Dubrovnik, I can do that; the historical society guided tour stops right underneath my living room window on Mondays, so that one I can do. But this world is yours. Yours and Mom's. It isn't mine. I don't belong here."

"Exactly," I said. "You're from the outside. So you see things from a different point of view. You keep catching things the rest of us miss."

I added, "Me and Carter and Calliope, sometimes we can't see the forest for the trees. You're the only person in this house who figured out what Mars and Saturn meant. You're the only one who ever thought to ask why World War III wasn't fought with nuclear weapons. And you're the only one who could have gotten me out of that building yesterday. It's *because* you're not inside the Bureau. It's *because* you've lived this whole other life. You see things the rest of us can't. We need you, Leo. *I* need you."

We sat in silence for awhile, lost in thought, before the rumbling of my stomach alerted me to the fact that Carter and Calliope were the only ones who had gotten lunch.

"Oh," he said. "Crap. You didn't get an omelette. No, don't get up, I'll make one."

"I want to watch you do it," I said. "Show me."

He went back over to the kitchen and I followed, hopping up to sit on the kitchen counter and look down at him while he worked.

"Talk me through it," I said.

"Step one is to have the filling ready," he said, and I watched the tension leave his face as he began pulling the ingredients back together. We were back in the world that he knew. "An omelette only takes about thirty seconds to cook all the way through, so whatever is going inside of it has to be prepared beforehand and waiting for you."

"Step two is prepping the eggs." He pulled over a glass bowl full of golden liquid, wonderfully flecked with visible chunks of black pepper, and scooped out a small amount. "An omelette for one person only takes about two or three eggs. Any more and it takes too long to cook and turns leathery. This is as much as you want."

"And then you add a little milk, and some salt and pepper. Not too much salt, since there's bacon in the filling. And Carter added some thyme and chives." He sliced a generous pat of butter and let it sizzle and hum in the pan for a few seconds, holding the pan by the handle and turning it so the melted butter coated the whole surface, then poured in the eggs.

"This is the tricky part," he said. "Because it looks like you're scrambling them, but you're not. You have to let it form that browned skin so it all stays in one piece." And I watched as he deftly swirled the pan while smoothing and spreading the egg mixture out with the spatula as the wet golden egg mixture softened and lightened into opacity. It was all over very quickly. Then he scooped the leeks and bacon into the center of the egg mixture and slid it onto the plate, folding it over as he went, and handed it to me. "That's how you make an omelette."

"You eat that one," I said. "Let me try."

He started to object, then saw the stubborn look on my face and yielded without a fight. I mimicked his movements exactly, swirling the butter until it sizzled but hadn't yet browned, pouring in just the right amount of egg mixture, and gently moving it around the pan with the spatula until it formed a perfect yellow circle, then carefully adding the filling, folding it over and scooping it onto the plate.

"I know how to make an omelette now," I said.

"Only because I showed you what to do," he said.

"Exactly," I told him. "That's exactly my point." I took a bite of the omelette I had made myself. "This is amazing," I said. "I'm sorry I gave you shit about the leeks."

"Reggie—"

"I wasn't born knowing everything about Richard Nixon, Leo. You weren't born knowing how to make an omelette. We had to learn. But we're smart people who learn fast. And you'll have Carter, Calliope and me on Comm with you the whole time. If I can make a totally delicious omelette without screwing it up, you can do this. I know you can."

"You know what the difference is?" he said. "The omelette wasn't shooting at you."

"That's fair."

"The omelette didn't murder our dad."

"I hear what you're saying."

"The omelette didn't manipulate the Timeline to cause fifty-six million innocent people—"

"I get it, Leo, we're on the same page, you can stop now."

"I'm just saying."

"I know."

"I'm scared, Reggie," he said. "This is terrifying."

"I'm scared too," I said. "We all are."

"And you don't really have any idea if this is going to work."

"No."

"I'm Katharine Bellows' son; it's possible they might have me in their database even though I'm a civilian."

"It's possible."

"And even if you bring home these photos, there's no guarantee that they'll find anything in them that helps us."

"I realize that."

"And going back to 1972 could be incredibly dangerous."

"I know," I said. "But we can figure all of that out together. The only thing you need to do is walk into the lobby of that building, give them your real name and tell the truth. You can do that."

"You make it sound easy."

"You can do this, Leo. I know you can."

"Can we come down now?" I heard Carter shout down the stairs. "Are you done fighting?"

"We're done, come back," said Leo.

"Oh thank God," said Calliope as the two of them clattered down the stairs. "Are you in?"

I looked at Leo. Leo looked at me.

"Yes," he said finally. "I'm in."

CHAPTER FIVE

LAST OF THE TIME AGENTS

Two and a half hours later, with no word from Leo, I began to wonder if I had made a terrible mistake.

"How much longer do we wait before we just find an empty broom closet, Short-Hop inside and hope for the best?" asked Carter, only half-joking. He was sprawled out on the couch while Calliope packed up supplies from Carstairs' cabinet and I paced anxiously.

"We can't," said Calliope. "It's a secure facility. Short-Hops don't work. You can only get there through their own private transport lab or by walking in through the front door. Visitors have to go through a background and security check with a full-body scan and then a resident or staff member has to vouch for you. Grove's going to have to agree to see Leo and sign an authorization form just to get him into the building."

"What if he doesn't?"

"He will," said Calliope firmly. "Reggie, where's the Gemstone drive?"

"Upstairs, in my room," I said. "It's plugged into my handheld."

"I'll go get it," she said. "We'll want to send it to Congressman Holmes along with the photos."

"Grab the file on my bed, too," I called to her as she went upstairs. "I took down the evidence wall in case they want it."

Carter turned to me as soon as she was gone.

"Truth, now," he said. "Is there really anything Grove can do?"

"Truth? I don't know," I said. "He's been friends with Holmes for decades and he's technically the only licensed Bureau agent left in the United States, so he's our best hope by a mile. A lot depends on how convincing he thinks this evidence is. And a lot depends on figuring out the identities of Saturn and Mars. But if there's anything he can do, he'll do it. For Calliope if nothing else. He owes her."

"They seem remarkably close," he said, looking upstairs after her.

"Calliope got placed with Grove right out of the Academy and never left," I said. "She could have gone up for agent certification any time in the past decade and aced it, if she wanted to. Mom used to push her about it all the time, said she's a hundred times too smart for her job – which is true – and that she was wasting her potential staying a tech forever. All the other techs on our floor are like twenty years old. It's a job you grow out of fast. And Calliope's the smartest person I know."

"But Grove didn't want her to leave, so she didn't. He is – *was* – the head of the department, plus our floor's senior Field Agent, and Calliope is his right hand. He would fall apart without her, and he knows it. He pays her an exorbitant salary and dotes on her like family – even though he hates absolutely everyone else. It's a complicated relationship. Not that his fondness for her isn't genuine, but it's definitely in his best interest to keep Calliope in a job that by rights she should have left eight years ago."

"What's he like?"

"Growly and short-tempered," I said. "Brilliant, but grumpy as a troll. Don't rub him the wrong way. Leo is a Bellows, and a civilian, so he'll give him a pass. He hates stupid people, and he assumes everyone younger than him fits into that category, so Calliope's the first tech – and one of the only human beings, frankly – that he's ever approved of."

"If he hates everyone so much, what makes you think he'll stick his own neck out for your parents?"

"He may be a grouch," I said, "but he's also a government man. He's loyal. He came up through the Academy with them and he worked side-by-side with my mother for decades. He's not as wild about me as he is about Calliope, he thinks I'm a pain in his ass – *this is not a place for you to comment* –," I added quickly, holding up my hand to silence the sarcastic retort I could see forming on his lips – "but I was his apprentice. If Leo Bellows shows up out of the blue at Sweethaven to discuss his missing family, Grove's going to let him in."

"You hope."

"I hope."

Calliope came bounding down the stairs just then, her wrist Comm flashing green.

"Leo rang in," she said. "He's inside. They're ready."

"All right," I said, as Carter stood up and the three of us moved to the center of the room. I took Carter's hand and he took Calliope's, as she slung her giant pack over her back and tapped her Comm.

"Clear," she said, and then we were gone.

We emerged from the Slipstream in a large, sterile-looking white room – alone except for Leo, and a gray-haired man in the flowing white tunic and pants of a Sweethaven patient. A man I thought I'd never see again.

"This is exactly the kind of irresponsible, idiotic behavior I have come to expect from Regina," he grumbled, "but I'm surprised at you, Calliope. I would have hoped to find you doing a better job keeping these children out of trouble."

She didn't answer, but jumped down off the platform, and in three long strides she had reached him and flung her arms around him.

"You goddamned curmudgeon," she said, tears in her eyes. "I've missed you too."

~

As Calliope had confidently predicted, and I had cautiously hoped, Grove had immediately come running when he heard that Leo was there. The lengthy delay that had caused me to go crazy waiting for word from Leo had a very simple explanation. Sweethaven patients were not permitted to use the transport facilities without permission, but Grove – who had been stuck inside that building for a year and a half, bored to madness – knew exactly when the security guards in that hallway took their breaks.

He had hustled Leo away to his living quarters, gotten as much of the story from him as he could while they waited, and then briskly led him to the transport lab at exactly seven minutes after three, walked in, took the scribbled piece of paper Calliope had sent with Leo, entered the coordinates she had written on it, and pulled us through.

Once we were inside, Calliope carefully talked Grove

through the process of erasing our transport coordinates from the system – so he'd be able to do it again later on his own when he jumped us out – and a few short minutes later we found ourselves seated on the floor of his room, drinking tea and telling him the whole story.

He had followed the Bureau shutdown and the rumors of my parents' alleged treason, but had been unable to get any more detailed information than what was being reported on the news. He was wild with curiosity about what had really happened, and it turned out that our guess had been correct – since he had never left Sweethaven, he had been left out of the investigation almost entirely.

"A few questions at the very beginning," he said, "and that was it. Everyone wanted to know if I knew where Katherine Bellows had gone. Everyone wanted to know how it was that my apprentice was sent on an administrative mission without my signing off on it. But once they checked the sickbay records and realized I was here – and unconscious, to boot – when you were sent to 1972, they eventually left me alone. And while I suppose it's a relief not to be under FBI surveillance, the fact that everyone I know *is* being watched means no one can tell me anything."

"But you're all right?" said Calliope anxiously, and he smiled at her – actually smiled, and I realized he must have been as worried about her during their long separation as she was about him.

"You worry too much," he said. "I'm fine. I was on bed rest for a few months, and my recovery was slow, but I'm perfectly well now. I'm only still here because I'm still on a regimen of daily infusions to build my tolerance back up so my organs can withstand Slipstream radiation again and get back out into the field."

"Grove," I said uncertainly, "I don't know if that's—"

"I'm too young to retire," he said firmly. "I'm not done yet. When the Bureau gets reopened, I want to be able to go back to work."

"I don't want you to overexert yourself," said Calliope.

"I won't," he promised. "Truly. I'm being careful."

He looked at me then, stern and appraising.

"I never thanked you," he said finally. "In fact, I think I yelled at you. But you were right. I saw the reports afterward. If you hadn't pulled me out when you did, I would have been caught in the Slipstream when I tried to jump out later and I would have been killed. You did the right thing. I'm very impressed with you," he said in a gruff voice, as though trying to conceal some emotion, and I beamed.

"That's the nicest thing you've ever said to me," I said.

"Don't let it go to your head," he retorted.

"I don't want to be the buzzkill here," said Carter, finishing his tea and setting down his cup, "but we haven't really explained to Agent Grove what we need him for."

"It's perfectly obvious," Grove said. There was just a hint of disdain in his voice, and I hid a smile, shooting Carter a glance that said, *I warned you.* "The Sweethaven transport lab is the only way to get you back to 1972. And you have to get those police photos."

"There's way more than just the photos," I said. "I have a whole data drive of my dad's Gemstone research, and a wall full of other documents besides. If you can get it in front of Congressman Holmes, it might be enough to open a Congressional investigation. That's our only chance to get the Bureau re-opened."

"It's a sound plan," he said slowly, thinking it over. "I agree with you that the photos are the clincher. They're the only hard proof that United Enterprises was involved. Get the originals too, I don't trust that police detective. He's already screwed this up once."

He looked at Carter suddenly. "Your apartment," he said. "Did you clear it?"

"What do you mean?" asked Carter.

"When you went on the run," he said. "Did you pack up? Did you follow evac protocols?" Carter looked from him to me helplessly.

"I . . . no, I just—I didn't know I wasn't coming back," he said. "I was just looking for Reggie."

"So your whole apartment is full of Slipstream radiation and Bureau tech?" asked Grove incredulously. "Just sitting there, waiting to be caught? And you were an Embed, so you had a built-in cargo drop too, I'd imagine. Good God, young man, did no one brief you on emergency evacuations?"

"I didn't *evacuate*. I was force-jumped," he repeated again, but Grove wasn't listening.

"He has to clear out," Grove said to Calliope. "Torch the apartment if you have to. What about you?" he said to me.

"I packed up all my tech," I said.

"Where are your clothes?" he asked. "Everything you got from Wardrobe. Everything that came through the Slipstream with you."

"It's all still at the apartment," I said guiltily, "I just grabbed a bag and ran."

He heaved a disappointed sigh.

"We'll take care of it," interjected Calliope reassuringly. "We'll clear the apartments. We can't torch Reggie's place at the Watergate – it's too suspicious with the break-in right next door – but we can sweep it and clean all the stuff out. The trace radiation will fade in a few days if we remove everything that came through the Slipstream."

"Okay," said Carter. "So we'll split up. I'll go to my apartment, Reggie will go to hers, then we'll go see Detective Barlow, grab the photos and come back."

"Calliope can stay here and monitor," I said, nodding. "Leo can go back to the safe house."

"I'll stay here," said Leo. "In case she needs help."

"None of you can stay here," said Grove. "It's far too dangerous. The three of you are under investigation, you already know that, and if he" – nodding at Leo – "wasn't already, he sure as hell will be soon, now that they know Regina slipped into and out of the building right underneath their noses. If any of you are recognized, it's over."

He turned to me as if a sudden thought had struck him. "Regina, you said your mother told you that you were safe in 1972," he said. "Did she say why?"

"No," I said. "She was weirdly vague about it. But insistent."

"Well," he said, "I trust Katherine Bellows. I think all four of you should go. I can drop you in a hiding spot I've used before. You'll work faster if you split up, and it's safer than trying to conceal any of you here."

"If Calliope doesn't stay to work the console," said Carter, "then how will we get back?"

"We'll set a rendezvous point," said Grove. "I'll drop you in on the day after you and Regina left, and I'll pull you back from the same coordinates at midnight that same night."

"How will we contact you to let you know we're all together and ready to jump?" asked Carter.

"You won't," he said. "That's the tricky part, unfortunately. There's no way for you to contact me without them tracing it. The next time the guards go on break, in" – he checked his watch – "forty-two minutes, I can sneak you in, jump you back to 1972, set return coordinates, and jump you back out at midnight. If you're not all together, I can't help you. Leo is going to have to leave the building the way he came in, which means I need to pull you back here in less than one hour, my time."

"Why?" Leo asked. I answered for him, the truth of our situation slowly dawning on me.

"Shift change," I said, and Grove nodded approvingly. "If you leave while the guards that checked you in are still on duty, they'll just wave you through. If they switch over and it's a new pair who don't recognize you, you'll get scanned again."

"So?"

"So you'll be covered in Slipstream radiation," said Calliope, realizing. "They'll be onto us."

"So *no matter what*," Grove said, his voice low and serious, "be back at midnight. I can't help you if you're not. Leo has to leave this building through the lobby in one hour or we're done for."

~

"Be honest," said Leo to me as we entered the pristine whiteness of Sweethaven's transport lab. "What are the odds of this working?"

"If we can all get back by midnight so he can pull us out in time to shove you out the front door?" I said. "Surprisingly, not that terrible. He only needs about three minutes to drop us in, then turn right around and pull us back and send us back to the safe house."

"Three minutes for him, eight hours for us," said Leo. "God, your job's weird."

"I'm sending you to Ivy City Yard," Grove said to Calliope from the control console. "Can you navigate them all from there?"

"I'm on it," she said.

"Thank you for this," I said to him over my shoulder as I stepped onto the transport platform.

"Don't thank me until my part of this is done," he said. "Thank me after Congressman Holmes gets the Bureau reopened. We're a long way from out of the woods yet."

"Typical Grove," I said. "Always finding something to be grumpy about."

He glowered at me from behind the console, but I could almost – *almost* – imagine that there was a twinkle in his eye as he did it.

"All right," he said. "Be back at these exact drop coordinates, at exactly midnight – all four of you – or I can't help you."

"We will," I promised. "Thank you."

"Good hunting," he said, and saluted us. Leo took my hand, and then we were gone.

CHAPTER SIX

SATURN

"Are you sure this is the right place?" said Leo, looking around nervously as we stepped out of the Slipstream into darkness. I smelled dirt and metal and I could hear the far-off hum of industrial machinery.

"I know this place," said Calliope. "This is one of Grove's favorite spots in the city."

"Where are we?" asked Carter.

"Ivy City," she said. "It's a run-down industrial neighborhood in northeast Washington. We're in a warehouse across the street from the Chesapeake and Ohio Railroad's main repair facility."

When our eyes adjusted to the darkness, we saw that she was right. The darkness opened up into a vast, cavernous space with the rusting shells of forgotten old train cars piled in shadowy corners.

"Follow me," Calliope said, and led the way to a hulking old boxcar sitting in the corner, its center doors open, and climbed in. "It's safe," she assured us before anyone could say what we were all thinking, and we reluctantly stepped in after her. Once we were all in, she closed the door, shutting us into pitch-blackness, until the metal box suddenly flared into brilliant light, and I saw that Calliope had pulled two adhesive lighting strips out of her bag and attached them to the wall.

"Home sweet home," she said, and sat down on the metal floor to rummage through her backpack.

"Couldn't he have sent us to a nice hotel or something?" said Leo.

"No," I said. "This is perfect. Grove uses this place all the time. It's remote enough that we can leave our stuff here safely without it being found or stolen, and we can transport in and out with almost zero HIO impact. Plus, even if someone on this end is looking for us, it will be almost impossible for them to follow us here."

"Why?"

"Because between this desolate graveyard of scrap metal and the Watergate Hotel," I said, "is Union Station. And train stations are very, very easy places to lose someone in."

"Here's how it will work," explained Calliope, pulling four envelopes of cash from her pack, taken from Carstairs' emergency supply cabinet.

"Trains come to Ivy City Yard for maintenance all day and night. The schedules have been programmed into your handhelds. When they're done, they leave here and go back to Union Station."

"You'll get on an empty train here and ride it into the city. Then, when you're finished and ready to come back, take a cab to the train station – switch cabs at a hotel if you think you're being followed. Check the schedule, find the next train headed this direction, then use this cash to buy a ticket for whatever the train is on the platform next to it. Then hop inside as soon as the coast is clear."

"It's perfect," I said.

"It's creepy," said Leo.

"I'm with Leo," said Carter. "I don't like it. There's only one exit and too many places to hide. If someone is tracking us, we could come back here tonight and find it crawling with U.E. agents."

Calliope dug a flat metal disc out of her backpack triumphantly. She set it on the ground, tapped her Comm a few times, and a small green light on the disc began to blink.

"You didn't think I left all Agent Carstairs' goodies in the safe house, did you?" she said. "This little beauty will block any scanner from picking up signs of our Slipstream radiation."

"What does that mean?" asked Leo.

"They won't be able to spot that we're here," Carter explained. "We'll be hidden from their equipment."

"But they won't be hidden from ours," she said, handing each of us a wrist Comm. "Put these on."

"What are these?" Leo asked.

"They're thirty-year-old wrist Comms from Dad's storage closet," I answered, a huge grin dawning on my face, "and U.E. won't be able to pick up their frequency."

"The beauty of planned obsolescence," said Calliope, without looking up from her bag. "The companies that sell you tech equipment get you to buy new models every ten minutes by making your new stuff incompatible with your old stuff. Which means the only way to outsmart United Enterprises is by using technology they haven't seen in so long their scans won't even recognize it. This is how we're going to communicate with each other."

"It's very . . . clunky," said Carter dubiously, examining the black plastic-and-metal wrist cuff he was now wearing.

"Think of it as retro," said Calliope. "I'm sure someday soon they'll come back in style. And you only have to endure it for one day; I think you'll survive."

"So what's the plan?" asked Leo, pulling up a wooden crate and sitting next to Calliope. Carter pulled another one out of a far corner for me, and sat down on the floor beside it.

"We split up," I said. "In and out. Fast as we can. I'd rather have us sitting on our asses waiting here for four hours than run the risk of being late and missing the transport at midnight. We'll get done quicker if we divide and conquer."

I dug through the pile of supplies Calliope was unpacking and handed a small metal canister to Carter. "You'll have to sweep both the apartments," I said. "Yours and mine. Pack up my suitcases – take all the clothes and everything in the vanity case in the bathroom – everything that came through the Slipstream."

"I have to touch your underwear?" he said dubiously.

"No, you *get* to touch my underwear," I said. "You're welcome. Take all my stuff over to your apartment. Grab whatever you want to take with you – any tech or personal effects you want to keep – then torch the rest. Make sure you detonate this *inside* the cargo transport so it shorts out and severs the Slipstream connection. We have to get rid of any evidence that might connect you to the Bureau."

"Got it," he said.

"What about me?" said Leo.

"You're on reconnaissance," I said. "We need to know if John Dean has any links to United Enterprises. You have to go to his apartment while he's at work and see what you can find. We need hard evidence linking U.E. to Gemstone that Grove can take to Congress."

"You want me to *break into the White House Counsel's apartment?*" he said, horrified.

"You don't have to break in," I said. "You just have to scan it. Bureau scanner data is admissible as court evidence. We have proof that the Watergate wiretaps traveled through the Slipstream. What we need to prove next is that John Dean did too."

"Meanwhile, I'm going to go annoy those crime scene photos out of Detective Barlow. Calliope, you set up shop here and stay on Comm with all of us. It's 3 p.m. local time now. We'll meet back here absolutely no later than 11:30 so we're packed and ready for Grove to pull us out at midnight. Got it?"

Everyone nodded. Calliope handed each of us a small, bulging knapsack from her huge pile of supplies accumulating on the floor of the train car.

"I've got a bag of tricks for each of you," she said. "Full of fun things from Carstairs' Magical Closet of Wonders. We've got everything from scanners to stun pistols, there's some protein bars in there if you get hungry, a portable shield to mask your Slipstream radiation, all kinds of good stuff.

"Look through it on the train, make sure you're clear on how it all works; the controls aren't in the same places and the settings are different from what you're used to. Do an inventory on the train. Leo, your bag has instruction manuals in it, call me if you have questions. All of you better get this stuff back to me in one piece."

"What happens if—" Carter began.

"Don't finish that sentence, Carter," I said warningly.

"I have to, Reggie," he said gently. "What happens if one of us doesn't make it back?"

We all looked at each other uncomfortably for a long

moment after that, shuffling our feet. Nobody knew what to say. It was the question we were all avoiding.

Splitting up was the only way to get everything done in time, but it was risky. None of us were combat-trained. Leo was a stranger in a strange land, Carter was a research aide, Calliope had no field experience, and I was only an apprentice who had kicked and screamed to avoid getting sent on this mission in the first place.

This is a really bad idea, a voice whispered in my head. *You're going to get one of them killed.*

"We're not leaving anyone behind," I said firmly, breaking the uncomfortable silence with more confidence than I felt. "We're all making it out of this alive. We're all going back. Is that clear? We are leaving together or not at all."

I paused, then added, "Don't go anywhere without telling Calliope exactly where you are, keep your wrist Comm switched on with the tracker live at all times, and come right back here the second you're done. Our first priority is getting each other home safely. That's more important than the photos or the apartment or anything else. We came in together, and we're going home together. Got it?"

Everyone nodded. I took a deep breath.

"Okay," I said. "Game time. Let's go."

We each took turns hugging Calliope, then left her in the train car, closing the door behind us. Instantly we were plunged into darkness again and had to feel our way through the maze of train cars until we could see the daylight shining through the open warehouse doors. We followed the train tracks to Ivy City Yard, where a number of trains lay waiting. I pulled out my handheld.

"Okay," I said, "we're looking for a passenger train with one engine and six cars. The engine is 4017. It's leaving in six minutes for Union Station to pick up passengers on its way to Baltimore."

"We should split up here," said Carter. "We should each take different train cars. Just in case. If one of us is spotted, hit your Comm and we'll come running."

He shook hands with Leo, then hugged me. I hugged Leo too.

"So this is what you do all day," he said.

"No, these are recent developments," I said. "I used to stare at a computer screen and drink coffee all day. Nobody was ever trying to kill me. It was great."

"It will be over soon," he said, with unconvincing optimism, and kissed me on the cheek.

"Go read your instruction manuals," I said. "Try not to electrocute yourself."

"See you at midnight," he said, and we went our separate ways.

~

I kept an eagle eye opened for the blond man with the newspaper all along the whole trip from Ivy City Yard to Union Station, and from there to the police station where Detective Barlow worked. But either I had successfully shaken him off, or he was better at concealing himself, because to my relief, I saw no trace of him the entire time.

Barlow was visibly displeased to see me, but made an effort at a polite greeting which I waved off.

"The photos, Barlow," I said coldly, following him back to his office, where he pulled an envelope out from his desk drawer and handed it to me.

"Here you are," he said. "Just as promised. Nobody needs to know about the, you know—"

"The part where you handed over evidence requested by the FBI to a total stranger and let him just waltz right out the door without even getting his name?" He bristled at that, but had the good grace not to respond, just looked away sulkily.

"We need the originals too," I said. "You clearly can't be trusted with them. This is sensitive information."

"I can't give out the originals, ma'am," he said. "They're police property."

I pulled the folded-up sheet of paper out of my pocket that Calliope had spent the morning working on and passed it over to him.

"This is not a request," I said. "It's an order."

He glared at me.

"Fine," he said. "I'll have to go down and get them from the evidence room. It might take awhile."

"I'll wait," I said.

"I can have them messengered to your office."

"No," I said. "I'm staying right here until they're in my hands. If you want me out of your hair you better find them fast."

He turned irritably and headed down the hallway.

"You didn't offer me any coffee," I called after him. He stopped and turned.

"I'm sorry," he said, straining for politeness through gritted teeth. "Can I get you some coffee?"

"I'm good, thanks."

He stomped off.

I pulled the envelope of photos out of my purse and began leafing through them. At first, there didn't seem to be anything in them that was new information – at least not to someone who had watched the whole burglary play out while hiding across the hall. I flipped through shot after shot of the DNC offices, straining my eyes to see if the burglars had left any clues behind. Then I stopped, frozen, photo in my hand, and felt the gears in my head stop turning and click into place.

Buried inside the stack of photos of the room itself was a close-up photo of one of the wiretaps the police had confiscated. And there, clear as day, I saw it.

A logo engraved in black plastic, an imposing capital U hovering over a letter E.

The wiretaps that the Watergate burglars had planted in DNC headquarters hadn't just come through the Slipstream. They had been manufactured by United Enterprises.

"I was right," I whispered to myself, ecstatic. "I was *right*."

This was it. This was the evidence we needed. Once these photos were in the hands of Congressman Holmes, we were home free.

I was so exuberant when Barlow returned – reluctantly handing over to me the second packet of photos – that I forgot to be unpleasant to him, just shot him a sincere expression of thanks, took the photos and bolted. I paged Calliope the second I got outside.

"You're kidding," she said when I told her, and laughed in delight. "It *worked*."

"I'm on my way back now," I told her. "I'll grab a cab for the train station right away."

"Wait," she said, "I have a better idea."

"What's that?"

"You have two sets of photos," she said. "Let's bring back the originals for Grove, but I can think of somebody else who would be very interested in the second set."

"Oh my God," I said, realizing. "*Woodward and Bernstein*."

"United Enterprises already exists in this time," she pointed out. "It's nothing big yet, but it's a real company. They might spot something you've missed, some link between U.E. and John Dean that we haven't been able to find. At any rate, it's worth a try."

"You're a genius, Calliope," I said. "You're a saint. You're a national treasure."

"I know," she said. "Now go. Hurry. We didn't budget for any unscheduled detours and I can't exactly call Grove and tell him to hold the transport for a last-minute change of plans."

"It's only five now," I said. "I'll be fine."

"There are only a few more trains tonight," she said. "Just make sure you're on one of them."

"I promise," I said, looking over my shoulder nervously as I crossed the street to hail a cab. I felt suddenly apprehensive and double-checked to make sure my wrist tracker was still on. I felt better with Calliope knowing exactly where I was, and it was broad daylight after all, but I'd had enough unsettling experiences walking around alone in 1972 that I was a little leery, exhaling with relief when I stepped out of the taxi at the *Washington Post* building, looking around and deciding that I had not been followed.

I had hardly gotten a chance to give my name to the receptionist when Bob Woodward stepped out of one of the nearby offices and spotted me.

"Regina!" he exclaimed, worry and astonishment on his face. He took my arm and pulled me into an empty conference room. "Get Carl," he called over his shoulder to the receptionist. "Right away."

While we waited for Bernstein, he drew the blinds closed, blocking off the windows that opened out into the rest of the office. He didn't say anything to me but his body language was tense and highly-strung. Carl arrived less than two minutes later, closed the door behind him, locked it, and sat down with his notepad.

"I'm going to tell you a lot of things," I said, "and some of them are going to sound crazy, but I'm going to ask you to trust me enough to hear me out. You'll be able to corroborate everything I say once you know where to look."

"Can you tell us what happened to you last night?" said Bob. "We've been worried sick."

Last night, I thought. Twenty-four hours for them, several days for me, a year and a half for Carter. Sometimes it still made my head spin.

"I was . . . in hiding," I said carefully. "I can't tell you where. There were two men in a car parked outside the restaurant – they had been following me – and another, a blond-haired man hiding his face behind a newspaper. He seems to turn up everywhere I go. A friend of mine – somebody I trust – came to the restaurant to warn me that I'd been spotted and to get out. There wasn't time to stay and warn you. He had to get me out of there before the men in the car took me."

"Are they dangerous?" asked Bob. "The men who were after you. Is your life in danger?"

"Yes," I said. "Mine, and others. You have no idea how high this goes."

I pulled out the crime scene photos I'd gotten from Barlow and set the packet of copies on the table, keeping the originals in my purse for Grove.

"You cannot let these out of your sight," I said. Bernstein took them out of the envelope one by one and laid them out on the table.

"Where did you get these?" he said.

"They're the police photos from the break-in."

"I know what they are," he said. "I asked where you got them."

"From a man named Detective Barlow," I said, "and he can't know that you have them or that you've spoken to me. I'm going to leave these with you, and trust that you'll be able to make use of them, but there's one in particular I want you to see," I pointed to the close-up photo of the wiretap.

"This device was manufactured by a company called United Enterprises," I said, "and you probably haven't heard of them yet, but you will. They didn't just sell illegal wiretapping equipment to these burglars. They've been in on the plot from the beginning. They're the ones that concocted the entire Gemstone plan."

"They arranged for Gordon Liddy to take it to the White House – to Dean's office, specifically. I'm confident that Dean is their man on the inside and that if you dig around, you'll find a connection between him and this company. I don't know what it is yet, but I know it's there. United Enterprises paid for Operation Gemstone and they paid to plant those bugs in the DNC office and a whole lot more besides. They're desperate for Nixon to be re-elected."

"This company is in bed with Nixon?"

"I don't know what Nixon knows," I said. "But I know that United Enterprises wants to get Nixon re-elected in '72 and Ronald Reagan in '76, and if that happens, all hell will break loose."

"What does that mean?"

"They're in the war-mongering business," I said. "They want a president whose strings they can pull. All of this – the spying, the secrecy – it's not just to discredit the Democrats. It's to buy Republican loyalty. They don't just want to keep Nixon in the White House, they want him to *owe* them.

They're trading favors. They're pulling strings to keep Nixon in power so that when they come knocking, Nixon will have to take their calls."

"Everything you've uncovered – you're on the right track, about all of it. You have to keep digging. You have to find the link between this company and John Dean, and you have to get the truth about the Watergate break-in out there. Nobody else will if you don't. But be careful. They've killed to keep this secret already."

They looked at each other.

"Start again," said Bob, "from the beginning. Take us through it step by step."

~

It was nearly ten o'clock before I finally looked at my watch and realized that if I didn't leave soon, I'd miss the last Ivy City train.

"I have to go," I said. I shook hands with Carl, then Bob walked me out to the elevator.

"Let me give you a ride," he said.

"It's okay," I said. "I'll take a cab. It's safer. They know I've met with you at least once. You're probably being watched too. I'd imagine your phones are being tapped. We shouldn't be seen together outside this building."

"I'd feel better if I knew you were somewhere safe," he said. "Cabs are risky."

"All of this is risky," I said. "I'll be okay."

"How will I reach you?" he said. "If I need to see you again."

"The photos should get you what you need," I said. He shook his head.

"That wasn't what I meant."

His eyes were very blue, I found myself noticing for the first time, and remarkably intense.

"Are you on the run?" he asked me.

"Yes."

"Do you have a safe place to stay?"

"I do. I can't tell you where, but yes."

The elevator door opened just then and I stepped into it. He got in with me.

"Please be careful," he said, not looking at me, as he pushed the button marked "Lobby" and the elevator began to descend. "I know I don't have to tell you that, but I'm telling you anyway. I don't want to find myself writing your obituary."

"I thought that was a whole other department," I said.

"Don't joke," he said. He did turn and look at me then, his warm eyes earnest.

"I'm being careful," I said. "I promise."

"Okay," he said. "I trust you."

And then suddenly, startlingly, out of nowhere, he hugged me, hard and tight, and pressed a kiss on my cheek. Then he pulled away abruptly, as if he had even surprised himself. Neither of us quite knew what to say after that.

"Well," I said finally, "I suppose I better go back upstairs and hug Carl now or he'll feel left out and it will throw off your whole working relationship."

Bob laughed, all tension gone. I laughed too.

"I've never met anyone like you, Regina Bellows," he said as the elevator reached the lobby and the door opened.

"I get that a lot," I said, "but usually as an insult. So thank you."

"Stay safe," he said again, and I nodded.

"I'll try to contact you if I find out anything more," I said. "In the meantime, just keep digging. I'm counting on you guys. Don't screw it up."

He laughed.

"If I had a dollar for everyone in this building who's said that," he said.

I reached out my hand and he shook it.

"Goodbye, Regina," he said. "It's been an honor."

"Goodbye," I said. "Thank you for everything."

The elevator doors closed on him looking after me with worry in his eyes, and I knew he was thinking the same thing I was thinking.

We were both wondering if we would ever see each other again.

The trip back to the train station was mercifully uneventful. A passenger train from Union Station was scheduled for maintenance and departing in ten minutes – the last of the trains on Calliope's list. I had cut it uncomfortably close

I bought a ticket for the train adjacent to it, using my 1972 cash per Calliope's instructions, then waited until the conductor's back was turned and darted across the rails, slipping into the empty train through an unlocked door. I sat down on the floor of the nearest compartment, so I couldn't be seen through the windows, and tapped my Comm to page Calliope.

"It's done," I said. "They've got the photos. I told them everything."

"Reggie!" she said, nearly shouting. "You're the last to call in. I've got Carter here too."

"I'm on my way back now," I said.

"Me too," said Carter in my ear. "Are you on the train?"

"Yes. Car 12."

"I'm in Car 8. Stay where you are, I'll come to you."

"Any word from Leo?"

"I'm here," said Leo's voice. "I got back about eight. I'm with Calliope."

"How did it go at Dean's apartment?"

"Not quite like we expected," said Calliope. "I don't think he's the one we're looking for."

"Are you sure?"

"There were definite traces of Slipstream radiation attached to objects all around his apartment," said Calliope. "But only certain things. If he had come through the Slipstream himself, the scanner would have lit up every single thing he'd ever touched or breathed on. But the levels were way too low. Just traces, really. And only attached to certain things. *This* pair of shoes but not *that* pair of shoes. The desk in his office but not the bookshelf next to it."

"So he's definitely been in contact with either Mars or Saturn," said Carter's voice over the Comm, just as the door opened and he entered, sitting down beside me and dropping his pack on the floor next to mine. "That's helpful."

"Hi," I said, smiling.

"Hi," he said. "Good to see you."

"Let's look at the scans when we get back to the safe house," Calliope said, "and see if we can figure out anything helpful from looking at which objects have trace radiation. Reggie worked for him, so maybe something will jump out at her that the rest of us missed. Carter, how did it go with you?"

"Well, I can now cross 'fire-bomb own apartment' off the list of things I need to do before I die," he said dryly, pulling his water bottle out of his pack and taking a drink. "I went over the place with a fine-toothed comb and the good news is I don't think anyone's been in it since I left. All my tech was still there. I snagged everything I could, pulled the fire alarm to get everyone else out of the building, then set the explosives and ran out with the rest of the crowd."

"And I don't have to ask how Reggie's day went," said Calliope. "Because I can see it myself."

"What do you mean?" I asked, puzzled.

"I don't want to toot my own horn," she said, "but sending you to the reporters was the first thing we've done that's actually created measurable results. I logged into the General Timeline through your dad's old handheld and it's going *crazy*. This whole Timestream is in flux. The system is beginning to self-correct. I can't tell if it was the photos specifically, or something you said, but there was a *huge* spike."

"So it's working," said Carter. "That's good."

"I'm cautiously optimistic," said Calliope. "But we haven't reached the tipping point yet. The system still isn't sure what it wants to do. Events on the Timeline are blinking in and out."

"We need to throw another rock in the pond, that's what Mom said," I told her. "The ripples aren't big enough yet."

"Yes," said Calliope. "We still haven't stopped the war. The war is still stable. We're getting closer and closer – whatever the reporters are doing is clearly nibbling away at it – but it's going to need another push from our end as well."

"Still," I said, "we did it. Good work, everyone."

"Back to the safe house after this?" said Leo.

"I think so," I said. "U.E. is going to be pissed as hell, and we should lay low for awhile until we know which way things are going. But once Congress reopens the Bureau, and Mom can come back, we'll have better resources to track Mars and Saturn and figure out exactly how to stop them."

"This is real progress," said Calliope. "I'm kind of amazed this went so smoothly."

"Christ," said Leo. "Don't jinx it," and they laughed like it was some kind of private joke.

I felt the train slow down, and I realized we were already back at Ivy City Yard.

"We're pulling in right now," said Carter. "Be there in five."

He stood up and walked towards the door, looking out the window. Then his expression changed, and a look of puzzled concern came over it.

"What?" I said. "What's wrong?"

"There's someone there," he said. "Blocking our entrance."

"What?" I said, jumping up to go look out the window next to him.

"It's okay," said Leo. "He works here."

"What do you mean?" I asked.

"Tall white guy, wearing jeans and a bright orange plastic vest thing?"

"Yeah," said Carter. "Has he been here since you got back?"

"Yeah, but it's okay," said Leo. "He's not a security guard or anything. He was working on one of the train cars in the yard when I got in, and there was no way for me to get across the street to the warehouse without him noticing."

"So I got off the train on the other side, snuck around some of the other engines until it looked like I was coming towards him from the street instead of the train, and then I pretended like I was lost and asking for directions. He snapped at me to go away and then as soon as his back was turned I ducked into the warehouse."

"What's he doing now?" asked Calliope.

"Just standing," said Carter. "Looking at his watch."

"Does he see you?"

"He sees the train," I said. "He doesn't appear to be looking at us."

I looked at the man in the orange vest for a moment, trying to figure out a way to navigate around him, when the last thing Carter had said clicked into my brain and my heart stopped beating. I reached out a hand without thinking and latched onto Carter's forearm. He yelped in pain as my fingers clamped onto him.

"Jesus, Reggie, *what*?"

"It's not a watch," I said hoarsely, pointing with a shaking finger. "Carter. Look. *It's not a watch.*"

And we watched as the man in the orange vest lifted his hand, spoke into the black band around his wrist and tapped it three times. Then he disappeared.

"Son of a bitch. It's a wrist Comm," I hissed furiously. "U.E. found us. Calliope, we're blown."

"*What?*"

"He transported out," I said. "I just saw it."

"Shit," said Calliope fiercely. "Shit, shit, shit."

"Did you recognize him?" said Leo. "Was that our guy?"

"No," I said. "I don't think that's Mars. I think that guy was just here to give the signal."

"Signal for what?"

"That we're all here," said Carter softly, as an ominous-looking dark van pulled up directly between us and the warehouse doors.

"We're screwed," I said to Calliope. "Carter and I can't get to you. And you can't get out."

"What do you mean, we can't get out?" said Leo in a voice laced with panic. "Why can't we get out?"

"Because," I said, watching out the window with my heart in my throat, "Eight U.E. guards just showed up between you and your exit."

They got out of the van, and as it drove away, I saw them split up into two teams of four. Guns at the ready, one team crept very slowly and quietly inside the vast train car warehouse where Calliope and Leo were hiding, while the other turned and began to move towards the train which had just pulled in. The train with me and Carter on it.

I pulled Carter down to the floor of the train car and we ducked beneath the seats.

"Damn," I said under my breath. "Calliope, where are you?"

"Same place where you left me," she said.

"Is the door to your train car closed?"

"Yes," she said.

"Can you lock it? Quietly?"

"I can try," she said.

"Good," I said. "Turn your lights off. There are four armed guards inside the warehouse right now."

"What?" she exclaimed in a whisper.

"And four more headed towards us," Carter said. "In case you guys were worried that we felt left out."

"They know we're here?" said Leo in horror.

"No," I said slowly, thinking it out as I spoke, retracing the guards' movements in my mind. "No. I think they *think* we're here."

"What are you talking about?" asked Calliope. "Carter, what is she talking about?"

Carter looked at me.

"The guards in the warehouse were stealthy," I said. "Hand signals. Moving slowly. If they had us on trackers they'd have charged in, guns blazing, and shot out the walls of Calliope's train car. But they didn't."

I risked a swift look out the window, lifting my head up just enough to see out of the corner of my eye. There were four guards down at the far end of the train, closest to the warehouse, guns drawn, slowly entering the first car. "It's the same on our end," I said. "They started down at Car #1, closest to the warehouse entrance, and they're going through one at a time. They're *hunting*. They don't know which car we're in."

"They can't be tracking our Comm frequency," said Carter, "because these things are a thousand years old. And we're all carrying around a scan blocker to mask our radiation trails. So either they have some way to hack into decades-old tech that Calliope didn't know about, or they didn't use tech to find us."

"The scan blockers work," said Calliope. "I'm watching the readouts right now. No trace radiation has escaped the filter. There's no chance of anyone finding us that way."

"I don't get it," said Leo. "Then how did they find us? No one knows we were here."

And then my blood went cold and I felt a pain clench my heart.

"That's not true," I said quietly. "There is someone. Someone who knows *exactly* where we are."

The silence that followed was awful. I couldn't look at Carter, but I could feel him looking at me. Through the Comm channel, I heard someone – I didn't know if it was Calliope or Leo – inhale sharply. Everything was very still.

Nobody said the thing we were all thinking. We all let it hang there. I felt like I had been punched in the stomach. I slid down the wall and sat back down on the floor of the train car.

Harold Grove.

"No," said Calliope finally. "No. There's another explanation. We just have to figure it out. We have to find a way out of this warehouse and—"

"There's no other way out of the warehouse, Calliope," I said dully, "and you know that. He dropped us inside a building with one exit. And now it's blocked."

"Stop saying 'he,'" she snapped.

"We're not doing this right now," said Carter. "Reggie, we need exit options."

"He sent us all over Washington D.C. to collect every last piece of evidence that might tie U.E. to Gemstone," I said to Calliope, ignoring Carter. "The original photos. That was *his* idea. Sweeping the apartments. And insisting that we all four go together, even at the risk of sending a civilian with no radiation immunity on a 140-year jump."

"We were idiots, we didn't even *think*. Of *course* this was what they wanted. There's no evidence that any agents were ever in this Timeline now. The Bureau's shut down, they control our whole building, and Carter just burned down his whole damn apartment to destroy the cargo drop that was the last working link to the Slipstream. We just did all of U.E.'s dirty work for them. And now we're trapped."

"He would never do this," she said. "He would never. He would *never*."

"Then how did they find us, Calliope?" I snapped. "You were on tech. You set the scan blockers. You covered our tracks. Did you screw up? Did you miss something?" The anger in her silence came in waves over the Comm.

"No," I answered for her, "you didn't. Which means the only person who could possibly have known exactly when and where to find us is the person who sent us there."

"Go to hell," said Calliope coldly, and was silent.

"What do we do?" Carter mouthed silently to me, huddled underneath the seat across from mine, and the petty annoyance at Calliope I was using to press my emotions down into the pit of my stomach evaporated, leaving a dark empty numbness in its wake. I felt hollow. Off in the distance, there were voices and clanging metal. The guards were moving closer. They had guns. We might die here. I should care, but I didn't. I felt nothing at all.

"I don't know," I said, my voice sounding dull and flat, even to me. I couldn't think about making a plan. I couldn't think about anything except Harold Grove's voice saying, "Midnight, don't forget."

Carter pushed the mute button on his wrist Comm, then knelt in front of me and muted mine as well.

"He's Saturn," I said, my voice expressionless. "Grove is Saturn."

"Yes."

"Okay," I said. "Here's the deal. I quit. I'm out. I can't do this. I'm going to stay on this train until either a guard comes in and shoots me or they send it back to Union Station, and then I'm going to just ride along, wherever it's going."

"Reggie—"

"Chicago, maybe. I've never been to Chicago. I think I'd like it. I like people with really strong opinions about pizza. I feel like I could be happy in Chicago."

"Reggie," said Carter, "I need you to stay with me here, okay? There are armed guards closing in and we need to get out of here. You're the leader. We need you to lead." He took my hand and squeezed it. "We need you to tell us what we're going to do."

"How the *hell* should I know?" I exclaimed. "What are my qualifications? Harold Grove was running a decades-long con to hide a massive Chronomaly from everyone in the Bureau and he was doing it ten feet from my desk. Right under my nose, and I never saw it. And I'm supposed to outsmart him *how*, exactly?"

"Reggie—"

"You don't understand," I said. "Everyone thinks that

just because I'm Carstairs' and Bellows' kid that I'm some super genius, but I'm not. I'm just a smart girl who's good at computers. We had one way back to our own time, and it was a trap. How the hell am I supposed to fix that? I'm not *magic,* Carter."

He sat down next to me and took my hand. We sat in silence for a few moments.

"I worked for him for five years," I said finally.

"I know."

"Calliope is never going to speak to me again."

"We can't worry about that right now."

I leaned my head back against the train car wall, sighed, then turned my Comm back on. So did Carter.

"Where the hell did you two go?" said Leo as the Comms clicked back to life.

"Sorry," said Carter. "That was an accident. But we're back now."

"Okay," I said, taking a deep breath. "We have two problems in front of us, so let's start with the biggest."

"The men with guns?" said Leo.

"Unfortunately, no," I said. "That's the small problem. The big problem right now is that we have no way to get out of 1972."

"Wait a minute," said Leo. "You're telling me there was no backup plan?"

"I would have told you if there was a backup plan," I said. "If I don't say 'Here's the backup plan,' assume there's no backup plan."

"So in that whole bag of tricks Calliope has been hauling around, there's nothing we can use to get home with?"

"No," said Calliope. "I have a dozen Short-Hops – you can go about six months at a time with those – but not nearly enough to get us from 1972 to 2112. No, for a big jump like that you need a device synced up to a real transport lab."

Something clicked inside my head. *A device synced up to a real transport lab.*

Those guards had black uniforms, not white, so they hadn't come from Sweethaven. They must have transported here directly from United Enterprises.

Which made them our ticket home.

"Wait a minute," I said to Calliope, the beginnings of a plan slowly beginning to coalesce in my head. "You have Short-Hops? You have them with you, right now?"

"Yes," she said. "The ones I swiped from the safe house. Didn't I tell you?"

"No," I said. "You didn't."

"You all have one," she said. "Didn't you go through your bag on the train like I asked you to?"

"Just to look for snacks," I said.

"Christ, you're predictable."

"Calliope, please tell me there's another train leaving Ivy City Yard tonight."

"The train three tracks over from you – the passenger train – is being prepped for departure now. Scheduled to leave in twenty-eight minutes."

"Are you packed?"

"Yes."

"Okay," I said. "You and Leo, use a Short-Hop and get on that train. Set it for just before departure. Carter and I will meet you. Leo, pick a number between one and five."

"Two."

"Great. Set coordinates for Car 2. Now go."

"Wait a minute," said Carter, looking at me. "Where are you going?"

I pulled the stun pistol out of the pack Calliope had sent with me.

"I have a really, really bad idea," I said.

~

It took another four full minutes for the first pair of guards to make it to our end of the train. Crouched underneath the seats, curled up into a tiny little ball, I watched with my heart pounding as four black-booted feet walked slowly down the aisle, then stopped.

They took the bait, I thought to myself triumphantly. We had left our packs, Bureau tech scattered around in plain sight, on the seats two rows away from the floor space where we were hiding – Carter on one side of the center aisle, me on the other. The guards had stopped exactly where I wanted them to and were bent over, their backs to us, looking down at the pile of gadgets on the seat.

I nodded at Carter. He nodded back.

We drew our stun pistols, crawled out into the aisle, and before the two guards even had a moment to register our presence, shot them both in the leg. They dropped to the ground immediately, immobilized but conscious. One reached for his Comm, but I was faster; I stunned them both in the chest, knocking them out before they could make a sound.

"Nice work," said Carter approvingly.

"Can you do that again?" I said. "Without me? When the second two come looking, can you get both of them on your own?"

"I think so," he said. "Two unconscious coworkers is way better bait than a bag of Bureau Comms. Why, where are you going?"

"Into the warehouse," I said, and he stared at me.

"What the hell are you talking about?" he said incredulously.

"They weren't sure about the train," I said. "I mean they can't have been completely sure we'd be on it. But they did know about the rendezvous point. They knew we had to come back to the warehouse."

"So?"

"So if it was you," I said, "doing a sweep of a pitch-black warehouse in the middle of the night, and you couldn't find any signs of the people who were supposed to be there, what would you do?"

"Call for help," he said, eyes widening. "Report in, confirm the drop coordinates, narrow the search."

I nodded.

"They're going to search this warehouse top to bottom and they're not going to find us," I said. "And then they're going to call Grove."

"And?"

"And I have to be there when they do. I need proof that he's Saturn."

"That's suicide."

"Not necessarily."

"Reggie—"

"Grove has been friends with Congressman Holmes for thirty-five years," I said. "How the hell am I supposed to get him, or anyone else, to believe me without proof? Even *Calliope* doesn't believe me."

He looked at me for a long moment, then nodded.

"Okay," he said. "Tell me what to do."

I pulled his Short-Hop, loaded and ready with five jumps, from the seat where we had left it as bait and handed it to him.

"Knock out the two guards when they come," I said, "then

Short-Hop them to the train with Calliope and Leo. Keep them there and wait for me. Zap them again if they start to wake up."

"You weren't kidding," he said. "This really is a bad idea."

"Tell me about it," I said.

"Don't be stupid," he warned me, as he crawled back under the seat again. "Just get what you need, fast, and get out."

"I know," I said. "I promise."

I put on my knapsack, set my Comm to stealth mode – the others would be able to hear everything I heard, and the device would record everything, but the incoming channel was turned off, leaving the device silent – then set my own coordinates. I took a deep breath, said a silent prayer, and tapped the Short-Hop's screen.

Instantly I was engulfed in blackness. As my eyes slowly adjusted, I found myself exactly where I had hoped I'd be – standing just inside the warehouse doors, concealed in a dark corner away from the guards. They had swept the front of the room first, and I could see their flashlights moving around in the dark away from me. I had to get close enough to hear – and record – without being spotted.

I waited in silence for a few minutes, watching the flashlights sweep the far corners of the warehouse. They were finishing up. They hadn't found us. They were annoyed. *Oh please*, I begged silently. *Please, be annoyed. Call your boss and tell him. Please, please, give me something.*

A flashlight beam glided over the wall above my head and I ducked down, huddled in a corner between two overturned train cars. It moved from floor to wall to floor and I realized that one of the guards was walking towards me.

"Bravo Team to Saturn," said the guard.

"Report," said a voice that was so unmistakably Harold

Grove's that I didn't realize until that moment how desperately I had wanted to be wrong.

Dammit, I thought. *Damn everything.*

I sent a silent apology to Calliope, who I knew could hear it through my silent Comm, and closed my eyes to blink back tears.

"We've swept the whole warehouse," he said. "There's no sign of them."

"What time is it there?"

"Quarter past eleven, sir."

"And the train?"

"Alpha Team is sweeping it now, sir, but they haven't reported anything."

"Run a scan," said Grove. "One of them never left the building. She's still there. Did you look inside the train cars?"

"Yes, sir. And we've run scans. There's no trace of agent activity; no radiation and no trackers. Like they were never here."

"Damn her," said Grove, his voice an unsettling mix of anger and something that might have been affection. "She's covered their tracks somehow. You're just going to have to start kicking open doors, then. They're inside that building, or they will be soon."

"What do we do we don't find all of them?" said the guard. "If they're not together."

"Shoot the boys," said Grove. "They don't matter. But Mars wants Regina Bellows alive."

"And the other girl, sir?"

There was a silence.

"Don't hurt her," he said finally. "You can stun them both, but I don't want the girls harmed. That's an order."

"Yes, sir."

"Report back again in fifteen minutes."

"Will do, sir.

And the Comm clicked off.

I pulled out my Short-Hop and jumped, landing in a dingy freight car on a moving train. Leo and Carter were huddled together next to the pile of black-uniformed bodies, talking quietly, while Calliope sat alone in a corner, staring at the wall. All three were startled by my arrival.

"Strip them," I said. "Keep everything. Uniforms, weapons, scanners, all of it. Where are we headed?"

"Calliope said this train is on its way to Baltimore," Leo said. "We have about two hours."

"Good," I said. "That gives us plenty of time. We have about half an hour before these four start to wake up."

We worked in silence for a few minutes, stripping each guard down to their underwear and frisking them carefully. Carter and Leo and I worked on uniforms and set all their tech aside for Calliope. They all wore earbuds and Microcams, had stun pistols in their holsters and wicked-looking laser rifles strapped to their backs, and – most importantly – transport Comms.

All of this went into Calliope's pile. She watched us in silence for a moment from her corner before her curiosity got the better of her, and she rose to walk over to our side of the train car and see what we had collected.

Once the four guards were entirely stripped down, Carter helped me lay them out on the floor, in pairs, limbs entangled with each other in a grotesque dance.

"Calliope, I need two Short-Hops," I said. "Programmed for the coordinates Carter and I just left. We need Bravo Team to think Alpha Team is still sweeping the train to buy ourselves a little head start."

She didn't acknowledge that she had heard, but wordlessly

pulled the devices out of her pack, tapped on the screens a few times, then tossed them to me without even looking in my direction. I set one on top of each pair of guards, then stared at them.

"How do you turn them on without touching the thing and getting yanked back with them?" asked Leo.

"I don't know, exactly," I said. "I didn't think that through."

"You could grab the guy's hand and use his fingers to push the button. Then you're not touching the Short-Hop," suggested Carter.

"But I'd be touching *him*," I pointed out. "I'd still get yanked."

"What if you lifted up his foot," said Leo, "and put the thing under his heel, and then dropped his foot, so then when it pushed the button you wouldn't be touching it?"

"Or you could put it next to them," said Carter, "and roll them over."

"Oh, for the love of God," snapped Calliope, pulling out her handheld. "They have a remote setting," and with three clicks all the guards were gone.

"Thank you," I said, but she had already gone back to scanning one of the U.E. transport Comms and pointedly ignoring me.

We watched her work in silence for awhile as the train slowly chugged along towards Baltimore.

"I've tried," Carter said to me very quietly, "and Leo's tried, but . . ."

And he gestured in Calliope's direction helplessly.

"Really?" I said incredulously. "Me? Calliope's having emotions and you think *I'm* the one to go talk to her?"

"Not under regular circumstances, no," he admitted, "but Leo and I couldn't even get her to look at us."

"Good Lord," I said.

"Why do you look more uncomfortable about this than about charging into the warehouse to spy on armed guards?"

"Reggie Bellows," I said. "Pleased to meet you," and against his will he let out a tiny snort of laughter. I sighed and looked over at Calliope, still tinkering with the wrist Comm. "Here goes nothing," I said to Carter, and walked over to sit down next to her.

"Hi," I said.

Silence.

"Can I help?"

"Do you know what you're doing?"

"No."

"Then no," she replied coldly, without looking at me. I gestured helplessly at Carter and Leo and started to get up and leave, but they both waved me back down. I watched Calliope work in silence for a little while, her irritation at my continued presence almost palpable. A few minutes went by before I spoke again.

"I'm sorry," I said finally. "I'm sorry you had to hear him say those things."

"Stop talking right now," she said in a cold, dangerous voice. "Stop."

"It wasn't an I-told-you-so," I said. "It was to get evidence for Holmes."

"I'm not doing this with you right now."

"Calliope, I had to. You know I had to. I needed proof."

And then Calliope snapped.

"I swear to God, Regina Bellows," she said, flinging the wrist Comm in her hand onto the floor of the train car with a loud clang. "If you say *one more word* after I've asked you twice to stop talking, I'm going to throw you out of this train."

"All right," I said, finally losing my patience. "That's *it*. I am *done* having this fight with you. I'm over it. You can stomp and shout at me all you want to, but you know what? He was my boss too. He was my mentor too. He went to school with my parents. You don't have a monopoly on being devastated here."

"You do not get to act like I did this to you, like you're the only one this is happening to," I went on. "Leo and I grew up in that office, Calliope. We've known Harold Grove since we were born, and now we've just found out that he might have killed our dad. So don't lose your shit in my face like I'm the one that did this to you. You want to be mad? Be mad at *him*."

"It's not you," she said after a long moment, and I could see her unbending slightly. "I'm not mad at you. I'm mad at *me*."

I looked at her curiously, and she looked back at me for the first time. There was weary resignation in her eyes. She looked ten years older than she had that morning.

"The Chronomaly was concealed for years by someone at the Bureau who was logging in every single day to reconfigure the Timeline manually," she said. "And then the very day Harold Grove is taken off active duty is the day the mask starts to slip, and suddenly the Chronomaly is visible. You want to know why I'm angry? I'm angry because I missed that."

I didn't say anything, but put my arm around her.

"It should have been so obvious," she said. "Right from the beginning. He must have panicked when he woke up in sickbay and realized he had no Timeline access and no security clearance. He would have known that the Chronomaly was becoming visible. He would have guessed that you and your mother had found it, and that was why you were sent to 1972."

A pause. Then she continued, "So he did the only thing he

could do. He started the rumor that Carstairs and Bellows had planted the Chronomaly themselves. He couldn't cover it up anymore, so the next best thing was to let it get out in the open and blame it on somebody else."

"And shut the whole Bureau down while he was at it," I agreed, "so nobody could go back and undo all his work."

"He's always been good at thinking on the fly," said Calliope. "It's a very Harold Grove plan."

"I know."

"I wish it wasn't."

"I know."

"We played golf together," she said. "Did you know that? He taught me how to play golf."

"I didn't know that."

"He spent Christmas with my family twice," she said. "He sent flowers when my grandmother died."

"Calliope—"

"I was nineteen when I started working for him. He was like a dad to me. He taught me everything I know."

She turned to me, eyes shining, and it suddenly occurred to me that I had never seen Calliope cry. "He's a good person, Reggie," she said. "This can't be who he really was. He can't have been this person all along. I would have seen it."

"Calliope, we don't know who he really was," I said gently. "We only know what he showed us. We only know the face he put on at work."

"And now you're telling me he was a traitor. And that fifty-six million innocent American and Chinese citizens died so he could help some company get rich. This man I've worked for my entire adult life. He's a monster."

"Find me a better answer then," I begged her, tears suddenly heavy my eyes too. "Seriously. Anything. The craziest idea you have, I'll take it. I don't want it to be true either, Calliope. Because if it is? If Saturn was Grove all along? Then that means all these years he's been committing treason right under our noses. He was doing all of this from ten feet away. Logged into the same computer system. You were right there. He was hiding from everyone, Calliope, but he was hiding most of all from you."

"He's not Mars, at least," said Leo, who I noticed had suddenly drifted over towards us. "That's something."

Calliope turned and looked at him sharply.

"What do you mean?" she said. Leo looked down, suddenly shy.

"Well," he said uncomfortably. "I mean, I might be wrong. It might mean nothing. But I just thought – well, Mars is really the one who started the war, right? So we don't actually know if Harold Grove had anything to do with what happened to Dad, or to all those other people. Maybe he was just the cover-up."

"'The cover-up for a war that killed fifty-six million people," said Carter. "He was complicit in genocide. I know he meant a lot to all of you, but we can't forget that."

"We're not," said Leo. "She's not. I didn't mean that. All I meant was . . . Calliope, maybe it wasn't all a lie. Maybe he wanted you to think he was a good person because he wanted to believe he *was* a good person."

Leo's voice was reasonable, patient. "Maybe once, long ago, he did a terrible thing, and found himself under the thumb of this company, and he's been stuck there for years. Maybe he's desperate, and he's afraid, and he's trapped – but maybe he's not a monster."

"You heard him on the Comm. We all heard him. He told the guards not to touch you. He didn't want anyone to hurt you. He's still Saturn, he still has all that blood on his hands and he still needs to be stopped, but maybe, also, there's a tiny part of him that's still the man you wanted him to be. Would that help? A little?"

"I never thought of it like that," I began to say, before I realized that neither of them were listening to me. They were looking at each other. And then Calliope did the least Calliope thing I had ever seen her do. She stood up, dusted herself off, wiped the tears from her eyes, and walked over to Leo. Then she placed her hand on the back of his neck, pulled his face down toward hers, and kissed him.

Watching someone kiss your brother is uncomfortable for all kinds of reasons, and I wanted to look away, but Carter and I were both so totally astonished – in fairness, I think, so was Leo – that we just stood there, staring, jaws on the floor, as Calliope kissed my brother and my brother kissed her back.

"You've been with them a lot longer than I have," I whispered to Carter. "How long has this been going on?"

"As far as I was aware, for the past fifteen seconds," he said. "I had no idea."

"That can't possibly be true."

"Well, all right, I admit I did harbor some idle wonderings—"

"I knew it. You were holding out on me."

"I assumed you paid attention to the behavior of other human beings and that eventually you'd pick up on the context clues yourself. The more fool I."

"I had three days, you had eighteen months."

"I'm thinking an April wedding, tulips and hyacinth, bride and groom in white linen, wine and seafood reception to follow at Leo's restaurant."

"Are you hiring yourself as wedding planner?"

"I'd be an amazing wedding planner and you know it. I'd be so much better at it than you. If you were in charge the wedding reception would be just everyone sitting around on couches eating protein supplements with no pants on."

"This is quite a day for kissing," I said. "Ask me why. Ask me who else got kissed today."

"Oh my God," said Carter, eyes widening. "You kissed that cop?"

"Gross," I said. "No. Woodward. And *he* kissed *me*."

"You made out with a reporter?"

"We didn't make out. It was one kiss. In the elevator. On the cheek. When he was afraid he was sending me off to my death. It was very romantic."

"No journalistic integrity, that guy."

"You're just jealous."

"I should call his boss. That's so unprofessional."

"You will not call his boss."

"Plus, how will Carl feel? Poor Carl. You should go back and kiss him too. You don't want to be the woman who comes between them."

"It was a kiss on the *cheek*, you're making this way too big a deal."

"You're the one who brought it up out of nowhere."

"I was just *sharing*," I said. "It was just a *coincidence*, I thought it was *interesting*—"

"You wanted to make sure everyone in this train car knew that you got kissed today? Fine, you win, congratulations, this is *your* big day, don't let these two jerks ruin it for you."

"I hate you."

"Mazel tov to you and Mr. Woodward. I hope your first baby is a boy and you name him Carter. How do you feel about double weddings?"

"Shut up."

"*Both* of you shut up," snapped Calliope, pulling away from

Leo and turning the full force of her irritated Calliope glare on Carter and me. A switch had flipped inside her, and she was back to herself. The sadness was still there in her eyes, but she was brisk and competent and focused once more, and a part of me wondered whether there was a chance that she and Leo were actually, against all probability, really good for each other. Maybe he would teach her what he had learned, as Leo Carstairs' son, about how to live while carrying around a hole in your heart. Maybe over the past eighteen months, while they waited for me, she had been the one who made him braver. Maybe it made a weird kind of sense.

"The fact is," I said, "that regardless of what motivated Harold Grove, he's not the one we have to worry about right now. We need to find Mars."

"And how do we do that?" said Leo. "We're stuck in the 1970's."

"No, we're not," I said. "Everybody, pick a uniform and put it on."

"Wait a minute," said Leo. "What's happening?"

"There's only one working transport lab left in the country that can take us home," I said. "And these uniforms are going to get us there."

"Where?" said Leo suspiciously.

"The belly of the beast," I said, tossing him an armored vest. "We're going inside United Enterprises."

CHAPTER SEVEN

MARS

"This is just the *worst* idea," grumbled Leo as Carter strapped the laser rifle to his back for him and straightened his jacket.

"What's the plan once we're inside?" said Carter. "Just Short-Hop out to the safe house?" Calliope shook her head.

"It's a secured building," she said, "blocked for transport in or out except using their own equipment. The guards' transport Comms are pre-set, we just need to push the button and the system will jump us back, but to get anywhere else we'd need to set coordinates from scratch from their main control room. Which they'll hardly just let me waltz right into. No, it's going to have to be old-school. Right out the front doors. We can Short-Hop once we're two hundred and fifty feet away from the perimeter."

"Oh, if that's all," said my brother irritably.

"If Calliope says that's the only way out, Leo," I said, "then that's the only way out."

"It's the only way out," said Calliope.

"We'll be gone before you know it," I said, trying to sound more reassuring than I felt. "We just need to look like guards for long enough to get ourselves to an open door. It's a huge corporation. People come in and out all day long. We just need to find a door."

"Okay," said Carter dubiously. "This better work."

"What's your better idea?" I said.

"Not marrying a reporter, for one thing. Writers keep crazy hours; the kids would never see their dad . . ."

"Oh, for the love of God, Carter, *I am not marrying Bob Woodward.*"

"Do *not* start this again," Leo interjected before we could get going. "You can fight all you want once we're back at the safe house."

"Everyone ready?" asked Calliope. We all nodded. She looked over at me. "You give the order, boss," she said.

"Okay," I said, raising my left wrist with my stolen U.E. guard Comm. "Go." And I hit the transport button, and braced for disaster.

~

My first glimpse of the inner workings of United Enterprises was remarkably anticlimactic. I stepped through the Slipstream back to my own time and found myself in a tiny, blindingly white room, about the size of a broom closet.

I blessed their trillion-dollar corporate budget that provided individual private transports for each on-duty agent (the U.S. government only had one in our whole building) because it meant that we had all landed with zero HIO interference. Nobody had seen us. It had worked. We were almost home.

Now we just needed to get out of the building.

I tentatively pushed open the door and peered out into the hallway. It was white out there too, pristine and immaculate. The guard's helmet shielded my eyes as they adjusted to the bright light. I was in a long corridor full of white doors, all closed, with a massive metal double door at one end and a glass one into the control room at the other. I stepped outside.

"Anybody else land inside a box?" I heard Leo say quietly, and realized the rooms must have been soundproofed; I could only hear him through the Comm.

"Me," said Carter.

"And me," said Calliope.

"Come outside," I said. "I'm in the hallway."

After a moment, I saw a door open, far away down at the other end, and a black-uniformed figure stepped out of it. Then another, right across from me, and another three doors down. We stood there tentatively for a moment, staring at each other, before one of them removed a helmet and revealed a head of springy golden curls. It was Calliope. Then we all took our helmets off.

"I thought for a second you might be real guards," said Carter in a very low voice as he and the others came towards me. "Damn helmets, you can't see anyone's face through them."

"Exactly," I said, grinning.

"I was expecting a crowded transport lab and guns drawn when we landed," said Calliope. "This is much better."

"Let's not stand out here," I said, waving everyone back into the tiny white room I had come from, packing our four bodies in like sardines in a tin can. "Okay, Calliope," I said, closing the door behind us. "Exits."

She pulled her handheld out of her pack and tapped on it a few times.

"We're on the twelfth floor," she said, scanning the building to pull up a layout map, "and there are no interior stairwells. But . . ." She looked at me. I looked at her. We both said the same thing at the same time.

"*Sidewinders.*"

"Oh great," I said. "That's the last thing we need."

"What are you two on about?" asked Leo. "What's a Sidewinder?"

"It's the world's most sophisticated elevator," said Calliope. "The whole building is constructed around it so it can move both horizontally and vertically. And it's secured. You can't just push a button. If it doesn't recognize you, it won't even open the door."

"And it's the only way around the building," said Carter. "And we're on the twelfth floor. Hooray."

"So now what?" said Calliope, looking at me.

"I don't know," I said. "We'll have to figure something out on the fly. Helmets on, people, we're going for a walk."

"We're just going to go wandering through this building in our stolen uniforms and hope to God we don't get caught?" said Leo. "That's your plan?"

"That's all I've got so far," I said. "If you have a better idea I'd love to hear it."

He didn't say anything, but he put his helmet back on. I pushed open the door from the transporter and the others followed me outside.

The metal door at the end of the transport corridor led to the master control room, which was bustling with activity. There was a grid onscreen that corresponded with the rows of transporters, lighting up red and green as agents came and went. Nobody appeared to notice us – the room was full of guards coming and going, and while not all of them wore helmets, enough of them did that we managed to sneak past unnoticed. The guards we passed gave us perfunctory head nods of greeting, a gesture we instinctively mimicked.

Outside the transport lab, all was steel and glass and white. The building looked like a very expensive fish tank. As we stepped out of the lab into the heart of the building, we found ourselves in open space. There was a central atrium, as high as the top of the building itself (which was too many floors up to count), ringed with glassed-in offices and solid steel doors that led, presumably, to more hallways.

"I wonder how big the paychecks are that come with these offices," murmured Leo at my side, as we marched two-by-two down the hallway. "This is a lot nicer than your building."

"Tell me about it," I said. "I don't even have a window."

The mezzanine corridor felt a little too exposed, so we turned left and made our way slowly through the interior hallways. We wandered aimlessly for ten or fifteen minutes while I desperately looked around for anything that might help us get out of there. And then, rather abruptly, I got my first look at the Sidewinder as we found ourselves suddenly facing a chrome-and-white elevator bay, staring up at an imposing-looking metal door.

A door with a small black panel on the wall next to it.

I turned and stared at Calliope, feeling giddy.

"Calliope," I said. "The scanner. Look."

"What about it?" she said.

"Waist level," I said. "Not eye level."

"What are you—?"

"The Sidewinder doesn't do retinal scans," I said, voice rising with excitement. "It scans *security badges*. It can't tell the difference between us and our uniforms." I pulled the badge from my stolen uniform and swiped it across the silver panel on the wall next to the door. A green light flashed twice, and the door whooshed noiselessly open.

I was so relieved I almost laughed with delight.

"Welcome," said a soothing, computerized female voice as we stepped inside. "You have 1A elevator clearance. What is your purpose?"

"There are no buttons," said Carter, puzzled. "What the hell kind of elevator is this?"

"How do you tell it where you're going?" asked Leo.

"You don't," I said. "It tells you."

"Welcome," the voice said again. "You have 1A elevator clearance. What is your purpose?"

"Leaving the building," said Calliope. "Main exits." The voice was silent for a moment, and we looked at each other nervously.

"Scans indicate your shifts are not yet completed," said the voice. "Permission to leave the building must be received from shift supervisor."

I felt all three of the others turn slightly accusatory eyes towards me. This was a scenario I had not, in fact, considered.

"'Steal a uniform and a transport,' you said. 'We'll just walk out the front door,' you said." My brother's voice was an exasperated sigh, and I glared at him.

"Look," I said, a little defensively. "First of all, watch your choice of words inside the sentient elevator. Second of all, I'm flying blind here."

"What is your purpose?" asked the elevator again, and I closed my eyes, frantically straining for a solution. *Come on,* I begged the universe, *come on. Give me something.* I heard Carter say something but I wasn't listening. I scanned through everything I knew about this building, about its layout, about

Sidewinders – which wasn't much – trying to think of a way for us to get out of the building.

We couldn't leave without our uniforms, or we'd be recognized. We couldn't leave *with* them, or we'd set off alarms for walking out the front door before our shifts ended. Either way, we'd never make it 250 feet from the perimeter without being caught.

I was thinking so hard that it actually took me a second to realize the elevator was moving. I snapped out of my reverie and looked at the others. Calliope and Leo were smiling at Leo, who shrugged.

"Welcome back," said Calliope to me. "You missed it."

"Where are we going?"

"I figured this elevator was too small – and too expensive – to be used for cargo," said Carter. "But they got desks and conference tables in here *somehow*. So there must be a second – hopefully less opinionated – elevator somewhere in the building."

"Nice work," I said approvingly, just as the Sidewinder came to a graceful halt and opened its doors. We stepped out and found ourselves in a less elegant, more utilitarian-looking hallway, facing a massive steel freight elevator door, with ordinary buttons outside it. Carter swiped his badge and pushed the "DOWN" button and we waited a minute, listening to the comfortingly old-fashioned sound of the heavy metal box rising up from the floor.

The steel doors opened and we stepped inside, relieved to find it a perfectly ordinary elevator. I pushed the button marked "GROUND FLOOR" and we began to descend. After a few moments we found ourselves in a wide concrete hallway with a big set of rolling warehouse doors at the end, and an ordinary door marked "EXIT" beside it.

I took a deep breath, walked over to it, and swiped my badge.

The door opened.

Air. Trees. Streets. Cars. Buildings.

No guards.

"Oh my God," said Leo. "You did it. We're free."

"Badges," I said, holding out my hand, and everyone pulled theirs off and handed them to me. "I'll leave these inside," I said, "so we don't trip the alarm."

"Good call," said Calliope, and she stepped out the door.

"Leo, you're with Calliope," I said. "You guys turn right and cross the street, then keep walking that way. Carter, go left. I'll go straight. We'll draw less attention if we split up. As soon as you hit 250 feet, jump back to the safe house. We'll rendezvous there. Got it?" Calliope and Leo nodded. "Okay," I said, double-checking that the coast was clear. "Go."

They assumed their best stern U.E. guard postures, put their helmets back on, and walked out the cargo door. I set their badges down on the floor, and stood up to see Carter looking at me with his arms folded across his chest and a stern look on his face.

"You didn't take off your own badge," he said.

"I will," I said. "I'm going to. Go ahead; I'll be right behind you."

"You think Mars is in the building," he said. "Or at least a clue to who he is. And you want to roam around the halls in your stolen guard uniform and see what you can find."

"And you stayed behind to stop me."

"No," he said, with a wry half-smile. "I stayed behind because U.E. security guards always work in pairs."

"Carter—"

"I'm in this," he said. "I'm your partner. That's the deal.

Where you go, I go. Where you lead, I follow. If you say we put our helmets and badges back on and take a stroll through the headquarters of United Enterprises, then I'm with you. Just . . . you know, try not to get us killed."

"I'm doing my best, I swear. I know it might not look like it."

He sighed and held out his hand. I gave him back his badge and he clipped it back on. "One condition," he said. "The second I see you do something reckless, and I mean the *second*, I will drag you back down here and shove you out that door if I have to carry you kicking and screaming. I am not letting you get yourself killed. Clear?"

"Clear," I said. "I'm not going to be stupid, I promise. I just want to look around."

"All right," he said with a resigned sigh, pulling his helmet back on. "Let's go."

～

Back in the glassed-in atrium hallway, we strolled slowly around the perimeter to get the lay of the land a little better.

"The other guards just look like they're walking around," I said. "I vote we just do a slow loop floor by floor and see if we see anything interesting."

"That sounds like a good place to start," he said. "Left or right?"

"Left," I said.

We turned left and walked slowly, purposefully, the way the other guards did, as though patrolling the hallways. My eyes darted left and right from behind the visor of my security helmet. There was nothing out of the ordinary on this floor, just people sitting at computers. We walked the whole circumference of the atrium. Then we went to the floor below and did it again. Nothing.

We had no trouble getting from floor to floor in the elevator, which meant that so far nobody at United Enterprises had caught onto the fact that those four guards had not actually returned inside their own uniforms. I definitely didn't want to be in the building when they figured it out, but I also knew that if I left now, I might never be this close to Mars again.

I was going to have to be the one to go to Congressman Holmes. It was all up to me now – to clear my parents, to turn in Grove, to hand over the Watergate crime scene photos, to reveal the truth about the war.

I thought back to that first meeting (which felt like a thousand years ago) where my mother and Director Gray and I sat in the Bureau Council Chambers across from the Congressional Time Travel Committee and I told them what the Timeline readings were showing us. Holmes liked me. He trusted me. And I think, deep down, he felt guilt about what happened to my father. I wanted to believe that he would listen, if I came to him with proof. But Grove alone wasn't enough. I had to give him Mars too. I had to give him something about U.E. that he could use.

We walked for awhile longer before we circled back around to the elevator bay again. It was empty; Carter stopped walking and leaned against the wall.

"Cover me for a second," he said. "My head is itching like crazy."

I kept watch down the hallway while he quickly pulled off his helmet, sighed with relief, ran a hand through his short dark hair, and then – wrinkling up his nose and looking very much like a little boy asked to finish a much-hated chore – put his helmet back on.

"It's only been like half an hour and I already hate this thing," he said. "How do these guys do it all day long?"

"No idea," I said, taking mine off and gathering up my hair for a moment to let the chill hallway air cool off my sweaty neck. I desperately did not want to put the helmet back on – it smelled like metal and perspiration and my coffee breath – but we had to keep going.

"What's next?" asked Carter, as if reading my mind. "We could do this for forty-something floors and not find anything."

"I know."

"We don't even know what we're looking for. We can't just walk up to someone and ask where Mars is."

I stared at him.

"What?" he said. "You've got your 'Sudden Idea' face on again. What did I say?"

"We can," I said. "We can."

"We can what?"

"We can ask where Mars is," I said, grinning at him, and I swiped my security badge on the panel outside the Sidewinder. The robotic woman's voice greeted us politely again and asked our purpose.

"We're looking for Mars," I said. Instantly the wall behind us lit up, and we turned. It had become a floor-to-ceiling digital computer screen. It began to flash rapidly through a series of images.

"What's it doing?"

"Scanning all the security feeds," I said. "It must be synced to everybody's ID badges. So you can either tell it where you're going, or you tell it who you're looking for and it takes you directly to their current location."

"That's . . . sinister," he said.

"But at the moment, convenient."

"Agent Mars is currently on floor Eighty-Seven," said the soothing voice. "Please provide your Restricted Access Level security code in order to proceed."

"Goddammit," I muttered under my breath. "I hate you, you stupid computerized elevator with your stupid questions and your stupid security codes." The freight elevator wouldn't help us this time – there was no way an unsecured cargo lift went up to the Restricted Access Levels if the Sidewinder required an additional password. And there were no stairwells.

"Reggie," Carter whispered in an urgent voice. I was only half-listening, trying to rack my brains for some way to access floor Eighty-Seven if neither the Sidewinder nor the freight elevator would take us there. "Reggie," he said again, pulling at my sleeve.

"Hang on," I said. "I'm thinking."

"Reggie," he said, his voice slow and soft. *"Turn around."*

I turned around.

The video wall had located Agent Mars' nearest security camera feed. It showed a gleaming, airy white hallway, skylights overhead – floor Eighty-Seven must be at the very top of the building. The digital projection was so detailed that I felt, uncomfortably, as though I were standing in that white hallway. I knew it was a one-way feed, but I felt naked and exposed, glaringly out of place in my black uniform.

Directly in front of us was a pair of glass double doors. A very pretty young woman sat at a desk and behind her was a glass wall into the most grand and opulent office we had yet seen. Though everything was white, it was lush and ornate in a way the rest of the building was not. Where the hallways and even the atrium were chilly, this room was elegant and refined. A huge white desk, heavy and intricately carved, sat in the center, flanked by white leather chairs, with thick white carpet underneath.

"Please provide your Restricted Access Level security code in order to proceed," said the elevator voice again. We ignored her.

Behind the desk was a high-backed white chair, facing away, with its back to us. A hand reached out for a white china teacup sitting on the top of the white desk, and Carter and I looked at each other.

"That's Mars," I said, my heart in my throat. "Mars is *right there.*"

"Please provide your Restricted Access Level security code in order to proceed."

Turn around, I begged the hand holding the teacup. *Oh please, oh please. Turn around. Let me see your face.*

We watched, praying for something to happen. A Comm screen pinged on the pretty receptionist's desk. We couldn't see who she was talking to, but it was a brief conversation, and she rang off.

And then the miracle happened. She turned around from her desk and tapped on the glass behind her. The hand set down the teacup and waved her in. My pulse was pounding. I clutched Carter's arm. *Oh please, oh please.*

We saw the chair slowly turn around.

There, clad in a perfect white suit, legs crossed elegantly as she sipped her tea, sat Beth Rutherford.

"Holy shit," I whispered. "Oh, holy shit."

"Oh, *no,*" said Carter.

"Please provide your Restricted Access Level security code in order to proceed," said the elevator.

"Let us out," said Carter, and the elevator door whooshed open. I couldn't move. "Walk normal, Reggie," he murmured under his breath, shoving me out of the elevator.

"Carter—"

"Transporter corridor," he said. "It's soundproof. Go. Walk. Now."

I held my head high, trying to walk steadily and purposefully like the U.E. guard whose uniform I was wearing, but I could hardly breathe inside my helmet.

Mars was Beth Rutherford.

She was Mars, god of war. She had planned this whole thing. All this time – while I was hunting through two different centuries for the mastermind behind the World War III Chronomaly – she had been sitting in the desk right across from me. For three months I had typed her memos and tolerated her snippy remarks about my punctuality. I had watched her endure a litany of endless indignities from people like Gordon Liddy and might even, if she had been a different sort of person, have pitied her for it.

And all that time, she was pulling the strings behind everything.

For three months, the enemy I was hunting had stared me in the face, and I didn't even know it. She was ruthless and brilliant, and I was powerless against her. What chance did Carter and I and a handful of antiquated gadgets from Calliope have against this corporation, against a person like that?

Mechanically, without even noticing where I was going, I followed Carter, retracing our steps back through the control room into the transport corridor, where he pulled me inside the first open door and shut it. We pulled off our helmets and stared at each other. Nobody said anything for a long time. Finally Carter broke the silence.

"You have worse luck with bosses than anyone I've ever met," he said, which struck me at that moment as so hysterically funny that I burst out laughing. I laughed and laughed and laughed, tears streaming down my face. I laughed until it crossed the line over into a kind of mania, as though all the tension and anxiety and panic of the past weeks and month had finally broken the dam.

I've lost it, I thought to myself. *I've officially lost it. Goodbye sanity.*

Carter watched me, an expression of growing concern on his face, until the laughter and the tears merged into some weird, gulping hybrid and I was laughing and crying and hyperventilating a little and beginning to feel like I might faint.

"Come here," he said, and he put his arms around me, and I laugh-cried into his shoulder until I felt my hysteria subside. "It makes a weird kind of sense," he said thoughtfully, his sensible voice soothing. "We were close. We were on the right track the whole time. We had narrowed it down to the Counsel's office. We just assumed we were dealing with Dean. But this explains everything. The trace radiation, the U.E. wiretaps, the Gemstone link – all of it. It makes perfect sense."

"Beth Rutherford was the real brain in that office all along," I said into his shoulder. "She ran that place. Dean could never have snuck a conspiracy this big past her without her knowing it."

"But she could certainly have snuck it past him."

"It makes sense," I said. "I don't know why I didn't see it."

"Because she's very, very good," said Carter. "Come on. We've seen what we needed to see. Let's head back to the safe house. Calliope and Leo will be wondering where we are. And we need to figure out a plan to get to Beth."

Something he said pinged the back of my brain.

I pulled my hand away. Carter stared at me. "What?" he asked, concern in his voice.

The safe house.

I paged Calliope. No answer. Then Leo. Nothing. I tapped my Comm frantically, over and over, but neither of them picked up.

"Reggie, what is it?" said Carter.

"Oh no," I said. "Oh no, oh no, oh no."

"Reggie," he said. "Tell me."

"We jumped from there," I said. "Calliope wrote down the home coordinates and sent them to Sweethaven with Leo." His eyes widened as he realized what I meant. "He jumped us from the safe house, Carter, *Grove knows where the safe house is.*"

"*Dammit,*" he said fiercely. He pulled out his own Comm and tapped at it, but got nothing.

"We have to go back," he said.

"No. We can't. It's a trap."

"Then we need to get out of the building," he said. "We can take what we have to Congressman Holmes. The photos and your recording of Grove, and the Gemstone file. We'll walk out of here and go straight to his office."

"Gemstone," I whispered, feeling my chest contract. "Oh no."

"What about it?" he began to ask, but stopped short when he saw the look on my face. "Reggie," he said slowly. "*Where's the Gemstone drive?*"

"Calliope had it in her bag when we left the safe house," I said, "along with the evidence wall."

"Where is it now?" he asked.

"I don't know," I said. "I don't remember. But I think—" I stopped, going back over it in my mind. "I think she left it with Grove," I said in a small voice.

"Grove has your evidence wall, and Gemstone," he said. "And presumably the first set of police photos. And the entire Bureau database."

"And the safe house coordinates," I said, closing my eyes, swallowing my tears, and realizing for the first time just how badly I had screwed up.

We had obliterated every trace of time travel agent involvement in the Watergate affair and in Gemstone. We had stolen police evidence, burned down Carter's apartment, and destroyed everything that had come through the Slipstream that could possibly be traced back to the 22nd century. Harold Grove had set a trap and we had walked right into it. And then we had handed him every single piece of evidence he didn't yet have.

"So what do we tell Holmes?" said Carter.

I shook my head, feeling the tears welling up, feeling the hysteria rising again.

"We tell him nothing," I said. "There's nothing we can do. I could go shoot Beth Rutherford in the head right now and it would stop nothing. There's *nothing* we can do from here, Carter, don't you get that? We can't stop her. We can't fight her. We can't fight this company. Holmes isn't going to help us. Telling the truth about U.E. isn't going to help us. None of that means anything anymore. We went all the way back to get those photos for nothing."

"The photos," he said, and he looked at me suddenly. "Reggie. *Reggie.* The photos."

"I told you," I said wearily, without opening my eyes. "Holmes won't do anything with the photos."

"Not those photos," Carter said. "The other set."

"What are you talking about?"

"You said we walked into Grove's trap," said Carter. "That we followed his steps exactly. We did everything exactly like he asked."

"We did."

"No," he said, voice rising with excitement. "*You didn't*. You did one thing that wasn't in Grove's plan. And he doesn't know."

I opened my eyes. I stared at him.

"Woodward and Bernstein," I said. "I forgot."

"We're not sunk yet, Bellows," he said. "That's our ray of hope. You gave the photos to the reporters and it *worked*. Calliope said so. That means—"

"That means we can still stop this thing," I said, feeling my pulse quicken and the dull ache of sorrow in my chest slowly fade away. "But we can't do it from here."

And suddenly I knew what I had to do . . . and where I had to go.

"We have to go back," I said. "Back to the beginning."

"Back to '72?" he said. "To the Watergate?"

"No," I said slowly. "The *real* beginning. I have to get to another Timeline where I know Beth Rutherford will be. And then I have to get *this* Beth to follow me in, without knowing where she's going."

"You can't," breathed Carter, eyes wide. "You can't be serious."

"Carter—"

"You're going to create a Double Incongruity? *On purpose?*"

"It's the only way," I said. "We have to erase Beth Rutherford from history so the Timeline can rewrite itself. It's like a forced restart."

"We could get caught inside the Incongruity with her," he said. "We could die there."

"There's no 'we,'" I said. "You're staying here. We have no way of getting into the Bureau lab to do a Rewind if something goes wrong. I can't risk both of us. I'm going in alone."

"Like hell you are," he said, eyes flashing. "I'm your partner. I'm not letting you fight Beth Rutherford alone."

"You can't come with me where I'm going," I said. "It's twenty times more dangerous for you."

"Why?" he said, suspicion dawning. "Where are you going?"

"To the only other place in all of time where I know I'll find Beth Rutherford," I said. "I'm going to the Sharpeville Massacre."

CHAPTER EIGHT

THREE MINUTES

"This is a terrible plan," said Carter's voice from my Comm two hours later, as I found myself army-crawling through a dusty air vent.

"Whatever," I said. "You have the easy job."

"Bait is the *worst job*."

"You're such a whiner."

"It's not even a *job*. It's something that gets eaten."

"Think of it this way," I said. "Your reward is that as soon as you're done being bait, you can leave. Plus, you got the fun part. You got to do the science experiment."

"That's true," he said, brightening considerably.

We had made our way from the shiny white upper stories to the grimy and dim lower floors where the real work was done, to the lowest subbasement of the building our 1A elevator clearance would allow us to go. There, Carter raided a disused storage room and I formulated the plan that had since split us up and sent me into the air vents, gingerly carrying the unholy concoction he had cooked up with a handful of sugar packets from the mess hall pantry, an empty cardboard toilet paper roll, Carter's stun pistol on its highest heat setting, and the gunpowder from the bullets in the guard's sidearm that I had carefully pried apart with pliers.

"I have the worse job," said Carter. "I might get shot at."

"*Might*," I said. "Whereas I *definitely* have climbed a tiny metal ladder through the building's air filtration system up from Subbasement-D to the 14th floor, lugging the kindergarten craft project from hell, so your argument has no standing. Where are you?"

"I'm almost there," he said. "I'm just a few feet from the door."

"Me too," I said. "Unless I made a wrong turn somewhere, I should be right above the transport lab in just a minute. Be noisy, okay? So I can find you."

"If this works, it will be plenty noisy," he said, and as I crawled through the metal tubing – dusty and spidery from decades of disuse – I closed my eyes and prayed that this would not turn out to be a giant catastrophic disaster.

"I'm outside the door," Carter said. "Are you close?"

"Hang on," I said. "I think I see the vents."

Transport labs are aggressively climate-controlled – the equipment is highly sensitive to heat, and the rooms are generally on the chilly side, well-ventilated and dry. That meant if we could get into the vent system unnoticed, I should be able to find the right room by watching for the right kind of grates.

"I see it!" I whispered. "Okay, I'll be right above it in five seconds."

"Tell me when you're in place," he said, "and go fast. I don't want to get caught lurking."

"I'm here," I said, peering down through the grate at the room below. I was above the transport lab's control room. Five white-coated techs were scattered around the room at the consoles. All was still and quiet. No one was looking up at the grates. Nobody had heard me.

"Are you ready?" I asked Carter.

"Ready," he said. "Go."

I took a deep breath, used my stun pistol to light the fuse, and let Carter's misshapen homemade smoke bomb – gunpowder and sugar heated together with a cardboard casing – drop to the floor, at the exact moment that Carter, clad in a head-to-toe biohazard suit over his guard uniform, charged through the door, discreetly elbowing the decontamination alarm on the wall to release a screeching klaxon wail, which reverberated hideously off every wall of the metal rectangle I was trapped in. Then, the final touch. Carter, who could not resist a dramatic flourish when it was presented, took a deep breath and shouted into the now-chaotic room.

"*Fire!*"

It was a thing of beauty. The control room fans had already spread the smoke through the room by the time they heard it, and even though there were only a handful of people inside, they did a credible job of creating a stampede to get out the door. This part had been Carter's idea, and it worked marvelously. They were so panicked that nobody stopped to log out of their computer or take anything with them. They just bolted.

The second the last one was out the door, Carter closed it behind them and I dropped down from the ceiling.

"Locks," I said over my shoulder as I raced over to the controls. "Shoot out the panels so they can't get back in."

He pulled out his U.E. laser pistol and a beam of white light shot out, neatly frying the electronic locking mechanism on the main transport lab door. My hands flew over the control panels at the main console.

"Are you in the system?" he asked.

"Oh yeah," I said. "This is the high-end version of the crappy system they sold the federal government. This baby's gonna do exactly what I tell her."

The transport system at United Enterprises was a thing of beauty, all sleek white panels and muted lighting. I ran my fingers over the touch-screen controls, fighting down a feeling of irrepressible envy towards the lucky bastards who got to use these computers every day. Whereas setting space-time coordinates from the Bureau's main console was a laborious process that required specialized tech skills like Calliope's, the lab at U.E. was so quick it practically read my thoughts.

"Okay," I said to Carter, "the doors from the guard transport hallway are sealed. Go do your thing."

"How long until they figure out how to un-disable it?" he asked.

"If we're really lucky," I said, "nine minutes."

"So, plan on five?"

"Three," I said. "Run." And I could hear him as I worked, running down the hallway and shooting out the control panels of every transport – except for one. I set the transport coordinates for the white box at the farthest end of the hallway.

Then, with a tiny pang of regret for the gorgeous technology I was destroying, I pulled out my laser pistol, aimed it at the screen of the console next to me, and fired. It blackened and shattered with a viscerally satisfying bang, and the lights around it went dark.

Bang. *That's for my dad,* I thought, feeling a surge of energy run through me.

I shot out the next one.

Bang. *That's for those seventy civilians in Sharpeville.*

Bang. *That's for the city of Beijing.* Bang. *The Washington Monument.*

Bang, bang, bang. *That's for the twenty-two million Americans and thirty-four million Chinese people who died so you could build this company.*

Every small explosion felt like a tiny act of rebellion. Beth Rutherford and this company had destroyed so many lives. It felt good to destroy something of hers in return. It felt good to fire beams of hot white light into glass and metal and watch them explode. It felt like I was taking something back that she had stolen from me.

The sound of pounding at the door and the high-pitched keening of laser drills snapped me back to reality.

"They're coming!" I yelled at Carter as I shot out the last console with a shattering crash.

"Almost there!" he yelled back. "Two more!"

"Hurry!"

The room was now a blackened, smoking heap of broken glass and metal – all except one console, which controlled the one transporter Carter hadn't blown up, and a discreet black panel in the corner labeled "Emergency Transmissions Only." I had torched every piece of equipment that would allow anyone to interfere with that transporter. If Beth Rutherford wanted to find me, the absolute only choice in front of her was to walk into a white box and push the button without knowing where she was going.

"Nice work," Carter panted, running back into the middle of the smoke as the pounding on the outside door got louder. "What's next?"

I showed him the console where I had loaded the two

jumps. He didn't have the years of fluency with this computer system that I did, but he was smart, and I had made it simple.

"You're going to send me through," I said, "and then you're going to send her through on a time delay. I need a head start to find the second Beth. And then you're going to lock onto the Comm you're wearing and you're going to jump yourself out."

"I'm setting your second jump to send you to Croatia. They don't have extradition treaties with the United States and if you tell Marcus at the restaurant that you're a friend of Leo's, he'll help you hide until I can come find you. Got it? Jump her when she enters the box, then jump yourself. Immediately. She'll bring backup and they'll try to shoot out this door."

The pounding on the doors got louder and louder.

"Three minutes is up," he said. "It's time." And he wrapped me in his arms, hard and tight, and kissed the top of my head.

"I'll find you," I said. "When this is all over, I'll come find you. Just be safe. Don't do anything stupid."

"You either," he said. "Ready?"

"Ready."

I slammed my hand against the "Emergency Transmissions Only" panel in the corner and heard a reverberating hum as it opened a building-wide audio channel.

"This is Agent Regina Bellows of the United States Time Travel Bureau," I said. "I have a message for Beth Rutherford."

I heard my voice over the Comm system in the transport lab and out in the hallways. The pounding on the doors paused, as though everyone in the building was listening. And I knew that up there, dozens of floors above me, she was listening too.

"You're not a god," I said, and as I spoke I felt a wave of white-hot anger rise up inside me, swallowing the panic, swallowing the fear. Nothing in the world existed right now except for Beth's face, hovering before me in my mind.

"You're a monster. You rewrote Time and killed fifty-six million people. You may call yourself Mars, but I'm Nemesis. Goddess of vengeance. I'm here to rain down a metric shitload of righteous divine retribution on those who show arrogance before the gods. And I'm *inside your fucking house*. You want me? Come and get me."

Then I pulled out my stun rifle, aimed it at the Comm system, and fired. A deeply satisfying, deafening shriek exploded through the building-wide intercom.

I looked at Carter. Carter looked at me.

"All right, Nemesis," he said, grinning at me. "Showtime."

"Good hunting," I called over my shoulder as I sprinted out of the control room.

"You too!" he yelled back, and as I ran I heard the sizzling sound of laser heat on metal as he sealed the control room doors behind me.

I could already hear the sound of shouting voices outside the transport corridor – they were resetting the lock already, they'd be inside in a matter of seconds. I ran past the smoke-blackened doors until I found the one pristine, closed white one and sealed myself into a soundless white tomb just as the hallway door flew open and a stampede of heavy boots charged into the transport corridor.

I closed my eyes, took a deep breath, and then I was gone.

CHAPTER NINE

REMEMBERING WHERE YOU'VE NEVER BEEN

I landed hard, losing my balance as I stepped out of the Slipstream and collapsing with a thud on hot dusty ground. If Carter's end of the plan worked, I had two hours before Beth Rutherford would crash through and land on this exact spot, which wasn't a lot of time. Still, I wasted ten or fifteen precious seconds just to lay there and catch my breath.

The air around me smelled of dust and tar and heat. I listened hard – shouting, like that of a crowd, but far away. Some English, some in a language I couldn't make out. Singing. Lots of voices, but muffled at a distance. Maybe I hadn't been spotted.

I jumped up, dusted myself off, and looked around. I was on flat, dry ground patched with bits of dead grass, standing behind an empty, unmarked military-looking jeep. There was nothing except dry grassland stretching away in front of me, with the faint shapes of a town in the distance. No people. The noises must be coming from behind me.

I checked my HIO meter. 1.8.

Not bad, I thought to myself approvingly. First crisis averted. I hadn't been seen.

I crouched low and peered around the side of the jeep. There was a decrepit shack about fifty feet away, surrounded by tattered fencing. A few men stood near the doorway, gesticulating wildly. As I moved around the corner of the vehicle, I finally saw what they were pointing at, the source of all the voices I had heard. Stretched far away across the dusty field in front of the shack was a vast crowd of African faces, thousands upon thousands strong, holding small paper booklets in their hands. It was an extraordinary sight. It was nothing at all like seeing it in photographs.

My coordinates had worked. I had beaten Beth Rutherford here.

I looked out at the vast sea of humanity stretching out in front of me and I let the singing and voices wash over me. "You are not going to die today," I whispered, with more hope in my voice than I felt, trying to send it through the air, over the crowd, towards the seventy people whose lives would be lost when the shooting started.

I had lied to Carter, a little. I had told him the plan was to create a Double Incongruity centered around Beth Rutherford. That was true. But that was only half of it.

I was here to stop the Sharpeville Massacre.

I was here to save not just the fifty-six million victims of the Third World War, but the people who were going to die right here, today: Seventy unarmed African civilians – and Agent Leo Carstairs, who had been shot in the back trying to save them.

I was going to bring my father home.

I inched around the other side of the jeep to get a better view. A cluster of police officers stood in the front of the station, collecting paper passbooks from the quiet and orderly crowd as they filed up one by one to patiently submit themselves for arrest. So far, all was just as it should be.

Then one of the figures detached himself from the cluster and moved away, very near where I was hiding. My heart sped up a little and I pressed myself against the hot metal of the jeep. It would be just my luck to get spotted by a police officer thirty seconds after landing and ruin the whole plan.

But it appeared I was in luck; he had only stepped away for a smoke. He pulled out a cigarette from his pocket, and as he lifted it to his mouth I saw him discreetly tap away on a wrist Comm disguised as a watch. My heart sped up even further as he turned his back towards the police station, staring off into the distance, facing towards me.

It was my very first look at my dad.

I knew him from my mother's family albums, of course, and from the handful of documents in the Bureau archives that were redacted enough for my security clearance level. But to see him three-dimensional, living, breathing – not a ghost trapped in amber – was disorienting in the extreme.

He wasn't all that much older than me. He looked so much like Leo. Achingly so. Fairer skin and much more blond than his son, but the sweep of the hairline, the nose, the jaw, the ears, I knew them all by heart. They were my brother's. And, I realized suddenly, mine.

This was the best opening I was going to get. I took off my U.E. helmet and weapons, stashed them inside the jeep out of view, and approached him.

"Agent Carstairs," I said, and he stared at me.

The range of expressions that overtook his face were dizzying. First surprise, then suspicion, then a baffled recognition, as though he knew my face from somewhere but couldn't quite place it.

"If you are . . . who I think you are," he said hesitatingly, "then I don't understand how you could possibly be here."

"I'm with the Bureau," I said. He was still staring. "I have to talk to you," I said urgently. "Alone. I need to tell you what's about to happen. You felt something was wrong when you landed here. Something felt off."

He nodded.

"It is," I went on. "Something is very wrong. And I'm here to try and stop it."

He looked at me for a long, long moment, and I could see the wheels turning. I could see him trying to decide whether or not he could trust me. And then I watched something click, and he smiled.

"I'll be damned," he said softly, and there was something almost affectionate in his voice as he added, "Follow me," and led me inside the hot, dingy metal box that served as some kind of outbuilding of the police station.

Once inside, he slammed the door shut and bolted it. "Low voices," he said quietly. "Thin walls." I nodded. "How's your mother?" I looked up at him sharply, startled. He grinned. "You have her eyes," he said. "My nose, but her eyes."

"Yes," I said, smiling back at him. "I do."

"What's your name?"

"Reggie. Regina."

"Regina. Of course. Of course *her* grandmother wins out over *my* grandmother."

"Your grandmother's name was Mildred."

"Mildred is a *classic* name. And your brother? Christopher?"

I froze.

I had always known, of course, that my brother was named after my father, but had somehow never put two and two together. No one had ever told me that Leo's name was not originally supposed to be Leo. It felt desperately wrong to lie to my dad, yet I couldn't see any way to correct him without telling him it was because he was supposed to die here and his son would bear his name as a memorial. I hesitated.

"Yes," I said after a moment, seeing him look at me curiously. "Christopher."

"Does he work for the Bureau too?"

"No," I said. "He's Europe's most successful restaurateur under thirty," and my dad burst out laughing.

"That's fantastic," he said. "Don't tell me any more. I want to be surprised. Don't give all the good stuff away."

He pulled a chair out for me and waved me into it, then sat down across from me.

"Okay," he said. "Tell me."

"You were right about Gemstone," I said, and his eyes widened. "You were right about everything."

~

It took me nearly an hour to tell my father everything we had learned – that Beth Rutherford and Harold Grove had been working on both sides of the Timeline to create, and then conceal, a Chronomaly of staggering magnitude to promote U.E.'s rise as a global power. His money had been on John Dean too; he, also, had never seen Beth Rutherford coming. And he was heartbroken but unsurprised about Grove.

"Your mother," he asked. "Does she know?"

"I don't think so," I said. "I haven't seen her since she went on the run, a few days ago. Or eighteen months ago. Or twelve years from now. Whenever it was. But anyway, she didn't know then."

"She'll be devastated," he said. "They were at the Academy together. They've been friends since they were fourteen."

"I work under him," I said. "Or, I did. I was his apprentice."

"It must have been awful, when you found out."

"It was," I said. "It was like a nightmare."

"And you said the other one, the woman – Mars – you said she'll be coming through the net here? Why? What's special about this place?"

"I sent her here to create a Double Incongruity," I said. "It's the only way to erase her from the Timeline. Her younger self is here already."

"I don't understand," he said, and that was the moment I realized that I had used up all my time, I had arrived, I couldn't stall for a moment longer. I couldn't explain what was about to happen without saying the thing I desperately didn't want to say. I swallowed hard, took a deep breath, opened my mouth to speak, and choked on the words. No sound came out. I gritted my teeth to try again.

But I was reckoning without Leo Carstairs.

"Oh," he said, instantly comprehending. "Oh, she's good. She's *very* good. Something's going to go wrong today, isn't it? I'm going to die and it's going to look like an accident. That's brilliant."

He shook his head in grudging admiration. "I knew something felt wrong," he said. "It wasn't just that the crowd was bigger than it was supposed to be. It was something in the air. It was—"

"Menace," I said.

"Yes," he said approvingly. "That's it exactly. I was expecting chaos, but I felt something much uglier and more dangerous than that. I didn't know what it was."

"It's Beth Rutherford," I said. "It's because she's here."

"You've got to hand it to United Enterprises," he said. "They cover their bases. This is a flawless plan. Is this all because of Gemstone?"

"No," I said, a slow, cold realization dawning over me. "I thought it was, but no. It's bigger than that. It's all connected." I felt the world slow around me as the final pieces of the puzzle snapped neatly into place. I closed my eyes.

Beth Rutherford had been running this plan on two parallel tracks – one running backwards from the 22nd century and one speeding forward the 1970's – until they had collided in 1981 with the Third World War. It was all one endless loop of cause and effect. In the future, Beth Rutherford decides to build an empire, so she sends herself back to the past to groom a tiny security company into a global empire. She concocts a plan called Gemstone and gets the White House to sign off on it, maneuvering John Dean and Gordon Liddy around like pieces on a chessboard.

Gemstone opens the door for rampant sabotage of Democratic campaigns, assuring a Nixon win and placing the Reagan administration firmly in Beth Rutherford's pocket. Then – when she launches her war, pitting the United States against China – she's the first in line to pick up the pieces on both ends and profit by trillions of dollars, building U.E. into the indestructible Goliath it remained until this day.

But a century later, young Leo Carstairs uncovers the existence of Gemstone, and a twenty-five-years-younger Beth Rutherford – unable to shut down his investigation by pulling Colin Daisey's strings – executes a cold-blooded murder, flawlessly camouflaged as an accident.

And not just to prevent him from tracing Gemstone back to United Enterprises.

It was to prevent the future that would come about if he had lived.

Because if he had lived, I realized, my father would have become head of the department, over Harold Grove, when Mom was promoted to Deputy Director. Grove could never have pulled off the cover-up with Leo Carstairs looking over his shoulder.

If he had lived, it would have been my father, not me, sent to rescue Grove from the spike in Ohio that almost killed both of us. It would have been him in front of the Congressional Time Travel Committee, revealing that the Third World War was a Chronomaly. It would have been him, with two decades of field experience, sent back to 1972 to fix everything. He would have tracked down Beth Rutherford, spotted the Chronomaly, unraveled the entire conspiracy and prevented the war.

But he didn't. Because he died here instead.

Beth Rutherford's entire empire – the future she had killed tens of millions of innocent people to obtain – was built on top of my father's dead body.

"None of it was a coincidence," I whispered. "The Mandela crisis pulling all the black agents into the same Timestream; Mom getting benched; Daisey ignoring everyone's warnings; your transport not working. All of this was *planned*, Dad. This is an assassination."

"How many people are going to die unless we stop it?" he asked. "I don't mean me, I mean everyone else. How many?"

"Seventy-one today," I said. "And fifty-six million more in twenty-two years."

"All right," he said, nodding. "What do we do?"

"We have to find the first Beth Rutherford before she picks

up a rock and starts a war," I said. "And then we have to go back to the spot where I dropped in and catch the second one."

"And create a Double Incongruity."

"Yes."

"Force-restart the Timeline, basically, without her in it."

"Yes."

"That's insane," he said. "*Insane.*"

"Dad, there's no other—"

"No, I love it. You really are my kid."

I felt tears welling up in my eyes, and instantly he was on his feet and his arms were wrapped around me.

"If I died here," he said. "then I died before you were born. I never got to do this. I never got to be your dad."

"I'm only twenty-five," I said into the shoulder of his jacket, voice muffled. "We still have time."

"Katie did a good job," he said, and I could tell he was crying a little too.

I heard the soft buzz of the alarm on my Comm.

"Ten minutes," I said.

"Okay," he said. "Tell me what to do."

~

We decided to split up, with my father pulling a few of the Sharpeville police officers he had befriended to fan out with him and discreetly begin searching through the crowd for young Beth Rutherford. We had the element of surprise on our side with at least one of the Beths; this one, the one here to throw the rock, had no idea we were coming for her.

I watched him slip out of sight, then hoisted my U.E. guard rifle and walked back to the spot where I had come through the Slipstream to wait for the other Beth – the pissed-off one who was out for my blood. I had seven minutes left, by my calculations, until the drop coordinates. It was the longest seven minutes of my life. The heat, the wind, the rising tension. I watched the endless procession of Sharpeville citizens walking up to the police station steps and handing over their passbooks to submit themselves for arrest.

Please, I thought to myself, *please let me be able to save these people.*

All seventy-one of them.

There was a soft ping! on my Comm, signaling an incoming transport, and my heart pounded like a bass drum in my chest. I pressed my back against the army jeep behind me, took the safety off my rifle, and pointed it at the spot where I could still see my own footprints in the dust. *Come on, Beth, you crazy sociopath,* I thought, *don't fail me now.*

Then the Slipstream shimmered into view before me. I took aim. I slipped my finger onto the trigger.

Then the Slipstream opened, and out stepped Beth Rutherford.

Holding a knife to Carter's throat.

CHAPTER TEN

DOUBLE INCONGRUITY

I froze.

"Hello, Regina," said Beth pleasantly. One arm was wrapped around Carter's waist, from behind, almost intimately. The other held a wicked-looking serrated blade at his jugular vein, pressed against his skin just hard enough that I could see the slightest pressure would draw blood.

"Let him go, Beth," I said. "I'm the one you want."

"Here's the problem with that," she said. "You managed to cause quite a bit of property damage in my building, which was *deeply* vexing, and I'm not at all in the mood to grant you favors. If your little plan was to lure me through the Slipstream to some undisclosed location, well, fine, I'm here, congratulations. But if you thought I wasn't going to arrive without some kind of insurance policy, that was very stupid."

"Please," I said desperately. "Let him go. You don't need to hurt him."

"Lower your weapon," she said. "You have no idea how to

use that thing. Someone might get hurt. Why don't you put it down?"

"Don't do it, Reggie," said Carter sharply. "Do not listen to her."

"Carter—"

"Don't be an idiot," he said.

"Yes, Regina," said Beth. "Please, do try not to be an idiot."

"If I put down the gun," I said, "will you put your knife away? So we can talk?"

"Set it on the ground," she said, "and put your hands up."

"Reggie, no!" Carter snapped at me and then winced. I had hardly seen Beth move her wrist but suddenly I could see the faintest trickle of blood snake down the blade of the knife.

"Okay," I said. "Okay. I'm putting it down."

I set the rifle down in the dust and put my hands up.

"Kick it over to me," she said, and I did. In one graceful motion, she knelt to the ground, Carter still wrapped in her arms, then switched the knife for the gun so quickly that we had no time to react. She pushed Carter over towards me, the rifle trained on both of us.

"Kneel," she said, pulling a wooden crate out of the back of the jeep and dusting it off, "and put your hands behind your back."

We did.

"All right, Regina," she said, setting the crate in the sand facing us, and sinking gracefully onto it, crossing her legs and leaning back against the door of the jeep in a posture of supreme relaxation, for all the world as if she were holding court in that posh U.E. penthouse office. The rifle lay in her lap, casually pointed at our heads. "You wanted to talk. Let's talk."

I looked at her, sitting there on that crate, her white suit still impeccable as if somehow resistant to dust, not a hair out of place, and I told her the truth.

"When I first met you," I said, "I thought how depressing it was that someone so brilliant was stuck filing paperwork all day for a man whose job you could do with one hand tied behind your back. I thought, 'I wish Beth Rutherford had been born in another time so she could really be who she was meant to be.'"

"And then, when I saw you behind that desk, when I realized that you were Mars, that you were the one we were chasing, you know what? There was some sick part of me that felt *relieved*. That felt some weird sense of satisfaction that there was more to your life than the White House Counsel's Office. If ever anyone was born to be a super villain, it was you."

"I take that as a compliment."

"It was."

I felt her relaxing slightly, and took the risk of shifting my position, sinking down onto the dirt to sit cross-legged in front of her. If you ignored the gun, we were just two people having a conversation.

"And now," I went on, "I find out you did all of this to get rich. What a letdown. You're not even *interestingly* evil. You're just like everybody else."

She looked at me appraisingly, her dark eyes thoughtful and with a flicker of unexpected amusement.

"You're *disappointed* in me," she said. "I'll admit that's not the reaction I was expecting."

"I expected more from you," I said. "Money. So pedestrian."

"I hope you realize we don't need to be enemies, Regina," she said. "You're an extraordinary agent. We could use someone like you."

"I'm nothing like you," I said. "I would never do the things you did."

"Wouldn't you?" she said softly. "There's nowhere in all of history that you wouldn't go rewrite time, if you could? To get back what was taken from you? Are you quite sure?"

Carter and I looked at each other. I swallowed hard. There was nothing visible behind and around us but dust and metal shacks. The jeep shielded the crowds from view. And we knew we had destroyed the Comm system that sent her through, blocking her from seeing her own coordinates when she jumped. But there was something in her voice that unsettled me.

Did Beth Rutherford know where we were?

"I dedicated my life to building United Enterprises," she went on. "Thousands of hours of field work over decades went into crafting this company." She leaned forward, as if imparting a great secret to me. Against my will, I found myself drawn in.

"Time is delicate," she said. "It's fragile. It needs to be handled carefully, like precision clockwork. We tried nearly a hundred different methods of manipulating the Timeline until we found one that managed to remain stable. If you don't think I found it distasteful, being forced to make use of incompetent children like John Dean and Gordon Liddy, maneuvering them with the utmost care while keeping my eyes demurely cast down towards the floor and calling them 'sir,' well, then you have no imagination. But still, despite all my best efforts, the only tactic that worked – that stabilized the future the way I wanted it – forced me to cover up their clunky, half-witted espionage attempts so it wouldn't discredit President Nixon. So I swallowed my pride and I let Gordon Liddy win. Because in the end, I got what I wanted."

"He died in the first D.C. bombing," I said. "That must have been satisfying."

She dismissed that idea with an impatient wave of her hand.

"Oh, for heaven's sake, Regina, I'm not a monster. The war was a side effect. A terrible one, I'll grant you. I didn't *set out* to kill fifty-six million civilians. Genocide is so . . . inelegant. No, what I needed was a President in my pocket, and the Third World War was how I got him. It was simple. I didn't foresee that Reagan would suspend the 23rd Amendment and serve four terms, but it worked magnificently in my favor. United Enterprises had the ability to predict, and provide him with, everything he wanted."

"In exchange for him giving you everything *you* wanted."

"Naturally."

"All that time," I said, "going back and forth, living two different lives – running a massive corporation from the top floor and then stepping back in time a century and a half to be hit on by old men and treated like half a person. Aren't you tired yet?"

She laughed.

"I wasn't *forced* to take that job for John Dean," she said. "I fought for it. I moved all the chess pieces around the board to clear that space. I sat across from him and offered soothing advice when he was at his wit's end. I made gentle suggestions that he later remembered as if they were his own. I *ran* him, Reggie. That wasn't a punishment. That was the *point*. He was completely under my control. All those men were. But because I was a woman – and not even a particularly pretty one – they couldn't see it."

She looked me up and down. "You," she said thoughtfully, "interest me enormously. You see, the Gemstone Chronomaly was very nearly stable. It required a high level of patching in a few key places – that kept Grove fairly busy – but more and more it appeared to be a promising long-term solution. The war put United Enterprises right where I wanted it – it made us a world power. Our technology, our security guards, our private transport access . . . I didn't create the best products because I wanted to be rich, Regina, I became rich because what I built was the best."

"And then *you* came along – with your clumsy, dogged persistence and your need to prove yourself. Always interfering, always in the way, but so deftly that it took me a little while to be sure of you."

"When did you figure out I was from the Bureau?" I said.

"Oh, that?" She dismissed the question. "I knew the first moment I met you. You were visible from a mile away. No, what I didn't know was *why* you were there. Whether you could be safely ignored until your mission was completed and you went away again – as other agents have – or whether I needed to dispose of you before you became a nuisance."

"I know there's not a lot we agree on," I said, "but I think we can get together on the fact that you did not stop me from becoming a nuisance."

Beth burst out laughing. Not a diabolical villain chuckle, but a real laugh, hearty and unforced. *She likes you,* I thought, *you didn't think she liked you but she does,* and a treasonous corner of my brain was irrationally flattered and pleased by it. I remembered our brief moment of kinship when Liddy was drunk and hitting on us, and I wondered what she had been like before she became the wall of iron she was now. I felt myself grow dangerously close to not hating her.

"You and me," she said. "Think what a team we could have been. Think what we could do together."

Somewhere in the back of my mind, a sane and logical voice was screaming and pounding on the wall and yelling, *Stop! Stop!* But I was like a bird hypnotized by a cobra. She looked at me, I looked at her, and I forgot about Carter, about my father, about Sharpeville, about everything in the world that wasn't Beth Rutherford.

"Look at me," she said softly, as though I was capable of doing anything else, and she rose from her seat to come over to me. She was very close. She knelt down right in front of me and touched my cheek with her hand. She had the greenest eyes I had ever seen. I had forgotten that anyone else in the world existed. I had forgotten who and what and where I was.

You don't have to kill her, I thought. *You don't need to erase her from the Timeline. Maybe there's still good in her. What if she turned herself in? What if it ended here, peacefully, and we all went home, and nobody had to die?*

"Put the knife down, Beth," said the voice of Leo Carstairs, and the spell was broken. I snapped back to reality with a jolt to see my father standing behind Beth with the barrel of his gun pressed to her temple. It took me a second to realize what he had said, and then I looked down.

She must have picked the knife back up when she came over to me, because now it was pressed against my left breast, had already sliced through the fabric of my shirt and was about to pierce the skin. She had slipped it there so gently that I had not even noticed it. I recoiled, violently, looking up at my father, and remembered with piercing clarity all the things that Beth Rutherford had done, all the lives she had destroyed, and why the thing we were about to do was necessary.

"Murderers tend to be very charismatic," he said in a nonchalant voice, picking up the knife and holding it out to Carter, who threw it as far away from us as he could. "They often have extremely attractive, compelling personalities. But whatever she might say to you, it's important that you remember this woman is not your friend. This woman is here to kill all of us."

"Your hired muscle is very opinionated," she said. "If he were one of mine, I would dock his pay for insubordination, but I suppose to each her own."

I looked from her to him and back again, and felt a surge of wild delight take over my body. *It had worked.*

"You have no idea where we are," I said exultantly. "You don't recognize him."

She dismissed it with a hand wave.

"It doesn't matter," she said. "My tracking coordinates have been sent to the U.E. cargo transport and there's an entire army of security forces on their way. So unless you've got an army of your own, besides the President's butler" – with a dismissive gesture towards Carter – "and your blond arm candy over here, you've got about three minutes before all three of you get a bullet through the forehead."

"The blond arm candy," I said, "is my father."

She froze.

"Agent Leo Carstairs, United States Time Travel Bureau," he said, pressing the gun closer to her temple. "Welcome to Sharpeville, Ms. Rutherford. And Ms. Rutherford." And that was the first time any of us noticed the body lying in a heap at his feet.

"Don't worry," he said, "she's still alive. Just unconscious."

It was unquestionably the most deliciously satisfying moment of my entire life. Beth's entire face went pale and contorted in horror.

"Oh, you stupid, stupid girl," she breathed. "You have no idea what you've done."

"I know exactly what I've done," I said, and stood to go look at the second Beth Rutherford, unconscious on the dusty ground. She was younger than me, and she hadn't grown into her imperiousness yet.

She looked ordinary. She looked like someone I would like. She was wearing khaki pants, a loose white shirt and a headscarf which had come loose in her fall. I knew she was dangerous, and that stunning her was the only safe thing to do. Still, there was a part of me that wished I had met her.

"You've trapped us in a Double Incongruity," she said. "We could all die."

"You know what?" I said, walking right up to her and staring her down. "I don't care if I die. I don't. Seriously. I only care if you do. Because without you, there's no Gemstone. No United Enterprises. No World War Three. All of it goes away. You're the brains behind this whole thing and I want you erased from Time like you never existed. If I can have that, I don't care what happens to me."

From a great distance, I heard a terrific rumbling, and the telltale sound of a helicopter. Carter and I looked at each other. It was starting.

"Let's get them inside the police station," said Carstairs. "Both of them. I don't want to take the chance of either of them getting back out into the crowd."

Carter hoisted the unconscious young woman over his shoulder unceremoniously while my father and I, guns drawn, ushered Beth inside and closed the door, locking it behind us.

"Carter Hughes, Leo Carstairs. Leo Carstairs, Carter Hughes," I said as soon as we were inside. Carter gave a little wave with the one hand that wasn't holding onto the unconscious second Beth, and my father nodded back politely. "Carter, tie them up," I said as soon as we were inside, gesturing to a pair of chairs in the corner. "Find some rope or something. Dad, you have to call Mom. That's what happens next."

"Okay," he said, "you just tell me what to say."

I told him everything I remembered. I told him what he would say, and what she would say, and about Colin Daisey yelling in the background.

And then I gritted my teeth, and let it happen.

Carter held my hand as I stood silently by as my mother screamed at Daisey to send backup, pleaded with my dad to leave, and I watched him say all the things I had told him to say, so that they could go into the emergency transmission logs, so I could read them two decades later after they were declassified, so I could travel back here and feed him his lines. It was a perpetual circle. Were they my words given to him and then back to me? Were they his words given to me and then back to him? I didn't know.

As he talked, a faint dull hum in the distance grew louder and louder, more insistent, until it resolved itself into the sound of a huge caravan of military vehicles, with a chopper overhead.

And then it clicked.

Leo Carstairs had sent that transmission because he knew he was about to die. And how had he known that? Because something had felt wrong to him about the trucks. He had mentioned the trucks in his transmission. Jenkins had seen him staring at them oddly when he first transported in. But I had been blind. It was so obvious. I hadn't put it together.

I suddenly knew what my father had known – how he had realized he was about to die.

Those trucks weren't South African police forces. They belonged to United Enterprises. They were never supposed to be here.

They had camouflaged themselves as well as they could, but Leo Carstairs would have known he was looking at a

22nd-century vehicle. He might even have known they came from United Enterprises.

And it was after he was caught staring at the tires on one of the vehicles that the first bullets began to fly. I was not at all sure that was a coincidence.

"Sir, is this line secure?" my father said into his Comm.

"I'm the director, Carstairs, of course it is," snapped the irritable voice of Colin Daisey. "Why would you—"

"I think there's another agent in the field, sir," my dad interrupted, repeating the line exactly as I had quoted it to him from the transcripts. He was looking at me as he said it, and suddenly something clicked inside my brain.

This had always been the part that didn't fit. Mom, of course, had investigated thoroughly – so had the Bureau – and no trace of any registered agent had ever been found. Daisey dismissed it as paranoid. But he had said it. Carstairs had said there was another agent in the field.

And he had said it while looking at me.

There *was* another agent in the field. But he wasn't referring to Harold Grove, who had never been here, or Beth Rutherford, who had never worked for the Bureau. He wasn't referring to Carter either, since I hadn't actually mentioned that Carter was one of us.

The other agent in the field was *me*.

Me, without my tracker, so I wouldn't show up even as a Ghost when Mom scanned the Sharpeville Massacre for traces of interference. She was still pregnant with me when that happened, I realized with a jolt. She had no idea that the second agent she was hunting for was one of the twin fetuses inside her at the very moment she was scanning.

The other agent was me, crashing into a Timeline I was never supposed to have entered.

"Oh my God," I whispered. "Oh no, oh no, oh no."

"Reggie, what is it?" asked Carter, worry on his face. My father finished the call and switched off his Comm, turning to me.

"What happened?" he said.

"I didn't realize it before," I said, hysteria bubbling up and causing me to babble. "I mean, from the transcripts. Because I wasn't there. I didn't think. But just now. Mom. When you called in. When she said the readings were off-the-charts crazy."

"Regina, slow down," said my father, placing both hands on my shoulders. "Take a breath."

"It's not because of Beth," I said urgently, "and it's not because of the crowd, or the extra soldiers. That wasn't it. We thought it was, but it wasn't. That's the *effect*. Not the *cause*. That's not what created the spike. The spike is *me*. Me meeting you. *I'm* the thing that wasn't supposed to happen. *I'm* what's going to make the whole thing unravel. Dad, I was standing here with you while you talked to her. I could hear her voice."

"And . . ."

"And she was pregnant with me when she called you," I said. "I'm in my own Timeline." They all stared at me. "Dad, it's me," I said desperately. "*I'm the Chronomaly.*"

There was a silence.

"What does it mean?" said Carter softly.

"It means she has to get out of here before the Incongruity hits," said my father. "Or the Timeline rewrites itself and erases her too. And if she's erased, then that undoes the entire Timeline she's been fighting to repair."

"And she'll die."

"No," said Beth. "She'll never have been born."

And she laughed at that, a giddy, delighted laugh. "My

Lord," she said, "you do know how to keep things interesting. A *Double* Double Incongruity. Who knows what could happen."

"What's going to happen?" said Carter.

"I don't know," I said. "But I've been here for two hours. So whatever it is – it's started already."

And then, as if we had delivered our lines and given some great cosmic stage manager her next technical cue, the entire world went black.

I don't mean it got dark suddenly. I mean the entire world literally blinked out of existence for a moment, there was nothing except empty void, and then blinked back in again. Everything was gone, I was alone in the darkness, and then I was back in the dusty South African police station with Carter and my father and both Beth Rutherfords.

"What the hell?" exclaimed Carter.

"It's starting," I said. "The Timeline is destabilizing. We have to get out of here before the Incongruity hits."

I forced myself not to look back at Beth Rutherford. I did not want to feel anything. I did not want to think about the fact that I was leaving her here to die.

I pulled out my U.E. transport Comm and took my dad's hand. "We're going to land at United Enterprises, in my time," I said. "We left one working transporter. We can get out of the building through the freight elevator and then Short-Hop out once we're clear."

He nodded. Carter pulled his Comm out too.

"You go first," he said. "Don't try to pull one over on me again."

"I won't," I assured him. "I want to get all of us home safe."

"Good," said Carter. "Because we still have to find Calliope and Leo."

"Leo?" said my father, some unreadable emotion in his voice.

I had forgotten my earlier lie about my brother's name – and was trying very hard not to think about where he and Calliope were right now – and busied myself with my suddenly nonfunctional transporter. No matter what I pressed, the screen stayed dark.

"Come on, you piece of crap," I murmured, "you've gotten me this far, we're almost done."

"What's the matter?" said Carter.

"It's not working," I said.

"Let me see," he said. I moved closer to him so he could look at it. The second I dropped my dad's hand, the screen lit up and the INITIATE TRANSPORT button blinked a merry green.

Then we knew.

"No," I said desperately. "No. Let me try again." And I seized my dad's hand.

The screen went dark again.

"Try mine," said Carter, taking my dad's hand in his. And we watched as his screen went dark as well. A creeping sensation of cold began to close around my heart.

Then everything went dark again, this time for much longer. The darkness was cold, and I fought down a rising panic as I realized I was running out of air. By the time I blinked back into the dusty sunlight, I was panting for breath. So was Carter.

"Your brother's name is Leo," said my father once we were all back.

"Yes," I said slowly.

"I mean, it was Leo before – when you first got here, before all of this – and it's still Leo now," he said in a gentle, sad voice.

"I don't know what you mean," I said.

"Yes, you do," he said.

"Dad—"

"You have to leave, Regina. Go. Before everything collapses."

"But you'll die," I said.

"We don't know that anymore," he said. "Beth Rutherford is unconscious. She can't throw the rock. You've already changed the story. And if the Incongruity hits, and erases her, then this was just a regular day's work and I go home just fine."

"But—"

"You can't bring me back with Bureau equipment," he said. "The Slipstream won't open for me. You need to get out before you're trapped."

"I can't leave you here," I said, tears spilling down my cheeks.

"Yes, you can," he said. "You have to."

He pulled me close to him then, and held me tightly. There were tears in his eyes. And mine. And Carter's.

"I'm going to fix this," I said. "I'm going to think of something."

"I believe in you," he said. "If there's a way, you'll find it."

"Oh my God," snarled Beth. "You're *nauseating*, all of you."

"Want me to knock this Beth out too?" said Carter. "Please?"

The deafening roar of military vehicles was upon us, and I knew we were surrounded. "No," I said. "There isn't time. Unfortunately. Dad, you have to go. Right now you're supposed to be walking the line with the local cops. Keep them cool. Don't let the U.E. forces get into their heads. And for God's sake, don't let anybody start shooting."

"Whatever you say, kid," he said, grinning at me, tears in his eyes. "You're the boss."

Then he hugged me again and headed outside.

"Reggie, are you ready?" said Carter.

"Ready," I said. "Let's go."

"Oh, before you leave," said Beth, in a deceptively mild and sweet voice. "Just one small thing."

"Not interested," I said.

"Oh, I think you will be," said Beth. "There are, I believe, twenty-six United Enterprises security vehicles currently surrounding this station, following my tracker. They're in stealth mode, which means they're dressed and armed like locals. The police here will be told they're reinforcements from Johannesburg, sent to keep the Negroes in line."

I winced. "You've been in the 1970's too long," I said to her. "You're way too comfortable with the words 'keep the Negroes in line.'"

She didn't dignify this with a response.

"There's a black unmarked civilian car traveling with the caravan of military vehicles," she said. "It should be parked right outside the door to this building. And I think there's something inside the trunk of the car that you're very much going to want to see."

"Reggie," said Carter warningly, knowing it was too late, seeing the decision on my face before he even spoke. "Don't listen to her. We need to jump. You need to get out of here. You have a Double Incongruity closing in on you. We have to get you home."

"What's in the trunk of the car, Beth?" I asked.

"That would be telling," she said. "But believe me, you're going to want to see."

"Don't do it, Reggie," said Carter. "It's a trap."

"I know."

"There are armed men outside."

"I know."

"Suit yourself," said Beth with an infuriating air of magnificent nonchalance. "I can have it delivered." And she knocked three times on the metal wall of the shack.

There was a silence.

Then someone on the other side of the wall knocked back.

My whole body felt cold all over. *We should jump,* I thought. *Right now. Before it's too late.* And yet, there was something she wanted to show me before I left her here to die . . . was it real, or was she hypnotizing me again so that this time, when she slipped the knife into my heart, I would never see it coming?

Go.

Stay.

Go.

Stay.

I looked helplessly at Carter. He looked back at me.

Then the door swung open, kicked by a booted foot with such force that it popped the rather half-assed bolt altogether, and two United Enterprises guards entered, guns drawn. Before them were two people in black U.E. guard uniforms with black bags over their heads. I couldn't see their faces, but even before Beth spoke, I knew.

"Thank you," she said. "Good work, you were very prompt. You can take the hoods off now." The guard roughly yanked away the black fabric.

It was Leo and Calliope.

CHAPTER ELEVEN

THE LOUDEST NOISE IN THE WORLD

They were alive.

Dirty, bedraggled, bound and gagged, but conscious and alive.

"Oh thank God," I said, and Carter clutched my hand.

"All right," said Carter. "Now tell us what you want in exchange."

"What we have here, darling," said Beth, "is a standard hostage trade. Now. You have something that I want – or rather, some*one* – and it seems that your adorable naïvete about Harold Grove's willingness to help you has leveled the playing field somewhat in my favor, because I have something you want. Two of them, in fact. You're getting much the better deal."

"Let them go, Beth," I said.

"I'd love to," she said. "Truly. As soon as you release the other Beth, put a rock in her hand, and let her do what she came here to do. Then I'll have one of these very nice young men take me back to my office before the Double Incongruity hits and takes me with it. Once that happens, we will be very pleased to return your brother and Harold's coffee girl. If you're quick, maybe we'll all get out of here before the Incongruity hits."

"You know I can't let you leave," I said to her. "If the Incongruity hits you, it erases you from the Timeline, and takes the Third World War and United Enterprises with it."

"Precisely," she said. "You can see how we'd have a bit of disagreement over that."

"The answer is no," I said, more firmly than I felt. She sighed.

"Regina," she said patiently. "This is not a negotiation. There is only the easy way and the hard way. The easy way gets us all out of here much faster and involves you being cheerful and cooperative. The hard way is . . . well, not as nice."

She reached out her hand, and one of the guards pulled out a stun pistol from his holster and handed it to her.

Then she shot my brother.

I screamed out his name and ran to his side, my heart racing in my chest, catching him just in time before he hit the ground. *Oh please,* I begged as I stumbled under his dead weight, my arms wrapped tight around him, *please be breathing. Please be okay.*

"A little to the left," Beth said to me in a cool voice. "You're a bit in my way."

"Leo," I said, ignoring her, slapping his face to wake him up. "Leo!"

"Suit yourself," said Beth, exasperated, and then she shot Calliope.

I couldn't catch Calliope without letting go of Leo, so I

watched, helplessly, as her body crumpled to the ground. I lowered Leo gently and checked both his pulse, than Calliope's. Carter moved towards me to help, but she turned her gun on him.

"Darling," she said. "I really wouldn't."

"Don't, Carter," I begged. "She'll do it."

Carter stopped moving, raised his hands over his head, and knelt on the ground.

"Very good," said Beth approvingly as I shook Leo and Calliope, blinded by tears of panic, desperately trying to revive them. They were both still breathing, but barely.

"They're still alive," Beth said. "This was only at about 75%. However, they will need emergency medical attention within the next, oh, I'd say twenty minutes, or their hearts will begin to fail. So I'd encourage you not to waste any more of their time by trying to think of ways to get the drop on me, and just go release the other Beth so we can all be on our way."

I looked down at the fallen bodies of Leo and Calliope. I had to get them home. I had to get them to a doctor. But if I let Beth Rutherford walk out of here, it would all have been for nothing, and seventy-one people would be dead in a matter of minutes.

"Time is ticking," said Beth. "I'd make a decision, and fast. Who are you going to watch die today, your brother or your father?"

Then the world went black again, and I felt a tremor inside the Slipstream. I couldn't keep my balance, and the air drained from my lungs as I fell into the endless darkness. I plummeted for a long time – who knows how long – before I suddenly felt rough dusty ground reappear beneath me. Panting for air, lightheaded, I lay on the ground for a long moment before I felt strong arms pulling me up. I stood, and dusted myself off.

That was when I noticed the unconscious bodies of Beth's U.E. security guards, lying in a heap on the ground.

"What . . ." I began, looking around me, but didn't finish. The rest of the words evaporated from my mouth when I turned and saw Beth Rutherford behind me, lying on the ground, unconscious. My father stood over her, laser rifle in hand.

"It was three minutes the last time," said Leo Carstairs. "They're getting longer."

"What the—"

"The ripples from the Incongruity," he said. "I saw you. I saw you all go down at the same time."

"Reggie," said Carter, who I realized had been the one to pull me up and was still holding onto me. "It didn't affect him. When we all couldn't breathe. Your dad, everyone else in the crowd, it didn't affect them."

"No one in the crowd would be able to feel it," I said. "The effects of the Incongruity are only dangerous to people who are in Flexible Timelines. Everyone who's where they're supposed to be is fine."

And then I froze, as I heard the words come out of my mouth. I stared at Carter. Carter stared back at me.

"No," I said. "No. She didn't throw the rock. It was all supposed to be okay. Beth didn't throw the rock."

"I'm sorry," said my father. "But Carter is right. I'm in my Timeline. That's what it means. Even without Beth Rutherford, I was always supposed to be here at this moment on this day. I'm in the right place."

He looked around at the crowd of people. "The Sharpeville Massacre is real, Reggie," he said. "That's what it means. You have to let it happen."

"I can't," I said. "I can't let innocent people die. I can't let you die."

"You have to," he said. "You have to correct the Timeline. That's our job, kiddo. That's what we do. That's who you are. You're Agent Regina Bellows of the U.S. Time Travel Bureau and you have a war to stop."

"Remember what you said to me at the Lincoln Memorial?" said Carter to me, taking my hand. "That sometimes part of this job is standing by and letting terrible things happen, to set the Timeline right? We're here. We've arrived. It's time. We have to get them home."

My father nodded.

"You don't know what happens after this," he said. "None of us do. Maybe this is how it was always destined to be. Maybe the Sharpeville Massacre is such a horrific atrocity that the rest of the world finally sits up and begins paying attention to what's happening in South Africa. Maybe seventy people die today to free a whole nation."

"Seventy-one," I said.

"We don't know what happens next, Reggie," he went on gently. "But if the Incongruity isn't touching me, then I'm where I'm supposed to be. And you have to go."

Then, suddenly, the Comm in my pocket – the one Calliope had given me from Dad's safe house stash – crackled to life.

"Reggie," said a voice I thought I'd never hear again. "Reggie, can you hear me?"

"Mom?" I exclaimed in shock.

"Reggie, the war is unraveling," she said. "The whole Timeline is correcting itself. I don't know where you are but you're at a crisis point and you have to get out before you're stuck."

I looked at my father's face. There were tears streaming down it.

"I'm in Sharpeville," I said, voice choked with sobs.

There was a silence.

"Leo?" she said softly.

"I'm here, Katie," he said. "I'm right here."

"Reggie, you can't pull him out," she said wearily. "I've tried. I tried so many times. The Slipstream won't open for him."

"She knows," said Carstairs. "I told her."

"Get her out of there, Leo," said my mother. "Get our daughter home."

"I will," he said. "I promise."

He pulled me close one last time and kissed me on the forehead. "She's something, isn't she?" he said to my mother.

"She's her father's daughter," she said, and her voice broke my heart. "Reggie, you have to jump, now. The Incongruity is almost on top of you. Where's your necklace?"

"What?"

"The necklace I gave you," she said impatiently. "Do you have it with you?" My hand moved instinctively to my throat. I had slipped it around my neck in 1972 and completely forgotten it ever since.

"I'm wearing it," I said. "Why?"

"Don't lose it," she said.

"Mom, I'm coming home," I said. "I'm going to see you again. I promise."

"Go," she said. "You have to get out. Jump now."

Then there was a silence. "Goodbye, Leo," said my mother, and even though that was all they said, there was something in the air that was so intimate that I felt like I was intruding.

"Goodbye, Katie," said my dad.

Then another blackout hit, worse than the last, and I lost my balance. My father caught me and stopped me from falling as I gasped for breath. When the world reemerged, I could see him looking at me, with infinite love and sadness and compassion in his eyes, and we both knew.

He was meant to die in South Africa. This was the end of the road.

My necklace had come untucked from the neckline of my shirt in the fall, and my father reached out and took the two pendants in his hand, and looked for a long moment at the one he had given my mother.

"'Time is a tree/This life one leaf,'" he said quietly, reading the words from the small silver disc. Then he knelt down, picked something up from the ground at his feet, kissed my cheek, and pressed it into my hand. I looked down at it.

A rock.

A craggy-edged, dirt-crusted, fist-sized rock.

I looked at my father.

"No," I begged him, my eyes filling up with tears. My voice was choked with sobs, barely coherent, but he knew. I shook my head frantically – *No, no, no* – but he nodded at me firmly. *Yes.*

"I can't," I said. "I can't. There's no one to Rewind you. No one on the other side to pull us out, no lab to come back to."

"I know."

"That was the whole reason I came," I said. "To stop this. I came here to stop Beth Rutherford from throwing that rock."

"No, you came here to stop the war," Carter said gently. "And you did. Or, you're about to. The Double Incongruity will fix it. The Timeline is unraveling. It will erase Beth and set everything right. But you have to throw the rock, so your father will die, so everything he said to your mother will go into the Congressional records, so she'll hide his Gemstone files, so that she and the Bureau will forget all about them until you tell her about Project Opal, and then give them all to you. It starts and ends with you, Reggie."

Carter put his arms around me. "I'm sorry," he said. "I'm

sorry. I'm so sorry. But he's right. Your father's right. You have to throw the rock."

"But he'll die," I said.

"He knows that," said Carter, and I could see there were tears in his eyes too. "He knows. It's not your fault."

"I'm ready," said my father. "It's okay."

"They'll all die," I sobbed. "I was supposed to save them."

"The Sharpeville Massacre is real, Reggie," my father said gently. "You were never going to be able to stop it. You saved fifty-six million lives today. But you can't save these people. You can't save me. You have to let it happen. It's time, Reggie."

I looked at Agent Leo Carstairs, tall and blond and dashing, with his bright kind eyes, and I looked at the rock in my hand, and then I looked back at him.

"I'm sorry," I said, and he wrapped his arms around me in a crushing embrace.

"No," he said. "No. You did everything right, sweetheart."

He kissed the top of my head over and over and over. "You did everything right."

Then he let go of me, tears in his eyes, and turned to Carter.

"It took me a little while," he said, smiling. "But I finally figured out who you remind me of." Then he hugged him tightly. "Thank you," he said. "For everything. When you get home, tell your dad about this. Agent Hughes deserves to know that his son helped save the world."

He turned to go.

"Wait," I said desperately. "Dad. Wait."

I pointed to the two bodies on the ground at our feet. "It's Leo," I said. "Leo is here. Your son helped save the world too."

"*Leo?*" said my father wonderingly, and he knelt down to where my brother lay on the ground. He stroked Leo's cheek and kissed his forehead. I couldn't watch, and turned away to bury my face in Carter's chest. "I can see it," he said in amazement. "He looks just your mother."

"He looks like you," I said.

"You two take care of each other," said my father. "And tell Katie—" He stopped. I turned back to him. "She was the greatest adventure of my life," he said softly. "Tell her that."

"I will," I said.

"Keep that necklace safe for me."

"I will. I promise."

Carter squeezed my hand.

"Reggie," he said gently. "It's time."

I nodded, wiping the tears away from my eyes.

"Goodbye, Dad," I said. "I'm really glad I met you."

"Good hunting, Agent Bellows," he said, and raised his hand to me in the old Bureau salute. Then he turned and walked away, back to the line of fire, back to the men with guns. He stood there, waiting. Like an actor in the wings, ready for his cue.

"Carter," I said, voice choking on sobs.

"I'm here," he said. "You're not alone. I'm right here."

The world blinked into darkness again, cold and grasping and hungry, and the void began draining the air from my lungs. I felt dizzy and weak, like I was drowning, flailing for breath. When I came back, I had lost so much oxygen that my knees gave out and I sank to the ground. Carter, who had fallen during the blackout, crawled over to me and put his arms around me.

"Reggie," he said, "it's time. The Incongruity is almost on top of us. We have to get out."

He knelt beside two of the fallen U.E. guards and pulled off their wrist Comms, then grabbed their stun rifles and two helmets. He linked the still-unconscious Leo and Calliope's hands together and clipped one of the stolen Comms onto Leo's wrist, then the other onto his own.

"Helmet on," he said, tossing it to me, "and have your rifle ready. I don't know where we're going to land. If anyone asks, we're U.E. guards escorting these two prisoners. Got it?" I nodded. He knelt down and picked up the rock, which had fallen from my hand in the blackout.

"I'll do it," he said. "If you need me to. I can do it."

"No," I said in a numb voice. "It has to be me." He nodded, compassion in his eyes.

"Okay," he said, and squeezed my hand. "Let's go home."

I took a deep breath, then took the rock from Carter's outstretched hand. I raised it, wound up my shoulder, prepared to throw. My father nodded at me, and I could see his mouth moving.

Three.

Two.

One.

Go.

I threw the rock. It crashed with a deafening clang against the metal roof of the police station, and I felt the world go crazy. As the next blackout hit, Carter threw his arms around me and pulled me down to the ground, pushing the buttons on his and Leo's wrist Comms at the same time.

Then the darkness closed over me, and we were gone.

CHAPTER TWELVE

THAT EVER I WAS BORN
TO SET IT RIGHT

Darkness.

For a long, long time, that was all there was. Darkness and cold. I felt the oxygen slowly leaving my lungs, and a heavy pressure beginning to coalesce inside my body.

This is dying, I thought. *This is what dying feels like.*

I am not brave, not really. I never have been. I think acts of desperation and adrenaline sometimes look like bravery, even when they aren't. But the important thing to know about me is that I'm not a heroic person. I had told Beth Rutherford I was willing to die to stop her war, and I had meant it.

But alone, in the dark, feeling my heartbeat slow and my organs begin to compress and my breathing slow to a standstill, all I wanted was for it to be over quickly and painlessly, and to believe it hadn't all been for nothing.

Please, I begged whoever might be listening in the cold

darkness of the Slipstream as it closed in around me, *fix it. Fix it so those fifty-six million people get to live. And if you can, please don't let this hurt too much.*

And then I closed my eyes, and I let the darkness close over my head, like I was peacefully drowning, and as I let go, I heard, far off in the distance – as though guiding me out of this life into the next – the sound of my mother calling my name.

~

"Regina."

~

I floated through the darkness, not breathing, not moving. It was like a waterless drowning, this dark force that pulled me down into a deeper darkness. It was useless to resist. It was useless to kick and splash and struggle. All I had to do was let go.

~

"Regina, wake up."

~

The second voice was somehow both closer and farther away – still muffled, as though coming from underwater or a very great distance, but louder than before.

I know that voice, I thought dimly, floating through the darkness, listening to my slowly fading heartbeat. *Whose voice is that?* I couldn't remember. I couldn't remember anything.

But the voice was pleasant, and I felt consoled by it. I was being welcomed into the afterlife very gently, by these loving voices calling my name.

~

"Can't somebody wake her up?"

~

Something jarring, in the soft soothing darkness.

Go away, I thought sleepily to the harsh, sharp voice that pierced the womb-like peace of the Slipstream as it guided me away. *Can't you see I'm busy dying over here?*

But it didn't go away.

It kept talking.

It got louder.

I couldn't pick out all the words, but I could feel them, hard and crystalline, slicing through the blackness and pulling me, against my will, in the other direction. I opened my eyes, and the world exploded into gold-and-white light. I squeezed them closed again, willing the darkness to swallow me up again, but it didn't. I felt my heartbeat revive. I took a deep breath, and felt my lungs fill with air. I opened one eye again, just the tiniest bit.

The world was blindingly white and blurry, and I could see a glowing golden shape looming directly in front of my face.

I moved my lips and a cracked, hoarse whisper came out.

"Are you . . . an angel?" I whispered to the golden shape, as my eyes slowly came into focus.

"For Christ's sake," said Calliope. "How hard did you hit your head?"

"Calliope," I said, the last shreds of darkness falling away as the world came back to me. I blinked and looked around. I was in a hospital bed, in a pristine white room. Across from me were two white couches with dark shapes curled up on them.

Carter and Leo.

Everyone was home.

"We're okay," I whispered. "We made it."

Calliope grinned. "Bet your ass we did," she said.

I shifted a little as I sat up and suddenly became aware of a heavy, warm weight beside me. There was somebody else curled up next to me in the bed. I rubbed my eyes, vision clearing, and turned to look.

It was my mother.

She was sound asleep, head pillowed on her arm. Her hair was disheveled, she had no makeup on, and she was wearing the cotton pants and sleeveless shirt she wore around the house and sometimes slept in. I wondered how long she had been there.

I watched her sleep for awhile before I reached over and tapped her on the shoulder.

"Mom," I said softly. "Mom."

Instantly, she awoke.

"Reggie," she said, smiling, tears in her eyes, and she stroked my hair.

"Hi," I said.

"Hi," she said back.

"Where am I?" I asked, struggling to sit up. "How long have I been out?"

Calliope was at my side in an instant and gave me her arm, helping me to shift so I was sitting upright.

"You're in sickbay," she said, "and it's been three days."

"The others were up and around yesterday," said my mother,

sitting up and sliding out of the bed to stretch her back. "You were at the center of the Incongruity, so the Slipstream radiation hit you the hardest."

I only half heard her. I was too busy looking at her shoulder, which was smooth and unmarked. Something about that felt wrong and strange to me, but I couldn't put my finger on it. Something was missing. *What was it?*

"Mom," I said softly.

She turned, mid-stretch, and looked at me, then saw what I was staring at.

"We have a lot to talk about," she said with a smile. "Calliope, wake up the boys."

Calliope leaned over to shake Carter gently.

"Carter," she said. "Wake up."

"I'm awake," he said sleepily, without moving.

"Reggie is awake, Carter, we need to talk."

"Reggie?" he said, bolting upright from the couch and flailing a little to sit up.

"I'm right here, Carter," I said. He pulled a chair over next to the side of the bed and sat down in it, taking my hand in his.

"You scared the shit out of me, Bellows," he said. "Don't ever do that again."

I started to say something but was distracted by a noise in the corner, where it appeared that Calliope had opted to wake my brother by smacking him on the head.

"Your sister's awake, lazy ass," she snapped. "Get over here."

Leo bolted off the couch so fast he almost tripped, and ran to my side, half-climbing over our mother to get to me and wrap me in an enormous bear hug.

"Hi, sis," he said, kissing the top of my head with tears in his eyes.

"Hi, bro," I said back, swallowing tears of my own.

"Oh, Lord," said Calliope. "*Emotions*."

"Calliope, let's go hunt down some coffee for everybody," said Carter, holding the door open and waving her out of it. "Let's give them a minute."

"Thank you, Carter," said my mother. "Coffee would be wonderful."

They left and closed the door behind them.

"Where's Dad?" I said as soon as we were alone together, and my mom stroked my hair.

"I'm sorry," she said. "But you did the right thing. You had to throw the rock. The Sharpeville Massacre restabilized the Timeline after the Incongruity hit."

"He died," I said, tears spilling out of my eyes. "He died *again*."

"It was different this time," she said. "There was no army of U.E. security forces storming the police station. There was no Beth Rutherford. There were only about five thousand civilians there instead of twenty thousand."

"What happened?"

"Reggie—"

"Tell me what happened."

She sighed.

"It was horrific," she said. "The police saw a crowd of African citizens marching toward them and opened fire without even stopping to ask what they were doing there. They didn't know or care that it was a peaceable protest. They were firing bullets into the back of a fleeing crowd. Carstairs saw a white police officer draw his rifle to take aim at an unarmed girl and he shot the man in the leg to stop him. That was when Jenkins jumped in and pulled him out. And the rest you know."

I felt sick.

"I tried," I said, tears streaming down my face, "I tried to fix it."

"You couldn't," she said. "Reggie, there was nothing you could do. Carter was right when he told you to throw the rock. The Timeline corrected itself. This was what was supposed to happen. The Sharpeville Massacre was a watershed moment in the fight against apartheid. It woke people up – not just in South Africa but all over the world. It took an atrocity of that magnitude to get people to sit up and listen."

"How many people died?" I asked.

"Sixty-nine," she said.

"It was seventy before," I said. She nodded.

"He couldn't save everyone," she said. "But he saved that girl."

"And you," said Leo, "saved fifty-six million people."

I stared at him, then turned to my mom.

"It worked?" I said.

"It worked," she said. "You were right. The Double Incongruity worked."

"We did it," I said softly, incredulous. "We did it. We stopped the war."

"You did," said my mother. "We're in a whole new world now."

And then I remembered what I had noticed before. I reached out a hand and touched the soft olive skin of my mother's shoulder, where there were no marks at all, and I looked up at her.

"You don't have a scar here," I said.

"No."

"You used to have a little scar from where they placed your subdermal tracker," I said. "All my life you had it. And then the last time I saw you there was a big, ugly, messy scar in its place where you dug it out."

She didn't say anything, just looked at me and nodded.

It had worked. The Timeline had corrected itself. No scar. No subdermal tracker.

No United Enterprises.

Which meant only one thing.

"Mom," I said, urgency creeping into my voice. "Mom. *You didn't come through the Slipstream.*"

She shook her head.

"No," she said. "I didn't."

"The Timeline rewrote itself with you on this side of it," I said. "Only the people who were stuck in the Incongruity remember what happened. Me, and Leo, and Calliope, and Carter. I'm right, aren't I? We're the only ones who actually remember."

"That's right."

"So how do you know all this?"

She didn't answer, but reached into her pocket and pulled out a thin filigree chain. My hand instinctively went to my neck and that was the first moment I realized my necklace was gone.

"The pendant from Carstairs is real," she said. "I've had that for almost thirty years. The clock is something else entirely."

"Ruth 3:11," I said. "The hands of the clock. It meant something."

She nodded.

"To remind you that I was still out there," she said. "That we were still working together. Both literally and figuratively."

She turned the silver hands from 3:11 to midnight and the clock face popped open. I peered inside.

"What the hell?" I said. "It's not a pendant. It's a *data port.*"

"I don't remember any of what happened in your Timeline," she said. "It's all on this."

"She was filing field reports the whole time she was gone,"

said Leo, "and syncing them to that thing around your neck. She knew the only way to get the information back here to the other side was for it to travel through the Slipstream with you."

"You sounded almost like a real agent when you said that," my mom laughed, ruffling his hair. "You're a natural."

"He was amazing, Mom," I said. Leo looked away, embarrassed, but I didn't care. I had wasted twenty-five years of my life living half a world away from him and hardly being able to carry on a conversation for longer than five minutes, and I was suddenly full of things I wanted to say. "He was brave," I said, and I took his hand in mine and squeezed it. "He saved my life. He was a hero. You would have been so proud of him."

"I already am," she said. "My kids saved the world."

"Carter and Calliope did the hard stuff," he said.

"You got me out of that building," I said. "You're the only one who could have done that. We couldn't have done any of this without you."

Carter and Calliope reentered with a tray of coffee cups and pulled up chairs next to us.

"Are you guys done having feelings at each other?" said Calliope. "Have you briefed Reggie yet?"

"The mushy part is over," said Leo. "I know human emotions cause your cyborg processing chip to short-circuit—"

"Excuse me if I didn't want to pull up a chair and make popcorn to watch you three have a private family conversation that didn't involve me—"

"Since *when* do you stay out of—"

"That's enough out of both of you," said Carter. "Don't make me send you to separate couches. Reggie has been conscious for like ten minutes and she probably has a million questions."

"I do," I said. "The field reports on the data drive – you've all seen them?"

"I have," said my mother, "and Calliope has too. She built it for me."

"You knew what it was?" I said to her. "Why didn't you say anything?"

"We couldn't risk you drawing attention to it," she said. "If you thought it was just a necklace, then everyone else around you would think it was just a necklace. If you started getting insane about it, Beth Rutherford would have seen right through you."

"So you know all of it," I said to my mother. "They've filled you in on what happened to us, but you also know all the things you - I mean the other you - didn't tell me. The things we didn't know."

"I can tell you now," she said. "You'll want to know where I was after I left you in 1972. What I was doing."

"What were you doing?"

"Hunting Harold Grove."

"Did you know?" I asked. "Did you know he was Saturn?"

"I suspected," she said. "There weren't many agents who could have managed a patch that size on their own. But Grove was top of our class in Chrono-Engineering. And it was a puzzling coincidence that the day he went off active duty was the day the Chronomaly first revealed itself. So I followed him. Every mission he took in the 60's and 70's, I followed him and I watched. And then I began to realize that everywhere he went, the same woman appeared in the background."

"Beth Rutherford," I said softly. Mom nodded.

"She was there in Ohio," she said. "At the library, when you pulled Grove out. Calliope synced your field reports to the necklace too. We watched the Microcam footage."

"The woman he was talking to," I said, realizing. "She walked away and then I pulled him out. That's why he was so pissed at me. He was there for a meet with Beth and I got in the way."

"That's right."

"I still don't understand how he got mixed up in all this," I said. "He still feels like the wrong fit. He's not a power-hungry psycho like Beth was. Did he just get into it for the money? Auction off his integrity to the highest bidder?"

"Oh," said my mother. "No, Reggie. That wasn't what happened. No, I stumbled onto it almost by accident when I was following him. I overheard a conversation when he didn't know I was there."

"Beth Rutherford was his sister," said Calliope.

"His *sister*?"

"It was her idea," Mom said. "All of this. She concocted the entire thing. I suspect – and this is not in any way to defend his actions, obviously, but it does change things – that in the beginning, he only got into it to protect her. I think he found out what she was up to and he was afraid she'd be arrested for treason, so he tried to cover her tracks from inside the Bureau."

"And then years went by, and things got more complicated, and before he knew it, he was an accessory-after-the-fact to Carstairs' murder and then he was in too deep to get out. And it changed him. It became who he was."

I looked at Calliope, who was stone-faced and dry-eyed.

"You wanted to believe in him," I said. "You wanted it so badly. To believe he wasn't a monster."

"I don't think he was a monster," said my mother. "I think he was desperate, and it made him reckless. I think he was willing to cover up the deaths of fifty-six million people to keep someone he loved from being executed for war crimes.

Beth wanted power. Grove just wanted to protect Beth. It isn't defensible, but it's human. He couldn't see right and wrong anymore."

"What happens to him now?" I said. "The Harold Grove on the other side of the Slipstream doesn't exist anymore, since the Timeline is different, so the one on this side hasn't actually done anything, but it still feels wrong for him not to pay for all those lives."

My mother shook her head.

"There is no Harold Grove on this side of the Slipstream," she said. "Their parents never had any children. That was the system self-correcting."

"Oh," I said.

Harold Grove didn't exist. Beth Rutherford didn't exist. They were not, never had been, real to anyone except the people right here in this room. I thought about that for a moment, trying to sift my complicated feelings about it.

"Wait a minute," I said suddenly. "I still work for the Bureau, right? If there's no Harold Grove, whose apprentice am I?"

"Oh man," said Carter with a grin. "We have a lot to show you."

~

After browbeating the medic on duty into letting me out of bed to walk around and stretch my legs, Mom took my arm and led me out of the room. Carter and Calliope followed, along with Leo, who had been granted a visitor's pass. Apparently without United Enterprises guarding their proprietary technology with a borderline violent obsessiveness, the Bureau was like any other government building where properly scanned civilians could come visit their sisters at work.

"Pardon me, ma'am," said a uniformed medical aide to my mother as we stepped out into the hallway. "Deputy Director Gray would like a word with you, if you're feeling well enough. But he says if it needs to, it can wait."

"No, I'm fine," said my mother.

"*Deputy* Director Gray?" I whispered in her ear, and she grinned broadly and winked at me.

"Damn straight," she said. The medical aide tapped on his wrist Comm.

"Sir," he said, "Director Bellows is on her way."

"Gray? As Director? Please!" my mother sniffed derisively under her breath. "Your old Timeline was a *mess*," and we followed the aide down the hallway. I couldn't help laughing as we stepped into the elevator.

"Try not to say too much," said Calliope. "You've been out for three days and you're a little fuzzy-headed, so use that as your excuse if you get lost."

"What do you mean, if I get lost?"

"We're through the looking-glass, Reggie," said Carter. "Everything in this world is different. Your mom has briefed Gray and the Congressional Committee, so they've seen her field reports, but it's all been classified. The four of us are the only ones who remember what really happened."

"But we came through the Slipstream," I said. "Where does everyone here think we were?"

"On a routine patch in the Gerald Ford administration, where we were hit with a Timequake," he said. "We've all been laid up for about two days, although you were unconscious the longest. And Calliope made something up about your brother being an amateur historian."

"Yeah, if anyone asks," said Leo, "you called me with a question and the line was open when the Timequake hit so

I got stuck with you. I can't imagine how anyone bought it, but as soon as Mom was looped in, she smoothed it all over."

"Who the hell is Gerald Ford?" I said.

"No idea," he said. "Apparently a president."

"Christ, I've got a lot of homework to do," I sighed.

"Tell me about it," said Carter.

"You don't know the half of it," said Calliope. "I've got ten times more catching up to do than you two."

"What do you mean?"

"Wait and see," said Carter with a grin. "It's a surprise."

We stepped out of the elevator and I found myself in a totally alien world. Gone were the vast, drafty, utilitarian hallways of our United Enterprise-built skyscraper. Gone were the dusty beiges and grays. There were marble floors beneath my feet, vaulted ceilings above my head, lush dark wood and brass fixtures all around me.

"What is this place?" I said. "This isn't our building."

"It is now," said Carter.

"No World War III Chronomaly means a lot less patching," said Calliope. "You'll be astonished how much smaller the Bureau is. They don't need hundreds of agents anymore."

We followed her down a corridor lined with oil paintings.

"It looks weirdly familiar," I said. "I have the strangest feeling I've seen it before."

"You have," said Carter. "You've been seeing pictures of it for years. This is the National Archives."

I felt tears welling up in my eyes. Leo squeezed my hand.

"The city is still here," I said. He nodded, eyes shining.

"Yes," he said. "It's all still here."

We had stopped in front of a mahogany door with a brass plate labeled "20TH CENTURY."

"Now remember," Calliope said, pushing it open, "Leo, you know nothing."

"Got it."

"Carter and Reggie, say as little as possible. We're all three supposed to be on leave for the next two weeks. When in doubt, fake a headache. Don't answer any questions until we've had a chance to get caught up on our homework."

"We know," said Carter.

I didn't answer. I just stared.

It was a big, bright, open room, bursting with sunlight and bustling with activity. And there, to my left, I saw three doors in a row with brass nameplates.

AGENT REGINA BELLOWS.

AGENT CARTER HUGHES.

AGENT CALLIOPE BURNS.

"Surprise!" said Carter under his breath.

I looked at Calliope and felt the tears welling up again.

"Don't get sentimental on me," she said. "This is gonna be no picnic. You have three weeks of medical leave to teach me everything these guys think I learned in five years at the Academy."

"Calliope—" I started to say, but couldn't find the words.

Calliope Burns had always been too smart for her job. She was brilliant and tough and irreplaceable as Grove's assistant, and her loyalty kept her at his side, prepping missions and filing reports and making coffee, long after she had outgrown her position.

And more than anything else so far – more than my mother becoming Director, more than finding at least one of the ruined landmarks of D.C. still standing – this was the moment it finally sunk in, all the way down to my bones, that we had really, truly, rewritten time.

In a world with no Harold Grove, Calliope had gone up for Field Agent certification.

I said her name again, trying to think of a way to put my feelings into words, but couldn't.

"Shut up," she said. "You're embarrassing yourself."

But she was smiling.

"Agent Bellows!" interrupted a perky voice I didn't recognize, and I saw a dark head pop up from behind a cubicle wall in front of my office.

"That's your tech," murmured Carter. "I forgot her name."

"Deborah," murmured Leo helpfully into my ear. "I met her yesterday."

"It's so good to see you up and around again!" said the tech cheerfully.

"Thank you, Deborah," I said, making a mental note to spend some quality time in the next week digging through the personnel database to learn everyone's names.

"I did some hunting around while you were gone," she said. "And I found that old book you were asking about. I already put the digital version on your handheld – I thought you'd like some new reading material while you're on leave – but I found an original for you too. It's on your desk."

"Thanks," I said, and turned the doorknob to enter my very own office.

I had an office.

The other three followed me inside.

"I've seen theirs," said Leo. "But we didn't go inside yours without you."

"Doesn't look like we missed out on much," said Calliope with elegant distaste, looking around her. My office was a catastrophic mess, with papers and sweaters and tech equipment and coffee mugs everywhere. I loved it instantly.

"Mine is much nicer," said Carter.

"Yeah, Carter hung paintings," said Leo. "And he has a rug. You don't have a rug."

"Calliope's is boring," said Carter. "It's just a white box with some computer screens."

"It's perfect," she said.

"She's weirdly in love with it," said Leo.

"They suit us," said Carter. "It's kind of crazy."

"No, it's not," said Leo. "They're *your* offices. You're all still you."

I ignored them and made my way over to the desk, where I found a flat, square, climate-controlled glass box containing a battered paperback book.

All the President's Men.

By Carl Bernstein and Bob Woodward.

After holding it together through the insane emotional rollercoaster of the past hours – and days – the dam finally broke. I traced their names with my finger on the glass surface of the box and I burst into tears. I cried and cried and cried. Calliope discreetly closed the office door as my brother came around the desk and put his arms around me.

"They did it," I sniffled into his shoulder. "They really did it. They stopped the war."

"*You* did it, Reggie," he said. "This was you."

"You know," said Calliope, examining the book, "if you're really going to invest in an analog book collection you should pay more attention to quality. This one's only going to depreciate."

"Thank you, Calliope."

"Did you know that the paper used in 20th-century trade paperbacks deteriorates much faster than—"

"Thank you, Calliope."

"You should ask if the box has a UV sealant on the glass, otherwise—"

"Thank you, Calliope," I said, but I had stopped listening. Carter, on the other side of the room, was standing next to a large window, covered in a rich damask curtain, and held his hand out for me to join him.

"Come here," he said. "Come look outside."

I felt a little thrill of both anticipation and fear surge through me as my body was pulled, slowly, almost against my will, to the place where he stood. Then he drew back the curtain, and I got my first look at the new world.

"Look," he said softly. "Look what we did."

Carter took my hand. I took Leo's. Leo took Calliope's. We stood there together in silence for a long time, gazing out at the glowing white obelisk of the Washington Monument, rising up like a beacon from the green of the National Mall, as endless clouds of pink cherry trees bloomed all around us.

THE MAN IN THE PUB

Galway, Ireland, 1981

The pub was called The Quays.

It was named for Quay Street, where it sat, beckoning passersby with its cheery blue storefront that opened up inside to a multi-story maze of Gothic arches, dark wood, staircases and wide open spaces. It was early afternoon on a Tuesday, and business was slow.

At a small dark table in a small dark corner on the mezzanine, a very young man with very fair hair was drinking a pint of Guinness and reading a newspaper. There was a pencil sitting beside his glass, and from time to time he would pause, thoughtfully, and circle something or write a note in the margins. He was known here, and when he came here to read, the publican brought him his drink and left him in peace. He was quite alone. The pub was sleepy in the late-afternoon sunshine, with only the faintest comforting hum of voices above him and below him. Everything was still.

"You hate Guinness," said the voice of a woman, suddenly slicing into the silence, and he looked up, startled out of his thoughts. She was smiling, her voice somehow very dry and very fond at the same time. She was in her late fifties and exceptionally striking – tall and elegant, with long dark hair and an aristocratic profile, the kind that should be stamped on a Roman coin.

"You're very observant," he said, smiling back at her. "I thought I was covering it pretty well. I prefer cider, but apparently here they don't consider that sufficiently manly."

"May I sit?" she said politely, and he nodded.

"You're Leo Carstairs," she said, and he stopped smiling. "You're an apprentice agent at the United States Bureau of Time Travel, and you're here on a long-term reconnaissance mission connected to a ring of Irish-American gun-runners in the 1980's. You were born in a small town in Oregon called The Dalles. You have a scar on the heel of your left foot from a childhood injury with a piece of broken glass at the park. Your favorite food kind of candy is marzipan, because your grandmother Lydia used to have it at her house every Christmas."

The young man stared at her, recoiling slightly.

"I'm telling you all of this," she went on, "because I need you to believe me that I know you, and that you trust me. You don't yet, but you will. In your time, you and I won't meet for another three years. Which was thirty years ago for me."

"Are you from the Bureau?"

"Yes," she said. "But not your Bureau. Not yet."

He looked at her, for a long time, appraisingly.

"This has nothing to do with the job I'm on, does it?"

"No," she said. "But I need your help. You're the only person I can trust."

He sat back in his chair, newspaper forgotten.

"This is all pretty weird," he said. "Even by professional time traveler standards."

"I know."

"You'd better start at the beginning," he said.

She nodded and sat down, taking a long swig of his Guinness and then setting it down in front of her. When he made a gesture of protest, she smiled. "Oh please," she said. "You didn't really want it."

Against his will, he laughed. There was something about her he liked immediately.

"So what do you want with me, stranger who apparently isn't a stranger?" he said.

"I'm going to tell you a story," she said. "And I need you to tell me how it ends."

Hours went by. The publican was pleased to see that young Leo had made a lady friend, although she was a bit too old for him, really, though he could see even from all the way down here behind the bar that she still had an exceptional pair of legs and very pretty hair without very much gray in it at all, and so he wisely left them alone.

He sent young Mickey up with two pints on a tray, on the house, but told him to come right back and not to eavesdrop. Young Leo was in every afternoon, polite but solitary, and the publican thought it was a nice thing to see him coming to life a little bit with a pretty woman.

But the pints went untouched, as the pair were too deeply in conversation to notice Mickey at all.

"Who's the girl?" Leo asked.

"She's a covert asset," said the woman. "I can't tell you her name. And you absolutely cannot let her see your face or know that she's being watched. Stay concealed at all times. This is what she looks like. This is a file on her coordinates and movements. All you need to do is keep her safe."

"Who's after her?"

The woman paused. "I'm going to tell you some things," she said, "and it's very important, *it's crucial* – you can't comprehend how many lives depend on it – that you never, ever, for the rest of your life, tell me that I'm the one who told this to you. Do you understand?" He nodded.

"There's a war brewing," she said. "United Enterprises is hand-in-hand with an agent from the Bureau – my Bureau – and a political operative from the Nixon administration, I don't know who, to artificially concoct a war with China. It will start in less than twelve months, and by the time it's over there will be fifty-six million casualties, largely civilian. This girl, the asset in 1972, she and I are trying to stop it."

"And I need your help. She's undercover in the White House, and she may be targeted. She's trying to unmask a vast conspiracy called Operation Gemstone. It's vital that she be kept safe. It's vital. Everything depends on it." Her voice began to shake. "I need you to make sure nothing happens to her."

"This isn't an official mission, is it?" he said.

"No," she said. "It's off the books. And you can never, ever tell anyone about it. Especially not me. When we meet, I can never know that we had this conversation."

"Let me get this straight," he said. "You want me to take a leave of absence, concoct a cover story and go back to 1972 to protect a girl whose name I don't even know, in order to stop a war that hasn't actually happened yet."

"Yes," she said. "Good. You've got it."

"Ma'am, with all due respect, I don't even know who you are," he said. "You haven't told me your name. I couldn't check up on a single detail of this story if I wanted to. Why should I trust you? Why should I risk my life for this girl? It makes no sense."

"You're the legendary Leo Carstairs," she said. "Or you will be. You're an adventurer. You trust your gut. You don't care about sense."

She set down the Guinness in her hand and leaned forward. "Look at me," she said, her rich dark voice suddenly insistent. "What are your instincts telling you? Am I lying to you, or telling you the truth?"

He looked at her for a long moment – at her wise, steady eyes, at the steely grace in the way she held her head, at her straight back – and his heart turned over very unexpectedly in his chest, and three things became suddenly, sharply clear to him at the same time.

First, that she was telling him the truth, because she was a person who would only ever always tell him the truth. He did not know how he knew this, but he knew it down to his bones. The dark-haired woman would not lie to him.

Second, that despite the aura of unflappable competence and intelligence that emanated from every pore of her body, despite the fact that she was so clearly a person who could handle absolutely anything – still, he could see that beneath her steely surface she was absolutely terrified, more afraid than she had probably ever been in her life.

And third, that at this moment of desperate fear, with nowhere else to turn and no one to trust, she had crossed through time in search of him – Leo Carstairs.

He wondered, thirty years from now, in her time, what they were to each other.

He realized, with a flutter in his stomach, looking into her dark worried eyes, that he thought he already knew.

"Okay," he said. "I'll do it. I'll be your bodyguard."

He had expected – what? Gratitude? For her to collapse into his arms with tears of thanks? He didn't know. But instead she simply nodded approvingly, with the ghost of a smile, and he realized with a start that she knew him so well that she had known he would say yes before she even sat down at his table.

"How do I contact you if I need to reach you?" he asked.

"You can't," she said. "I'm relying on you to figure out what needs to be done and do it."

"Well, that's . . . not reassuring."

"I don't trust very many people," she said. "But Leo Carstairs is the only person who has never once let me down."

"That's very flattering."

"I'm not flattering you. I'm telling you the truth."

She got up from the table, passing a handheld device over to him.

"The files you need are here," she said. "The asset is staying at the Watergate and works in the White House Counsel's office."

"What's her name?"

"You can't know her name," she said. "It will disrupt her Timeline if I tell it to you."

"Well, that's cryptic," he said, but didn't push it. "What happens if someone tries to take her out?"

"You don't let them," she said, and there was something bloodthirsty in her voice. "Whoever you have to take down, however much blood you have to shed, you have to keep her safe."

"Tell me who she is," he said, unsettled by her fervor, questions swirling in his mind, but she shook her head and stood up from the table.

"By the way," she said. "when you get back to the Bureau, you should look into Operation Gemstone."

"I should?"

"Yes," she said. "You should. A time is going to come when a very great deal depends on the information you're going to dig up."

"What the hell is Operation Gemstone?"

"You'll know when you find it," she said as she turned to leave.

"Wait," he called after her as she descended the staircase. "I still don't even know who you are."

She stopped and turned to look back at him.

"I'm the love of your life, Leo Carstairs," she said. "You just don't know it yet."

And then she was gone.

The End

ACKNOWLEDGMENTS

I am a playwright by trade and training, and this is my first novel. I don't know if you guys know this, but novels have *a lot* of words in them. *The Rewind Files* is like eight times longer (by word count) than my last play, and the majority of it was written between November 2014 and May 2015, which means there were days when trying to get all those words out of my head almost broke me. The list of generous souls who held my hand, shepherded me through this process, read drafts, gave notes, cheered me on, and had my back is obscenely lengthy. For this, I apologize in advance.

First and foremost, to Chris Hanada and the extraordinary team at Axiomatic Publishing and Retrofit Films, all my love and devotion and gratitude and my firstborn child if they want it. I came to the world of publishing as clueless as a baby deer, but from my very first conversation with Chris I knew I was in the best possible hands. I am profoundly grateful for the countless hours he and his amazing staff put into this project, and for their faith in my work.

I belong to an online collective of women and women-identifying writers of extraordinary wisdom and humor, who pushed me when I needed it and gave me a safe space to stomp and yell when the words wouldn't come. I am grateful to all of them, but most particularly to Rowan, whose notes on gender and racial politics were invaluable to the Carter and Kitty scenes in *Past Imperfect*, and to Alice, whose magnificent resilience and beautiful words inspire me every day.

To Playwrights West, my theatre family in Portland, both for enriching my life with their creativity and for putting up with my insane decision to write a novel while I was supposed to be finishing script rewrites for my play *Dear Galileo*.

To Random Order Bakery & Coffeehouse on Northeast Alberta Street in Portland, Oregon, where I am currently sitting as I write this. Easily half of this book was written there while eating "Cylon Attack" breakfast sandwiches (bacon, kale and fried egg on ciabatta) and drinking endless cups of coffee. It is the Platonic ideal of Writer Coffee Shop: good coffee, real food (not just muffins), open late, serves booze, specializes in pie. I basically use it as my home office and they all deserve medals for putting up with me.

To Evan, Jesse and Sarah, my beloved trio since our college roommate days 13 years ago, my first readers, and the creators of a fake Change.org petition to nag me to finish *The Wayward Traveler* faster (the closest I'll ever come to understanding what it's like to be George R.R. Martin) – I love these weirdos with the burning fire of a thousand suns. My professional life was in complete upheaval during the year I wrote this book, and these three were unfailingly patient with my stress meltdowns, even though two of them were in the middle of planning their own wedding, which is really not a time that you should be forced to play career counselor to a writer who just left her day job and is now freaking out about it.

To my best friend Erin, an English professor at Ole Miss and the most brilliant person I know. She is the platonic love of my life and the light in every one of my dark places, from writer's block to deepest grief. I would not be who I am today without her, her husband Jordan, and our fifteen years of friendship.

To my grandmother Lydia, our family's original Watergate junkie, who died when I was five. I inherited, and used while researching this book, her copies of both the complete transcripts of the Nixon tapes, and *The Collected Speeches of Abraham Lincoln*. While it remains one of the great sorrows of my life that I never got to talk about Watergate with her, it is in her honor that Agent Carstairs hails from The Dalles.

To my brother Christopher, a film editor who works with Retrofit, who emailed me last summer to tell me the company was branching out into sci-fi publishing and said "Hey, you should send them your Watergate thing!" At the time, my "Watergate thing" was like four chapters and a pile of assorted shrapnel that I had started three years ago as a NaNoWriMo (National Novel Writing Month) project and never finished. It was by absolutely no stretch of the imagination *anything* resembling a book, and I was so resistant to the idea of letting a real publisher see it that he finally said, "*Fine*, send it to me and *I'll* send it to them."

A week later I had a publisher. This is why my siblings are my absolute most favorite people in the entire world: Christopher believed that I had a book inside me even before I did. To my sister Cat, my caretaker and my conscience, who makes me a better human; to my other brother Colin, my partner in geekery and favorite person to hang out and do nothing with; to my phenomenally generous and loving stepmom Debby, my most enthusiastic cheerleader; and to my awesome stepbrothers Michael and Charlie, who will be skateboarding through Europe when this book comes out and make me feel like a cooler person just being related to them – these people are the best family a writer could have. (If you are eagle-eyed, you will spot all their names somewhere in this book.)

Like Reggie, I too have one absent and one present parent; this book, like everything I write, is dedicated to the memory of my remarkable mother Theresa, who died of ALS in 2008 and whose grit, grace, wisdom, stubbornness, and ability to put idiots in their place without even mussing her hair, are deeply woven into Katie Bellows and all the women in this book.

But most of all, my thanks and love and gratitude to my incredible dad, without whom *The Rewind Files* would never have existed. It is not every father who shows his love for his daughter by giving her a 900-page book about Watergate for Christmas when she is 22 years old, which is why Ken Willett is the best. He drove me to and from college every year, and we spent many of those road trips between Portland and Walla Walla talking about Watergate. His memories of the way the scandal unfolded, of Grammy Lydia's conviction that this wasn't just a small-time botched robbery, of the way it changed American politics, were endlessly fascinating to me. He has also been my biggest champion as a writer; in eight years of writing plays he has never missed a single one of my opening nights. All the good men in this book have pieces of him – Leo, the fantastic cook who is always taking care of people; Carter, the empathetic listener who gently but relentlessly pushes Reggie to be her best self; and Carstairs, the selfless father with a fierce dedication to justice.

And last but not least, this book is dedicated to my teenage heroes, Bob Woodward and Carl Bernstein, and to all the men and women at the *Washington Post* who made their work possible. The fact that an unfinished NaNoWriMo piece of *All the President's Men* fanfic is now a real book you are holding in your hands (or on your screen) is the kind of thing that makes you believe dreams do actually come true.

RECOMMENDED READING & VIEWING

I have been a passionate, some might say "obsessive," Watergate junkie since I pulled *All the President's Men*, entirely at random, off a shelf in the reading nook of the Menucha Retreat Center in Corbett, Oregon, when I was a junior in college on retreat with my Confirmation class. I didn't feel like going outside to shoot hoops with the other kids during free time, but the only book I had on me was a Bible, so I pulled the first paperback with an interesting title off the shelf of faded paperbacks in the upper mezzanine reading nook, and that was it. I was hooked from page one. I read it during every retreat break, I read it on my bunk while everyone else was getting ready for bed, I read it at meals until I was asked to put it away and participate with the rest of the class, I read it when I was supposed to be preparing for Confession (none of which I subsequently confessed), and then when I had to put it back on Sunday afternoon before I got on the bus, without having finished it, I went straight to Powell's Books the next day and bought it so I could find out what happened next.

There would be no *Rewind Files* if there were no *All the President's Men*, far and away my favorite work of nonfiction and easily one of my all-time top three favorite books. Bob Woodward and Carl Bernstein's account of their role in unraveling the Watergate scandal is a magnificent piece of writing and is the perfect entry point for somebody who wants to learn more about these events. It's a crackling, tense thriller, rich in detail and dry humor, and it does a better job than any other book I've read of taking the reader through the journey of Watergate as it unfolded to the public.

Since I fell in love with Woodward and Bernstein fifteen years ago, I have amassed an entire shelf on my bookcase of Watergate-related books. By far my most-used source for historical information was Stanley Kutler's mighty tome *The Wars of Watergate*, which I got for Christmas from my dad one year when I was in college. Do not be intimidated by its vast size; Kutler's prose is sharp and snappy and intensely readable. My copy is full of orange highlighter and scribbled margin notes and post-it flags and folded-down pages and this book would not be what it is without it, particularly the chapters about John Dean and Reggie's job in the White House.

Some of these are books and films I revisited for research, while others were absorbed into my brain years prior and floated around in my head, informing the story. For purposes of giving credit where credit is due, I am sharing all of them here.

Books & Magazines

- *All the President's Men,* Bob Woodward and Carl Bernstein (1974, Pocket Books/Simon & Schuster)
- *The White House Transcripts*, Richard M. Nixon (Viking Press, 1974)
- *The Wars of Watergate: The Last Crisis of Richard Nixon,* Stanley J. Kutler (Norton, 1990)

- "I'm the Guy They Called Deep Throat," John O'Connor (*Vanity Fair*, July 2005)

- *A G-Man's Life: The FBI, Being "Deep Throat," and the Struggle for Honor in Washington*, Mark Felt and John O'Connor (Public Affairs Books, 2006)

Film

- *All the President's Men* (dir. Alan Pakula, 1976); I can't help it, the Woodward and Bernstein in my head are absolutely Robert Redford and Dustin Hoffman

- *Nixon* (dir. Oliver Stone, 1995); the John Dean in my head is David Hyde Pierce because of this movie

- *Frost/Nixon* (dir. Ron Howard, 2008), a filmed adaptation of Peter Morgan's marvelous 2006 stage play of the same name; the Richard Nixon in my head is Frank Langella because of this movie (I'm basically fantasy-drafting a Watergate movie at this point)

- *Our Nixon,* a documentary created from Super-8 home movies by three of Nixon's senior staff members (dir. Penny Lane, 2013)

Internet

My online sources were many, and the "Watergate" folder of bookmarks in my Firefox browser goes on forever, but I'll highlight a few standouts here:

- First of all, Watergate.info is a treasure trove of information, from audio files of the White House tapes to link roundups sorted by incredibly useful subheadings like "Burglars," "Deep Throat," "Impeachment," etc. It was here that I found the first-person account of Watergate burglar Eugenio Martinez describing the events of that night, a gold mine of useful details. I also learned, with great delight, that the Washington Post has helpfully archived Woodward and Bernstein's original Watergate coverage in a special online section, allowing me to read through their early articles in order, as they were first written.

- *Time* Magazine, BBC News, and South African History Online were my sources for details about the very real Sharpeville Massacre.

- I am indebted to the website of the Spy and Private Eye Museum, for photos of what the actual Watergate bugging devices looked like, and to the remarkably detailed and thorough Watergate section of author Michael Dobson's blog for a great deal of helpful information, including the best and most detailed breakdown I ever found of Operation Gemstone and its various components, none of which I made up.

- Some very lucky, very fancy writers have research assistants to ensure their historical accuracy. I, however, do not. I spent hours digging around Wikipedia for answers to weirdly specific questions like what year Diane von Furstenburg first showed wrap dresses on the runway and what the subbasements of the White House looked like in the 1970's. If you happen to spot massive historical inaccuracies in this book, let's all just say they're Chronomalies, shall we?

ABOUT THE AUTHOR

CLAIRE WILLETT is an award-winning playwright from Portland, Oregon. The Rewind Files is her first novel. Her plays include Dear Galileo, which will receive its world premiere in Portland in August 2015; "One of Everything," a dance/spoken-word collaboration with choreographer Briley Neugebauer; The Demons Down Under the Sea, an adaptation of "Annabel Lee" by Edgar Allan Poe; the Scottish folk musical Carter Hall (with Grammy-nominated Nashville songwriter Sarah Hart); the chamber opera The Witch of the Iron Wood (with Portland composer Evan Lewis); How the Light Gets In; Frankie and Clara; That Was the River, This Is the Sea (with Gilberto Martin del Campo); and Upon Waking. She was named the 2011 Oregon Literary Fellow for Drama and has received awards from the Regional Arts & Culture Council and the Oregon Arts Commission. Claire is a proud company member of the Oregon writers' collective Playwrights West and one of the founding artists of Portland's annual citywide Fertile Ground Festival of New Work. She holds a B.A. in Theatre from Whitman College (Walla Walla, WA) and is a graduate of the Paul A. Kaplan Theatre Management Program at Manhattan Theatre Club in New York City. She currently lives in her hometown of Portland where she collects Liberace memorabilia, spends way too much money at Powell's Books, freelances as a marketing and development consultant for arts nonprofits and spent eight years as a Catholic youth minister. Find her online at www.clairewillettwrites.com, on Facebook at @clairewillettwrites, or on Twitter at @clairewillett.

ABOUT AXIOMATIC PUBLISHING

Axiomatic Publishing is the book publishing arm of Retrofit Films, a Los Angeles based film and television production company. Each of our book series is created by an emerging author, and we are dedicated to using our years of development experience to help our writers bring their stories to life.

For exclusive discounts, giveaways, and latest news on titles, sign up for our mailing list at our website!

Twitter: @axiomaticpub
www.axiomaticpublishing.com
www.retrofitfilms.com
Questions? Feedback? Typos?
editor@axiomaticpublishing.com

THE REWIND FILES BOOK CLUB QUESTIONS

(Spoiler alert! Don't read these unless you've read the book!)

- How did you *experience* the book? Were you engaged immediately, or did it take you a while to "get into it"? Were you able to picture the Time Travel Bureau offices? How about DC in 1972?

- What surprised you most about the concept of time travel as portrayed in this book?

- Do you feel that Reggie *changed* by the end of the book? Did she grow or mature? Do you feel she learned something about herself? What was it?

- Do you find all the *characters convincing?* Are they believable? Compelling? Are they fully developed as complex, emotional human beings--or are they one-dimensional?

- Is the **plot** engaging—does the story interest you? Is this a plot-driven book: a fast-paced page-turner? Or does the story unfold slowly with a focus on character development? Were you surprised by the plot's complications? Or did you find it predictable, even formulaic?

- How did you feel about both the *protagonist and antagonist* being women?

- What *passages* strike you as insightful, even profound? Perhaps a bit of dialog that's funny or poignant between Reggie, Calliope and/or Katie? Maybe there's a particular comment that states the book's thematic concerns?

- Which *character* did you most relate to and why?

- Which two *characters* were your favorite **relationship**? (Can be romantic, friendship, familial, adversarial, etc.)

- Did you feel that Katie handled the situations in this book well as a *parental figure*? Do you feel that she acted more as a mother or more as a boss towards Reggie?

- There is a noticeable theme in the book of characters being put in a box by society (past and future) for who they are. Whether it be African-Americans or women time travel agents, the book reminds us how unrestricted history was for Caucasian men. How did this make you feel?

- Which characters do you particularly *admire or dislike?* What are their primary characteristics?

- Did you agree with **Reggie's decision** to investigate Grove while knowing Calliope was listening? What do you feel this situation did to each Reggie and Calliope and also their relationship?

- Would you have done something different from what **Reggie/Calliope/Leo/Katie/Carter** did at any point? Were you disappointed in any of their decisions?

- Who in this book would you most **like to meet?** What would you ask—or say?

- **Consider the ending.** Did you expect it or were you surprised? Was it manipulative? Was it forced?

- If you could **rewrite the ending**, would you? If so, what would you change?

- If you were to **talk with Claire Willett (author)**, what would you want to know?

Made in the USA
Middletown, DE
29 April 2020